"Think you know Barbie? Think again; in this delightful, fast-paced, compassionate, and well-researched story, Renée Rosen skillfully takes everything you think you know and turns it on its head, telling us the real story of the feisty, strong, original woman who created America's most loved and most hated doll. Choose this one for your book club if you want the conversation to flow. I promise you everyone will want to talk about this excellent and fascinating book."

—Elizabeth Letts, #1 *New York Times* bestselling author of
The Ride of Her Life

"*Let's Call Her Barbie* is a riveting read for anyone who loves historical fiction, strong women (real and otherwise), Barbie the doll, *Barbie* the movie, or stories about the American dream. As an avid lover and collector of Barbies—at a time when society often looked as harshly at me as it once did the doll—this story spoke to my heart and spirit and made me love my beloved Barbies even more. The first must-read of 2025! It's DOLL-ing!"

—Viola Shipman, *USA Today* bestselling author of *The Page Turner*

"Bold. Tenacious. Resolute. Renée Rosen's *Let's Call Her Barbie* vividly brings to life the incredible journey of Ruth Handler, the woman behind the iconic doll. Through impeccable research and masterful storytelling, Rosen captures Handler's fierce determination and the challenges she faced as a woman breaking barriers in a male-dominated world. Impossible to put down, this is a riveting portrayal of a flawed yet awe-inspiring visionary. I thought I knew Barbie's story, but Rosen's unflinching portrayal of the doll's meteoric rise, and the players behind it, proves there's much more to this tale. An absolute must-read."

—Karma Brown, #1 international bestselling author of
What Wild Women Do

PRAISE FOR THE NOVELS OF RENÉE ROSEN

"Renée Rosen is my go-to for whip-smart heroines who love their work."
—Kate Quinn, *New York Times* bestselling author of
The Briar Club, on *Park Avenue Summer*

"Richly detailed and meticulously researched—historical fiction readers
will love *The Social Graces*!"
—Chanel Cleeton, *New York Times* bestselling author of
The House on Biscayne Bay, on *The Social Graces*

"A scintillating, beautifully written peek into the life of one of America's
most fascinating women. . . . I absolutely could not put it down."
—Kristy Woodson Harvey, *New York Times* bestselling author of
A Happier Life, on *Fifth Avenue Glamour Girl*

ALSO BY RENÉE ROSEN

Fifth Avenue Glamour Girl

The Social Graces

Park Avenue Summer

Windy City Blues

White Collar Girl

What the Lady Wants

Dollface

LET'S CALL HER *Barbie*

RENÉE ROSEN

BERKLEY

NEW YORK

BERKLEY
An imprint of Penguin Random House LLC
penguinrandomhouse.com

Book design by Kristin del Rosario
Interior art: Stripes © DivinHX/Shutterstock

Library of Congress Cataloging-in-Publication Data

Names: Rosen, Renée, author.
Title: Let's call her Barbie / Renée Rosen.
Other titles: Let us call her Barbie
Description: First edition. | New York: Berkley, 2025.
Identifiers: LCCN 2024014839 (print) | LCCN 2024014840 (ebook) |
ISBN 9780593953631 (hardcover) | ISBN 9780593335680 (trade paperback) |
ISBN 9780593335697 (ebook)
Subjects: LCSH: Barbie dolls—History—Fiction. | Mattel,
Inc.—History—Fiction. | Handler, Ruth—Fiction. | Ryan, Jack,
1926–1991—Fiction. | LCGFT: Historical fiction. | Novels.
Classification: LCC PS3618.O83156 L48 2025 (print) |
LCC PS3618.O83156 (ebook) | DDC 813/.6—dc23/eng/20240405
LC record available at https://lccn.loc.gov/2024014839
LC ebook record available at https://lccn.loc.gov/2024014840

First Edition: January 2025

Printed in the United States of America
1st Printing

To Barbie lovers everywhere.
May we all continue to feel empowered and inspired
by her for generations to come.

LET'S CALL HER BARBIE

PART ONE

Thinking Small

My Sources Say No

1956

"Pop Goes the Weasel" is what Ruth hears when she opens the conference room door. She's jet-lagged but refuses to succumb on her first day back from vacation. Too excited to have slept on the plane, she's operating on coffee, cigarettes and pure adrenaline. She's carrying the foot-long carton that rode in her lap on the flight from Switzerland to Los Angeles and cannot wait to reveal what's inside. Her gut tells her she's on the cusp of something big, but even Ruth Handler can't imagine the Pandora's box she's holding in her hands.

Elliot, her husband and business partner, is at the far end of the table, plucking the strings on a red Uke-A-Doodle, the first toy he ever invented. He's not jet-lagged, because unlike Ruth, he slept on the plane. Nothing comes between Elliot and his sleep. Seated next to him is an engineer fresh out of Harvard, the ink still wet on his diploma. He's futzing with a jack-in-the-box, the clown's head bobbing on its coiled spring. He shoves the clown back inside, closes the lid and cranks the handle for an encore as another weasel goes *pop*. To his right is a man who rowed for Princeton in 1947 and is now loading a round of caps into the chamber of a toy pistol.

Across from him is a Cornell graduate, class of '51, who's shaking a Magic 8 Ball and praying over it with eyes closed as if his life's happiness depends on the answer. To an outsider, they look like a bunch of men goofing off, but they are highly skilled Ivy League engineers, and making toys is a serious business, especially here at Mattel.

"Good morning, gentlemen," Ruth says, taking her seat at the head of the table. One by one the toys are exchanged for protractors, compasses and pads of paper. Gesturing to the empty chair, she says, "I see your ringleader is missing."

Only Jack Ryan can get away with being late to a meeting. No one else would dare keep her waiting. The rest of them fear her, and with good reason. She's their boss and is well aware that they call her Ruthless behind her back, which she secretly likes. Ruth is petite, only five foot two, and yet she looms larger than Elliot in many respects. Always fashionable, she sports a smart hairstyle, cropped short with a thick row of dark bangs. She's a purposeful woman, the sort who makes men say idiotic things like *Smile* when they pass her on the street.

Finally, the door swings open and Jack swaggers in like he's six feet tall rather than five feet, eight inches—three of which he's inherited from his imported Italian elevator shoes. He's been with Mattel for about a year now, ever since Elliot lured him away from the aerospace enterprise, Raytheon. Jack's only thirty and is already a vice president overseeing the research and development department.

While Jack settles in, Ruth lights a cigarette, fisting up the empty pack of Winstons she opened the night before on the plane. She'll cut back, she promises herself, but not today.

When everyone's ready, Ruth takes charge of the meeting. Topping her agenda is Mattel entering the doll market. They've wanted in on this lucrative piece of the business for ages but haven't seen a clear path forward. Until now. She's got the answer and it's going to turn the doll world on its proverbial head.

"We all agree that there's a glut of baby dolls on the shelves right now. The last thing anyone needs is another doll that blinks or cries or wets itself." Ruth speaks at a measured pace, to keep from jumping right in. She feels like a racehorse waiting for the starter bell. "What we need is this—" She ceremoniously places the box on the table, lifts the lid and removes the plastic doll inside. "Gentlemen, meet Bild Lilli."

The room falls silent. Not a peep out of them. Instead, they shift in their chairs and clear their throats as they take in the doll—her perky blond ponytail, the pin curl resting on her forehead, her long shapely legs, slender waist and ample pointy breasts. Dressed in hot pants and a tight sweater, Bild Lilli has come-hither eyes that command the room's attention. All twelve inches of her.

"Well"—Ruth drums her fingers—"somebody say something."

For years now Ruth has wanted to create a grown-up doll, but she's not a toy designer and her stick figure drawings never convincingly conveyed her concept. She'd all but given up on the idea until she spotted Bild Lilli in that souvenir shop in Lucerne. Actually, it was her daughter who saw her first. At fifteen Barbara is too old to play with dolls, but she still collects them. Ruth and Barbara were mesmerized by Bild Lilli. There she was. Like she'd been waiting for Ruth to find her.

Ruth bought one for each of them and ran outside to show Elliot. "See? This is what I've been talking about."

"Oh, c'mon, Ruthie," he said, smirking, "we can't possibly make a doll like this."

But he should have known better than to say that. She took it as a challenge, and Ruth has never backed away from a chance to defy expectations. He learned that early on when their budding company needed someone to make deliveries and Ruth volunteered. "No way," said Elliot. "You can't drive a truck." So what did she do? She rented a Dodge pickup, her high heels barely reaching the clutch. Did she care about the men standing by, laughing, placing bets that she couldn't back it out of the lot? So what if it took her almost a dozen tries. She'd be damned if she'd ever let anyone dictate what she can or can't do.

"Give me one good reason why this doll won't work," she said to Elliot. They were still outside the souvenir shop, standing on the sidewalk.

"I'll give you two reasons." He pointed to Bild Lilli's breasts.

"Ah, Ruth," Jack says now, "I don't know if you noticed this little detail or not, but ah, that doll"—he cocks his head to the side—"ah, she's got tits."

This sets off a round of hoots and howls, all of them following Jack's lead: grabbing at each other's chests, making lewd comments. She can't afford to let this meeting get away from her. But they're not letting up. They're not even hearing her. Exasperated, she reaches for the cap gun on the table, aims for the ceiling and fires off three shots. Everyone jumps with a start as the air fills with the scent of sulfur.

"You all sound like a bunch of goddamn boys in a circle jerk." She's learned to talk to them this way, to show them she speaks their language and is just as tough as any man. "Of course she has tits. That's the whole goddamn point. She's not a *baby doll* kind of doll."

"Then what exactly *is* she?" asks Jack. "She looks like a hooker."

"She's not a hooker," Ruth insists, though he's not wrong. Jack Ryan knows a prostitute when he sees one. Bild Lilli is based on a risqué German comic strip character who turns tricks while amusing her male admirers. "She's a gag gift," says Ruth. "They sell her mostly to men. You know, like a sex toy."

"So now you want us to make sex toys?"

"Of course not. Jesus." She slaps the table, heat welling up inside her. She's getting flustered, and if she's not careful, they'll mistake her passion for being overly emotional. She needs to be practical, logical. Drawing a deep breath, she backs up and starts over. "We say we want to be in the doll market, and I'm telling you, this is the way to do it. Think about it—we give little boys toy guns, toy soldiers and building blocks. And what do we give little girls? Baby dolls. Little boys can pretend they're grown men, brave soldiers. And you know what little girls get to play? They get to play *mommy*. They get to play *house*. That's it."

"And what's wrong with that?" asks Jack.

She looks at him, and at this roomful of men, and drops her cigarette in an ashtray, grinding it out with more force than needed. "You all might find this hard to believe, but not every little girl wants to grow up to be *just* a housewife and mother. There's more to being a woman than that. If you hand a little girl a baby doll, she's going to make believe she's a mommy. But if you hand her something like this"—she holds up Bild Lilli—"she can pretend she's a young independent woman. Maybe she'll make believe she's going to her office, or out on a date, but she sure as hell's not gonna pretend she's changing a diaper or pushing a stroller."

She ignores the way Elliot's eyebrows hike a bit higher each time she speaks. Clearly, she's going to have to crystalize this for them. "Just think how much the world's changed since the war ended. Anyone want to guess what happened when those soldiers returned home to the ever-loving arms of their sweethearts? I'll tell you what happened—they got busy making babies. Do you realize how many babies were born in 1946?" She poses the question and provides the answer. "Over three million. And that number has grown every year since. Our population has been exploding over the past decade. Right now, in this country, there are millions of little girls between the ages of three and ten. And next year there'll be even more. Many of those girls are simply too old for baby dolls, and there's no toys for them. We can fill a huge hole in the marketplace by introducing a doll they can relate to." She scans the room, eyeing them hard.

Elliot offers an admiring smile, because even though he's not sold on the idea of this type of doll, he appreciates her rationale and can't deny that she's identified something they can capitalize on.

"Gentlemen," she says, "we are sitting on a goddamn gold mine, and yes, that gold mine just so happens to have tits."

Jack sits up a little straighter. "You're serious? You want us to create a doll like *this* for *little girls*?"

"That's right." Pulling a fresh pack of Winstons from her pocket, she unravels the cellophane so quickly, it's like she can't get her next cigarette lit fast enough. "This is a million-dollar idea if ever there was one." She hears herself sounding so self-assured, but even as she speaks, she's aware of all the ways a doll like this could go awry. She knows the kind of time, the man-hours, not to mention the money it will take to bring this doll to fruition. If she's wrong, if it fails, what will that mean for the future of Mattel? What will it mean for her? Will the rest of the industry laugh at her, thinking, *It figures a woman would come up with something like this*?

Sure, everyone here knows there'd be no Mattel without her, but to the outside world, she's just Elliot's wife. Maybe they think she keeps the books or answers the phones. They don't see the behind-the-scenes work she does, the business maneuverings, the negotiations she pulls off. Hell, she doesn't even have her name on the door. Mattel is a combination of their former business partner Harold "Matt" Mattson's name and Elliot's—*Matt* and *El*. This doll would at least give her something tangible to show for herself, to say, *See, I did this*. And there's a part of her that needs that kind of recognition, and despite her doubts, she's ready to take a chance on this doll.

"We'd be fools to walk away from this," she says, ramping up her argument. "This is our chance to create a new segment in the marketplace—it's untapped. No one even knows it exists yet."

Jack picks up the Magic 8 Ball. He shakes it, glances down and sighs. *"My sources say no."* There's a ripple of laughter. "Sorry, Ruth, interesting idea—it's intriguing—but a doll like that would cost a fortune to produce." He shrugs, case closed. "Let's move on."

After the meeting, Ruth goes into Jack's office, located next to hers. She stands in his doorway with Bild Lilli in one hand and a freshly lit cigarette in the other. Jack's office is tidy. There's a credenza in the corner, fully stocked with top-shelf liquor, and a bearskin rug in the center of the room. He sometimes sprawls out on it to stretch his back or to take a nap, which he believes is a critical part of the creative process—though he'd ream his engineers if he ever caught them sleeping on the job.

Ruth clears her throat, and he looks up from his drafting table. "Why were you so quick to reject this doll?"

"Why? Because." He doesn't say anything more, as if it's understood.

"Don't you see what this doll represents? She radiates a different kind of energy."

"Yeah, she radiates sex." He holds a metal ruler in the air, waving it like a sword.

Ruth takes a pause. She has to be smart about this. If this doll is going to get off the ground, she's going to need Jack on her side. The others, even Elliot, will listen to him. A year ago, when Jack joined Mattel, he was a fresh burst of energy, like a little bouncy ball. There's a childlike playfulness to him that they needed. Together Jack and Elliot went on a toy-making spree, turning out a whole new crop of music boxes, plastic guns and other marvels that spun and whirled and flew off the store shelves.

"Let me ask you something," he says. "When you were a little girl, would you have played with a doll like this?"

The answer is right there. She doesn't even have to reach for it. "No," she says. "But only because I never played with dolls." It was true. Dolls were too frivolous for her, as were most toys. If she'd been apt to *play* with anything, it would have been her brother's Lincoln Logs. At least she could build with them and have something to show for her efforts. The irony that she's ended up in the toy business is not lost on her. "But we're not talking about me here," she says. "We're talking about an entire segment of the population that doesn't have a toy they can relate to."

"And you think they're going to relate to a doll like this?"

"Do you know how many times I caught my daughter putting on my lipstick, playing in my high heels? Little girls can't wait till they're old enough to wear makeup and fancy clothes. That's the genius of a doll like this."

Ruth rarely gets excited about anything, which is not to be confused with her getting agitated. He's witnessed that side of her plenty of times. But seeing her so animated now is enough to make him give the doll a closer look. He sets the ruler aside and, holding out his hand, gestures for the doll. He bends Bild Lilli at the waist and perches her on the edge of his desk. Speaking directly to the doll, he says, "I think I dated you once."

"That wouldn't surprise me." Ruth aims her gaze toward the ceiling.

Jack is a Casanova who plays around on his wife, claiming they have an *understanding*. He's been sleeping his way through the women in the office since the day he started. What they all see in him, she will never know.

Jack moves the doll's arms up and down. He removes her shorts to investigate the hip joint mechanics, and then the snug sweater to see how the arm joints work. He twists her head off, looks inside.

"Well?" she asks.

He shrugs, screwing Lilli's head back in place. "There's too many design issues."

"Jesus Christ, Jack—you designed Sparrow and Hawk missiles for the army and now you're telling me you can't design a twelve-inch doll?"

"Is this some sort of a challenge?" He sounds offended because he *is* offended. His entire career has been built on his reputation as a brilliant engineer, and if the war hadn't ended, he'd still be making rockets and missiles. Jack never planned on being a toy-maker, but he knew he had to reinvent himself. Thankfully Mattel came knocking before Raytheon started laying people off. Now he needs to carve out a new niche, prove his abilities all over again. "You think it's so simple to design a doll like that?" he counters.

"I don't see why it's so damn hard."

"For starters, look at the face." He hands the doll back to Ruth. "Look at how detailed and intricate the design is. The blue eye-shadow, the red lips, the rouge on her cheeks—no machine can replicate that. It would all have to be done by hand. And the same thing with the hair. It's rooted into the scalp. And that's all got to be hand stitched. It would cost way too much, and honestly, I can't think of a manufacturer here that would even know *how* to do it."

"What about making it overseas? In Japan?" She eyes his luggage in the corner, a Val-A-Pak slumped over his suitcase. Jack is leaving for Tokyo that evening to investigate manufacturing options for a talking wristwatch. Before he has a chance to object, she thrusts Bild Lilli back at him. "Just take her with you and see if you can find someone—anyone—over there who can reproduce her."

Jack reaches into his pocket for his compact tape recorder, which accompanies him everywhere, even to the men's room, where he sometimes does his best thinking. He presses the button and speaks into the tiny mesh box: "Look into doll reproduction. Per Ruth." He clicks off the recorder. "This is a long shot, you realize that, don't you? And it has nothing to do with my ability to design a twelve-inch doll."

Their eyes meet and she cracks a smile. Here is a man who once sat in on highly classified meetings at the Pentagon, but now he works for her, and she's charging him with the task of designing a doll. A doll with tits.

The Wisdom of Razor Blades

Jack is on a Pan Am flight—window seat—his gaze alternating between his view of the Pacific Ocean and the stewardess's legs each time she walks up and down the aisle or stops to refill his wineglass. Such are the hardships of first-class travel. But it's a nice perk. Especially after spending three weeks in Tokyo knocking on doors. Joined at the hip with his translator, Jack repeatedly tried to convey the idea of reproducing Bild Lilli, whom the Japanese businessmen deemed indecent. Just when he was about to give up, he found Kokusai Boeki Kaisha, the only manufacturer willing to take on such a *risqué project*—their words according to his translator, not Jack's.

He had returned to his hotel room that night after a little celebrating. It was midnight his time, eight o'clock the previous day back home. He knew Ruth would already be in the office. When he'd placed that telephone call and told her the good news, he'd heard her clap all the way from Los Angeles. They kept the call short since it was $12 for just the first three minutes, but after he hung up, he heard Ruth's voice over and over again: "You did it, Jack. I knew you could. Hurry home. We've got work to do."

Though Ruth's only forty, just ten years older than Jack, he tends to think of her as a mother figure. Sure, he challenges her from time to time, but still, he seeks her praise and approval as if hoping to fill the void where his own mother—his father, too—remain silent and withholding. Not long ago, Jack had devised a preprogrammed player harmonica that Elliot said was too similar to the toy saxophone he'd been developing. But Ruth had called it brilliant, making Jack beam and grow taller on the spot.

After his call with her that night, he'd hardly slept, which was nothing new for him. He actually cherishes his bouts of insomnia. They make him feel powerful compared to lesser men who can barely function on anything under eight hours. He's at his best when running on four hours a night, or better yet, three. Long after the national anthem has been sung and all that's left is the TV test pattern, Jack comes alive. His creativity is at its full strength. His best ideas have always been hatched just before dawn. Or after a nap, which doesn't count as sleeping in his book.

That night in his hotel room, he'd thought about all he'd accomplished in Japan. He'd found someone to make the doll and now all he had to do was design her. Ideas were already coming faster than he could sketch them on the Imperial Hotel stationery. After that initial inspired burst, he'd called the front desk asking for more paper and a bourbon. The bar was closed for the night, and he could have bought a case of booze for what he spent on a bottle, not including the extra 50 yen for the bellboy who delivered it to his room. But it didn't matter. He happily sipped his drink and sketched and dreamed.

"More wine, Mr. Ryan?" The stewardess bats her long lashes.

Women are naturally drawn to him. They say he looks like Dean Martin. He has that same dark hair, but Jack's face is more diamond shaped, with a wide forehead and pointy chin that grows even more pronounced when he smiles, as he is doing right now.

"Peachy," he says, as she leans over and refills his glass once more.

While Jack is getting the stewardess's telephone number, Ruth is back in Los Angeles with Charlotte Johnson, the only fashion designer in L.A. willing to meet with her. Ruth spoke on the telephone with seven other designers, but at the first mention of making doll clothes, they said they weren't interested. In a last-ditch effort to find someone, Ruth went to the Chouinard Art Institute. Charlotte is an instructor there, but unlike the old saying *Those who can't do, teach*, Charlotte is quite accomplished. Attractive, tall and slender, she's a former runway model turned Seventh Avenue hotshot with her own label. It was only after relocating to Los Angeles that she started teaching while trying to establish a new roster of West Coast clients. But Charlotte is soon to be divorced and she needs the extra income, which is the only reason she's even entertaining the idea of moonlighting for Mattel.

Ruth now sits in Charlotte's tiny kitchen at a green Formica table with two mismatched chairs. There's a seashell ashtray between them, and two sweating glasses of lemonade.

"Before we get started," Ruth says, retrieving a stack of papers from her briefcase, "I'll need you to sign these."

"What exactly am I signing?" Charlotte asks. She has a soft, high-pitched voice that makes her sound like she's always standing on her tiptoes.

"Just some Do Not Compete forms. Confidentiality forms, a Nondisclosure Agreement," says Ruth.

Charlotte grabs a pair of glasses and fogs the lenses with her breath before wiping them clean. She shuffles through the forms, thinking these precautions are ridiculous. Who is she going to tell? If anything, she doesn't want her colleagues knowing she's desperate enough to make doll clothes.

But Ruth has her reasons. Louis Marx, "the Toy King," owns one of the largest toy companies in the country, but that's partly because he steals his best ideas from Mattel and everyone else. He goes to Toy Fair—the big annual trade show in New York—just to see what the competition is up to so he can make knockoffs to sell at a lower price. Marx has even sent his spies into Mattel to snoop around under the guise of applying for a job, so they can't be too careful.

After Charlotte signs the forms, Ruth double-checks the signature lines. Satisfied that she's protected the doll's secrecy, she reaches into her briefcase for Bild Lilli. Since Jack took her doll to Japan, Ruth has borrowed her daughter's, and with a "Ta-dah" she presents Bild Lilli.

"Oh, my." Charlotte takes the doll and adjusts her glasses for a closer look. "This is *not* what I was expecting."

Her reaction is not what Ruth was expecting, either. She thought Charlotte—another woman—would be wowed by this doll. Instead, she seems as skeptical as all the men at Mattel. Ruth takes a sip of lemonade and notices the kitchen wall clock indicating she's running late for her daughter's play, but she can't leave yet. She has to sell Charlotte on this first. She's running out of options and she needs someone to design clothes for this doll. She tells Charlotte about discovering Bild Lilli and how Jack has just secured a manufacturer in Japan. "Of course, we're going to redesign and reengineer the doll and make her our own, but this gives you the general idea we're going for. Now we just need to figure out how to dress her."

"So I'd be designing clothes? For *this*?"

"Yes, but I don't want ordinary doll clothes. I'm looking for real stylish outfits—high-end designs."

Charlotte sits with this for a moment. "So you're looking to turn this into a fashion doll. Sort of like a paper doll—"

"Exactly!" Ruth feels like she's finally getting somewhere. At least Charlotte gets the concept. "As a matter of fact, I based the whole idea of an adult fashion doll on paper dolls. My daughter used to play with paper dolls all the time."

"*I* used to play with them. They've been around forever."

"So you know all about those flimsy tabs."

"Just awful," she says. "They never hold the clothes in place. And they always tear."

"And the cardboard cutouts"—Ruth shakes her head—"they're about as much fun as a stick. But just imagine playing with a doll that has *real* clothes. Made from the finest fabrics, with *real* buttons, *real* zippers, *real*—"

"Wait—" Charlotte stops her with a laugh, revealing a slight gap between her front teeth. "Buttons? Zippers? There are no buttons or zippers small enough for this kind of design. They don't exist."

"Then we'll create them." She owns a company full of inventors. If they can create cap guns, why not zippers? "You design them, and Jack will figure out how to make them. Trust me, he's a genius. A pain in the ass sometimes, but still a genius."

Charlotte sits back, folds her arms, fingers drumming along the sleeve of her blouse. "This sounds like an awful lot of work."

"I know." Ruth looks around Charlotte's tiny bungalow with its chipped Mexican tiled foyer and secondhand furniture. "But I'll make it worth your while."

Charlotte considers this. For months now she's been struggling, skimping on groceries, worried about keeping the electricity on and gas in her car. Depending on what Ruth's willing to pay, this could allow her to breathe a little easier, allow her to sleep at night.

While Charlotte examines Bild Lilli again, Ruth packs up her things, thinking that if traffic isn't too heavy, she can still make the opening curtain.

"Just exactly how *worth my while* were you thinking?" asks Charlotte.

"I don't know—how's $5 an hour sound?"

"How about $6?"

"Done."

Charlotte looks at Ruth and smiles. "Why, this doll's just a marvelous little thing, isn't she?"

By the time Ruth enters the high school auditorium, the curtain is up and they're already halfway through the first act of *A Tree Grows in Brooklyn*. The room is dark, with dust mites stirring in the spotlights near the stage. Ruth and another guilty parent, a father clutching his fedora, inch down the center aisle looking at the backs of heads. She finally sees Elliot and her son, Ken, in the center of the third row. After sidestepping her way to the vacant spot next to Elliot, she calls even more attention to herself with the squeaking hinges on her seat. But at least she's in place to applaud when Barbara, in the role of Katie Nolan, finishes singing "Look Who's Dancing."

"I got here as fast as I could," she whispers to Elliot before the applause dies down. "My meeting ran late, and traffic was murder." Barbara sees her and smiles as Ruth blows her a kiss.

"You tell that to your daughter," he says, keeping his eyes on the stage.

She wants to say, *At least I'm here. That's more than my mother would have done.*

Her mother already had nine children by the time Ruth was born, and a husband who spent most of his time at the gambling tables. At forty, the last thing Ida Mosko needed was another baby. After six months Ida had had enough. That's how old Ruth was when her mother handed her infant to her eldest daughter, Sarah, and said, *Here, you take her. You raise her.* Sarah was a newlywed, old enough to have been Ruth's mother, and while Ruth loved her sister, that didn't change the fact that her own mother hadn't wanted her.

It wasn't until Ruth held Barbara for the first time that she realized what her mother had given away. Barbara was beautiful and magical, and she was hers. The feel of her baby in her arms evoked such mixed emotions, elation and despair. It left Ruth wondering how you could carry a child for nine months, shield and protect them inside you, only to take one look and say, *No thank you. Send that one back.*

Aside from pure, unwavering love, nothing about motherhood had come naturally to Ruth. How could it have? She was raised by her sister, a woman who worked every bit as hard as Ruth works now. Sarah ran a drugstore in Denver with a soda fountain in back and was far too busy to play with and nurture her baby sister. From a young age Ruth never wanted to be a bother or a burden, lest Sarah give her away, too. Ruth did chores without having to be asked. She bagged garbage and hauled it to the street, cleaned the litter box for a reclusive tabby that rarely came out from hiding. In the winter she shoveled the drive and walkways, in the summer she mowed the lawn, in the fall she raked leaves and in the spring she planted flowers. At ten she was already stocking shelves and unpacking deliveries at Sarah's store. For as long as she could remember, Ruth has equated being useful and productive with being lovable, or at least keepable.

When Ruth had Barbara, she was starting from scratch. She made herself blow those raspberries on her tiny belly, had to remind herself to bounce Barbara on her knee, to speak baby talk though it made her feel ridiculous. A grown woman saying *goo-goo* and *gah-gah*, playing peekaboo and patty-cake.

But none of that meant she didn't love Barbara, and showing up late for her play isn't a measure of how much she loves her now. Ruth may not be a model mother herself, but she would have sooner given away an arm than one of her children.

After the play they celebrate at Punch & Judy, Barbara's favorite ice cream parlor. Elliot and Ken are on one side of the booth, Ruth and Barbara on the other. Ruth glances at the menu and suggests they get a Moron's Ecstasy for the table—eight scoops of ice cream, eight different toppings: hot fudge, butterscotch, caramel, raspberry syrup, marshmallow fluff, cherries, nuts, and whipped cream.

"You kids know why they call it a Moron's Ecstasy, don't you?" says Elliot. "Because only a moron would eat the whole thing by themself."

They have a laugh over this, and when the monstrosity arrives, they each grab their spoons. Ken holds his like a sword. "En garde," he says, digging in only to let out a high-pitched "Ooh" a moment later when the ice cream goes straight to his head.

After Ken's recovered, Elliot taps his spoon to his water glass. "And now, ladies and gentlemen"—he holds the napkin dispenser up like a statuette—"the Oscar for Best Actress in a High School

Musical goes to"—he pauses while Ken drums the tabletop—"Miss Barbara Joyce Handler."

Barbara giggles while they applaud and shyly buries her face in Ruth's shoulder.

"Take your bow, Miss Handler," Ruth says, kissing the crown of her head. "You were wonderful, darling. Just wonderful." With her lips still pressed to Barbara's hair, Ruth breathes in the scent of her daughter's shampoo and then breathes in the full moment before her—everyone is in a good mood, no one is sulking, no one's fighting. What a rarity. Since Barbara turned thirteen and thought she was all grown up and knew better than her mother, Ruth hasn't been able to do anything right by her. The slightest thing can set her off. It's like throwing a match into dried kindling. But for now, Ruth's sweet little girl is back, and when she looks at her family, all she sees are perfect little pods of contentment.

Later that night, as Ruth and Elliot are getting ready for bed, she tells him about her meeting with Charlotte. "At one point I thought she was going to turn me down," she says, turning around so he can unclasp her pearls. "But then—thank God—we started talking money . . ."

While she's recapping her negotiations and brushing her hair, Elliot changes into his pajamas and sets his alarm clock. He's listening because he always listens to what she says, although right now he's troubled by what he's hearing.

". . . and then Charlotte *finally* agreed to do it. Isn't that terrific?" When he doesn't respond, she pauses her hairbrush midstroke. "You're not still upset with me for being late to the play, are you?" Barbara isn't angry with her—why should he be?

"No, no." He shakes his head. "Are you kidding me? Tonight was wonderful. I haven't seen the kids so happy in ages."

"Then what's wrong?"

"I'm just surprised you're already consulting with this Charlotte woman. Jack hasn't even designed the doll. You don't even have a name for it yet. Don't you think it's premature to be worrying about doll clothes?"

She smiles and goes to his side, sitting next to him on the bed. "I have a gut feeling about this, Elliot. Call it intuition or a marketing hunch, but you have to trust me. I know this doll is going to be a huge hit." She's crunched the numbers, has analyzed the market every which way possible. She knows what she's doing. "Don't you see? The clothes are like razor blades."

"I don't follow."

"Think about it. Where does Gillette make most of their money? Got news for you, it ain't on the razors. It's on the blades. Trust me, the real money is not in the doll. It's going to be in her wardrobe."

Huge but Not Gigundous

Elliot still isn't sold on the doll, but now that Ruth has Charlotte on board and Jack has secured KBK for manufacturing, they can get down to business. She hopes Elliot will eventually come around, but for now, it's just the three of them.

Mostly they work in the evenings, after Charlotte finishes at Chouinard and Ruth and Jack have taken care of their regular workloads, which haven't eased up and won't. Ruth goes from meeting to meeting, and in between there are mountains of paperwork, sales calls and a host of financial matters to deal with. Jack barely has time for lunch and is busy overseeing more than 200 engineers and developers, tweaking their designs, troubleshooting malfunctions and keeping the pipeline full of new toys.

The doll is different, though. They're not even sure yet why that is. Maybe because the risks are so high and the potential rewards so unfathomable. If this doll works, she'll line all their pockets. But for now, they're just burning money and man-hours on a concept whose intricate design has never been done before. Sure, they have Bild Lilli as an example, but she's only a jumping-off point.

The three of them speak their own distinctive languages. Jack is the technical guy, Charlotte more the aesthetics and Ruth is all business, though she tries to contribute creatively. Both Jack and Charlotte are talented artists and can express their thoughts in drawings, which puts Ruth at a disadvantage. One night, already punch-drunk from hours of work, they howl-laughed over Ruth's attempt to sketch the doll's foot.

"That looks like somebody ran over it with a truck," said Jack, clutching his sides.

"How is that possibly a foot?" said Charlotte, holding her chest.

"It's got toes," said Ruth, dabbing at her eyes, barely able to get the words out.

Other times they're serious, locked in passionate debates over things like hair and eye color. They can go hours over shades of fingernail and toenail polish, the kind of plastic to use and how many points of articulation their doll should have. They bat around names—*Miss Fashion Plate, Fancy Fashion Franny, Little Miss Model* . . . But by far, the biggest discussion is about the doll's anatomy.

"Oh, c'mon, Jack," Ruth laughs when he shows her his drawing, "you gotta make those tits smaller."

"Okay, all right." Jack flips his sketchpad back around and makes some modifications.

"Smaller," she says after glancing at his revised sketch. "I mean it, Jack. They're still too big."

"You're no fun," he says and takes yet another stab at it.

Soon dinner arrives and there's a sea of Chinese take-out cartons with chopsticks jutting out, and packets of soy sauce are strewn across the conference room table. Night after night, they order pizzas, deli sandwiches, hamburgers or Chinese. While they're eating, Elliot comes in to see how much longer Ruth will be.

"I'm almost done," she says.

"That means another hour or two," he says, not unkindly but because he knows his wife and how easy it is for her to lose track of time when she's working.

"Hey, Elliot," says Jack, "while you're here, I could use a man's opinion. Ruth thinks these tits are too big."

Elliot laughs as he looks at Jack's rendering, both front and side views. "They're huge, but not gigundous."

"See," says Jack. "They're not too big."

After Elliot leaves, Charlotte, who has been lost in concentration, looks up from Jack's mechanical drawings. Her brow is furrowed. "Guys, we got a bigger problem than her boobs. I'm looking at the doll's dimensions. You've given her the equivalent of a twenty-four-inch waist."

"Because we want her to have an hourglass figure, right? Isn't that the whole idea?" Jack's loosely basing this doll on a real woman, a beauty from his past who stood five foot nine and weighed a svelte 110 pounds but was still curvaceous.

"Okay, but look at this." She turns the sketchpad around to show them both. "You've got her at eleven and a half inches tall, a half inch shorter than Bild Lilli. She's one-sixth the scale of a real woman, but you're forgetting there's no such thing as one-sixth scale in the thickness of fabric. Fabric is fabric. In order to make anything with a waistband, it's going to require the bulk of the fabric plus whatever fastener we're going to use. That means you have to make her waistline smaller than normal just to compensate for the thickness of the fabric. Otherwise, it'll make her look bulky, stocky."

"Why didn't you say something sooner?" he asks.

"I didn't think about it until just now. I've never worked on something this size."

None of them have. It's all trial and error. And lately, it's been more about errors. Every detail on the doll has been a challenge. Jack almost pulled his own hair out trying to invent the doll's hair. Every monofilament he tried failed in testing—some deteriorated in the rooting process, some attracted moisture and grew moldy, some wouldn't hold the color dye. Finally, Jack consulted a team of Dow chemists who had devised a special polyvinylidene chloride substance called Saran, and that finally worked. The next hurdle was sourcing the right kind of plastic for the doll's head, the torso, the arms and legs. Everything was either too hard or too soft, and they tinkered for months, heating and then cooling polyvinyl chloride, trying to figure out the right combination of plasticizers for this doll. And even now they're not convinced they've gotten it right. Despite what Greiner & Hausser, the makers of Bild Lilli, were able to do, Ruth, Jack and Charlotte are going to take their doll many steps further.

Jack hasn't slept in thirty-three hours. He isn't tired. Not in the least. He's exhilarated and hyperaware of his senses. It's like he can hear a baby crying five miles away, can see beyond the walls of his office to the cars zooming by on Century Boulevard. There's a sharp, frenetic crackling reverberating inside him that doesn't let up and would make anyone else want to jump out of their skin. But this is Jack.

This is how he gets when he's fully engrossed in a project. And he cherishes it, riding the wave for as long as it lasts. Because he knows this surge will be followed by the bottomless crash, where the current suddenly shuts off and he's left feeling listless and hollowed out. It's a worthless kind of emptiness that negates whatever achievements might have preceded it. And that's when he enters the long black tunnel, and it can take him days, weeks or even months to find his way out.

But for now, he is fully alive, and he's done the work of five men. The walls of his office are papered with mechanical drawings of legs, arms, necks. He's prepared side views of the torso in elevation, in vertical cross-section views, in perspective views. He's defining points of articulation. He's tinkering with the longitudinal bores placed inside the legs that interact telescopically with a set of pins in the base of her feet, allowing the doll to balance in various positions with the help of a stand. There are a million decisions to be made, and they come down to him. He feels a little mad, like Dr. Frankenstein creating his monster. But this doll is no monster. No, when he's done with her, she will be a goddess.

There's a knock on the door. It's Ginger, his secretary. She's tall with a prominent and ever so slightly hooked nose, thick brown hair and an even thicker waistline. Jack does not find Ginger attractive, which is why he hired her, a conciliatory gesture for his wife, Barbara, after getting into trouble with his secretary at Raytheon.

If only Ginger were the answer to Jack's troubled marriage. He appreciates how hard it is for his wife to stay married to him. He's sure she'd be better off without him, and he'd leave her if it weren't for their two young daughters and his father. James J. Ryan, despite his own countless affairs, believes divorce is a mortal sin that will send his son straight to hell. Jack worships his father, forever seeking his approval, so divorce—at least in his father's lifetime—is out of the question.

"This just came in from legal," Ginger says, holding up a stack of papers. "It's about the licensing agreement with Greiner and Hausser."

Jack ruffles his hair and sighs. "Okay, let's hear it."

Ginger begins to read the two-page memo advising Jack and Ruth to secure a licensing agreement with G&H for the rights to base the doll off Bild Lilli. Jack doodles more legs on his sketchpad while listening to her read, taking in every word:

". . . therefore, regarding patent infringement surrounding the marketing of this particular doll . . ."

Ginger is a godsend—his personal gatekeeper and the keeper of a secret she knows nothing about. Innocently she takes copious notes in meetings and reads them back to him, along with every long-winded interoffice memo, every newspaper article of note, every patent registration form he has to complete. And it's not that Jack can't read. He's not illiterate. At a young age he was diagnosed with word blindness, meaning that he can read a menu, road signs, even simple phrases, but when strung together in sentences and paragraphs, words make no sense to him. He gets tangled up in anything too long. Everything turns to double vision, as if his eyes have been dilated. Other times the sentences form wave patterns, or individual letters will appear more like symbols. He's never read a book cover to cover and would never have graduated from Yale had he not cleverly organized study groups wherein other students did the reading and reported back to him. He inherently understood everything that they themselves were struggling to comprehend. Even as a child, he had the ability to see things three-dimensionally. A born engineer, he's always interpreted the world in terms of interconnected systems and structures. This keeps him just a few steps ahead of everyone else.

". . . and based on my preliminary investigation," Ginger continues, "there are substantial similarities between the G and H product and the proposed product for which we are . . ."

Throughout his life, Jack's kept his secret and found ways to

work around this obstacle. Doctors' excuses claiming vision problems allowed him to take exams orally, and now Ginger seamlessly
and unknowingly fills in all the blanks for him here at Mattel.

She's never questioned why her boss insists she read to him.
She'll do anything for him, anything at all. He's the first man who's
ever made her feel important, and after a lifetime of being invisible
to men, that does more for her than he'll ever know. Unlike her
father, Jack remembers her birthday and even sends her flowers.
And last year on Valentine's Day he gave her a heart-shaped box of
chocolates. Of course, he did that for all the other women in the
office, too, but still . . .

"However," Ginger continues, "there are concerns about the
prior art, and therefore, I would strongly recommend . . ."

After she finishes reading to him, Ginger observes him already
leaning over his drafting table, eager to get back to work. "You really love working on this doll, don't you?" she says.

"You kidding me? I'm in heaven." He laughs. "I'm creating the
world's most perfect woman."

"So you really think she's perfect, huh?"

"She will be when I'm finished with her."

Even before Ginger's closed his office door, Jack is back at work,
examining and reexamining his calculations. To achieve the look of
an hourglass figure and get past the added bulk of the fabric, Jack's
had to trick the eye, create an optical illusion. On paper, the doll's
measurements are absurd: 39"-18"-33". The same is true for the
doll's feet. *What grown woman wears a size three shoe?* But anything
larger will look clown-like. The littlest details have tripped him up,
like the doll's hands. After Jack consulted with a sculptor to get
them just right, Charlotte so astutely pointed out that they wouldn't
work with the clothes.

"You'll never be able to fit her hands through the sleeves. You can't have her fingers spread out. They have to be together and narrow, like this." She demonstrated.

"Wait," said Jack. "Don't move. Hold that pose." Charlotte's hands were exquisite. How had he not noticed before just how long and tapered and elegant her fingers were? He reached for a Polaroid, capturing her hands from every conceivable angle before regrouping with the sculptor and saying, "Those are the hands. That's what I want."

Jack is now lost in thought when Ruth enters his office without bothering to knock. "I had a thought on the name. What about Lady? The Lady Doll." She smiles, shoulders thrown back. "It's simple, and to the point."

"Lady?" he laughs, tucking a pencil behind his ear. "As in *Lady and the Tramp*?"

"Oh, shit." Her posture sags. Why are all the good names already taken and why is this so hard? She's been grinding her brain, going over every alliteration, every imaginable combination. Nothing feels right. Ruth glances down at Jack's drafting table. "Let me see what you're working on there."

"Just trying to finalize the features for her face."

She leans in closer. Whereas Bild Lilli has a severe expression, a cunning, playfully naughty look about her, Jack is designing a beauty queen.

"She's too pretty," says Ruth.

"There's no such thing as *too* pretty."

"She can't be *that* pretty," Ruth says. "She has to be attractive, yes, but she can't be so beautiful that little girls can't relate to her. They have to be able to see themselves in this doll. That's the whole point of her. Little girls have to look at this doll and be able to picture their own futures."

"But the nose," says Jack, "now, that's a beautiful nose."

"That's the problem. It's *too* beautiful."

"I suppose you think her lips are too pouty," says Jack.

"As a matter of fact, I do. And those cheekbones are way too high."

"Anything else you'd like to ruin?"

"Yeah. While you're at it, tone down her eyelashes. They're too fluttery."

"Too fluttery my ass."

But he ends up doing as she says, because they both recognize that when it comes to collaboration there's always a little give-and-take. They push and nudge their ideas forward, each hoping the other will see their brilliance. It's a dance, and they don't mind stepping on each other's toes. They have an uncanny ability to work in unison, to harmonize and build on each other's ideas. When Jack says the doll should be freestanding, she suggests they create a base for her, and he designs one that is virtually invisible. When Jack wants to give her long hair, Ruth wants it in a topknot pony-tail. Each one lays down a rung on their ladder that ultimately results in a race to the top, for Ruth Handler and Jack Ryan are nothing if not competitive.

The Power of Pink

1957

After another long day, Ruth pulls out of the Mattel parking lot in her new pink Thunderbird convertible, a present from Elliot for their nineteenth wedding anniversary in June. He had it custom-painted for her in the shade she selected. And it's not that pink is Ruth's favorite color—it's that her sister taught her early on that a woman in business has to be tough as nails inside while still appearing feminine on the outside. "If you come across too hard," Sarah said, "you're a ballbuster, and no one wants to work with a woman like that. But if you're too soft, they'll roll right over you. This way, you keep them guessing. They don't know what to make of you. Striking that balance between the two will be your secret weapon." Ruth took her sister's words to heart and watched her in action, noting the way Sarah would always let the men hold the door for her, lift boxes and crates and anything they deemed too heavy for a woman. Sarah could smoothly haggle with a vendor—a firm tone under a laughing voice. She dressed neatly and modestly but was never without her bright red lipstick. Even up until the very end. A pang hits Ruth in the chest—even after a decade she still misses her big sister. Sarah is the reason why Ruth wears her pearls every day, why, no matter how busy she is, she makes time for her weekly manicure.

Forty-five minutes later, she pulls into the long drive of their Beverlywood home on Duxbury Circle. It's a big house on the cusp of Beverly Hills. They bought it in 1955 after their first big success, the Burp Gun, which sold more than a million units the year it launched. It was the first time they felt *rich*. The floodgates had opened and, admittedly, they went a little overboard. They were suddenly in the big leagues. They had a financial advisor, life insurance policies—they felt like grown-ups. The freedom of seeing something in a store window and saying *I'll take it* was irresistible. Ruth went from buying off the rack at the May Company to shopping the exclusive Los Angeles boutiques and owning half a dozen Chanel suits. Elliot got the Mercedes-Benz he'd always wanted. They started traveling first-class and took family vacations to London and Paris. They hired a driver to take the children to and from school, partly because they were too busy to do it themselves, and partly because Elliot worried about kidnappers, given their newfound wealth. And then, of course, they bought the house, which they promptly tore down to the studs and rebuilt. Elliot designed the entire place with floor-to-ceiling windows and custom millwork throughout. *Better Homes and Gardens* called it a *modern marvel*. *Architectural Digest* said it was *fanciful*, with its spiral staircase encircling an actual two-story-high oak tree with toy birds perched on the branches. There isn't another house like it anywhere. It's certainly nothing like the home Ruth grew up in back in Denver, a one-story, two-bedroom clapboard with a tiny front porch and three wooden steps in varying degrees of rot.

The sun is about to set, streaking the sky red and orange, casting a warm glow above the rooftop. The sprawling lawn is flanked with palm trees, fig and pomegranate trees, too, and there's a swimming pool out back, which Ruth rarely gets to enjoy these days because the doll is taking up so much of her time.

They've been working on it for over a year now, and Ruth has long since given up on the hope of launching it at this year's Toy Fair. They're nowhere near ready. Jack's having problems with the arm sockets. Plus, they still don't have a name for it: *Molly Model, Make-Believe Belinda*—each one is worse than the next. But despite the hiccups, there is something magical and all-consuming about creating this doll. Each tiny victory is hard-won, the result of so many previous attempts that didn't work. When Jack finally got the hip joint to move right, when they got the hairline rooted correctly, when they figured out the perfect arch of the doll's foot, high enough to support the mules Charlotte was constructing, they celebrated like they'd won the World Series. On more than one occasion, they've broken out champagne and toasted with paper cups and coffee mugs.

But then there are days like today. The reason she's so late getting home is because that afternoon they received their first shipment of prototypes. They were so excited and couldn't wait to get the boxes open. But when Jack uncrated the first doll, they were speechless. *What did the translator tell KBK?* The doll looked Japanese, and her epicanthal folds were only part of the problem. They used the wrong plastic, and lo and behold, they gave the doll nipples. Jack nearly sawed off one of the doll's arms while trying to file away the areolae with his Swiss Army knife. Ruth would have been home over an hour ago had they not been on an overseas call with their translator and KBK, trying to sort out the whole mess.

Ruth's always been a hard worker, but everything's intensified since she began working on the doll. It used to be that by five, maybe six o'clock at the latest, she was done for the day, and she left her work at the office. They always made a point of having dinner together as a family. She played tennis at the club and met friends for lunch once, sometimes twice a week. She has no idea what happened to their mixed doubles game. It seems to have evaporated over the past few months, like most of their social life. She's been so busy, she missed Barbara's parent-teacher conference last week. It just completely slipped her mind. Ruth had her secretary send the teacher flowers and a note of apology. She probably should have sent them instead to Barbara, who claimed to be so embarrassed she didn't want to go to school the next day. She also missed one of Ken's piano recitals, but it couldn't be helped—she and Charlotte were sourcing fabrics. Admittedly there's not much balance in Ruth's life now, but it's temporary, just until she gets this doll launched.

Ruth enters through the front door, slings her pocketbook onto the marble table in the foyer and shuffles through the mail. Slipping off her heels, she pads on her aching feet through the living room, where the last traces of sunlight glint off the lid of the grand piano, Ken's fingerprints visible on the fallboard. Just beyond that, in the dining room, Elliot and the kids are finishing up dinner.

"Sorry I'm late," she calls out. "We had another crisis."

"We waited as long as we could," says Elliot with an apologetic shrug. "I didn't know when you'd get home. I had Edna keep a plate warm for you."

Ruth nods and plops down at her place at the table. It's heaped with schoolbooks and homework, as if they knew better than to expect she'd be home in time to eat with them.

"How was school?" she asks collectively as she pushes the books aside and rests her elbows on the table.

"I don't want to talk about it," says Ken, chasing a pea around his plate.

"Didn't you have tryouts today?" she asks.

"I *said* I *don't* want to talk about it." Ken drops his fork with a clank.

He is rarely gruff like this. Ken is a studious twelve-year-old with a crew cut, thick glasses and occasional clusters of acne. Ruth worries about him. He's a loner. More introverted than his older sister and thankfully less moody, too. Usually.

"And what about you?" She turns to Barbara, who has hardly looked up from her plate. "How did rehearsal go?"

"May I be excused?" Her request is directed at Elliot.

"Something wrong with the steak?" asks Ruth. "It's your favorite."

"I'm full," she says, scooting away from the table and heading out of the dining room, her feet falling hard, stopping just shy of an outright stomp.

"What's wrong with her?" asks Ruth, picking at some mashed potatoes left on Barbara's plate.

Elliot shrugs and cocks his head toward Ken, meaning *Not in front of him.*

Ken asks if he can be excused, too, and once he's out of earshot, Elliot says, "He didn't make the team, in case you didn't figure that out."

"I assumed as much." She props her forehead against her hand, massaging her throbbing temples.

"He'll be all right," says Elliot. "I talked him into joining the chess team instead."

She nods and realizes she's hungry, starving actually. She can't remember if she ate lunch that day. She takes a bite of Barbara's Salisbury steak.

"The kids miss you, Ruthie."

"I know." There's a stab of guilt just below her rib cage that makes her breath catch.

"You're never home anymore. You're not available when they need you—"

"Oh, c'mon, that's not true." But her defense is weak because they both know he's right.

"You're always working. Or preoccupied with work. It's taking a toll on them."

She drops her fork and pushes the plate away. "Don't you think I see how unhappy my children are? Jesus, Elliot, I feel guilty enough as it is. I don't need you to make me feel any worse than I already do."

"I don't want to fight about this, Ruthie."

She doesn't want to fight, either, but she does want to point out that coming home on time won't make Ken more athletic. It won't clear up his acne or cure his farsightedness. It won't make him more popular at school. Slowing down at work won't make Barbara more tolerant of the other cast members or of the classmates who she says *copy* her outfits even though they all wear the same poodle skirts and saddle shoes. Even if Ruth quit working altogether, she couldn't set things right for her children.

It's such a contrast to how she is at the office. There, she is a force. Decisive and sure-footed, she can make a $200,000 decision to switch shipping companies just like that. She can stand up in front of a roomful of men and tell them what to do. She can hire and fire people and change their financial futures with the stroke of a pen. At Mattel she's able to make an impact, whereas at home, she is ineffective. And nothing else makes her feel more worthless than that. Is it any wonder why she works as much as she does? At least she's not emotionally vulnerable at work, not looking to her staff to love and accept her.

Do You Want to Dance?

You seem to be in an awfully good mood today," Dr. Greene observes, indicating in his notes that Jack appears to be entering a bout of mania. His last manic episode had been four months prior. In addition to attending Group once a week with his wife, Jack also sees Dr. Greene privately. There are things he can't talk about in front of Barbara and a room full of loons. For example, today Dr. Greene wants to probe deeper into what he refers to as Jack's "hypersexuality syndrome."

"I like sex and my wife doesn't," Jack says. "Barbara and I have an understanding about this. She knows I go elsewhere for sex. Is that such a crime?"

Dr. Greene tilts his head before flipping to a clean page. "Do you remember your first sexual awakening?"

"No," Jack lies, knowing exactly when this occurred. He owes his sexual awakening to the Rockettes. He grew up in New York, where his father was a big developer, and one afternoon, twelve-year-old Jack accompanied him to Radio City Music Hall. While his father was busy with clients, Jack sneaked into the orchestra pit to watch the Rockettes rehearse. That kickline—those legs—oh, what they did to his young body, making it tingle and harden in ways he'd never known possible.

"Really?" says Dr. Greene. "No recall? None whatsoever?" He clears his throat.

Jack remains silent.

"How are we doing on the masturbating?" Dr. Greene asks.

"*We* are doing just fine with that. I've taken matters into my own hands," he says, knowing Dr. Greene won't appreciate his pun. Dr. Greene is concerned about frequency, the goal being to reduce the number of *incidents* to a *normal* range. But who's to say what's normal?

Now Dr. Greene changes the subject. "In our last session, you were talking about your childhood and your parents."

Jack sighs, then groans.

"You said your father is distant."

"My father is a cold, callous sonofabitch." But Jack still reveres him.

"And your mother?"

Jack laughs. "Lily Ryan is a pretentious snob. She's all about appearances."

It's true. A perfect example was Jack's childhood home in Riverdale, on the fringe of Manhattan and the Bronx. Theirs was the largest house on the block, with a big circular drive, columns out front and ornate ironwork on the door. Unfortunately, the inside of the house did not match the grand exterior. His mother had a vision and was forever re-wallpapering, repainting, reupholstering, trying to get it just right. The result was a clutter of ladders and paint-splattered drop cloths all around. Jack often feels like he *is* that house, so appealing on the outside in his tailored suits and silk ascots, but on the inside, a mess.

"I recall you mentioned not being allowed to have friends over."

"Oh hell no. My mother wouldn't allow anyone *inside* the house. Even delivery boys had to leave stuff on the back porch. Having friends over was out of the question. Besides, she didn't approve of any of them, and if I was invited to their houses, she'd say, 'You don't want to mix with those sorts. Those people are commoners.'" Jack laughs sadly. "Everyone was a commoner or a loser, too bourgeois, too uncouth, too oafish, too *something*."

"That must have been quite lonely for you," says Dr. Greene.

"Can we change the subject, please?" The truth is, he's still lonely. Especially in his own home. His wife is right there, but he feels her flinch each time he touches her. It wasn't that way in those first few years—there was laughter, intimacy and sex, though never quite as much as he would have liked. Still, he thought they were good together, and yet, somewhere between having children and his work, they lost each other, the chasm between them impossible to cross, impossible to deny. She can't give him what he needs and vice versa.

Now he tries to fill that empty void any which way he can. Aside from insomnia bouts, he cannot sleep alone unless he's passed out, and Jack would sooner set his hair on fire than eat in a restaurant by himself. If only his mother had allowed him to have friends. It's because of her that he learned at a young age to live inside his head, and now, he's parked there.

Elliot leaves work early one day to run some errands before heading home. He's out back by the pool taking stock of the improbable fact that he, Elliot Handler, owns a home with a swimming pool and no mortgage. When he met Ruth, his pockets were empty. They were at a charity dance for B'nai B'rith and he borrowed a nickel from his friend to get in so he could dance with her. By the end of that first foxtrot, he was in love and didn't know what to do about it. She was out of his league. How could a kid from Denver's west side—who ran around town with a bunch of Jewish and Italian thugs—possibly win the heart of a girl like Ruthie Mosko?

Later that night, as they stood outside the Denver Lodge on Colfax Avenue, he dried his sweating palm on his pant leg before daring to hold her hand. His voice croaked when he asked if he could walk her home. He didn't have a car and she lived more than a mile away, but she agreed. So walk they did, her delicate hand in his. Elliot's head was swimming with excitement as he anticipated their first kiss. Oh, how he'd agonized over it, trying to figure out how to orchestrate it. When should he kiss her? For how long? Should it be a peck? On the cheek? On the lips? Something more intimate? Could he dare French-kiss her? While he was running all this through his mind, Ruthie stopped on the sidewalk, the streetlight glowing all around her, making her look even more angelic. They were just a few blocks from the lodge when she got up on her tiptoes and kissed him, long and soft and full of miracles. Elliot smiles remembering that moment and how she took charge then and forever since. She was even the one who proposed marriage. And thank heaven for that.

He goes to the toolshed and takes down the long-handled skimmer off the hooks on the side and collects leaves and insects floating on the water's surface. They have a pool boy who comes in twice a week, but Elliot likes taking care of the pool himself when he has time. He focuses on going after a coppery, iridescent-backed beetle in the shallow end.

Elliot knows he'd never have this pool or the house and for sure not a successful company without Ruth. Had it not been for her, Elliot and his friend Matt would still be working in a garage, *potchking* around with Lucite picture frames. It was Ruth who had the idea to go out and sell them. Eleven years ago, she made her first sales call, shlepping a sample suitcase she could barely lift into a home furnishings store. Before she'd even gotten the case open, the owner said he wasn't interested.

"Don't be in such a hurry to say no." Ruth held out a frame, explaining that Lucite was the latest thing. "I'm giving you first dibs, but if you're not interested, I'll just sell these to your competition." That man ended up placing a $3,000 order, and knowing she'd made him bend to her will set a fire under her. It was like a pilot light that to this day has never gone out.

She never lost her drive, even during the tough times, of which there were many. Just as their picture frame business was getting off the ground, the government needed all plastic products for the war effort. Apparently, the war effort needed Elliot, too, but he was thankfully never sent into combat. As soon as he was back home, Elliot and Matt started working with cheap lumber and wood scraps, designing dollhouse furniture. Once again—but now with two children in tow—Ruth went about selling those items and learning the toy business. She studied trade magazines like she was cramming for a test. She even took a train by herself to New York City to attend her first Toy Fair in 1945. She had no idea how enormous the toy industry was and just how much money there was to be made there.

After that Ruth convinced Elliot and Matt to go into business together. Their first year out of the gate they made $30,000, and they more than tripled that in their second year. By 1947, they'd made their mark in the industry with Elliot's Uke-A-Doodle, a plastic toy ukulele. Since they'd outgrown their little storefront, Ruth negotiated the lease for their first building. When their payroll hit one hundred people, Matt became overwhelmed. It was too much for him, and Ruth encouraged Elliot to buy out Matt's interest for

$15,000—it was a king's ransom at the time, and they'd borrowed the money from Sarah and her husband, Louie, to do it.

"What are you doing out here?" asks Ruth now, coming through the sliding glass doors. "Is everything okay?" She sets her purse and car keys on one of the lounge chairs. "I came out of my meeting and they said you'd already left for the day."

"I had to get the pressure checked on my rear tires. And I stopped by the travel agent. We're all set. Two weeks in Hawaii. A resort hotel right on the beach. We'll go whale watching and take a helicopter ride over Kauai—oh, and a boat trip along the Napali Coast. Doesn't that sound great?"

"When is this again?" she asks, sitting down on the lounge chair.

"We'll leave June eighth—that first Saturday after school lets out."

"Oh." Ruth chews on her lip, sighs with exaggeration.

The tone of her voice, the look on her face—he knows what's coming and he can't bear to hear her say it. "Oh, no, Ruthie. You cannot back out of this trip. The kids will be crushed. They've been looking forward to this for months."

"Okay, all right," she says, capitulating. "I'll go."

"And what? Sit in the hotel room and work the whole time like you did in Tahoe? In Niagara Falls?"

"That's not fair."

"Isn't it? Can you even remember the last time we went on vacation when you didn't spend half the time working? I'll tell you when it was, it was Europe—that was over a year ago—before you saw that damn doll." He lifts the net from the pool, flips it over, tapping it on the cement to empty his trappings.

"What do you want me to say? I'm trying to run a company."

"It's my company, too, Ruthie. You forget that sometimes." This comes out harsher than he intended. He doesn't like losing his temper. That tends to upset him more than the thing that infuriated him in the first place. Now his head is hurting; now he's aware of the stagnant air and the tightness in his chest.

"I have never forgotten that," she says. And she means it. But like so many creative types, Elliot's not necessarily a businessman. He's a dreamer, fanciful and childlike. And like Jack, Elliot can tinker with a toy forever. Without her pushing, nothing gets finished. Can't he appreciate the kind of pressure she's under? She carries their business on her shoulders.

"Ever since you found that doll you've been consumed with work. You don't have time for anything else—not even your family. You spend more time with Jack these days than you do me."

"Please don't tell me you're jealous of Jack."

"Of course not. God no." He takes a deep breath, tries to find the words to explain himself. "But I know what happens when two people collaborate on a project. There's a bond that no one else can penetrate. There's an energy, and I know you feel it. He does, too. It's like a private club that no one else can join. Didn't you feel that way when I was working with Matt?"

She was so busy selling, getting their business up and running, she never thought of it that way.

"So yes," says Elliot, ashamed to admit it. "I guess I am a little jealous of your partnership with Jack."

"Then work with us. God knows we could use your help."

He shakes his head. "I'm sorry, but I don't see why you're so hell-bent on making this doll. It's not going well, Ruthie. One week the hair's not working. The next, it's the arms. And you still don't have a name. You're going in circles. I've worked on a lot of toys, and when you hit this many roadblocks, the universe is trying to tell you something. It shouldn't be *this* hard. Plus, the whole concept of a doll like this, with the breasts . . ." He shakes his head again. "It just doesn't feel right. No one else has the guts to say it to your face, but we think you need to hit the brakes."

"Who's *we*?"

"The accountants, the lawyers, half the developers and engineers. There's too much risk involved."

"Oh, come on, we've always taken risks." Though, really, she's the risk-taker who then persuades Elliot to go along with the plan. "It's how we've built this company. It's why we're successful."

"That's not the only reason. You and I have different strengths that complement each other, and that's why we've been successful. I design and you sell."

And then she gets it. It's not only that he's jealous of Jack. "Do you resent me for trying to create a toy?"

"Don't be ridiculous."

"I'm serious. Do you?" He doesn't usually challenge her, and that's a big reason why their marriage works. She leads and he follows, happily, willingly. But then again, she's never veered into his area of expertise before. But she's not trying to take anything away from Elliot or upstage him at all. It's just that she's banking everything she's got on this doll's success, and when all is said and done, she wants it known that this was her idea, her vision.

"Ruthie, I've never told you how to go out there and sell, have I?"

"So you *do* resent it."

"Now you're insulting me. It's not about you designing, it's about *what* you're designing. It's a toy that doesn't make any sense." He hangs the skimmer up on the hooks. He's so angry he can't look at her right now, and he goes back inside the house to simmer down.

Ruth stays outside on the lounge chair, watching the droplets of water gathering on the cement beneath the net. With each fresh drip of water, she feels her family pulling farther and farther away from her.

They always vowed never to go to bed angry, but Elliot's already asleep by the time Ruth comes upstairs. She considers waking him to talk it out, but it's late, she's exhausted, and part of her thinks he should apologize, or at least meet her halfway. She feels like he's asking her to choose between her family and work.

She sits with this for a moment, trying to see it from his point of view. Maybe Elliot has some cause to be jealous of Jack. There is an intensity if not an intimacy that's developed over the past year or so. The two of them can fall into fits of laughter just as easily as they can be at each other's throats. When one of them gets an idea, the first thing they do is rush to the other's office to share it. There is passion—not of a romantic sort, but then again, who's to say what the difference is. You're giving your heart and offering up all that you've got inside.

What frustrates Ruth, though, is that an opportunity like this doesn't come along every day, and Elliot can't see it. If this doll is even half as successful as Ruth thinks she'll be, they will be set for life, and so will their children, grandchildren and great-grandchildren.

Ruth knows what it's like to have money one day, lose it all the next. Her sister's drugstore had plenty of ups and downs, and Louie often joined Ruth's father at the poker tables. Sarah never knew when he'd come home or if she'd be able to put food on the table the following week. Money for even the necessities was never a given. She remembers their electricity being turned off and having to rely on flashlights until Sarah had enough money to pay the bill.

The toy business is always a gamble, and this fear of scarcity is ingrained in Ruth. She would have thought Elliot would understand better than anyone. Has he forgotten how broke he was when they met? Does he forget the days when they were lucky if they had $18 in their bank account?

She glances at Elliot, feeling so distant from him even though he's right there. She can't remember the last time they made love. She's too tired in the evenings when his foot crosses to her side of the bed and touches her leg—his mating call. In the mornings, while fastening her pearls and applying her lipstick, she'll look at him through the mirror and say, "Want to tonight?" He understands the shorthand and always smiles, always says, "Sure." But when *tonight* comes, she's too tired, or he's too engrossed in a book or a television program. And another day goes by.

Ruth eventually dozes off into a restless sleep and is disoriented for a moment when the alarm goes off. It stirs them both, and even before she opens her eyes, their argument replays in her mind. She doesn't want something like a doll to come between them. Elliot is the best thing that's ever happened to her, and she loves this man in all the big and small ways. She loves his creativity and is endlessly fascinated by how his mind works. Only Elliot can point to a cracked sidewalk and see an old man's profile where everyone else sees broken concrete. He has the ability to spot the goodness in everything—even in her. She loves that he gives the best foot massages, loves that he never curses out other drivers when they're stuck in traffic and rarely loses his temper with the kids. He loves to laugh, and when he does, it makes her laugh, too. She loves that V-shaped patch of hair on his forehead, all that's left of his dark, lanky curls. And his smell. Elliot has a unique smell, clean and sun-kissed. And he never has body odor. Ever. In all the years she's known him, no matter if he's golfed eighteen holes, played six sets of tennis or been working with a blowtorch in a hot garage, he still smells good to her, welcoming and pleasing.

She scoots over to his side of the bed. "I'm sorry," she whispers into his ear.

Still half-asleep, he pulls her closer. "I'm sorry, too."

A tear slips from the corner of her eye and onto her pillowcase. She doesn't let herself cry often, finding tears to be a waste of time. But this morning's tears are her contrition because she realizes she's been taking him for granted.

"I'm sorry," he says again. "I just miss you, Ruthie. That's all."

This makes her cry harder as she buries her face in his shoulder, already growing damp from her tears.

"Shush." He soothes her, rubbing circles on her back. "It's okay, Ruthie. We're okay."

She breathes him in deeply, feeling her whole body expand as all her little hurt, empty spaces fill with his love for her. Nothing else feels as safe to her as Elliot, and at times like this, when she's so raw, she never wants to be anywhere but at his side, even as the voice inside her head is urging her to hurry up, get showered, get dressed and get to work.

Let's Call Her Barbie

One evening when Elliot stops in Ruth's office to let her know he's leaving for the day, he finds her and Jack in a panic. There's a bottle of scotch on her desk and half the room is wallpapered with giant sheets of paper filled with Ruth's handwriting: *Dilly-Dolly, My Big Dolly, Grown-Up Girly*. When Elliot asks what's going on, they tell him about a new doll that the Ideal Toy Company is releasing.

"And this isn't another Betsy Wetsy," says Jack, slicking his hair back with both hands. "It's an adult doll."

"What do you mean by adult?" asks Elliot.

"*Adult*-adult," says Ruth, her voice tinged with hysteria. "An adult, grown-up doll with high heels and a woman's body and—Jesus Christ, I can't believe this is happening."

"Wait a minute, hold the phone—what *exactly* do you know about this doll?" Elliot asks, ever calm, ever levelheaded and practical, never rushing to conclusions. "It might not be anything like your doll. When's it coming out?"

"A few weeks. A month. A year from now—I don't know," says Jack. "We just found out about it."

"First thing you two need to do is calm down," says Elliot. "For all you know, Ideal's still in the early stages with this doll."

"But we can't afford to take that chance," says Ruth. "This is what I've been afraid of all along. We have to be first to market. We have got to get this doll ready to go. No more delays. No more screwups."

"I think you're overreacting," says Elliot, which only makes her glare at him. "There's room in this market for more than one adult doll. Look at all the different baby dolls, all the toy guns. Everybody's got a jack-in-the-box, a bouncy ball. You'll see, it'll be okay."

"Easy for you to say." Ruth hates it when he's so logical, especially when her emotions take over. It makes her feel unhinged.

"Have either of you even seen their doll?"

"I'm trying to get my hands on one," says Jack. "I've got calls out to Revlon and—"

"Revlon?" Elliot makes a face. "The cosmetics company?"

"Ideal partnered with them," says Ruth. "They're calling it the Miss Revlon Doll. They're way ahead of us. We don't even have a name yet."

"Is that what this is all about?" Elliot gestures to the sheets of paper tacked up everywhere. "You're great with names, Ruthie," he says, trying to make her feel better. "You're the one who came up with the Uke-A-Doodle, and Mattel—that was you, too. It'll come. You can't force it."

"But I *have* to force it. We're running out of time. We *need* a name now."

"You two are making yourselves crazy," says Elliot. "Creativity doesn't work that way. Jack, you know that better than anyone. There's a reason why the best ideas come to you in the shower, or when you're out at the beach. You can't keep grinding over it in your head. C'mon, let's get out of here. You both need a change of scenery."

They end up shooting pool at a bar near the airport that smells of stale beer and whose lights flicker every time a plane takes off or lands. Unfortunately, getting them out of the office hasn't really helped matters. Now, instead of spiraling in her office, they're doing it in a bar. While Elliot and Jack are shooting pool, Ruth is anxiously swerving left then right on her stool, shouting out names. "What about Fashion Franny? Or Melody Model?"

Elliot's stayed out of it so far because this is their toy, not his, but he can't stand watching them go at it like this. Naming a toy is like naming a baby. A name attaches a personality to that child, and after coming up with endless possibilities, you look at your newborn and just know which one is right. A toy is no different. He hasn't wanted to overstep, but the ideal name is so obvious to him. All this time it's been right there, hiding in plain sight.

"You know," Elliot says, after Jack takes his next shot, "you both have some pretty important people in your lives named Barbara. You could call it the Barbara doll. Or the Babs doll. Or hey, even better—what about Barbie?"

Ruth stops fidgeting at the bar. Jack is still leaning over the pool table. They are frozen in place and looking at Elliot with their mouths open. *Barbie. Barbie. Barbie.* It's fun-spirited, bouncy, and perky. It's got a certain pizzazz and presence. It's perfect.

Jack straightens up, smacking his forehead. "Why didn't somebody think of that?"

"I just did," says Elliot.

"It makes perfect sense," says Ruth. "Our daughter, Jack's wife!"

"A tribute to both our Barbaras," says Jack.

"Oh, let's do it," says Ruth. "Let's call her Barbie."

It's settled. Finally. They stay at the bar and celebrate with bottles of Miller High Life—*the Champagne of Beers.* This is a huge step, and they're giddy with excitement and relief. With a name, their doll feels real. Now she's more than just a hypothetical, more than just a concept.

"C'mon," says Elliot, checking his watch and setting his empty bottle on the bar. "Drink up. It's late, and we got a lot of work to do on this doll."

"I don't believe it." Ruth looks at him, smiling. "Did I just hear you say *we*? Does this mean you're officially joining the doll team?"

"You mean the Barbie doll team," says Elliot. He laughs, accepting the fact that if he wants to spend time with his wife, he needs to embrace her Barbie doll.

Ten Fingers and Ten Toes

1958

Ruth is sitting at the conference room table beneath a cigarette cloud of her own making, watching Jack bounce a rubber ball off the wall—*thump, thump, thump. Thump, thump, thump.*

"Do you mind?" she says, pressing her fingertips to her skull.

"Mind what?" *Thump, thump, thump.*

"Jesus, Jack." She gets up and rips the ball from his grip.

"Well, then give me a cigarette or something. I gotta do something with my hands."

"Fine." She slides the pack to him.

They are awaiting the arrival of the next round of prototypes from Tokyo. Someone from the loading dock telephoned reception to say they'd arrived, and they had better be right this time. They've been working on Barbie for two years now. They wanted to launch her at this year's Toy Fair, the granddaddy of trade shows for their industry. It's held every March in New York City, but Barbie wasn't ready in time, so now she'll debut at next year's show—if they're lucky. At least they don't have to worry about the Miss Revlon Doll anymore. She scared the hell out of them until they saw what she looked like: an oversized head, a ridiculously high waist, a pancake of a bosom. She was just a glorified baby doll with lipstick and clunky high heels. Miss Revlon isn't even in the same league as their Barbie doll.

Charlotte tumbles into the conference room, her arms loaded down with fabric swatches, a measuring tape looped about her neck. Ruth has recently hired her full-time and at a premium salary of $15,000 a year.

"I want to run these by you both," says Charlotte, dumping her wares on the table. "Take a look and tell me what you think."

Splayed out before them are squares of cotton, velvet, rayon, taffeta and silk, some with tiny bees, tiny flower petals, wee itty-bitty plaids, stripes and houndstooth patterns. It's been impossible to find patterned fabrics small enough to work with Barbie's scale, so Charlotte's been creating her own step-and-repeat designs from scratch.

"Ooh, I like the polka dots," says Jack, reaching for the swatch, running it through his fingers. "They're peachy."

"Yeah," Ruth agrees, as she picks up another fabric square. "They're sweet. I like this pink-and-white-striped one, too."

"We can do some mixing and matching, too," Charlotte says, pulling out a chair and dropping into it.

Ruth looks at the dark circles beneath Charlotte's eyes, the lingering cough from that cold she can't seem to get rid of. The woman is exhausted, and Ruth feels responsible. She recently sent Charlotte to Japan so she could prepare the team of seamstresses who will eventually be mass-producing Barbie's clothes. Before that, Charlotte was in Paris for the fashion shows, seeking inspiration for Barbie from Balenciaga, Givenchy and Schiaparelli. Ruth knows she's asking a lot of Charlotte and frequently issues bonuses and other perks, like a company car, to pacify her and keep her from leaving.

Not that Charlotte has any such plans. Quite the contrary. If it weren't for Mattel, she's not sure what she'd do with herself. Charlotte's a night owl and often brings work home just so she has something to do in the evenings. She's tried dating, but men have funny ideas about divorced women and she's not looking for a roll in the sack.

After Charlotte collects her fabric swatches and heads back to her office, Ruth smokes another cigarette, wondering where the hell those dolls are. She's anxious because last month another disastrous shipment arrived from Tokyo. The doll's nose and cheeks were blistered up; half her fingers and toes were missing.

Jack had cursed and chucked the doll back into the box. He explained that the roto casting hadn't worked and that they were going to need people on-site to physically rotate the molds so the vinyl would spread out evenly, all the way to her fingers and toes.

"And what's that going to cost?" she'd asked.

"I don't know. And don't give me that look. I've been telling you all along that making a doll this size, with this degree of detail, has never been done before."

"If the Germans figured out how to do it, why can't you?"

"Jesus, Ruth, we've been through this a hundred times. Nobody's ever used this kind of plastic—not even the Germans. Bild Lilli's hard as a rock. And unless you want to pay the licensing fee to Greiner and Hausser, you need to back off and let me work this out."

There's a knock on the door and Ruth comes back to the moment just as Jack's secretary enters the conference room, carrying a large box. Ginger is a good three inches taller than Jack, and it's no secret that she has a devastating crush on her boss. She dotes on him and would probably feed him grapes while he lounges on his bearskin rug.

Jack takes the box from Ginger and sets it on the table. Pulling out his knife, he carefully slices through the Japanese lettering on the packing label. Ruth's shoulders stiffen; her gut feels like she's swallowed a fist. *What if it didn't work? Again?* They've poured so much money into this project: Jack's travel to Japan, Charlotte's, too, the KBK contract, Charlotte's salary, the lawyers, plus the sheer man-hours it's taken them to get this far.

And it's not just what it's cost the company. What about the price for her emotionally? Because of Barbie there is tension at home—arguments with Elliot, resentment from Barbara and sheer apathy from Ken, who's so used to his mother's absence, he no longer asks when she's coming home. Her entire family has made sacrifices on Barbie's behalf, and what if KBK can't get the doll right? Does she have the wherewithal to go back for another round? Ruth's frustrated and growing increasingly nervous about her ability to pull this off. And yet, giving up is not an option. She isn't one to fail. When things aren't going her way, she backs up and barrels ahead faster and harder than the time before. *Don't force it* means *Give it all you got.* She has a way of breaking things down, making people, circumstances and objects yield to her. Now she needs eleven and a half inches of plastic to do the same.

Jack cuts through the last of the tape, digs through the packing material and pulls out a doll, holding her up to the light for inspection. Ruth can't read his face. His expression hasn't budged.

"Well?" she asks.

"You tell me." He hands her the doll. She looks and looks and looks some more. There's not a single plastic bubble on her cheeks or forehead. Her hairline is evenly rooted. Her arms and legs move. She bends at the waist like she's supposed to. Like the mother of a newborn, she checks the doll, examining her closely. She has ten fingers, ten toes.

Ruth isn't one to squeal, but just then that's exactly what she's doing. It's reflexive and comes leaping out of her. The tension in her body is already unwinding like a spool of thread. She's on her feet now and standing so close to Jack it seems like they should hug or do something to commemorate this moment, but that would be too awkward. She's not one of his admirers, and yet she can't stop herself from pulling him to her. He lifts her off her feet and whirls her around, and the two laugh so hard their eyes leak tears of happiness and relief.

They're still recovering, still basking in their victory, when Henry Pursell, Mattel's general counsel, comes into the conference room.

"Look," says Jack, holding up Barbie. "Isn't she terrific?"

"That's, ah, that's great," says Pursell. "But what about the licensing agreement with Greiner and Hausser? I haven't seen anything yet."

"Don't worry about it," says Jack.

"Well, somebody around here has to worry about it. Before you two invest any more time and money into this Barbie project, you better make sure you've got the rights to transform Bild Lilli into your own doll."

"We'll take care of it," says Ruth. Eventually. Or not. Jack's confident that he's found a way to work around the patents, so they won't even need to enter into an expensive licensing agreement. Besides, they don't have time to deal with something like that. They need to keep things moving. And she knows how Jack operates. Just because they have this new prototype doesn't mean he's done tinkering. No, he's going to be looking for more ways to refine the design. In his mind nothing is ever finished. Everything can be improved upon whether that improvement is visible to the naked eye or not.

She looks again at the doll. There's both a sense of calm and a surge of power churning inside Ruth because they've made it this far and now she knows this is going to work.

Don't Call Her a Doll

Charlotte is drowning. Even with Mia, a sample maker who does all the sewing for her, the workload is too much for one person. Especially since Mattel keeps sending her back to Tokyo to oversee the production of Barbie's initial outfits: a zebra-striped swimsuit, a navy blue and white sundress with a front pleat, and a white wool fleece coat with stylish pockets and a martingale belt.

Ruth has promised to hire another designer. She and Charlotte have already interviewed several candidates but Ruth decided they were NMM—Not Mattel Material.

"We need someone who's tough like us," says Ruth. "Someone I can't make cry."

"That's asking a lot," Charlotte laughs. "You make half the men around here cry. But," she says, "I might just have the right person for this job."

It's her former student Stevie Klein, though the last time Charlotte saw her, Stevie was indeed on the verge of crying, beating back tears. Just three months before graduation, Stevie had sat in Charlotte's office saying she was dropping out of school. Charlotte suspected Stevie's reason but didn't want to shame her into admitting it. The truth was that Stevie was pregnant, a pregnancy that she would lose a few weeks later, along with the man who'd impregnated her. But degreed or not, Stevie Klein had been Charlotte's most promising student at Chouinard.

Stevie stood out from the beginning because she was left-handed. At first Charlotte couldn't imagine how Stevie would overcome such a disadvantage, which ranged from minor to severe. With only right-handed school desks, Stevie sat sideways, forced to write almost upside down, the underpart of her forearm all the way to her elbow smudged with pencil lead. There were no left-handed needle threaders, and no left-handed scissors, either, so it was harder for Stevie to cut a straight line. To create a classic herringbone stitch, she had to work in reverse, from right to left. Even the numbers on her tape measure were upside down when she held the base in her left hand. Yet, with all these strikes against her, Stevie excelled, turning her weaknesses into her greatest strengths. It might have taken her longer to cut her patterns, but they were more precise than anyone else's. She didn't just measure a model once; she measured twice to make sure her readings were accurate. Perhaps it was because Stevie was left-handed that Charlotte noticed how innovative she was and that she possessed a rare type of ingenuity. In Basic Sewing class, Stevie created bound-button holes and preferred double darts over a single dart, even though they were more time-consuming. She would hand stitch her zippers, making them virtually invisible, and Stevie had been the first of Charlotte's students to master the princess seam. She had a flair for the dramatic, inherently understood that different fabrics behaved differently. She knew the emotional properties of colors, and no one had to teach Stevie Klein that form follows function. Plus, she's one tough cookie.

S tevie is standing behind a long counter at a diner on Pico Boulevard where she's been waitressing for the past year, unable to
find work in her field no matter how hard she's tried. Coming off
an eight-hour shift, she'd sketch new ideas over dinner before sitting down at her sewing machine till late at night, working up new
designs to take out into the world. On breaks, she'd change out of
her uniform in a tiny bathroom stall, put on one of her own designs
and rush to an interview. On her days off, she'd knock on every door
she could find, offering herself up as an intern, as an apprentice—
willing to work for free just to gain some experience. But without a
degree, no one's taken her seriously. Her roommate and former
classmate, Vivian Ross, landed a paid internship with Rudi Gern-
reich at R.G. Designs. She'd tried putting in a good word for Stevie,
but nothing came of it.

Now Stevie is staring at the last dregs of catsup dripping from
one upside-down bottle into the waiting mouth of another when
she looks up and sees her old instructor, Mrs. Johnson. She's accompanied by a short man and an even shorter woman, or maybe
they just appear that way since Charlotte, like Stevie, is unusually
tall for a woman. At first Stevie thinks they've just happened
into the diner for an early lunch, but no, they've come to see her,
and their timing is good, because after she finishes with this last
catsup bottle Stevie can finally take her break.

When she steps out from behind the counter, the short man
gives her the once-over and whistles through his teeth. "My oh my."

"Down, boy." Mrs. Johnson smacks him on the shoulder.

"Pay no attention to him," says the other woman.

"Does he bite?" asks Stevie, and when the man grins, scanning her body, she calls him on it, "Hey, Short Stuff—my eyes are up here."

"Ha-ha." The man laughs, delighted by this. "You're a feisty one, aren't you?"

Stevie plants her hands on her hips. "Buddy, you have no idea."

"Ooh, I like her," the woman says as if Stevie's not standing right there.

At this point, Stevie is formally introduced to Jack and Ruth. All of them, including Charlotte—formerly Mrs. Johnson—are now on a first-name basis. They take a booth in the back, the one with the torn-up turquoise seat cushions. Stevie doesn't have a clue what's going on, and while they're making small talk about the traffic on Sepulveda Boulevard, Jack plucks sugar cubes from a little dish next to the salt and pepper shakers and begins building an igloo.

"Charlotte here tells me you were her best student," says Ruth, tapping a pack of cigarettes against the table.

"She was," says Charlotte. "She's a natural-born designer."

This is somewhat true. Stevie caught the design bug early, mostly out of necessity. When she was growing up, her father sold *World Book Encyclopedias* and money was tight. Not wanting to wear secondhand clothes, she convinced her parents to buy her a used Singer sewing machine, a big clunky one with a treadle base that she still has to this day. With the help of a neighbor lady, Stevie taught herself to sew. She had a feel for it almost immediately and became a good seamstress and then an excellent one.

Still, Stevie can't take in Charlotte's praise and continues to blame herself for messing up her career in such a spectacular way. Foolish girl, she thought she was in love. But the universe had a different plan and she learned her lesson. Never put a man first; never let them take you off course. Because of a man, she never graduated, and her dream of being a fashion designer has been packed away, along with her final project: a wedding gown she'll never wear.

The other waitress heads their way with coffees. She has a bad case of knock-knees and walks with a seesaw-ish back and forth stride that sends every cup sloshing on her tray. How she never spills a single drop is a miracle and the sign of a woman devoted to a lifetime of waiting tables. It's enough to make Stevie cry, as if seeing her future self.

"So what brings you down here?" she asks.

Ruth leans forward and clasps her hands, revealing an enormous emerald ring on her finger. "We're coming to you with a terrific opportunity."

"It's all top secret. Completely under wraps," says Jack, who's still working on his igloo, which is now beginning to take on the shape of a castle, complete with a tower and steep walls. When he gets to the last cube, he fetches another dish of sugar from a nearby table, meticulously placing one block and then the next.

"What I'm offering you," says Ruth, "is a chance to design an entire line of clothing. And accessories. All high-end fashion, from casual to formal wear."

"Wait—you're offering me a job? A *design* job?" Stevie's eyebrow rises as she tries to keep a check on her expectations. If this is a joke, she's not finding it funny. Stevie looks at Charlotte for confirmation.

"We'd be working together along with *him*." Charlotte gives Jack a hitchhiker's thumb, frowning playfully. "Technically, he'd be your boss, but you'd be working directly with me."

"We can't give you any other details just yet," says Ruth, picking a fleck of tobacco off her tongue. "You're going to have to trust me—and Charlotte. And take a leap of faith."

"But one thing we *can* tell you"—Jack pauses, leans in conspiratorially, looking both ways as if about to cross a street—"you'd be designing clothes," he whispers, "for a doll."

So it is a joke. Stevie collapses back in her seat.

"I know what you're thinking," says Charlotte. "I felt the same way at first, but this isn't just another doll. She's not like anything you've ever seen before."

"But that's all we can share with you right now." Jack brings a finger to his lips, his eyes crinkling as he smiles. "We've probably said too much already."

"It really is an exciting opportunity," says Ruth. "I wouldn't waste your time—or mine—if it wasn't. And we'll start you off at $200 a week."

Stevie suppresses the urge to gasp. She isn't sure she's heard correctly. Ruth's offering her $200 a week? To design a line of clothing? For a doll? She looks at Charlotte to see if they're serious. *My God, they are.* At the diner she's only making 65¢ an hour plus tips, and that isn't enough to live on. Vivian had to cover Stevie's half of their rent last month, and her greatest fear is being forced back into her parents' home. She has a cavity that needs filling, and just that morning she paid for three gallons of gasoline with nickels and dimes. Her car—an old clunker—is prone to overheating and needs a new battery.

Stevie hopes her face doesn't give her away when she says, "I'll need to think about it." But at $200 a week, there's nothing to think about.

The following Monday at 08:00 hours Mattel speak, the office officially opens. A line is forming out the door with a hundred or more employees waiting to be let inside. Some drink coffee from thermoses and smoke cigarettes; some make small talk with those around them while others keep to themselves, reading their morning newspapers. Mattel has almost eight hundred people on its payroll. They range from young to middle-aged, a mix of men and women, some Mexicans, some Negros, and Orientals. When it comes to Mattel's hiring practices, discrimination is not a factor. Qualifications are all that matter. One by one, each person shows the armed guard their badge, even though he knows most of them by name. The women open their pocketbooks so he can take a look inside before allowing them to proceed.

An hour later, at 09:00 hours, Stevie reports to Mattel for her first day of work. After turning onto Rosecrans Avenue, she arrives at a large one-story white building in a desolate industrial area out by the airport. Pulling into the parking lot, she sees the dreaded haze of steam rising from the hood of her car. As her windshield clears, she hears a thunderous roar and looks up to see an airplane overhead, coming in for landing, so low in the sky she can make out the *TWA* on its tail.

Charlotte asked Stevie to arrive an hour later than normal. There's no line now so she walks right into the building, where she's stopped by the uniformed guard. He rifles through her pocketbook, cluttered with Life Savers wrappers, used tissues, a lipstick, her empty wallet and whatever else has settled to the bottom. The guard nods to the woman behind a plate glass window, who asks for Stevie's driver's license, returning it after a quick glance. Finally, a heavy metal door opens, and Stevie is advanced through a turnstile to the lobby. There's classical music playing, which seems odd given that she's staring at a display case filled with toys: a ukulele, a carousel, a honeybee with wheels, and several plastic guns.

A perky receptionist with auburn hair and freckles appears out of nowhere and, without warning, snaps a Polaroid of Stevie. While fanning it to speed up the developing process, she rings for Charlotte. The receptionist glances at the Polaroid and her smile dips ever so slightly as she holds up what is quite possibly the worst photograph ever taken of Stevie. Her face looks distorted; her nose is too long while her mouth and cheeks appear squished in. It's like her face is a piece of chewing gum stuck on the bottom of someone's shoe.

The receptionist slides the photo into a clear sleeve of a badge, which she hands to Stevie. "You'll need to have this on you at all times."

Stevie wants to ask for a do-over, but that seems vain, and so she slips the lanyard badge about her neck and follows the receptionist down a hallway where Charlotte is waiting for the handoff.

"What's with all the security around this place?" Stevie asks.

"Oh, you'd be surprised how competitive the toy business is. A lot of industrial espionage goes on."

"Ooh"—Stevie pretends to nibble her fingernails—"sounds very sinister."

"Don't laugh. There are spies everywhere."

This is true, and Mattel is even more cautious than other toy companies because Jack and several others are former aerospace engineers. Now the details of the toys they're making are as secretive and guarded as any military operation.

Charlotte gives Stevie the grand tour, starting with a long-paneled wall she calls Mahogany Row. "This is where Ruth and Elliot sit. Jack's office is back there, too, next to Ruth's." They walk through a maze of workstations, separated by brightly colored partitions. There's a series of slanted drafting tables, strewn with T squares, mechanical pencils and compasses. Charlotte points out where the engineers and developers sit. The model makers, next to them, are testing the sound bars for a xylophone, their tinny nursery rhyme competing with Chopin's piped-in Etude in C Minor. The sales and public relations departments are across from them, next to the legal and accounting departments.

"And here—here we are." Charlotte does a little pivot, welcoming Stevie to an area in the very back corner. "You'll sit over there," she says, pointing at a workstation that appears to be a dumping ground for unwanted folders, boxes, a beat-up desk blotter, staplers and other stray office supplies. "Don't worry," says Charlotte. "We'll get someone to clear all that out." She pauses before a doorway and motions for Stevie to follow her. "And I'm right in here."

Charlotte's office is packed with stacks of fashion magazines, pattern books and fabric swatches of every imaginable shade from the same *Standard Color Reference of America* they used at Chouinard. Bolts of fabric are tucked off to the side, leaning against the wall next to a sewing machine. Her desk is cluttered with pencils, pincushions, measuring tapes and ashtrays. In short, everything Stevie would expect to find in a fashion designer's office. Nothing about any of it feels toylike to her.

Charlotte pulls out the customary confidentiality forms that have become standard practice for anyone who comes within ten feet of Barbie. Once Stevie signs them all, she finally meets the doll, which is not the chubby, cherub-like toy she'd been expecting.

Observing Stevie's reaction, Charlotte says, "So now you understand why I came to you." Proudly she holds Barbie up to the light. "You put in two years designing clothes for her, and you'll be able to write your own ticket." Charlotte exchanges the doll for an oversized sketchpad. "Now, these are just preliminary," she says, flipping to the first page, "but I want to give you an idea of the kind of clothes we're talking about."

Charlotte points to drawings of several dresses, and the sketches are as sophisticated and detailed as any designer flats she's ever seen. She almost forgets they're talking about doll clothes. Stevie is beginning to see a real angle for herself, and as she wedges the possibility open just a sliver more, she's flooded with a dream she thought she'd let go of. But now, after almost a year of rejection, the designer inside her is being nudged awake. This doll she's dressing is basically a woman—albeit a miniaturized woman, but still a woman. She won't really be making doll clothes; rather, she'll be creating a line of haute couture for a teeny-tiny person. And she's being paid to do so. She's already jumping ahead, imagining how she'll use Barbie's clothes in her portfolio when she applies at real design firms. Though it's been a circuitous route, she feels light and ebullient with the prospect of finally being back on track with her career.

Charlotte turns the page on her sketchpad and Stevie looks at the finely drawn undergarments and laughs.

"Is something funny?" asks Charlotte.

Stevie is still laughing. "It's just, I mean, c'mon—a bra and girdle? For a doll?"

Charlotte's not laughing. She leans forward. "Let me give you some advice—never *ever* refer to Barbie as an inanimate object. Or call her a *doll*. Ruth will go berserk if she hears that."

I t doesn't take long for Stevie to fall into a routine at work. By week two, she knows the drill. Each morning at 08:00 hours she arrives, sees that Ruth's pink Thunderbird is already there, the engine cooled, no longer ticking. Taking her place in a long line of coworkers, she waits to have her pocketbook inspected and flash her badge. She pushes through the turnstile, greeted by a blast of classical music, then heads to the galley kitchen, where she waits in another line for the coffeemaker. More often than not, Ginger will cut in front of everyone. "Jack needs coffee," she'll say by way of explanation, and the line will part for her like the Red Sea.

By 09:00 hours, the place is a madhouse. Mattel's engineers and developers, encouraged by their fearless leader, Jack, behave more like a bunch of teenage boys. From their workstations they fire slingshots at each other, lob toy hand grenades over their cubicles and soar paper airplanes carrying flirtatious messages to the nearby secretaries. Squirt gun fights are frequent, and at some point every morning, Gina in sales will sneeze three times in a row, followed by a chorus of *gazoontites* coming from all directions.

Because their offices are in the middle of nowhere, Mattel has a cafeteria for its employees. Everyone eats there, even Ruth and Elliot. It isn't free, but for a buck or two you can get a full lunch. Women wearing lab coats and hairnets scoop out the day's offering, which is always some sort of Mexican cuisine, loaded with jalapeños and chilis. Almost everyone keeps a stash of Rolaids in their desk drawer to combat the inevitable heartburn. At 14:00 hours, Elliot changes the soothing classical music to marching tunes, believing that "On, Wisconsin!" and "Stars and Stripes Forever" will ward off the afternoon slump.

When the clock hits 17:00 hours, it's quitting time and Stevie heads to the nearby beach with Mia, their sample maker, and Patsy from accounting, whom she's become friendly with. Sitting with the other women on oversized blankets, they watch the guys play volleyball. The men take off their shirts, baring their suntanned muscles as they show off, spiking and diving into the sand, hoping to impress the ladies.

One day, an engineer they call Twist—his real name is Anthony Wheeler—scores a point and gives Stevie a smile and a wink as he dusts sand off his chest and broad shoulders. He's very handsome, but Stevie's not interested, still too raw from her breakup with Russell.

She can't believe how close she came to making the same mistake her mother made. Stevie's done the math. Her parents married just seven and half months before she was born, and while she's always known they love her, she often wonders if they ever loved each other. She can't remember a time when they didn't sleep in separate beds, in separate rooms. Other than *Tonight Starring Jack Paar* and *Perry Mason*, they seem to have no shared interests. Her father can be gruff, which bothers Stevie more than it does her mother. He's not a violent man, just a deeply unhappy one, no matter how hard her mother tries to please him. She pulls off minor miracles in the kitchen, making a cheap cut of meat tender and savory. She can turn a can of Campbell's Tomato Soup into a zesty spaghetti sauce. Her specialty, though, is desserts: chocolate pudding, lemon tarts, devil's food cake made with buttermilk. Stevie expected her parents to divorce once she was on her own. After all, they're both still young and attractive, and Stevie could picture them remarrying, finding genuine love the second time around. But they're still together and fairly miserable. When asked why she doesn't leave, Stevie's mother said, "Where am I gonna go?" She has no money, no means of supporting herself. She's trapped, and Stevie vows she'll never let that happen to her.

Russell did her a great favor by walking away, though she's still scarred by it and terrified of getting pregnant again before she's ready. So now, when handsome Twist is giving her the eye, she merely smiles back to be polite. She allowed a man to derail her career once before; she won't let it happen again.

Stevie is still new to the company and isn't yet aware of just how much interoffice canoodling goes on at Mattel. There's Blythe in inventory, who was caught performing fellatio on Herky from sales in the men's room. Leah in reception is having an affair with Alex in production, who is also having a thing on the side with Connie in payroll. After hours, Phil from the mailroom has *done it* on the conference room table with Millie from shipping. And, of course, there's Jack, who has the uncanny ability to make each girl in his harem think she's special. Ruth knows about all the hanky-panky going on but doesn't say anything because, after all, she, too, is sleeping with one of the owners, who just so happens to be her husband.

The Learning Curve

For weeks now all Stevie's done is execute Charlotte's ideas. She works up sketches and flats for Charlotte's concepts, and upon Charlotte's approval, Stevie creates the patterns. Once Charlotte approves those as well, Stevie hands them off to Mia, who lays them out in muslin and does the pinning, the cutting and sewing. When they have a sample on the fitting doll—a headless three-dimensional torso of Barbie's body—Charlotte tells Stevie which fabrics, which buttons, and even what color thread to use. She feels more like a lackey than a designer, and Charlotte has picked up on this.

"Patience, Stevie," she says. "There's a learning curve here. Trust me, designing clothes in one-sixth scale is tricky. It took me forever to realize that if I want details like topstitching, pockets, even collars to look right, I have to measure them against Barbie's head instead of her body."

"But that doesn't make any sense."

"Actually, it does. There's a lot of optical illusions at play here," she says. "The only way Jack could make Barbie *look* proportional was to cheat everything else. That's why her head is so large. It's why he made her neck extra long and so narrow. Honestly, we couldn't even hold our heads up if we had those same proportions. And yet, on Barbie, it works." She taps out a cigarette from her pack and strikes a match. "Something else I learned," she says, leaning into the flame, "is stitches per inch. Normally, you'd allow six, seven, maybe even ten stitches per inch, but for Barbie"—she pauses and shakes out the match—"it's more like twelve or sometimes even fifteen stitches per inch. You have to remember to make adjustments for things like seam allowance and your thread weight. You can't use a regular thirty- or forty-weight thread. It's too thick. Your thread needs to be eighty, ninety, or even higher if you can find it. And on top of all that, Barbie's clothes have to look sophisticated but still appeal to kids—so they need to be easy enough to button and zip and slip on."

"I get it. I can do all that."

"I know you can. And you'll get your chance." Charlotte props the cigarette in the corner of her mouth, squints one eye to shield it from the smoke. "Trust me, there's plenty of work for you to do. Just be patient."

A few weeks later, after being at Mattel for almost a month, Stevie finally gets a chance to present her own designs. She's worked late every night for the past week and didn't get home until after midnight the night before. She'd lost track of time, double- and triple-checking her measurements, perfecting her concepts.

Now, at last, she goes into Charlotte's office with her sketches in hand. She loves the outfit she created and is certain that Charlotte will be impressed and take off the training wheels. She's almost giddy when she presents her design, a purple A-line dress with a sweet Peter Pan collar.

Charlotte adjusts her glasses and examines the flats. She isn't saying anything. There's no *Wow* or *My goodness*. None of the reactions Stevie's been expecting. Instead, her heart feels a pinch when Charlotte reaches for her pencil and starts jotting down comments in the margins.

"This is a good start," says Charlotte.

A start? But it's finished, thinks Stevie.

"What about a name?"

"I'm calling this *Apple Delight*." She points out the apple repeat pattern on the fabric.

"Nah, sounds too much like a recipe. You can do better."

Can she? That was the best she had out of a list of twenty. And by the way, no one said a word that day in the diner about coming up with names. They name each outfit like it's a lipstick or nail polish, names like *Golden Girl* and *Evening Splendor*.

"What about *Apple of Her Eye*?" Charlotte suggests. "Oh, and where are we at on the accessories?"

"I have a pocketbook for her—see?" Stevie indicates the sketches on her drawing pad and, as a bonus, holds up a teeny-tiny handbag that she mocked up, made from a paper binder clip. She had to get creative because nothing on such a small scale exists. She remembers sitting at her desk, fiddling with the binder clip when she got the idea. After covering it in some leftover fabric and replacing the pinchers with a delicate chain, she had a Barbie-sized pocketbook.

"Hmmm." Charlotte taps her pencil and turns the page, expecting more, but it's blank. "Oh." She looks up, her bottom lip curled under. "What about the interior? Where's the lining?

The lining? Stevie didn't realize she had to be *that* detailed for a pocketbook the size of a postage stamp.

"There has to be a lining," Charlotte says, dipping her chin, peering at Stevie from above her eyeglasses. "And where are her shoes? Barbie can't leave the house without shoes. Think about it,

Stevie. Does Barbie need a hat? What about jewelry to complete her outfit?"

Stevie is bent over her sketchpad, taking notes, her ears beginning to burn. She took this job for the money, thinking it would be a breeze and possibly a foot in the door, but if she can't design clothes for a doll, how is she ever going to create real outfits for real women?

Charlotte has now grabbed her own sketchpad, her pencil moving back and forth. "Why don't you start working off this." She rips the sheet from the pad and hands it to Stevie.

She's growing hot and clammy. This meeting has gone south and she's feeling that she's failed, that she's right back to being Charlotte's lackey.

As she gets up to leave, Charlotte says, "Wait, where are you going? I've got something else I'd like you to take a stab at."

"What's that?"

"I've had an idea for something. It's been knocking around in my brain for weeks now, but I don't have time to get to it. I'm thinking of something classic. Something like this—" Charlotte pulls out a folder and hands Stevie a magazine spread. "Think you could work off that?"

Stevie studies the photograph of a sleek model in a Chanel suit standing outside a Paris café.

"That's just a jumping-off point," says Charlotte. "Take this and run with it. Make it your own."

And that's what Stevie does. Returning to her workstation, she pins the photograph up on her wall and reaches for her sketchpad. It's Chanel, so it's a timeless design, and Stevie could replicate it, scaling it down for Barbie. But instead, something takes over her, or maybe it's Stevie giving herself over to the illusion of Barbie being more than a doll, or maybe not a doll at all. It's like slipping into another dimension. It frees up her pencil as she imagines all the places Barbie might wear this outfit. In her mind, she follows Barbie around for the day, seeing her riding up in an elevator of some make-believe office building, someone bringing her a cup of coffee. Barbie's the boss, so she's taking telephone calls and attending meetings. She goes to lunch with colleagues at the Formosa for dumplings. Back at the office, Barbie checks her appointment book for what's on tap that afternoon, and in the evening there she is, sitting in Hamburger Hamlet with a group of glamorous friends, sipping an ice-cold gimlet. It's all so silly, and yet it allows Stevie to push the concept, and in the course of an hour, she's found ways to make this suit more versatile. She'll keep the collarless cardigan jacket and the sheath skirt, but the blouse isn't quite right, it's too stiff for Barbie. Instead, she'll design two separate tops—one for the office and one that's more elegant for evening. She's picturing navy blue, shank buttons, a decorative hat and a charming little hatbox. Before the day is out, Stevie has countless sketches rendered for a design she's calling *Commuter Set*.

While she's working away, she senses a shift in the energy as Jack approaches, pausing at Mia's workstation to ask about her son's broken arm. He congratulates Huntly on taking first place in last weekend's regatta and thanks Melody for her inventory report. It's like he's going from workstation to workstation planting seeds of joy and goodwill.

"How are you doing over here, kiddo?" he asks, stopping at Stevie's desk.

God, how she hates it when he calls her that.

He takes one of her sketches, holds it up to the light. "Hmmm." He brings a finger to the tip of his chin. "I'm afraid that cuff's too narrow."

Stevie folds her arms. "Maybe you could wait till I'm finished before you start criticizing what I'm doing." It comes out harsher than it should. After all, Jack is her boss. More specifically, her boss's boss, but she doesn't like this guy. Something about him rubs her the wrong way.

"Just thought I'd save you some aggravation further down the line," he says, amused by her indignation. "I made a similar mistake once upon a time. Trust me, Barbie's hands will never fit through those narrow openings."

"I realize that." Actually, she hadn't even considered that, but dammit, he's right. They're far too narrow. "I'm not finished yet." She yanks the sketch from him with a little too much force and the corner rips.

"Well, I guess you showed me, didn't you?" He smiles, and before walking away, he says, "Better get used to a little constructive criticism, kiddo. Don't take it so personally."

I just don't like the guy," Stevie says to Patsy that night after work. They have decided to forgo the volleyball game and bonfire at the beach and have instead ended up at a taco joint for margaritas. They're sitting outside at a bright orange picnic table, surrounded by a trellis of bougainvillea. There's a basket of chips, lined with greasy waxed paper, and a dish of salsa. Stevie resists, knowing that if she starts on them, there'll be no stopping.

"You gotta get to know him," Patsy insists, propping her sunglasses up on her head. She has high cheekbones and a smile worthy of a toothpaste commercial. "Give him a chance. Seriously," she says. "You will love Jack. He's a great guy. I mean it. And he's a genius. He told me once that his IQ is 140."

Stevie laughs. "And you believed him?"

"I'm not kidding, he's brilliant." She tucks her long blond hair behind one ear and leans in closer still. "Can you keep a secret?"

"Yeah, sure," says Stevie, licking the salt from the lip of her glass.

"He gave me my first orgasm."

"Who? Jack?" Stevie nearly drops her drink.

Patsy nods, her eyes growing wide. "I mean, I *thought* I'd had an orgasm before, but then I was with Jack. The first time I had sex with him I thought, 'Oh my God, now I get it. Now I get why sex is such a big deal.' And man oh man can he kiss. Hands down, Jack Ryan is the best kisser ever."

Stevie is stunned and a little nauseated. She can't imagine kissing Jack, let alone having sex with him. "But he's so short."

"Don't let that fool you," says Patsy. "He has more inches where it counts." She giggles. "I'm serious, the man is extremely well-endowed."

Stevie shakes her head to clear the image. "But wait a minute"— she reaches for her first chip—"he's married, isn't he?" She recalls seeing pictures of his wife and two young girls on his desk.

"Well"—Patsy shrugs—"yes and no."

"How is someone married and not married?"

"He and his wife have an understanding. And he's completely up-front about it. He told me right away—he said, 'You know I'm married, right?' And his wife knows he fools around. Like I said, they have an understanding."

"How convenient." Stevie dips another chip in the salsa.

"One thing you need to know about Jack," Patsy says, sounding very serious, "he never lies. Not about anything. He told me right away that he doesn't believe in monogamy."

"That's charming—Jesus, Patsy, how long have you been seeing him?"

"*Was*. I *was* seeing him. It's over now. But we were together for"—she tilts her head, calculating—"I don't know, maybe six months or so."

"What happened?"

"Oh, I was madly in love with him, but he told me it was time for him to move on."

"And you're okay with that? You have to see him every day." Stevie helps herself to another chip and then another after that, promising herself it's the last one.

Patsy laughs. "He's still a great friend. I can talk to him about anything. And if I need help with something, he's right there. He fixed my oven the other day. There was something wrong with the starter jet or something like that. Anyway, he's generous and kind. Honestly, he's one of my favorite people on the planet."

Stevie gives this a moment to settle in. She's nervously eating at this point and takes one last chip before nudging the basket away. "Does Ginger know about you two?"

"Oh, poor Ginger."

It's no secret that Ginger is pining away for Jack. And she's not the only one. There's Mia, Wendy, Gina, Laura and half the secretarial pool. And now Patsy, too. All of them swear that Jack is an excellent boss. Especially if you're a woman. If you work late one night or come in over the weekend, you'll find flowers or a box of chocolates on your desk the next day. Some of the women have taken his gestures as a sexual overture, but they've been wrong. At last year's Christmas party, Ginger had too much to drink. Jack drove her home, only to have to pry her hands off him before tucking her into bed. The next day she claimed amnesia. Another girl who'd undressed and waited for Jack on his bearskin rug was tenderly handed back her clothing and told she'd make some other man very happy. She resigned one week later.

Patsy puts her sunglasses back in place. "Don't be so hard on Jack. You gotta get to know him better."

On the drive home that night, Stevie is still stunned by Patsy's confession. *Patsy and Jack?* She can't comprehend it and that business about orgasms. She's not sure she's ever had an orgasm, but according to Patsy it's the sort of thing that if you've had one, you'd know it. The only man Stevie's ever been with is Russell, and given what happened, she links sex with pregnancy, not with pleasure—and certainly not with orgasms.

Earning Her Keep

As Ruth's leaving for the day, she sees Stevie's light on in the back. She's noticed that Stevie is usually among the last to leave, and even when she goes to the beach after work with the others, she'll often return to the office for an hour or so. Ruth respects Stevie's work ethic. She was much the same way when she was starting out, although Stevie is more focused than Ruth was at her age. At twenty-one, Stevie already knows where her talents lie, whereas Ruth was still trying to figure that out.

Ruth was practically raised inside her sister's drugstore and fountain shop. Since they couldn't afford a babysitter, Sarah brought young Ruth to work with her. While Sarah and Louie loved her, they'd just gotten married and wouldn't have taken her in by choice. Never wanting to be a burden and feeling she had to earn her keep, Ruth went to work at the store when she was just ten years old. She polished the glass and mahogany cases that housed everything from hearing aids to Bromo-Seltzer. Ruth watched her sister at work. Sarah knew all the customers by name and gave their children lollipops. She met with vendors peddling Epsom salts, glycerin, licorice powder and all kinds of snake oil products. Sarah washed and squeegeed the front window herself and did her own displays for holidays and special sales. In time, Ruth helped with all that and more. By age twelve she was in the back, working as a soda jerk, making chocolate phosphates, ice cream sodas, malteds and banana splits. Every day after school she headed straight for the fountain shop. Her friends gathered there, too, crowding into the booths and around the circular marble tables. She never felt subservient waiting on them. Just the opposite. She took great pride in bringing them extra sprinkles and chopped nuts or adding a splash of cherry syrup to their Coca-Colas. She saw it as a way of being useful to them—a theme that would guide her through adulthood. *Be useful, be helpful and they'll keep you around.* If not for that soda fountain, Ruth feared she'd have nothing to offer in the way of friendship.

As she grew older, Ruth assumed she'd open her own drugstore and fountain shop one day. Then she started helping at her brother's law practice. She found the work fascinating and decided she'd go to law school, but when she turned nineteen that all changed after she went on vacation to California. Ruth fell in love with Los Angeles—the sunshine, the mountains, the beaches. It was a wonderland. Sarah, who initially didn't approve of Ruth's courtship with Elliot and who wanted to keep them apart, had encouraged Ruth to stay out there and get a job. The job she landed was typing up movie scripts at Paramount Pictures, making $25 a week. Much to Sarah's chagrin, it wasn't long before Elliot followed Ruth out there. And despite having a boyfriend who was waiting for her to get off work, Ruth often stayed late, looking for extra jobs and ways to make herself useful so Paramount would keep her on.

"Burning the midnight oil again?" Ruth calls out to Stevie.

"Oh, I'm just organizing these new patterns for Mia," she says. "I never seem to have time during the day."

"Well, don't stay too late." Ruth hears herself and it takes her by surprise, even makes her a tad bit uncomfortable. She's usually not this solicitous when it comes to her staff.

I t's almost nine o'clock by the time Ruth gets home that night. She's exhausted and still preoccupied with work. She sees Elliot and Barbara in the family room. Her daughter is stretched out on the sofa, her reddish-brown hair framing her face, her bare feet propped up on the glass coffee table, pink toenail polish chipped. She's leafing through *Bazaar*. If only Barbara spent half as much time on homework as she does on fashion magazines.

Ruth goes over to Elliot, who's reclining in his favorite chair, parked in front of the television set. He's watching that Steve Mc-Queen program he enjoys and is so engrossed he barely stirs when she kisses the top of his head. She turns toward her daughter but hesitates, uncertain as to the best way to greet her, the way she'll find the least offensive. Barbara's too old for a cuddle and would surely wipe her cheek dry if, God forbid, Ruth kissed her. Finally, she opts for a friendly, nonconfrontational "Hello?" It's tentative, comes out more like a question.

Barbara looks up from her magazine as if being pulled away from something monumental, about to discover the Holy Grail or the eighth wonder of the world. She doesn't say anything.

"Everything okay?" asks Ruth, tiptoeing about the land mine.

"Fine. Everything's just fine."

"Doesn't sound so fine to me."

With that, Barbara tosses her magazine on the table and storms off to her bedroom. A moment later the door slams.

"What's eating her?" Ruth asks. "Did she and Allen have another fight?"

"We should be so lucky." Elliot shakes his head and goes over to turn off the TV before he tidies up the coffee table, where Barbara's magazine has jostled some coasters and kicked up ashes from the ashtray. "Unfortunately, I think the lovebirds are just peachy," he says, borrowing one of Jack's pet phrases.

Neither Ruth nor Elliot is crazy about this new boyfriend. On the surface, Allen Segal is a nice Jewish boy, just what they would want for their daughter. But Allen is three years older than Barbara, wears his hair like Elvis Presley's, smells of cigarettes and never looks them in the eye. He works in a sporting goods store and seems awfully fond of kayaking and miniature golf. Ruth has a sneaking suspicion that Barbara dips into her allowance when they go out and sometimes gives Allen gas money.

After fixing herself a drink and taking a few fortifying sips, Ruth climbs the curving staircase and goes to check on her daughter. After a deep breath, she knocks on Barbara's door and accepts the irritated "Whh-aa-tt" as permission to enter.

Ruth finds Barbara lying on her bed, her back to the door. For a long time, they sit in silence, aware of each other's breathing. Ruth isn't sure what to say, and this is unlike her. She never second-guesses herself at work, never doubts herself this way with anyone else. Only Barbara has this kind of power over her. She can't even pinpoint when or how this started. There was a time when Barbara never would have talked back to her. As a young girl she was nothing but grateful and loving. How many times did Barbara curl up in Ruth's lap, asking to hear the same stories about the movie stars Ruth met when she was a Hollywood secretary? "Did you really meet Lucille Ball and W. C. Fields, Mommy?" Or, back when they couldn't afford a sitter, how Barbara loved to accompany Ruth on sales calls, being introduced as "my new assistant." What happened to that little girl? And more importantly, what happened to the young mother who couldn't bear to be away from her daughter for even a few hours? Now she walks on eggshells with her own child.

She wonders if she ever made Sarah feel so apprehensive. She doubts this because in Ruth's eyes, Sarah could do no wrong. The real person to ask would have been Ruth's mother, but when Ida Mosko was alive, she hardly acknowledged Ruth as her daughter.

She's still haunted by the time Sarah and Louie went to Fort Collins for a few days and left ten-year-old Ruth with Ida. The whole concept of mother versus big sister was something Ruth grappled with. No one ever hid the truth from her. She knew this wasn't her grandmother's house, it was her mother's, the same house that her nine siblings called home. The six boys doubled and tripled up, sharing bedrooms, and the three girls did the same. But there was never any room or a bed for Ruth and she couldn't understand this, especially now that Sarah was married and had moved out.

She was fascinated and bewildered by her mother. Who exactly was Ida Mosko and why did Ruth feel a strange sense of attachment to her—almost a primal need to be close to her? She followed Ida from room to room, always underfoot, watching as she sat at the kitchen table peeling potatoes, chopping onions. As soon as that task was completed, she picked up the broom, or a dustrag, or a basket of laundry. She never stopped moving. Never did Ruth see her mother resting, doing nothing.

Her mother spoke no English. The only Yiddish Ruth understood was *gey avek*, go away, and *gey shfiln indroysn*, go outside and play. *Play* was as much a foreign word as the others. Ruth would watch her brothers Aaron and Muzzy climbing trees and flying kites, and it all seemed so pointless. You climbed the tree only to climb back down. You got the kite in the air only to have it crash a few feet away. *What did that accomplish?* When Ida told her daughter *gey avek, gey shfiln indroysn,* Ruth didn't budge. She wanted to be where her mother was, wanted to help set the table, dry the dishes, fold the laundry, mop the floor—whatever it took to prove she was a good girl, a helpful girl, a girl worth keeping. But her mother didn't want to keep her, and when Sarah and Louie returned, Ruth and all traces of her were packed up. That was that. She had failed to win her mother's love.

Her mother and father are gone now, but really, Ida's been dead to Ruth since the day she gave her away. That one turn of events has left its footprint in her life, affecting her more than she realizes. It's why she's built such a hard shell around her heart, why she drives herself to exhaustion. Every day she wakes up thinking she has to be useful and productive in order to prove her right to exist.

"What do you want, Mom?" Barbara asks, tugging Ruth out of her past.

"What's going on, Barbara? What's the problem?"

"Nothing," she says in that way that indicates it's *something.*

Barbara is going to make Ruth work for it, but she doesn't know how to go about it. She's intimidated by her own child, and the longer she sits there saying nothing, the harder it will be to say anything. "I know you're upset, but sweetheart—" She dares to stroke Barbara's back, only to have her scoot away. "Well, I can't help you unless you tell me what it is."

"You won't do anything to fix it anyway, so what's the point?"

"Why don't you try me? Is it Allen? Did you two have a fight?"

Barbara slaps her pillow and flips onto her back. "No, it's not Allen. I'm surprised you even remember his name. Or mine for that matter." She stares at the ceiling, her lower lip crumbling, her pride refusing to give way to tears. "You're *never* here," she bleats. "No one else's mother has to work."

"Well, I don't *have* to work, either. I choose to work."

"And I hate that Edna makes us dinner every night."

"Would you rather *I* made dinner?" Ruth attempts a joke here because they both know she's a lousy cook.

Barbara doesn't even crack a smile. "I hate this stupid house. Why can't we live in a normal house like everyone else? None of my friends have stupid trees growing out of their living rooms."

"You used to love that tree." Ruth remembers when they first moved in, Barbara always had slumber parties with her girlfriends down in the basement, their sleeping bags at the base of the tree like they were camping out. She played down there constantly, and Ruth would find her leaning against the trunk, a book in her lap. Back then the tree was great, but now, like everything else, it's no good.

"And why can't I walk to school like a normal person? No one else has a chauffeur. It's humiliating."

"It's for your safety."

"I hate it," she says before returning to her original assault on Ruth. "And I hate that you're always at the office. All you care about is work. Sometimes I swear you care more about that doll than you do me."

"You know that's not true."

Barbara turns her back to Ruth once again. "I don't want to talk about this anymore."

"Okay, all right. Fine."

As she gets up to leave, Ruth scans the shelves of dolls that Barbara's been collecting since she was a little girl. Among them are porcelain dolls, rag dolls, oilcloth dolls and baby dolls in bonnets and nightgowns and oh my— At first glance Ruth thinks it's Barbie. But no, it's Bild Lilli. An uneasy feeling begins burbling in the pit of her stomach. Bild Lilli's cunning expression seems to know what she's thinking. It's unnerving. Despite all the work they've done, Barbie is still the spitting image of Bild Lilli. How is that possible? Had they forgotten what Bild Lilli looked like? Could they have subconsciously embedded her face and body in their minds, reproducing her to a tee? No, no. Impossible. They made countless changes to their design. Jack spent months and months working on her. They even hired Bud Westmore, a Hollywood hair and makeup artist, to consult on reshaping Barbie's eyebrows, softening her lips and eyes, reworking her hairline.

Ruth thinks about that licensing agreement her legal department begged her to secure. She never did it. Neither did Jack. She feels a little sick inside. Surely Jack made enough critical changes along the way, and she knows he's already applied for a patent for Barbie's construction. They didn't cross a line, *did they*? No one could accuse them of *stealing* the idea for Barbie. And even if they did, they couldn't prove it. Barbie is *not* Bild Lilli. They have nothing to worry about. Nothing at all. No, they're perfectly fine.

She takes a deep breath and looks again at her daughter, a little sausage of rage and adolescent angst. She pauses at the door, her hand resting on the light switch, wondering if she should turn it off or leave it on. "Barbie, honey, do you—" Ruth stops. She's caught her mistake, but it's too late.

Barbara flips over with a propeller-like force. "Don't call me that. I'm not your stupid doll."

That night Ruth lies awake in bed. She assumes Elliot is asleep when suddenly he flings off the covers.

"Did I turn off the pool lights?" he asks.

"I don't know. Probably."

"I can't remember if I turned them off." He's up now, stumbling over the pair of shoes at his bedside, always there in case of an earthquake, in case he needs to make a fast escape over broken glass. He slips into his bathrobe at the foot of the bed and goes to the top of the stairs, where he sees nothing but darkness. Not a pool light in sight.

"Were they off?" she asks when he returns to the bedroom.

"They were off." And within moments, his eyes are closed.

She's always known Elliot is a worrier. She'd love to disconnect that part of his brain prone to incessant concerns: *Do we have enough life insurance? What if the sprinkler system goes out? When did I last have the oil changed in my car?* It used to be endearing, and one day it will be again, but for now it baffles her. She doesn't operate that way. She's about speed and following her gut. Hesitation and apprehension kill inspiration just as surely as time kills deals.

She looks over at Elliot, already back asleep. So serene. It's a wonder he can sleep with so much to worry about. Ruth sits up in bed and reaches for her cigarettes. Elliot doesn't like for her to smoke in bed, afraid she'll burn the house down, but he's out now and nothing wakes him. She raises her knees, resting her elbows on top as she lights up, taking a deep, satisfying drag, wondering how she can make things right with Barbara. She accepts that her unconventional childhood explains why she isn't a conventional housewife and mother. But the very thing she is most proud of— growing a successful business—is the same thing her daughter resents.

"I'm a latchkey child," Barbara has repeatedly said, tears in her eyes.

But Ruth can't stay home waiting for her children to return from school. She'll never know how to fold a fitted bedsheet or how to tell if a cantaloup's ripe. She doesn't want to attend luncheons and PTA meetings. She has no desire to play bridge and mah-jongg. Ruth would rather play poker. In fact, she and Elliot have a standing game with two other couples, and she often feels she has more in common with the husbands than the wives.

Ruth's not a girls' girl. She knows Barbara wants her to be more like other mothers, and Ruth wants—well, she wants Barbara to be more like Barbie. *My goodness.* This is an epiphany, a branch of lightning already beginning to vanish as quickly as it's appeared. Ruth might not even remember it in the morning, but right now, in the darkness, it's clear that she thinks of Barbie as her daughter's alter ego. Or rather as the young lady she wishes her Barbara to be.

Avoidance Behavior

Jack returns from another trip to Japan to find that Ginger has changed her hair color. She's lightened it. And it brings out her eyes, which are bluer than he'd thought. It looks like she's lost some weight, too. He knows she's been trying to reduce. He's seen the Ayds caramels in her desk drawer that she nibbles during her coffee breaks. The box says *Ayds Reducing Plan. Lose up to 10 pounds in 5 days.*

His trusted gatekeeper is now leaning against his doorjamb, telling him that the weekly Barbie status meeting in the conference room has started. And he's late. Jack leaves himself a message on his tape recorder, grabs his coffee and tries to gather his thoughts as he heads down the hallway. The good news is that the Barbie master molds are close to being finalized and should be ready to go soon. The bad news is that it's almost rice harvesting season in Japan, and that means the farmhands that KBK hired to do the piecemeal work on Barbie will be returning to the paddies to harvest rice. So starting in September, KBK will shut down their Barbie operations for a month, possibly six weeks. He is not relishing the thought of telling Ruth.

From the hallway he sees everyone seated around the table. Twist is pitching crumpled-up wads of paper into the wastebasket; Frankie is waving his pencil, making it appear rubbery; Huntly is building a chain of interconnected paper clips. It's like they're all fussy little kids, incapable of sitting still.

And then there's Ruth, glowering at him. "So good of you to join us, Jack."

He saunters in and closes the door behind him, all smiles and forced lightness. "Are we having fun yet?" he asks.

Ruth grinds her cigarette down to a nub. "Let's get started, shall we?" She stands up and goes to an easel-backed drawing board in the corner with a big *Barbie Toy Fair Launch* scribbled across the top in thick black marker.

Toy Fair is getting closer. This trade show draws tens of thousands of buyers and sellers from across the country, and it's the one chance each year to introduce new products. Toys live and die depending on their reception at Toy Fair.

Never mind that they have two new Burp Guns, the H_2O Two-Stage Missile water rocket and the musical boxes and xylophone that Elliot dreamed up—everything and everyone is focused on Barbie. She's slated to debut in March at the '59 show. If they miss that, they'll have to wait an entire year, again, before they can effectively release her. They can't afford to have Charlotte, Stevie and Mia treading water for twelve months, and yet Ruth can't afford to let them go for fear she'll never get them back. Jack and his team could continue to test and tweak more prototypes for an eternity. They're already over budget on Barbie, and on top of that, Ruth worries that if they fall behind schedule, someone else—and not Miss Revlon—will beat them to market with an adult doll.

Tensions are running high as everyone feels time closing in from the other side. Elliot has a giant calendar tacked up on the conference room wall, and each day when he arrives, before he puts on his classical music, he crosses out another box in red marker and adjusts the days. They are 247 days away. It's July now. They have just over eight months. Ruth's brought on more people, moving key personnel from engineering and model making in the boys' toys divisions over to work on Barbie. Now nearly a third of their operating budget is devoted to getting Barbie off the ground.

Ruth begins running down her checklist. "Where are we at with the revised packaging?" she asks Sid Gravely in marketing.

Sid's in his late twenties and is already bald. His toupee nests on his head, never landing in the same spot twice. It's positioned either too far left or too far right, exposing the edges of his pink scalp, which everyone politely ignores.

"The revised packaging?" Ruth asks again, more insistent this time.

Sid's a smart guy and very good at what he does, but he's terrified of Ruth. Glancing down at his notes, he says, "We're, ah, we're almost there."

"Almost? What does that mean? And what about the final logo design?"

"It, ah. It's—it's, ah, coming along." Pinpricks of sweat are sprouting on his forehead.

Ruth shoots him an irritated look and then widens her gaze, taking aim at the entire room. "We need to finalize everything and get Japan started on production. We're running out of time, people."

This is not what Jack wants to hear—especially in light of his rice harvesting news, which will impact their timeline. So while Ruth is berating everyone, Jack tunes her out, taking note of Charlotte's new designer. Stevie's young, but she's a firecracker and smart as hell. He can tell she doesn't like him, which is utterly disconcerting. Unlike the other girls, Stevie doesn't give him long-ing glances, doesn't laugh at his jokes and doesn't linger after a meeting hoping to strike up a conversation. She does none of that. In fact, in the three months she's been there, he's never once felt like he's had her undivided attention. Whenever he's talking—even in a meeting—she seems to be doing something else, writing a note to herself, leafing through some files or source material. The fact that she won't give him the respect he deserves—he is her boss, after all—makes her intriguing, a challenge. He wants to win her over, but to what end, he can't say.

He wonders if she has a boyfriend. How could she not? He sees how Twist and the others flirt with her. She's a brown-haired, blue-eyed beauty with a dimpled chin like Ava Gardner. He bets her hair feels as good as it smells . . . *Jesus, stop it!* He shouldn't be thinking about her in this way. He shouldn't be thinking about her at all. This is what Dr. Greene would call "avoidance behavior." Jack doesn't want to think about rice harvesting, so he is thinking about Stevie. Jack Ryan is nothing if not introspective.

He forces himself to refocus on the meeting, hearing all the jargon tossed around about *play value* and *nature play pattern* toys versus *projection play pattern* toys. Ruth is now talking about fore-casts and inventory needs before she turns the floor over to Char-lotte.

"Here's the latest designs," says Charlotte, as Stevie lines up a series of outfits on the fitting dolls. The first one sports a strapless cocktail dress made of a white and gold brocade pattern. The dress is a close-fitting sleeveless sheath that zips up the back and hugs Barbie's curves. "It's a classic design," Charlotte says.

"I like it," says Ruth. "Now you just need to plus it up. What about a matching stole? Or maybe a wrap?"

While Stevie takes copious notes, Charlotte reaches for her

sketchpad and in big vigorous strokes knocks out a jacket with three-quarter-inch sleeves. "What about something like this?" She tears the sheet from her pad, sliding it across the table to Ruth.

Jack watches the two of them, Ruth and Charlotte, playing off each other, harmoniously as wind chimes. It's like there's some telepathic current flowing between them.

"Maybe dress up the collar," Ruth suggests. "Add some details on the sleeve."

"Maybe fur trim?" says Charlotte.

"Exactly what I was thinking," says Ruth. "And what about accessories?"

"Oh, I have a full line of accessories," says Charlotte.

Of course you do, thinks Jack.

Charlotte presents a gold clutch bag with lemony silk lining and a pair of brown open-toed pumps. Ruth loves them. *She fucking loves everything Charlotte shows her*. Much as he hates to admit it, Jack's feeling a little crowded out. It used to be the three of them, but now it's Ruth and Charlotte. And Stevie. Jack's sure it's just a matter of time before she worms her way into the girls' club. And that's what it is. It's a girls' club, but he wants in.

Growing up, he was never allowed in the boys' club. He was too short for most sports, aside from wrestling, which held no appeal. If he was going to get sweaty rolling around on the ground, it was going to be with a girl. Not that he had many options for that, either. The girlfriends would come later, and my how his life changed once he discovered how to unlock that treasure trove. Aside from his wife in recent years, the only women he hasn't been able to charm are Ruth, Charlotte and now Stevie, which floods him with concern. Is he losing his touch? What then? Right or wrong, the attention and admiration of women are the source of his confidence. His sense of identity is wrapped up in them as surely as his arms long to wrap around their bodies.

"And Jack." Ruth shifts her focus to him. "Why don't you bring us up to speed on your trip. Where are we at with KBK?"

Jack reaches back and gives his neck a squeeze. His collar is slightly damp. His head feels like it's in a drum and his voice sounds muffled as he reports back on the successful assessment of the Barbie molds. He knows he's talking, but the distortion is like feedback from a microphone. Finally, he gets to the tough part, the rice harvesting.

It's only the shrill sound of Ruth's "Are you fucking kidding me?" that clears his head. "You're telling me *everybody* who works on Barbie is going to shut down for an entire month so they can go harvest fucking rice?" Ruth's on her feet, leaning over the table, her venom directed at Jack.

He's got to recover some ground here. His entire team is watching. Even Stevie has her eyes on him. And he's not like Sid. He's not afraid of Ruth. "Yep," he says, now also standing, figuratively prodding her with a needle, trying to get under her skin. "That's exactly what I'm telling you. KBK is closing down Barbie production so they can harvest *fucking* rice." He's aware of Stevie watching him and he feels like he's performing for her, playing to her. Their eyes lock for the briefest of seconds before she breaks away.

"And nobody—meaning *you*, boy genius—thought to build this into our goddamn timeline?"

"Okay now, that's enough." Elliot stands up and places his hands on Ruth's shoulders, gently coaxing her back into her chair. "We still have time until Toy Fair," Elliot says. "When they're done harvesting, we'll have KBK bring on extra shifts if we have to. We'll have their people working round the clock, on weekends, too.

We'll have KBK do whatever it takes to make up the lost time and keep us on schedule. Okay?" Elliot's gaze travels around the room as he pauses on each of them, one at a time, to make eye contact. Placing both palms flat on the table, he says, "All right, then. Can we move on now?"

Aside from inventing toys, acting as the peacekeeper is perhaps Elliot's most important job at Mattel. He trails behind his wife, cleaning up the carnage from vendors she's upset, employees she's turned into a puddle of tears, bankers she's insulted. Without Elliot's diplomatic charms, Ruth's impatience, not to mention her ire, would have probably blown up Mattel years ago.

S tevie pulls out of the Mattel parking lot, grateful that she finally had the money to replace the battery and no longer has to hold her breath and pray each time she turns the ignition key. As she drives, her head is buzzing from the meeting earlier that day. She still can't get over how Ruth lashed out at Jack—and in front of everyone. Now she gets why they call her Ruthless. It was a little scary, but also impressive to see her in action like that.

Stevie's mother is just the opposite, so quick to apologize for all of life's upsets, taking full responsibility for anything that goes wrong in her father's world—it's her fault if he burns his tongue on the soup, if the newspaper sections get out of order. Her mother even takes the fall for things like the hot water tank going on the fritz, the flat tire he had on the freeway, the dog barking next door. Stevie knows it will never happen, but just once she'd love to see her mother show a little strength, take back a little power—power that she doesn't even know she gave away.

Her mind shifts back to the meeting. Jack certainly wasn't ruffled by Ruth. Stevie still doesn't like Jack, but she's admittedly curious about him. Ever since that conversation with Patsy, she hasn't been able to look at him the same way. *Jack Ryan, a masterful kisser, the giver of orgasms.* She must have been thinking about that in the meeting, because at one point their eyes met. It had sent an unexpected charge through her and she'd felt the blush rising on her cheeks.

Much to her annoyance, she's still thinking about Jack when she gets to her apartment. She and Vivian live in one of those newer structures that will later be coined a *dingbat. Casa Bella* is sprawled across the white stucco in gold lettering with a smattering of stars for a bit of added embellishment. The building looks like it's standing on stilts, and is divided into four apartments with an overhang that covers the cars.

Stevie steps inside, puts her keys on a little kitchen table and eases out of her heels, her feet soothed by the chill of the tiled floor. She can tell that Vivian isn't home yet because she hasn't tripped over her shoes, all the lights aren't on, and the hi-fi isn't blasting.

Though friendly at Chouinard, Stevie and Vivian became roommates out of economic necessity. After turning up to view the same West Hollywood apartment that neither one could afford, they decided to move in together and split expenses. As roommates they are compatible, but mostly because Stevie doesn't make a big deal about the peanut butter knife left out on the counter, the toothpaste clinging to the bathroom sink or Vivian's tendency to use the last of everything from shampoo to milk.

Grabbing a bottle of bitter lemon from the icebox, she goes out onto the balcony, which overlooks a pool. It's a warm evening and the two young boys from 1B are swimming, splashing about. As Stevie takes a sip from her drink, she catches herself thinking about Jack again, recalling how he looked at her in that meeting.

Or had she been the one looking at him? *Oh, just stop it!* But the more she admonishes herself not to think about him, the more she does. It's like telling someone *Don't think about the zebra in your bathtub.* The whole thing is so messy. She works for him, and besides, she'd have to get in line behind all the other women who adore him. And she most definitely does not adore him.

"Stevie? You home?" she hears Vivian calling.

"Out here."

Vivian joins her on the balcony. With sleek black hair to her shoulders and enormous dark eyes, Vivian's stylish and short, almost as short as Ruth and sometimes just as pushy. "So today I met the editor of *Glamour* magazine," she says, helping herself to Stevie's bitter lemon. "They're going to feature one of Rudi's swimsuit designs in their June issue. Isn't that exciting?"

"Yeah, that is exciting." She tries not to sound jealous. Last week it was the fashion editors from *Vogue*, and the week before, *Harper's Bazaar*. "Oh, and I had lunch today with Bob."

"Bob?"

"Bob Mackie. He asked about you. Said to say hello."

"Is he still at Paramount?"

"Yeah, and he's working on Marlene Dietrich's new picture. Isn't that great?"

"That's—that's really great." Bob was their classmate, and like Stevie, he'd dropped out of Chouinard before graduation. But Bob left because Frank Thompson hired him to be a costume sketch artist for the movies.

Bob and Vivian are in the center of the fashion design world, and while Vivian talks endlessly about her internship at R.G. Designs, Stevie is legally silenced, gagged by that mountain of confidentiality forms she signed. All Vivian knows is that she makes doll clothes for some toy company. Stevie can't even utter the words *fashion doll* without risk of getting fired. Unlike Charlotte and Jack, who have special clearance, Stevie can't bring work home, so she can't show Vivian the rabbit fur stole and blue bubble dress she's been designing or the white vinyl car coat with red fleece lining she's been working on with Charlotte. As spectacular and intricate as her designs are, at the end of the day, they're still just doll clothes. Stevie feels like a bit player on the design stage, questioning if she made the right decision and how, despite her $200 a week, Mattel is going to get her any closer to her goal of becoming a real designer.

Jack arrives fifteen minutes late for Group. He lost track of time and then got stuck in traffic. Despite the rice harvesting debacle earlier that day, he is a rising star at Mattel, but at home, he's in the doghouse, which is why he attends group psychotherapy with his wife. He's a lousy husband, he knows this. It's been years since he's been faithful to Barbara. He works too much, drinks too much, too. He does love his little girls, though, and yet he can't say he's a great father, either. He's never gotten the hang of being a parent. In many ways he's still a child himself, always getting into mischief and encouraging his daughters to do the same. He shows them how to roast marshmallows over the flame on the gas stove, he wakes them up when he can't sleep for a game of marbles or checkers. They are the little play friends who—thanks to his mother—Jack was never allowed to have.

When it's Jack's turn to speak, Dr. Greene says, "How are we doing with your *im-pul-siv-i-ty*?" He breaks the word into five syllables.

Jack is stuck on the *we* of it. *We* are not doing anything with his *impulsivity*, which is Dr. Greene's word for it, not Jack's. Jack knows what Dr. Greene wants to hear, what Barbara *needs* to hear, and so he says it: "I realize my actions have consequences." *There, that wasn't so hard, was it?* But he can't look at his beautiful wife because she'll see right through him. When it comes to self-control and good judgment, Jack lacks both.

He glances around the room at the other four couples, plus Dr. Greene, all of them sitting in a circle on folding chairs. Dr. Greene is wearing a pair of corduroy slacks the color of stadium mustard and a brown cardigan sweater. His legs are crossed; his foot bobs up and down. His loafer, having slipped off his heel, dangles in limbo. He looks bored, and if he isn't, he should be. What a sorry lot they are. The wife sitting to Jack's left cries in every session because her husband had an affair nine fucking years ago. The husband of the couple next to them has a fear of mirrors. He thinks something awful will happen to his wife if he looks at himself. *How crazy is that?* Jack seems completely sane in comparison and wonders how in the hell he let Barbara talk him into this.

Poor Barbara. He never should have married her. They met on Cape Cod and Jack was taken by the girl who attended the Parsons School of Design, enchanted by her talent, her creative flair and intellect. It didn't hurt that Barbara, with her lustrous chestnut-brown hair, beautiful smile and patrician nose, has the kind of upper-crust pedigree his mother approved of. If only she liked sex half as much as he loves her. And he does love her. In fact, if she'd let him, he'd *show* her just how much he loves her several times a week, but Barbara's not a physical person, and that's the only way he can express his feelings. So they miss each other, two stars shooting off in opposite directions. But still, he loves her more than any of the other women in his life. And right now, there really isn't anyone special. Yes, he had that fling with the cocktail waitress, but it petered out. There was Patsy and then Wendy from the office, but neither of those were serious things. The woman in Tokyo, Akari, was fun but limited since his Japanese consists of three phrases: *Is production on the budget, yes?*; *You be very nice business partners*; and *Would you like to do sex with me tonight?*

He will admit to being a little preoccupied lately by Stevie in the design department. She shows zero interest in him, but he keeps trying to get to her. She's like a mountain to climb, a riddle to solve, a challenge to be conquered. Beyond that, he's not sure what he wants from her other than some reassurance that at thirty-one, he's still attractive, still desirable.

Jack's wife is speaking to the group now, talking about her favorite sweater being destroyed by clothes moths, as if this has anything to do with their future. He studies her face, knowing that the real problem with their marriage is not his overactive libido, his obsession with work or even his drinking. It's his brain. He's convinced that something is not right up there. But man is he ever busy inside his head. The thoughts—some good and many very, very bad—crowd in on him, packing his skull so tight, it feels like his head might split in two. Oh, how he wishes he could just stop thinking. Is that asking too much? Isn't there such a thing as a happy medium between feeling invincible, like he can fly, and feeling like he wants to hurl himself off a rooftop? The highs are so high he can feel the sun's scorch, and the lows are bottomless, bleak and black. He's either miserable or elated. There's no in-between. Surely other people's minds don't torment them the way his does.

The only time he manages to escape and block out the noise is when he's lost in his work, concentrating so intently that nothing else can worm its way in. That's why he's given all he has to Mattel. To this doll. Right now, Barbie is his only respite.

The Living Laboratory

On the drive home from their monthly poker game with friends—one of their few social engagements to have survived Ruth's accelerated work schedule—Elliot brings up the subject of market research for Barbie.

"It's time," he says as they head down Laurel Canyon, surrounded by the Hollywood Hills. "You'll need it for the advertising. What about that guy we met? You remember the one—Aaron or Ernie."

"You mean Ernest? Ernest Dichter?" She laughs and flicks her cigarette out the little butterfly window. "You complain that I'm spending too much money as it is—well, let me tell you, Ernest is not cheap."

Ernest Dichter is what they call a psychological marketing consultant. He claims he can unlock what's inside the consumer's subconscious mind. His company, the Institute for Motivational Research, has supposedly convinced the public that bathing with Ivory soap makes people feel smarter, not just cleaner. Dichter is also the brains behind Chrysler's revelation that men prefer convertibles, while wives are partial to sedans.

"Well," Elliot says, "it's worth it to spend a couple grand to figure out how we're going to sell Barbie."

She thinks about this, recalling a time when they didn't have to pay anyone to tell them how to market a toy. It was just the two of them, putting their heads together. It was fun, exhilarating. She remembers when they were launching the Uke-A-Doodle, how they would stay up late at night, working on the catalogue copy, and how together they figured out the right description: *A colorful miniature ukulele with a built-in music box. Two toys in one. Turn the handle and it plays real music . . .* They didn't know any better and they did just fine, but with Barbie the stakes are too high, and Elliot's right—they need to bring in a pro.

The following week Ernest Dichter arrives in Los Angeles from New York. He's a bespectacled middle-aged man with a flat, boxy head and wiry white hair. His Viennese accent becomes thicker when he's had a few drinks. Once Ruth makes Ernest sign a series of confidentiality and Do Not Compete forms, they get down to business.

After giving Barbie a close examination, Dichter lights a cigarette held in a black onyx holder and simply says, "Interesting."

"Interesting? That's it? Don't you think she's unique?"

"Doesn't matter what I think." He blows a plume of smoke toward the ceiling. "Why don't *you* tell me what *you* think is so unique about this doll?"

"Isn't it obvious?" says Ruth. "Barbie offers tremendous play value, not to mention the fact that she promotes projective play patterns and—"

"Let me stop you right there." He seems amused and chuckles without making much of a sound. "Do not tell me from here." He points to his temple. "Tell me what it is about this doll from here." He thumps his heart.

"Okay," says Ruth, taking a beat, finding a way to put it into her own words. "I think a doll like Barbie—well, I think she can unlock the imaginations of little girls. They can pretend they're grown-up, just like their doll. And they can make their Barbie *do* whatever they want. She can *be* anything they want. She can be a career girl, a fashion model, she can travel the world. She can take those girls beyond their bedroom walls. I think she's empowering. Certainly more empowering than traditional dolls. She can pave the way for young girls to explore all kinds of possibilities." Ruth sees Dichter smiling, nodding. "No other doll on the market can do all that."

This little speech of hers makes Ruth think that if only her daughter had a Barbie doll growing up, maybe she would have dreamed a little bigger, a bit bolder, set her sights on something more interesting than Allen. Ruth looks at someone like Stevie, who's not that much older than Barbara and yet seems so much wiser. Stevie has a direction in life, a plan for herself that doesn't appear to revolve around a man. Ruth wonders where she went wrong with her daughter. Between Sarah and Ruth, Barbara's been surrounded by strong, ambitious women all her life. Did none of that rub off on her?

Dichter looks at the doll again. "I know what we're going to do. We're going to conduct a series of Living Laboratories."

"What exactly is a Living Laboratory?" asks Ruth.

Ernest tips the ash from his stemmed cigarette while explaining that he'd like to interview a number of young girls and their mothers. "And then, after we meet with them and show them this doll"—he gestures with the cigarette like a conductor's baton—"then we'll devise the marketing strategy based upon our findings."

Ruth is eager to get started. After all, if Dichter is good enough for Procter & Gamble and Chevrolet, there must be something to his methodology. Two weeks and a $12,000 contract later, Ernest starts conducting the Living Laboratories in an off-site location. He interviews a total of 147 girls and their mothers. He pays them each $5 for their time, and all are required to sign a confidentiality agreement. They are not to talk to anyone about this study. They cannot tell anyone about the toy they are about to see.

During the first round of interviews, Ruth, Elliot, Charlotte and Jack are seated in an adjoining room, separated by a two-way mirror. They keenly watch a dozen little girls, ranging from six to eleven years old, take their places at a long table.

"You are such lucky young ladies," Ernest says. "You're about to be the very first to play with a brand-new doll. Are you ready to meet her?"

Pigtails and ponytails swish with excitement, legs swing back and forth, the soles of their shoes barely sweeping the tiled floor. Ruth lights a cigarette and nearly forgets to exhale because this is her moment, her chance to see firsthand how little girls will react to Barbie.

"Here she is. This is Barbie!" He holds up a blond Barbie, dressed in a black-and-white chevron swimsuit.

The girls' eyes grow wide; some cover their mouths. Are they delighted or horrified? Ruth can't tell.

Ernest presents two versions of Barbie—blond and brunette—allowing them to pick which doll they want to play with. Each doll is dressed in a different outfit, which causes a bit of a scuffle, as two girls want the *Golden Girl* sheath dress and three want the *Nighty Negligee Set*, complete with a little pink stuffed dog. They grab, they scowl, and Ernest eventually makes peace, promising that they'll get to play with all the clothes.

Chewing on the tip of her pen, Ruth studies the little girls' body language, their faces, their smiles, and the way each one holds and caresses Barbie, how they brush her hair. She wonders what's going through their minds. And then something rather surprising starts to happen.

"Are you seeing this?" asks Jack.

"I'm seeing it," says Ruth, inching forward in her chair.

"What are they doing?" asks Elliot, although what they're doing is quite obvious.

After all the kerfuffle over who got which outfit, the little girls start removing Barbie's clothes, eager to see what's going on underneath there. They giggle. They blush. Ernest places more outfits on the table and the girls examine the various dresses, jackets, the tiny shoes, hats, gloves and pocketbooks.

On the other side of the two-way mirror, they listen as Ernest asks them deceivingly simple questions: "Do you think Barbie's pretty? Which outfit do you like best? Would you like to have Barbie as a friend?"

One girl says she wants to look like Barbie when she grows up. Another says Barbie is her new best friend and they're going to Paris. A third likes her fancy clothes. One of the girls has some reservations, insisting that Barbie looks mean and acts like a brat. Ruth quickly jots this down on her notepad.

For nearly a week they observe these interviews with different groups of young girls, and the feedback is just as Ruth suspected. Barbie sparks their imagination and lets them fantasize about who and what they want to become when they grow up. She's pleased with the results. So are Jack and Charlotte. Even Elliot admits he might have underestimated Barbie's appeal to young girls.

Ruth is more delighted than she is surprised. From the very beginning, she knew she was onto something. The little girls have only confirmed her hunch. They are clearly tickled and inspired, and they're speaking on behalf of girls everywhere. Ruth's already heard what she needs and is half tempted to cancel the rest of the Living Laboratories. But the following week, Ernest proceeds to interview the mothers.

When they arrive, Ruth is on the other side of the two-way mirror with Elliot, Charlotte and Jack. *There they are*, she thinks. *The old guard.* The mothers fidget with their pocketbooks, sip their lemonades and nibble at the plate of shortbread cookies. Ruth imagines they spend their mornings poring over cookbooks, planning dinner and trying to come up with new Jell-O recipes. Later they'll get all dressed up to go to the supermarket, gingerly maneuvering their carts, like a ladylike game of bumper cars. She envisions them standing over their ironing boards, relocated to the living room so they can watch *The Guiding Light* and *As the World Turns* as they press bed linens that no one ever sees. With the table set and meat loaves in the oven, they'll wait for their husbands and children to return. *Is that enough for them?* Ruth thinks about all the women her age, about their mothers and grandmothers, too—and about all the potential that's been stymied and wasted. She thinks about the novels that could have been written, the music composed, the scientific breakthroughs made, the diseases that might have been cured, and the political agendas that could have been set if only those women had been encouraged to follow their dreams.

When Ernest presents Barbie to the mothers, they snicker, roll their eyes and fold their arms as their disapproval ripples from one end of the table to the other. Ruth's shoulders go slack as her bravado begins to fray.

"This is supposed to be a doll?" asks one mother. "A doll? For young girls?"

"How can *that* be a doll?" challenges another. "It's a woman. And it has breasts. Disgusting."

"So you think breasts are disgusting?" asks Ernest.

The mother's mouth drops open. "That's a highly inappropriate question. But since you asked, yes, breasts are *disgusting* when given to young girls to play with."

"And if it's supposed to be a doll," says another, "why is it wearing eyeshadow and lipstick?"

"And would you look at those high heels," another says, shaking her head.

"Only hussies wear shoes like that," says the one next to her. "That doll looks like a prostitute."

Ruth sits back, crestfallen, as she smokes back-to-back cigarettes. She expected some pushback, but nothing this harsh.

Ernest clasps his hands behind his back and leans in ever so slightly. "So Barbie would *not* be a suitable doll for your daughters, is that what you're saying?"

That is indeed what they're saying. The women are chattering all at once and there is nothing but negativity spewing from them: *The doll's too sexual. What's wrong with ordinary dolls? Whoever thought this up is perverse. They should have their head examined . . .*

Ruth crushes out her cigarette and balls up her hands. The observation room is suddenly stifling, and her head feels like it's in a vise. Her worst nightmare is unfolding before her eyes. Mothers are going to derail everything. Three years of hard work are coming to a screeching halt. There's no way to come back from this.

"So," asks Ernest, interrupting the cross-chattering, "is it fair to say that you all agree that Barbie is too sexual?"

The consensus is yes. Except for one woman. "I'm sure you're all going to hate me for saying this," she says, "but I actually think that doll's kinda fun."

Ruth perks up. So do Elliot, Charlotte and Jack.

"She's very glamorous," the woman continues. "I just love all her

LET'S CALL HER BARBIE

clothes. And she's just so well put together and accessorized. If only I could get my daughter to dress a little more like her."

Another mother speaks up. "I can barely get my daughter to brush her hair."

"Or put on a clean dress," says another.

"I keep telling my daughter she'll never find a husband if she doesn't start dressing more like a young lady . . ."

"I've had that very same conversation with my daughter," says another.

"I nag my daughter constantly about her hygiene. I'll never get her married off at this rate . . ."

Ruth leans forward, pressing her fingertips into her forehead, which has begun to throb like she has a jackhammer going off inside her skull. It's 1958, for God's sake, and all they care about is getting their daughters married?

Ruth closes her eyes, listening to Ernest wrapping up the session. Elliot, Jack and Charlotte are murmuring among themselves, sounding frustrated and discouraged. Ruth feels sick inside. Just when Elliot's starting to believe in Barbie, Dichter undoes it all. She can hear it now: *Let's cut our losses, Ruthie. Let's quit before we lose our shirt on this doll* . . .

After the mothers leave, Ernest invites them all into the laboratory room.

"Well, that was a total waste," Ruth says, dropping into a chair and pushing the plate of cookie crumbs aside.

"Not at all," says Ernest. He appears pleased by what's transpired.

"Oh, c'mon," Ruth says, "you heard what those women said."

"They hate Barbie," says Elliot. "They'll never buy one for their daughters."

"I beg to differ," says Ernest with a smirk that makes Ruth want to claw his face off. "Those women just gave us a wealth of information. You only heard what they *said*, but I understood what they *meant*." Ernest begins to pace, his white tufts of hair jutting out, almost perpendicular to his body. "The mothers' number one concern is making sure their daughters can attract husbands. And what those mothers sparked to was Barbie's sense of style, her being so 'well put together.' You saw how those young girls brushed Barbie's hair, how they fussed over her outfits. All we have to do is convince the mothers that Barbie will help their daughters catch a husband."

They're all looking at Ruth, expecting her to explode—*That's not what Barbie is about. She's the opposite of all that*—but Ruth stays silent. Her mind has just latched on to something. She's not exactly sure what it is yet but she's working it, like fitting a key inside a locked door.

"You see," says Ernest, "Barbie will encourage their daughters to dress better, to pay more attention to their grooming. That is the message your advertising must convey to the mothers."

The locked door swings open. Ernest is right. All this time she thought they would be selling Barbie to little girls, but really, they'll be selling Barbie to their mothers.

Something Borrowed, Something New

Coming off the Living Laboratories, Ruth and Charlotte sit down with Stevie to discuss a new outfit for Barbie: a wedding dress.

"For Barbie?" Stevie is confused, her eyes shifting from Charlotte to Ruth. "But I was under the impression that Barbie wasn't supposed to—"

"This is all driven by the market research," says Ruth dismissively. "I'll dress Barbie in a clown suit if that's what it takes to get buy-in from the mothers." It's true, and even though Ruth's agreed to put Barbie in a wedding dress, that's as far as she'll go. There'll be no future talk of marriage. Barbie is still going to represent what it means to be a modern, independent woman.

"The wedding dress is going to be the centerpiece of Barbie's launch," says Charlotte.

"It'll be featured in the TV campaign and in all the print ads, too," says Ruth.

"So it has to be spectacular," says Charlotte. "Think you can do this?"

"Absolutely, I can do this," Stevie says. Of course she can.

She has already made a perfectly enchanting wedding gown, and back at her workstation, she opens her sketchpad, ready to re-create a dress she could design in her sleep. She's memorized every fold, knows how to work with the satin, the tulle, the cathedral train. She knows because it was her final project at Chouinard. She began working on it when she learned she was pregnant and Russell said he wanted to marry her. If he hadn't run out on her, she would have been married in that dress; she would have stayed in school, graduated at the top of her class, had the baby and kept going. She might not even have been showing yet by the time she finished school. No one would have known a thing. Even before meeting Ruth, Stevie knew it was possible—not easy, but certainly possible—for a wife and mother to have a career. But without a husband in the picture, her plan unraveled.

She shoves *what might have been* to the back of her mind and focuses on the wedding dress, thinking of the best way to convert it to Barbie's scale. She sketches ideas and drapes silk on a fitting doll, looking to see which way the fabric wants to move. It comes alive inside her head, and she's lost in all this when she hears Jack's voice.

"Need a coffee or anything?" he asks.

"What?"

"Coffee? Or maybe a belt of bourbon?" He half smiles and leans over her workstation, close enough that she can smell his musky aftershave. "I just thought I'd offer some moral support on the wedding dress. I know it's a lot of pressure. And we don't have a lot of time."

"It's okay. I can handle it." She looks up and his eyes grab hold of hers. They're a blue-green and she realizes she's never noticed the color before.

"Okay, then," he says, hesitating for a moment. "If there's

anything you want to bounce off me, just say the word." He smiles and swaggers away.

Stevie is aware of everyone—the men and women alike—watching him disappear around the corner, disappointed that he didn't stop by their workstations, too. This is the second time this week that Jack's come to see her. Two days ago, he dropped off a fashion magazine that the mail boy would have delivered anyway. She almost gets the feeling that he's looking for excuses to talk to her.

W hen were you planning on showing me this?" Ruth asks Barbara as she pours her morning coffee, fingernails clicking against the counter.

"They just handed them out yesterday," says Barbara. "You were working late. What was I supposed to do, call your secretary and schedule a meeting so I could show you? Or should I have just left it on your pillow for when you got home?"

"Don't be fresh." Ruth looks again at her daughter's report card. She used to be an A student. But now she's getting Cs and C minuses in every subject, from math to sociology. Her teachers' comments say it all: *Unsatisfactory. Needs improvement.* "I want you to spend less time with Allen and more time on your schoolwork."

"Why? What difference does it make?" She shakes out a bowl of cornflakes and uncaps the milk bottle. "I'm not going to college."

"The hell you're not."

"I'm-not-going-to-college," she annunciates emphatically. "I'm going to marry Allen."

"Over my dead body. You're not going to throw your future away on some boy. Especially not *him.*"

"You don't even know Allen." She slams the bottle down, and a dollop of milk escapes, landing on the counter. "Maybe if you were home once in a while . . ."

"Don't start on that, Barbara. I'm in no mood, and if your grades don't improve, I'm going to forbid you to see him, do you hear me?"

Barbara is still protesting as Ruth scoops up her keys and heads out the door. Twenty minutes later and stuck in traffic, she stews. Barbara is only seventeen; how can she even think about marriage when she has her whole life ahead of her?

By the time Ruth arrives at Mattel, she's still agitated, and her mood hasn't improved when she steps into the conference room for—of all things—the wedding grown presentation. She knows that putting Barbie in a wedding dress is a smart strategic move, but the whole idea of Barbie getting married makes her blood boil.

"Where's Jack?" she asks. "Somebody tell him to get his ass in here. I haven't got all day." It's warm and stuffy in the conference room. Her blouse is clinging to her skin. "And call reception and have them lower the air."

Half a cigarette later, Jack comes in. "It's about time," she says. "What's the matter, did you get lost or something?"

"Well, good morning to you, too," he says, taking his seat.

After Charlotte sets the stage, Stevie begins her presentation. She's been working on the wedding gown for weeks now and has incorporated all of Charlotte's suggestions: lengthening the train, embellishing the veil, adding more embroidery on the bodice. The sample on the fitting doll no longer resembles Stevie's wedding gown, which is a good thing. She doesn't need to be reminded of Russell every time she works on it.

Ruth plucks the fitting doll from Stevie and examines the dress up close. "That's it? That's all you've got?"

"What more should there be?" asks Stevie, looking at Charlotte, who's just as confused.

"Gee, I don't know," Ruth says sarcastically. "What would a bride possibly need besides a dress? Maybe a bouquet? A pair of shoes?"

"But this meeting was to review the gown," says Stevie, knowing she shouldn't challenge Ruth and defend herself, but she can't just sit there and take it. "I haven't even started on the accessories."

Ruth makes a disgusted hissing sound. "Ever heard of *something borrowed, something blue, something old, something new*?"

"But Ruth—" Stevie tries again.

"Whoa, Ruth," Jack says, cutting Stevie off. "C'mon, give the kid a break."

The kid? Stevie glares at him. "If you don't mind, Jack, I can handle this my—"

"She did a bang-up job on the gown, and you know it," says Jack. "She'll get to the accessories. Just back off."

Ruth doesn't say anything. Instead, she gathers her cigarettes and lighter and marches out of the conference room. She does this from time to time, abruptly walks out of meetings that aren't going her way. She'll make her exit, storming down the hall with that look in her eyes that makes everyone bury their heads in their work, praying they don't do anything to call attention to themselves. It's like being in the presence of a grizzly bear.

After the meeting adjourns, Jack stops by Stevie's workstation to check on her. She grips her pencil tight and keeps her chin tucked, her head down. "You didn't need to do that," she says, refusing to look at him for fear she'll burst into tears.

"Do what?"

"Defend me. I'm perfectly capable of taking care of myself."

"Oh, I'm sure you are," he says. "But I'd do the same for anyone on my team. I'd do the same for Twist or Frankie. I'm your boss, and Ruth was being a beast."

That softens her some, or at least enough to confess her bewilderment. "I just don't know what I did wrong. The meeting wasn't even about accessories."

"C'mon," he says, "let's get out of here."

"I can't," she mutters. "I've got too much work to do."

He reaches over, pries the pencil from her fingers and sets it down on her desk. "Trust me on this. I know when someone needs to step away from their work."

S tevie and Jack end up at the Brown Derby, sitting across from each other in an Old English–style booth, drinking dry gin martinis.

"Now, isn't this better?" he says after taking a sip.

Unwilling to let him know how grateful she is that he insisted they get out of the office, she says, "I don't usually start drinking before noon, you know."

"Don't worry. I plan on feeding you, too."

"Good, 'cause I'm starving."

"Wait a minute," he says, leaning forward. "Is that—could it be—is that a smile I detect?"

"More like a simper," she offers in spite of herself.

He sits back, arms folded. "You don't like me, do you?"

"Just because I don't flaunt myself around you like the other girls doesn't mean I don't like you." In fact, she doesn't dislike him, not like she did in the beginning. And she acknowledges that he has gone out of his way to show her a kindness or two.

"We could be friends, you know."

"Friends?" She cocks an eyebrow. "I've heard you have a lot of those."

"My, my," he tuts. "You seem awfully focused on me and the

other girls in the office." He takes another sip of his martini. "Just so you know, I have plenty of purely platonic female friends, too. And I happen to be a very good friend."

"If you do say so yourself."

"Well, the way Ruth went after you this morning, I'd say you could use a friend like me." He sits back, eyeing her. "There's that simper again."

She studies his face for a moment. His eyes look warm and friendly, his Irish complexion fair and smooth. "Actually, I think that was a half smile."

He clinks his glass to hers, holding her gaze. There's a moment of silence that is anything but empty. His pulse quickens; her breathing shallows. He's wondering if she has a boyfriend and she's wondering if the rumors about him being such a great kisser are true. He's thinking she is adorable. And smart. She's thinking that maybe he does look a little like Dean Martin after all.

Stevie clears her throat, blinks and excuses herself, heading straight for the ladies' room. *What in the hell just happened out there?* She splashes water on her face and stares at herself in the mirror. Her cheeks are flushed; her heart is still thumping like a little bunny. *You idiot, he's your boss. And he has a wife. Stop it, just stop it.*

When she returns to the table, they order: rainbow trout for her, the swordfish for Jack. Half an hour later, her stomach is still fluttering as she pushes the food about her plate.

"I thought you were starving," says Jack with a rascally grin. He knows he's gotten to her.

Stevie is quiet on the drive back to the office, and sitting at her desk, she tries to think about the wedding dress accessories, but her mind keeps ricocheting back to Jack.

The Juggling Act

The next day Ruth calls Stevie down to her office to do something she rarely does—apologize. She hadn't meant to lash out at her like that. She'd been surprised and even impressed that Stevie hadn't cried. If anything, she'd pushed back—respectfully, professionally. She'd actually behaved more professionally than Ruth had.

There's a light rap on her door. "Ruth?" says Stevie. "You wanted to see me?"

She motions her inside, gestures to the seat opposite her desk. "I wanted to talk to you about yesterday's meeting." She'd like to come right out and say she's sorry, but the words get stuck in her throat. Instead, she says something she's often thought but has never verbalized. "You remind me a lot of myself when I was younger."

"I do?"

She can't tell if Stevie is flattered or offended. "My first job when I left Denver and came out here was at Paramount Pictures. I was a secretary."

"That must have been exciting."

"It was." She reaches for a cigarette and lights it. "When I started I wasn't great at my job," she says, exhaling smoke from the corner of her mouth. "But I *became* great because, like you"—she points her hot ash Stevie's way—"I worked harder than the other stenographers. I went into work every day thinking of ways to be more efficient. The bosses noticed what I was doing, and I went from typing scripts to working for some big directors, like Alexander Hall. You think *I'm* a tough boss?" Ruth laughs. "My point is that I wanted to be the best at my job. Right now, Charlotte is the best, but you're going to surpass her one day. The main thing, if I can pass along some unsolicited advice, is that if you're going to be successful at anything—I don't care what it is—you have to learn how to bounce back from disappointments, rejections, false starts and even temporary failures. You have to find the strength to pick yourself up and keep going. When things go wrong, you need to change your plan, maybe change your approach, but don't you dare ever give up."

Ruth's secretary buzzes in, her voice staticky. "I have Barbara on line three. She says it's urgent."

Ruth sighs. "I have to take this." She pulls off her clip-on earring and reaches for the receiver. "Yes, Barbara?"

Stevie can hear Barbara's voice through the phone as she shouts at her mother about not wanting to ride with the chauffeur . . . wanting to walk with her friends to the picnic . . . Stevie's embarrassed to be overhearing this and makes a *should-I-leave* gesture, at which Ruth shakes her head. Trying to make herself invisible, Stevie looks around Ruth's office, which can only be described as playful elegance. The antique desk works surprisingly well with the modern pink leather sofa.

"Barbara, we've been through this," says Ruth, tapping her cigarette to the ashtray.

"Nobody's going to kidnap me," Barbara shouts back.

"That's right, because you're going to be safe in the car." Ruth actually agrees that the driver is a bit extreme. It's not like they're the Lindberghs. But Elliot, the worrier, insists, so she insists.

"But I don't want to be driven there."

"Barbara, I'm not going to discuss this with you any longer."

There's a screech coming over the phone, loud enough to make Ruth squint and pull the receiver away from her ear.

Stevie diverts her attention to the family photographs on Ruth's desk: framed pictures of the four of them. In one, they're standing before a mountain; another has a waterfall in the background; another looks like one of those professional family portraits. Stevie thinks how lucky those kids are to be growing up in such a loving household, going on family vacations. The only thing close to a family vacation for Stevie was tagging along with her parents to the encyclopedia conventions in places like Lincoln, Nebraska, and Eugene, Oregon.

Stevie admires what Ruth has been able to do. She has an adoring husband, two beautiful children and a thriving career. Stevie's mother could barely handle one kid, and any type of work or interests outside the house would be out of the question. Stevie is heartened by Ruth's example, because one day she would love to have a husband and family of her own, but not at the cost of her career. Ruth is showing her that it is possible for a woman to juggle all three.

"I'm hanging up now, Barbara. This conversation is over."

"But—"

"Goodbye, Barbara."

After setting the receiver back in its cradle, she says, "My daughter," with an exasperated shrug. Clipping her earring back in place, she says, "I just wanted to let you know that I think you're going to do very well here."

"Thank you, I'm trying."

"I know you are." She smiles, grinding out her cigarette. "How are the wedding accessories coming?"

"They'll be ready in time for the meeting."

"I have no doubt."

And that is as close as Ruth can get to apologizing.

Later that week, Stevie and Charlotte present the wedding set accessories—a bouquet, blue garter, pearl necklace, little white gloves and white shoes. Ruth seems genuinely pleased. It's as if the previous meeting never happened.

Now it's five o'clock and Stevie is exhausted. She grabs her pocketbook from her bottom desk drawer, says a quick good night to Mia, Charlotte and Patsy, waving to Twist and Frankie before heading down the hallway, past the turnstile and out to the parking lot.

It's especially hot, even for August, and her old clunker has been poaching in the sun all day. The pavement is giving off a wavy mirage-like haze and the leather seat sears her bare arms and the backs of her legs. The steering wheel is too hot to grip. She cranks down the window, and when she turns the ignition, nothing. She tries again and again, her foot pumping the gas pedal, all to no avail. The last thing she needs is car trouble, especially since she's recently replaced the battery. She's thinking she's going to have to call for a tow truck when Jack wanders over, and the sight of him evokes a smile. It's involuntary and already out there. He's seen it, and she's annoyed that he has this effect on her.

"What's the problem here, kiddo?"

"It's dead." She keeps her eyes straight ahead and sighs to indicate that no, she's not happy to see him, not one little bit. She squeezes the scorching-hot steering wheel as if holding tight to that thought.

"Well, let's have a look."

She gets out of the car and he steps in. After trying the ignition, he releases the hood and lifts it up, his shirtsleeves rolled to his elbows. "Yep," he says, nodding, "your spark plugs are shot." He snoops around a bit more, tweaking this coil and that. "Your alternator's about to go, too."

"Shit."

"Well, don't worry. Easy fixes, kiddo. Very easy."

"You know how to fix cars?"

"Please, I used to build missiles for a living." He slams the hood closed. "Gotta tell you, though, this one really ain't worth fixing. You need a new car." Jack dusts his hands off. "Come with me." He gestures toward his shiny black Alfa Romeo, parked next to Elliot's Mercedes.

"Where are we going? What about my car?"

"Don't ask so many questions. Just relax. Trust me."

She half expects him to wink, but instead she's the one who winks after she says, "Trust you? Yeah, about as much as I trust my car will ever start again."

They end up at the Bozzani Volkswagen dealership on Sunset and Broadway.

"This is a crazy idea," she says. "I can't afford a new car and I can't get a loan." She's already tried and was turned down. They said she needed a male cosigner, and Stevie's too proud to ask her father for help. After supposedly wasting his money on design school, she's reluctant to ask him for anything.

Jack cocks his head to the side and gives her a smile. "I can cosign for you."

"I can't let you do that. Besides"—she offers a coquettish shrug—"how do you know I'm good for it? I could skip out on my payments, and you'd be left with the loan."

"I'll take my chances."

"You're a gambling man, aren't you?" she says, wondering why she's giving him that same flirty smile she used to flash at Russell. "Seriously," she says, reining herself back in, "why would you do this for me?"

"It's not for you," he says. "It's for me. We have a lot of work to do on Barbie, and I can't afford to have you stranded on the side of the road somewhere in a broken-down car, unable to get to work. C'mon, let's just test-drive a few. Just for fun."

And it is fun. They take out several models, going from the Beetle Convertible to the Beetle Sedan to the Sunroof Sedan, zipping around corners, racing alongside the streetcar tracks and whirling past City Hall. And after much protesting on her part, Jack cosigns the loan for Stevie's cherry red convertible with the matching leatherette interior. She loves the new car smell, the radio and the whitewall tires.

When Jack presses the keys into her hand, she feels his fingers linger, her skin absorbing the gentle heat of his touch.

"I won't sleep with you because of this," she says.

"I don't recall asking you to."

Now she's embarrassed, wishing she hadn't been so presumptuous. "And you mean it?" she says, trying to recover. "There's no strings attached?"

"Not even a thread."

Put Her on Ice

R uthie, are you crazy?" Elliot drops into the chair behind his desk. The color has drained from his face. "You want to spend *how much* on the television advertising for Barbie?"

"Relax, Elliot."

"Relax? You're gonna give me a heart attack."

"God forbid, pooh, pooh, pooh," she says, warding off the evil spirit. "We already know the power of advertising on TV. We'll start airing in June, so it coincides with school letting out. That gives retailers plenty of time to place their orders at Toy Fair, get everything shipped and on the shelves in time for summer vacation."

"But you're talking about $125,000. Just for Barbie alone."

"I've crunched the numbers, and I'm being conservative when I say we should have Tokyo ramp up production to 20,000 Barbies a week—"

"Oh, Ruthie—that's an awful lot of—"

"Along with 40,000 outfits—"

"Oh God, you're killing me. I swear to God you are killing me."

"Trust me, Elliot. Remember what happened with the Burp Gun?"

How could he forget? It was the biggest gamble she ever took, and he had no choice but to go along with it. Back in 1955, Mattel introduced the Burp Gun. It was just an ordinary cap gun, but Elliot designed it as a machine gun, able to fire round upon round. It was quite the sensation at Toy Fair, and the orders practically wrote themselves. But once the Burp Gun got to the stores, it didn't sell. At the time, Walt Disney happened to be looking for a sponsor for his new TV show, premiering that spring. Disney wanted $500,000 for fifty-two weeks' worth of TV spots. At first Ruth dismissed the idea. *A TV commercial in the middle of March?* The only time anyone advertised toys on television was the two weeks before Christmas. Besides, if it failed, $500,000 could have put Mattel out of business. But then again, Ruth came from a family of gamblers, and with knots in her stomach, and Elliot hyperventilating, she decided to do it. As soon as the Burp Gun commercials began airing on *The Mickey Mouse Club*, sales took off. They filled over a million orders that year alone, and the Burp Gun is still their best-selling toy.

With just eight and a half weeks until Toy Fair, Ruth and Elliot arrive at a soundstage in Burbank. Mattel's advertising agency, Carson/Roberts, is about to shoot the Barbie commercial.

The amount of equipment and number of people needed to film one commercial is staggering. There's a Bell & Howell camera resting on a tripod, a dolly for the moving shots, a crane for the overhead shots and three enormous solar spotlights. There's a thick bundle of wires, cables and cords, taped down to the floor so no one trips over them. All the advertising agency people are there, along with the director, a tall skinny man with penny loafers. He has half a dozen assistants, plus the stylists, the prop master and the craft service people, who will feed them throughout the day.

There are dozens of Barbies on hand, some brunettes, some blondes, each dressed in various outfits. Ruth hovers while two stylists prep Barbie's hair. Another one steams her clothes and scrutinizes each item for any loose threads or imperfections that the camera and lights might pick up.

"Okay, people," says the director, looking at his shot list, "let's lay down the establishing scene." After some last-minute tinkering on the set and once all the dolls are in place, an assistant flips a switch and the spotlights kick on. The whole set goes dazzlingly and nearly blindingly bright. Ruth and Elliot can feel the heat from all the way across the room. The director rushes over to the set to tweak one of the Barbies, and by the time he takes his place behind the camera and looks through the lens, everyone sees there is a problem. The Barbies are melting. Under the heat of the lamps, their chins become elongated; their synthetic hair begins to wilt and weld together, forming helmets. Barbie's bangs are plastered to her forehead.

"Cut," the director calls out.

They replace those dolls, redo the set and push the spotlights off just a bit. They're all ready to go again. No sooner does the director call "Action" than the same thing happens again. The third time they try to film as quickly as possible. Halfway through the second take, the bridal Barbie's cheeks bubble up and blister. Ruth's entire body slumps. She feels like she's the director's chair folding in on itself.

"This is a disaster," says Elliot after another botched take. "I'm going back to the office. I can't watch this anymore."

After Elliot leaves, Ralph Carson, the numbers man, huddles with Ruth. "There's no way this is going to be an eight-hour shoot like we planned on," he says. "I'm afraid we'll be going into over-time."

"That's time and a half, isn't it?" asks Ruth, already calculating what this does to their budget.

"Afraid so."

"Well, that's bad news for you."

"For me?"

"I'm not eating the overtime costs. You are."

And that's the end of that discussion. Now Ruth has Carson watching the clock as closely as she is. After another forty-five minutes and two more fruitless attempts, they break for lunch. The entire morning has been a waste. There's a trash bin full of ruined dolls and outfits drizzled in plastic. Nothing with Barbie has gone smoothly. As a team, they were nimble, though; they always found ways to work through all the production hiccups and naysaying and overcame every other obstacle. This was supposed to be the easy part. She can't live through another setback. There has to be a way to make this damn commercial.

Maybe they need to bring in fans? But that would mess up Barbie's hair, flutter her clothes. Can they shoot without the spot-lights? Maybe lighten the film in postproduction? She's thinking, thinking, gnashing her teeth and her brain, but the director, his crew and the ad agency people are lined up at the craft service table, filling their plates with macaroni and cheese, roasted chicken, lima beans and rice pudding. *Why the hell am I the one trying to solve this mess when the people I hired are more interested in lunch?*

She can't bring herself to eat. Her stomach's upset, roiling from nerves and too much coffee. Instead, she reaches inside the ice chest for a bottle of Coca-Cola, and as she wipes away the conden-sation and takes a sip, an idea comes to her.

Turning to Carson, she says, "Why don't you keep the Barbies in the ice chest until it's time to shoot?"

"Are you serious?"

"You have a better idea? Let's put those Barbies on ice."

And that's what they do. The stylists gently wrap each doll in plastic, careful not to mess their hair or outfits, before plunging them deep into the ice. They work quickly to get each take before re-icing the dolls for the next setup. Barbies' little legs and feet are sticking up in the air like bottles of champagne.

Lovesick

1959

Another sixteen-hour day. Ruth is exhausted, running on fumes and nicotine. Her head is full of numbers, projections, schedules, phone calls needing to be returned. For every one item she ticks off her list, two more appear. She should be glad the day is over. Now she can go home and relax with her husband and children. But these days home feels like more work, a different kind of work. For her, it's harder work.

She'll have to watch herself, bite her tongue when she wants to mention something about Barbie or Toy Fair. When Elliot goes to tell her how he beat Marvin six–love, giving her the blow-by-blow of their tennis match, she'll force herself to listen, or look like she's listening. But the whole time she'll be thinking about the final mix for the Barbie commercial, wondering if they should have gone with a female announcer rather than a male. If Ken is sulking, staring at the same page of the book in his lap, she'll know she should go to him, ask what's wrong, ask for every detail of his day, but the thought is more draining than anything she's done at the office. And then there's Barbara, who'd probably prefer Ruth didn't say anything to her at all. When Ruth finally arrives home and steps inside, she wonders if they'd resent her even more if she said a quick hello and slipped upstairs to soak in a bath.

Ken is already sequestered in his room, while Barbara and Allen are in the living room with Elliot. The girl is lovesick. Barbara is only seventeen, turning eighteen next month. What does she know about love? Never mind that Ruth was sixteen when she met Elliot. That was different. *Ruth* was different.

She assumes this is just another Tuesday night. After all, Allen is always at their house. He's there for dinner twice, sometimes three times a week—not that Ruth joins them, because she's usually working late. But there's many a Saturday afternoon that she sees him lounging by the pool, even if Barbara doesn't feel like swimming. Ruth often finds him sprawled on the couch while Barbara sits beside him, *watching* him *watch* a television program she has little interest in. But tonight, there's a restlessness in the air. Something is looming, and Ruth senses that they've been waiting for her. She hasn't even poured herself a drink when Barbara announces her news.

"Allen and I are getting married."

Barbara is smiling full-on, but with each passing second that goes by without Ruth or Elliot speaking—saying anything at all— her brightness dims. Despite Barbara always threatening to get married, Ruth and Elliot are still caught off guard. It had seemed more like a taunt than a possibility. She and Elliot exchange looks: *How should we play this?*

"Married? My goodness. Isn't this a surprise. Mazel tov," Elliot finally says, getting up to kiss Barbara and shake Allen's hand.

"Really?" says Ruth, unable to pull off her husband's cheery delivery. "You two are getting married?" She might as well have said, *You two are going to rob a bank. How marvelous.*

"Yes," says Barbara, looping her arm through Allen's. There's something very possessive in the gesture, like she aims to put a lock on him. "We're getting married this June. Right after graduation."

Allen hasn't said a word. Barbara is driving this train, and Ruth knows she should keep quiet, but heaven help her, she can't. "Allen," she says, "how do your parents feel about this?"

"Ah." Allen blinks, dumbstruck. He's scared of Ruth, and she knows it.

"We wanted to tell you and Daddy first," Barbara says, gripping Allen's arm ever tighter.

"I believe I was talking to Allen," says Ruth, immediately regretting her tone. No wonder her daughter hates her. But she's not interested in being Barbara's friend at the moment. She lights a cigarette, snapping her Zippo shut with a loud *clack*. "Tell me something, Allen, how's the sporting goods business been treating you lately?"

"Um, what?"

"Ruthie—" Elliot gives her a *go easy* look, but it does no good.

"What do they pay you an hour?" Ruth asks. "A buck and a quarter?"

"Actually it's $1.15. But I'm due for a raise."

"Oh, good. A raise." She pauses, takes a dramatic puff off her cigarette. "Listen, I'm not gonna pussyfoot around here—what I want to know is how you plan on supporting my daughter after you're married."

"Mother!"

Ruth holds up her hand. "Do you want to go out and get a job, Barbara? 'Cause I'm all for that." Barbara is seething. Ruth can't stop herself. She needs to—*quick*—do something to spare her daughter from making this horrible mistake. The panic comes out as a rush of rage fueled by adrenaline, and now that she's started, there's no turning it off. "Allen, you still live at home, correct? With your parents? How much can you afford for rent each month? What about groceries? Have you ever seen, much less paid, an electric or telephone bill?"

"Mother!" There's a foot stomp this time.

Ruth's all in and there's no pulling her back. This is how she fights, and even the National Guard couldn't stop her now. "Let's face it, Barbara, you've been raised in a certain fashion. You might not like this big fancy house, you might say you want to live like, quote, 'a *normal* person,' but you *do* appreciate nice things. *Expensive* things. I just want to make sure that Allen can provide for you."

"Of course he can provide for me," she insists with another foot stomp.

"And, Barbara, what about college? Is that out the window now? Are you just going to sit at home and keep house?" Ruth goes for the jugular. "When was the last time you made your own bed, young lady? You know, you won't have Edna to pick up after you, do your laundry, clean your dishes . . ." Bull's-eye. Direct hit. But Ruth keeps it up, lobbing one objection after another until Barbara storms out of the room crying, leaving her fiancé standing there, pale and speechless.

W ell, that didn't go very well, did it?" Ruth says to Elliot later that night as she folds back the bedspread.

He pulls her into his arms and, as Ruth takes a shuddering breath, he says, "You could try apologizing, you know."

"For what? For not wanting my daughter to throw away her future?" Ruth drops her head to his shoulder. "She's about to make a terrible mistake. We can't let her do this."

"But we need to be careful," he says, meaning Ruth needs to control her temper. "Otherwise, we'll only drive her into his arms."

"I know, I know. I just—I couldn't help myself. She's a child, Elliot. She's nowhere near ready to get married. And to *him*?"

"We'll try and find a way to reason with her. Gently. Rationally. You're overtired, and that's not helping things. Try and relax and get some sleep."

Ruth nods and leans toward him, accepting a kiss before he turns out the light, leaving her in such darkness, it takes a moment for her eyes to adjust. She lights a cigarette, the ember tip glowing red. Elliot doesn't say anything about her smoking in bed. For tonight he allows it.

Her daughter is in love with love, with being a bride—with no thought as to what comes after that. Does Barbara *really* know Allen? How does he handle stress? Resolve arguments? Is he kind to strangers? Is he fair and honest? Generous with a dollar or stingy and watching every penny? Does he drink too much at parties? Leave his dirty socks on the floor? Is he a gambler like the rest of her family? And what about children? Will he be a strict father or leave all the disciplining to her? These are the things that no one tells you to consider when you get engaged. But further down the road, these are the very things that will make or break a marriage. Barbara is shortsighted, focusing only on things that are destined to change. Allen's looks will fade; his hair will thin as surely as his waistline will thicken. He may fall ill or on hard times. When everything about him that she initially fell in love with has disappeared, what will she be left with? And will that be enough?

What Ruth can't understand is why Barbara's in such a hurry. There's time for marriage and children. Time that she won't ever get back if she doesn't take it for herself now. Ruth wants her daughter to have opportunities, to be able to do more with her life than raise children and be Allen's wife. It won't be enough for her, but how can she get through to Barbara? It's not as if she can boss her around like one of her employees.

At the office Ruth calls the shots. At home, with her daughter, she doesn't. That last thought resonates with her. It's so obvious, but she hasn't realized it until just now. In that split second, she understands what it is about Barbie and that wedding dress that gets her so riled up. It's all about control. Ruth can't control Barbara, but she can control Barbie. Ruth might not be able to stop Barbara from getting married, but she can stop Barbie from doing it. Like most revelations, this notion will dance around her thoughts, coming and going, until she's ready to fully accept it.

She thinks Elliot's already asleep until he says, "You know, your sister didn't think I was good enough for you, either."

"Oh, please, you can't compare the two."

"No, of course not, but just think about what I'm saying."

After a deep inhale she remembers how much Sarah disliked Elliot in the beginning. Elliot was a talented artist, but all her sister saw was a poor scrawny boy with scuffed-up shoes and oil paint beneath his fingernails. There was no way he could provide for her baby sister. The one big fight Ruth and Sarah ever had was over Elliot.

Ruth had known from the start that Elliot was the right man for her. Even at sixteen, she knew how strong-willed she could be. She knew she needed a husband who was secure enough with himself to let her take charge. A marriage with any other type of man never would have worked. Sarah had balked when Ruth borrowed money to get their fledgling plastic business off the ground, but Ruth believed in Elliot, and more than that, she believed in herself. She'd gambled on Elliot, her starving artist, and she'd won.

"And don't forget," Elliot says now, "Sarah thought you were too young to get married, too."

Ruth can't deny this, but there's a big difference. Barbara is young for her years, far younger now than Ruth ever was. Barbara thankfully has had a much easier life than Ruth did, but privilege has made her daughter soft and impressionable.

Ruth has always been the opposite. Hard and immutable. When she first met Elliot, she was smitten by his good looks, his glorious head of dark ringlets and that smile. She thought it was just infatuation, but as they got to know each other, Elliot—soft-spoken, shy, congenial Elliot—found a way to break through her shell and soften her heart. But that makes sense. Imagine the impact of two hard objects colliding. They would have smashed each other to bits. Instead, it was his warm, gentle sensibility that melted her exterior. He had found that part of her that her mother took away and he'd handed it back to her. She trusted that Elliot Handler would never give her back; he'd never let her get away.

Toy Fair

The Mattel delegation—Ruth, Elliot, Jack, Charlotte, Sid and half a dozen sales reps, all of them men except for Gina— are at the gate about to board the plane for New York City. They're all energized, all of them anticipating Toy Fair. There's a triumphant feeling in the air. They've all been through so much together and are taking turns recalling all the ups and downs of creating Barbie.

"I will never forget the way you sawed those nipples off," says Charlotte, squeezing Jack's wrist as she laughs.

"Oh lord, and remember all the other prototypes," says Ruth, smiling, shaking her head. "I thought they'd never get it right."

"And what about those telephone calls with KBK," adds Elliot. "They're speaking to us in Japanese, while we're talking to them in English. It was a comedy of errors."

In the midst of all this laughter and whooping it up, Gina graces them with her daily allergy attack: "Awww-chew! Awww-chew! Awww-chew!" And just like in the office, they all shout "Gazoon-tite" and start laughing even harder.

Everyone's so upbeat, so ready to take this next step. Each year at Toy Fair there's always one or two hot new releases. And when a toy is hot, there's an energy field that swirls around it. A hot toy is all the buyers and manufacturers—envious as all get-out—can talk about. They all have the feeling that this year Barbie is destined to be *that* toy. She's going to steal the show.

When they land in New York, they head straight to the International Toy Center at 200 Fifth Avenue in the Flatiron District to begin setting up. For the next two days, all of them work side by side, preparing their booths, hanging signs and banners, all while keeping Barbie under wraps and away from Louis Marx and other spies. In the evenings Ruth and Elliot take the important toy buyers out for drinks and dinner. The night before the fair officially opens, Jack buys tickets for everyone to see *A Majority of One* on Broadway.

The next day, everyone is wound up and ready to go. It's March 9, 1959, and here they are, just hours away from unveiling Barbie. That morning, they all meet for an early breakfast at the hotel. There's a certain kind of magic buzzing about the table, each of them shimmering inside, filled with anticipation.

Ruth can't wait to start writing up orders. She's a natural-born saleswoman who thrives on the challenge of making someone believe they need what she's got. It's a game for her, like she's fencing with the customer, lunging and parrying; they want her to ship the order for free, she wants them to increase their buy and put up a big display in their store, they want their store mentioned in her advertising, she wants Mattel mentioned in theirs.

It's a hot, sticky morning in New York; the temperature is unusually warm for this time of year. Ruth's hair is frizzing from the humidity, and the short cab ride from the hotel to the show already has her flushed and overheated. Still, she can feel the adrenaline pumping through her.

They enter the exhibit hall and Mattel's presence is impossible to miss. They've rented out a good deal of real estate in the showroom for their standard toys: the Uke-A-Doodle, the Burp Gun and various other guns, music boxes and the H_2O Missile. But Barbie, their star, has her own room with a round table in the center, spotlighting three different dolls—one blonde and two brunettes. Blonde Barbie is dressed in her zebra-striped bathing suit, which hugs her breasts and hips. She sports gold hoop earrings and black high-heeled mules and holds a pair of white-framed sunglasses in her hand. One of the brunette Barbies wears the *Gay Parisienne*, a blue pin-dot taffeta bubble dress with a white rabbit fur stole. The other brunette Barbie is the centerpiece, the bride in the *Wedding Day Set*. There are additional outfits on display from the 900 series, including *Plantation Belle*, *Roman Holiday*, *Suburban Shopper*, *Sweater Girl* and *Enchanted Evening*.

One more cigarette, one more cup of coffee and the doors open. A flood of buyers and wholesalers from across the country enter the showroom, their dark suits and briefcases rushing in like a flock of crows. Elliot and Jack are already demonstrating the latest edition of the Thunder Burp Gun to customers from FAO Schwarz, while Ruth and Charlotte are in the other room with Barbie. Charlotte fusses with the outfits and Ruth is all smiles, her sales face in place, ready to greet her first buyer of the day.

"Jimmy!" She lights up, holding out her hand to him.

Jimmy Lowe owns a small chain of toy stores in the Midwest. He has a big round face, pitted with acne scars that make him look like a human sponge. After asking about his wife and daughters, it's time to present Barbie.

"Here she is," she says, pointing to the table of dolls. "This is our latest creation—the Barbie doll."

Jimmy's eyebrows rise and pull together. He looks at Barbie and back to Ruth. He chews on his lip. "This doesn't look like a doll to me." He releases his lip and starts scratching the side of his head. "It looks like a regular woman."

"Exactly!" Ruth smiles. "That's the point. That's the beauty of her."

When he doesn't say anything, she moves deeper into her sales pitch. "She'll retail for $3, and look—we have all these outfits for her." She shows him *Golden Girl* and *Cruise Stripes*. "These will be sold separately. Anywhere from $1 to $5 each."

She follows the shift in his vacant eyes. *What the hell is wrong with him?* There's no spark, not even a glimmer of excitement or intrigue. She pushes harder still. "These are real clothes, too. Not just regular doll clothes. The zippers work, the buttons button." She hears the desperation leaking into her voice. "Each piece was created by a real fashion designer. And see? Each outfit has a tiny Barbie label inside. Isn't that something? I tell you, Jimmy, Barbie's better dressed than I am," she says with a sickeningly sweet chuckle that makes her want to cringe. "We'll be rolling out twenty-two outfits for her by the end of this year. It'll be like razor blades," she says now, thinking this is the angle she should have started with. "That's where the money is."

He's back to chewing his lip.

"Jimmy, there's never been a doll like this before. She's going to allow little girls to fantasize and make believe they're grown-up."

"But I thought the whole point of toys was to let children be children. Let's not rush them into being grown-ups."

She sees where he's heading and so she tries a different tack. "But Barbie can teach young girls how to groom themselves." She hates how that sounds, like they're a litter of kittens. "Jimmy," she says, nearly exasperated, "don't you think your daughters would want to play with a Barbie doll?"

"You kidding me?" His spongy face goes all a-pucker. "My wife would pitch a fit if I brought that doll into our house."

After Jimmy leaves, Ruth tells herself it's just him. He's too old-fashioned and doesn't understand Barbie. She'll get him on board later. But Jimmy's argument is the basic sentiment she hears from the next several buyers. An hour into the show, she feels the ground beneath her about to give way. Usually one sale leads to another, the momentum builds and each deal gets easier, like she has a tail-wind. But now everything is sinking, and it takes more and more effort to keep her smile from going under, too.

By two o'clock that afternoon she has written up a few meager orders. There's a burning pit in her stomach until at last, she sees Lowthar Kieso entering the Barbie room. Lowthar is the head toy buyer of Sears, Roebuck and Company.

"Well, look who's here," Ruth says playfully, giving him a hug. "It's about time you made your way in here." He's going to be Barbie's savior. The other buyers always watch him and follow his lead. "Well," she says, after making her Barbie presentation, "isn't she something?"

"Ah, yeah. You can say that again." He adjusts his eyeglasses. "When I heard you had a new doll, this is not what I was expecting."

"That's because there's never been a doll like Barbie before. Sure, there's been paper dolls, but you can't compare them to a Barbie doll."

"I'm sorry, Ruth," he says, shaking his head. "I can't see this on our shelves. It's not for little girls. That doll has a woman's figure. If you don't mind me saying, it strikes me as indecent."

"Oh, come on," she says, "I never took you for a prude."

"Not a prude, Ruth. Just telling you, that's not appropriate for children."

"We've done a ton of market research," she counters, "and I assure you little girls adore her, and their mothers—"

He holds up his hand to silence her. "I'm sorry, Ruth. I gotta trust my gut on this. And my gut tells me this is not a doll for Sears."

She can't hear the rest of what he's saying, though she sees his lips moving. No toy stands a chance without Sears, Roebuck and Company. A full-blown panic begins welling up inside her. She's clammy, feeling suddenly woozy. How can it possibly be that Barbie is bombing?

After Lowthar makes his apologies and leaves, Ruth huddles with Elliot and the rest of the Mattel team. All the energy from breakfast has fizzled. Shoulders slumping, heads shaking, lips pursed, they are all stunned by the lackluster reception to Barbie.

"What the hell is going on? Look at this," says Ruth, fanning out the scant handful of orders. "What is happening here? Where are the orders? What are you all hearing on the floor?"

Jack sighs. "All I keep hearing is that Mattel has a doll that looks like a hooker."

"That's what I heard, too," says Sid, nervously adjusting his toupee.

"I'm sorry, Ruthie," Elliot says. "She's just not connecting with the buyers."

No one else says anything. They've been working on this project for three long, hard, maddening, exhilarating years. None of them know what they'll do next if this doesn't work. Especially Charlotte. She was hired specifically to work on Barbie. If there's no Barbie, there's no need for her. Or Stevie. Or Mia.

Elliot gets called away by a customer, and after the others return to the main floor, Jack stays behind with Ruth. He's angry and in shock. He can't comprehend this reaction to Barbie.

"You should hear them out there." He gestures toward the main room. "'Hey, did you see the doll with the tits?' I feel like someone just told me my kid's ugly."

"That's *exactly* how I feel."

She slumps into a chair. He takes the seat next to her. At the same time, they look at each other and say, "Shit . . ."

When she can't take it anymore, Ruth leaves the trade show early. Back at the hotel, the *Do Not Disturb* sign gets caught in the door, and she yanks it so hard, the cardboard handle rips off. She barely gets inside her room before the tears let loose. Stepping out of her heels, she stares out the window at the bustling city below. She hates New York. Even from twelve stories up she hears the horns honking, sees the endless chain of taxicabs and people on the sidewalks rushing to and fro. How can life just go on as if nothing happened? How could she have been so wrong? This is a financial disaster in the making. She thinks of the ramifications and of all the money they've wasted. She's watching three years of hard work unravel before her eyes.

She knows she's going to have to tap some reserve of strength to keep fighting, but she's not sure how to access it. She's gone back to that well to bolster herself so many times now, she fears she may have depleted the supply.

Elliot finds her an hour later, cried out and despondent. "I'm sorry," he says, stroking her back.

She rolls over and looks up at him, mascara smudged beneath her eyes. "I still can't believe they didn't like her."

"It happens," he says. "But you gave it your all. No one can deny that. Maybe it's the timing." He shrugs. "It's out of our hands now." Another shrug. "We'll cut our losses and move on."

This makes her wince. "At least the Burp Gun and the water rocket are selling."

"Yeah, but not enough to cover the losses on Barbie." He scrubs a hand over his face, thinking aloud. "I'm afraid we're going to have to lay off some people . . ."

A wave of nausea hits her.

"I'll get word out to KBK," he says, "and tell them to stop production. Halt the shipments, too. And we'll call the ad agency, tell them we're canceling the Barbie TV."

"No! We can't—"

"But we need to let them know we're not running the TV now. That alone will save us $125,000 on the media buy."

The thought of killing the TV campaign is what unlocks that reserve of strength she feared was all used up. She saw what advertising on television did for the Burp Gun. That was a gamble and they triumphed—it's what put Mattel on the map. She props herself up against the headboard. "I'm not canceling the TV."

"What? Aw, no, Ruthie, no. Now you're just throwing good money after bad."

It's at times like these—the crisis points in their lives—when she notices the greatest differences between the two of them. He gives in too easily. He doesn't fight, and she can't *not* fight. "We have to run that TV. We've come this far. We can't quit now. I can't give up on Barbie. I just can't."

Elliot drags both hands through his thinning hair and sighs. He knows his wife. She's not ready to surrender yet. "If we run that TV and it doesn't work, you need to promise me—and I mean this, Ruthie—no more. We're done with Barbie after that."

"That TV campaign is our last shot, Elliot. It has to work. It just has to."

One Card Left to Play

B ack in Los Angeles, the news of Toy Fair travels through the office like a piece of juicy gossip. Before the day is out— before Elliot and Ruth and the others have even boarded their plane—everyone at Mattel knows that the Barbie launch was a colossal failure.

The next day, staff members arrive for work, flash their badges and push through the turnstile as if they're attending a wake. They tuck their personalities away and keep their voices low, respectful. No one cracks a joke or pulls a prank on the guy sitting next to them. They keep their heads down and thank God they're not on the Barbie team. Despite Ruth and Elliot making the rounds first thing that morning, reassuring everyone that Mattel will weather this storm, there's a feeling that layoffs are imminent.

Charlotte hasn't slept in days, wondering what her next move should be, even though Ruth tells her not to worry. "You're not going anywhere," she says, standing in Charlotte's office, leaning against the closed door as if barricading her in, afraid she might bolt. "I'm not giving up on Barbie and neither should you. Elliot's already getting ideas for new dolls." Which isn't true, and they both know it.

Charlotte's not sure what direction she'll pursue if she leaves Mattel. The thought of teaching again isn't very inviting or lucrative, and she fears how the years she's devoted to Barbie will be perceived in the design world. She's let so many of her contacts lapse, her former clients have gone elsewhere and she'd be starting over from scratch. This is what's keeping her up at night, but she doesn't dare let it show at work. For now, Charlotte is doing what she can to keep up morale.

"Ruth still believes in Barbie," she tells Stevie. "And Elliot already has ideas for new dolls." Charlotte perpetuates the lie. "Before you know it, we're going to be busier than ever, so take advantage of this downtime . . ."

But Stevie isn't buying it. Everyone says Barbie is a flop, it's all over, despite what management is telling them. She feels gutted, like a promise has been broken. So much for *put in two years on Barbie and you can write your own ticket.*

Since she started at Mattel, she hasn't had to worry about money. But now, old fears are resurfacing. She hasn't been good about saving, because for the first time in her life, after paying her bills, she's had money left over to spend on herself. And unlike her mother, who has to justify every item on her grocery list with the exception of beer and beef jerky, Stevie doesn't have to answer to anyone. What a powerful, heady feeling it was that first time she walked into a store and bought a pair of shoes without first asking the price. She saved the box and for a week only wore them around the apartment, careful not to scuff the soles, taking comfort in knowing she could return them, which she never did. That was the beginning of treating herself to little things here and there that were previously off-limits. She still has the price tags on a new scarf and a pair of slacks hanging in her closet.

How can she give all that up? And if she loses this job, she'll lose her apartment. She'll have to go back to waiting tables and possibly be forced to move back home with her parents. That wouldn't just be a step backward—it would be a landslide into defeat.

For the first time since he started at Mattel, Jack calls in sick. Four days in a row. He gave everything he had to Barbie. He made her. Believed in her. She was going to make little girls happy, and in exchange Barbie was supposed to make him a rich man. Now his patent is worthless, and there'll be no hefty royalty checks coming his way. But more than that, Barbie gave Jack the recognition he never got at Raytheon. His word blindness aside, Jack's always known he's smart, even brilliant, but at Raytheon he was one of thousands of young, brilliant engineers. It was impossible to stand out. Barbie changed everything for him, especially since Elliot initially showed no interest in the project—Jack was the head engineer, the one everyone looked to. But Barbie's dead now, and no one will care about him anymore.

How can he face his team after this? He's a failure. Twist, Frankie, Huntly, they've got to be disappointed, and Jack hasn't got the strength to raise them up. He can't even get out of bed now. He's gone from being so energized that he'd stay awake for two and three days in a row, to sleeping fourteen, sixteen, even eighteen hours a day.

In his waking hours he stares blankly at the walls and the shadows, terrified by all he sees. He's surrounded by rage, all of it stemming from his own mind. It's unescapable. He's exhausted from trying to ward off the evil thoughts, and it's not long before his eyelids grow heavy and he has fallen back asleep. His wife can't get him up; Ginger can't, either. Finally, they turn to Ruth for help.

"Jack," she says, "I'm devastated, too."

And she is. Ruth's had her own demons to battle since they returned from Toy Fair. No one believes in Barbie anymore, just like no one believed in her. When she first arrived in L.A., everyone told her she'd never land a job at a Hollywood studio, and she did. Everyone, Sarah included, said *Don't marry Elliot, you'll starve to death.* How many times has she heard *don't*? *Don't start a toy company. Don't move to a bigger building. Don't hire on more employees. Don't build the new house. Don't advertise on TV. Don't make a doll with breasts.* She's heard *don't* and *can't* too many times. Thank God she didn't listen. She kept her own counsel—always has, always will.

Ruth still has one card left to play, and that's the Barbie TV commercial. There's too much already invested, too much at stake, to just let Barbie die on the vine. Ruth can't accept this failure. Especially not while trying to plan her daughter's wedding for a marriage she believes will be an even bigger disappointment than Barbie.

Ruth throws open the floor-to-ceiling drapes in Jack's bedroom, setting loose a swarm of dust mites and casting rays of light into his eyes. He groans, squinting as he props the pillows up behind him.

"We still have a company to run," she says. "We need you back. *I* need you back. Mattel isn't Mattel without you." She sits on the side of his bed and reaches for his hand. It feels like the right thing to do, but it's also too tender for them, so she breaks the moment and says, "Besides, who's gonna piss me off if you're not there?"

His hand goes limp in hers. He can't even crack a smile.

"And Barbie isn't finished yet," she says.

Jack groans in disbelief.

"Oh, c'mon, and there'll be new toys, new ideas, I promise you. But none of that will happen unless you come back to work."

"You don't understand—there's nothing more inside me." He can't imagine ever having another creative idea. Or feeling joyful again. He can't imagine feeling anything other than pain. His mind has locked him inside a torture chamber. There's no escape and he's too chicken to take his own life, so the next best thing is sleep. "I'm tired," he says. "I need to rest."

"What you need to do is to stop feeling sorry for yourself and get back to work."

He shuts his eyes again.

On the fifth day of Jack's hiatus, they bring in the big guns. Dr. Greene makes a house call. "Jack," he says, sitting in a chair across from his bed, "are you familiar with the term *manic depression*?"

Jack opens one eye, looks at the good doctor, wearing his customary gold corduroy slacks that ride up his calf when he crosses his legs, exposing a pair of white socks. *The man can't dress for shit.*

"Jack? Did you hear me?"

"Yes, I'm familiar with the term. My uncle had manic depression."

"Well, then, that makes sense. It does tend to run in families."

"My uncle was a raving loon," he says with more exertion than he's been able to muster in days. "I do *not* have manic depression."

And with that, Jack fires his doctor, and just to prove to Dr. Greene—and to himself—that he most definitely does not suffer from manic depression, he finds the energy to get up, get dressed and go back to work.

But Mommy, Why?

Awww-chew! Awww-chew! Awww-chew!"

"Gazoontite," one lonely voice half-heartedly calls out to Gina, trying to preserve all that's been lost.

It's back to business as usual, but without the pizzazz. Without the flair and excitement. No one bothers with squirt gun fights, no one's flying paper airplanes, everyone's waiting for the other shoe to drop. Ruth keeps herself busy, taking care of all the work she let slide while she was focused on Barbie. Plus, she is still finalizing plans for Barbara's wedding. Her days used to infuse her with a jolt of excitement and energy. Now by five thirty, six o'clock in the evening, she's ready to call it quits. The kids and Elliot like having her home for dinner again, but all she wants to do is crawl into bed.

The company makes it through the rest of March. No one has been fired. Ruth gives Charlotte and Stevie unconvincing pep talks while they idle away their days, reading fashion magazines, organizing patterns and fabric swatches.

By the time May rolls around, they've begun working on a new, more traditional doll. A baby doll with a twist. It's Jack's idea, and after a few cursory attempts, he figured out a way to make this doll speak. Her name is Chatty Cathy, and with the pull of a string, she'll utter phrases like "I love you." "I hurt myself." "Take me with you." Ever so slowly Jack feels his energy ramping back up, and eventually he applies for another patent for the voice box planted in the doll's belly.

At last it's June, and the day that Ruth's been both anticipating and dreading arrives. She steps inside her office and closes the door. It's not quite two o'clock and the Barbie television commercial is about to make its debut. Ruth is all alone on this one. Everyone else, even Jack, has moved on, trying to forget the whole Barbie mess. She adjusts the rabbit ears on her ten-inch portable TV until the reception clears, bringing Annette Funicello, Cubby O'Brien and Jimmie Dodd into her office.

While Ruth is anxiously awaiting the commercial break in L.A., it's five o'clock in Queens, and nine-year-old Chloe Martin is planted on the floor in the family room, glued to the television, watching her favorite program, *The Mickey Mouse Club*. When her mother comes in to check on her, she wonders if her daughter has changed the channel. There must be some mistake, but no, the dial is still on Channel 7. Chloe's eyes grow wide as the TV screen fills with images of a woman. *Technically it's a figurine of a woman. No, wait*—the mother is confused—*did they just say it's a doll?*

"Can I have one, Mommy?" Chloe asks even before the commercial is finished airing.

Her mother considers the Mr. Potato Head sprawled out on the rope rug before her daughter and then takes mental inventory of the toy chest teeming with Play-Doh, Crayola crayons, paint by numbers sets and puzzles. A child of the Depression herself, she's never denied Chloe a thing, but she doesn't care what this new doll costs, the answer is no. "No, you cannot have one of *those*."

While Chloe's mother is explaining why it's not an appropriate toy, it's a quarter past four in Chicago, and as soon as the Mouseketeers finish their tap dance, little Denise Watson sees Barbie for the first time. Nudging her mother awake from her nap on the sofa, she says, "Look, Mommy. Look at that doll. Can I *pulease* have a Barbie doll?" Denise's mother is sitting up now, groggy but also perplexed by what she's seeing.

Five minutes later, some 800 miles away in Denver, eleven-year-old Joyce Hinton is sobbing because her mother has already said she cannot have *that* doll. At the same time another little girl in San Francisco is also whining as she stands in the kitchen, asking, "But Mommy, why? Why can't I have a Barbie doll?"

But Mommy, why? That is the sound, like the beat of a drum, and it's growing louder and louder each time those little girls see Barbie on their television screens.

For the next week Ruth tunes in to *The Mickey Mouse Club* every day to watch her TV commercial and watch her dream fade further away. The commercial appears to have zero impact. There's no new Barbie orders coming in. It's as if it never aired at all. She feels more despondent each time it runs. It's like a candle burning out, the flame growing fainter until the final wisp of smoke.

Elliot was right. She should have canceled the advertising. She has a warehouse full of dolls and she hasn't a clue about what to do with them. She's crunched and re-crunched the numbers, seeing what the damage would be if they drop the price of Barbie from $3 to $2 to $1. It's no use. She knows they have to stop the bleeding and that soon they'll have to let the Barbie team go, including Charlotte and Stevie.

The thought of doing that makes Ruth sick. She cannot eat,

can't sleep, can't find the enthusiasm she needs for the new Chatty Cathy doll or Mattel's other toys. She can't find enthusiasm for anything. Not even her daughter's wedding. Especially not the wedding. Ruth might have been wrong about Barbie sweeping the nation, but she is certain that Barbara's marriage is a mistake.

Her daughter's eighteenth birthday came and went; her high school graduation was last week. Both milestones were eclipsed by this wedding. From the time Barbara was a little girl, Ruth dreamed of her daughter's wedding day. How proud, how happy and filled with love she'd be. Instead, she feels as though she's losing Barbara forever, and it hurts so much Ruth can hardly breathe. Barbara's bound to be scared, nervous. Ruth knows she was when she got married, and none of it had to do with her love for Elliot. But that's just how enormous a step this is. Her little girl thinks she doesn't need her mother anymore, when in truth, she needs Ruth now more than ever. But Barbara won't let her in. Ruth's alienated her daughter, all in the name of love, but that doesn't seem to matter, and now Ruth fears nothing between them will ever be right again.

The wedding takes place that weekend. The ceremony is held outdoors, overlooking the ocean, nestled on a velvety green lawn. Not a cloud above, the temperature an ideal seventy-three degrees. There's a beautiful chuppah, and rows of white chairs are on either side of the aisle, lined with ropes of pink roses. It's picturesque, every little girl's dream wedding. *And a complete charade*, thinks Ruth, wondering how she'll get through the next few hours.

The rehearsal dinner was tough enough, making nice with Allen's family, playing the role of the cheerful mother of the bride, even putting on an act for her own siblings, who came into town from Denver and Northern California. Tomorrow's brunch at their country club for the out-of-towners will be another challenge, but this right here is nothing short of excruciating. When Elliot walks Barbara down the aisle; when Allen stomps on the glass, which might as well have been Ruth's heart; when they're in the receiving line, Ruth is crumbling inside. The smiles, the kisses and hugs, the toasts and dancing—every bit of it is a separate hell.

When it's over, after their friends and relatives have boarded their trains and planes and gone back to wherever they've come from, Ruth falls apart. Every limb, every cell in her body, is drained. She crawls into bed on Sunday night before the sun's gone down and stays there until noon the next day. Despite Elliot's urging, pleading with her to get up and come with him to the office, she lies there in the bedroom with the curtains drawn.

For the first time she understands why Jack couldn't get out of bed after Toy Fair.

Ruth is grieving for both Barbara and Barbie. It's while she's feeling so low, so despondent, that she realizes something. She'd been moving so fast, working so feverishly, that she couldn't see what Barbie really meant to her. Or why. The doll was more than just a business opportunity. In her own way, Ruth had been hoping that Barbie would fix what she couldn't fix with Barbara. She missed her chance with her own daughter, but she still wanted Barbie to connect with all those little girls out there. She wanted Barbie to be their role model and show them what it meant to be feminine *and* strong. That if they want to get married and have children, that's fine, but they can still have a life of their own. Barbie was supposed to deliver a new, fresh message for the next generation to grow into. But now it's all over.

Eventually Ruth forces herself to get up and face what's left of the day. By the time she arrives at Mattel, it's two in the afternoon. She's still groggy, in a trance. "Off We Go into the Wild Blue Yonder" is playing as she heads to her office, telling her secretary she doesn't wish to be disturbed. Once inside, she leans against her closed door and begins to sob until her nose is stuffed, her eyes are burning and her chest aches. Work has always been her oasis, but not now. There are Barbie dolls and Barbie outfits everywhere. Mock-ups of all the print ads and point-of-sale materials they'd planned to deploy after the Toy Fair launch are piled on her desk, in the corner of her office, on the window ledge. She is surrounded by reminders of her defeat, of the mess she's made of everything. She doesn't know how to salvage Barbie any more than she knows how to fix her relationship with her daughter.

She's a failure as a mother and a failure in business, too. They're all laughing at her now. What a fool she was to think she could pull this off. It's all too much for her. She has no stamina left, no resilience. She's of no good to anyone, and with that thought, an old fear returns: No one will want her anymore. The people she needs the most will turn their backs on her just like her mother did. A bottomless hole opens beneath her, and Ruth is falling fast.

The phone buzzes. She ignores it. She can't talk to anyone right now. She lumbers over to her desk and reaches for a cigarette. Through the walls she hears a commotion going on next door in Jack's office and figures he's probably going at it again with Patsy or Ginger or God knows who. With fingertips pressed to her temples, she tries to drown out the noise, but it's growing louder, with more voices and laughter, too. It sounds like he's having a party in there.

Again, her phone buzzes. *Jesus*, now she's getting annoyed. Didn't she tell her secretary she didn't want to be disturbed? She goes to light a fresh cigarette, unaware of the one already burning in her ashtray. Her telephone rings yet again. She picks up the receiver and slams it back down. A moment later, there's a knock on the door.

"Go away. I'm busy."

"Ruthie, it's me." She hears Elliot from the other side of the door. "Why aren't you answering your phone? We need you right away. We're all in Jack's office."

She leans forward, the heel of her hand pressed to her forehead. She can't focus on another Chatty Cathy meeting; she hasn't got the energy for another brainstorming session, or for anything else.

"Just—just give me a minute, okay." She sighs and tries to center herself as she pulls out her compact, wipes away the smeared mascara beneath her eyes, freshens up her lipstick, just like Sarah taught her to do.

With a deep breath, she steps out of her office and finds she's walked into nothing but chaos. *What the hell is going on?* She's never seen so many people back here on Mahogany Row at one time. There's Stevie and Patsy, Mia and Charlotte. She spots Sid, Twist and Frankie, too. Everywhere she looks there are people spilling out of Jack's office and into the hallway. "Here she is," someone shouts, and there's an eruption of applause. Applause and hoots and whistles as she makes her way to Jack's office, utterly confused. She still doesn't get that this is about her.

Elliot sees her and reaches for her hand, pulling her inside. "Finally. There you are. The woman of the hour." He loops his arm around her as the cheering swells.

"What is going on?" she shouts above the commotion.

Jack is weaving his way toward her with a bottle of champagne. "We did it, Ruth," Jack says, filling a glass for her.

"Did what?"

"Barbie. You were right, Ruthie," says Elliot. "You were right all along." He takes her face in his hands and kisses her, which makes everyone clap even more. Holding her tight, he says, "Didn't you hear the phones out there? They haven't stopped ringing all day. Ruthie, my love, we can't fill the Barbie orders as fast as they're coming in."

Did she hear him correctly? She still doesn't quite get it, even as she looks around her at all the smiles, hears all the excitement and celebration. What's happened takes a moment to sink in, and when it does, Ruth nearly goes limp in Elliot's arms, and she can't stop the onslaught of tears. Sweet tears of relief.

PART TWO

Perfect Is the Enemy of the Good

Peacocks on Parade

1960

R uth removes the hard hat the contractor made her wear and pats her hair back into place before stepping inside her office. Despite the plastic sheeting tacked up everywhere, there's a film of dust on her desk, and the air is so thick with plaster and sawdust, she can taste it. It's noisy, too; the pounding and banging only let up when the construction crew take their lunch and coffee breaks. The expansion should be completed by the end of July—it's January now—and with the way Mattel is growing, Ruth fears they're still going to be packed in like sardines.

Having already abandoned her New Year's resolution—not even making it a full day before she cracked—Ruth reaches for a cigarette. She's bracing herself before checking the latest sales report, which landed on her desk while she was touring the new wing of their building. She worries that the past seven months have been a fluke, that this is the month when Barbie's sales will slip.

As she looks at the numbers, a sense of relief spreads in her chest, like a pat of butter melting in a hot pan. It's no fluke. They've sold 46,874 Barbies this past month, up over 11,000 units from December—and that included the Christmas season. She makes a note to have KBK ramp up production, suspecting they'll go from shipping 60,000 Barbies a month to 100,000 by the end of the year.

Each time those sales numbers grow, her peacock feathers fan out and she wants to climb to the top of Mount Baldy and shout, "Look at us now!" She was right about Barbie all along, and if Ruth Handler was a risk-taker before, it's nothing compared to the chances she'll be willing to take in the future. She will leverage this win for years to come, reminding anyone who challenges her that the doll everyone rejected at Toy Fair is now an undisputed smash hit.

At times Barbie's success is overwhelming for her, but it's even more so for Elliot, who went from worrying *if* the doll would sell to now worrying about keeping up with the demand. For the first time in his life, Elliot's having trouble sleeping. He's up at three or four in the morning, staring out at the swimming pool or pacing the hallway. He's already worried about finding a large enough venue for next year's holiday party.

"Hey, Ruth." Jack pokes his head into her office. "Our one o'clock is here."

"Be right there." She takes one last drag of her cigarette before stubbing it out.

To keep enough Barbies in the pipeline, Mattel is hiring like mad, both here and in Tokyo, where each Barbie undergoes a meticulous hair and makeup application process, all done by hand, from her eyeliner to her lipstick. Every fingernail and toenail is individually polished, every strand of hair is painstakingly rooted. All together this requires hundreds of artists, not to mention the hundreds of seamstresses who work on her wardrobe and accessories. Back home, Ruth and Jack are interviewing candidates to fill positions for engineers, developers, sample makers, production managers, sales reps, fashion estimators, even people who specialize in plastics.

With construction underway, they hold interviews in a trailer out in the parking lot. It's a tight fit inside with a small metal desk and three chairs. A kitchenette, with a coffeemaker and a tiny icebox, is off to the side. One by one, Ruth and Jack meet with prospects, quickly weeding out the ones they deem NMM—Not Mattel Material. They're looking for certain personality types—people who are entrepreneurial, competitive and driven. They're looking for feisty individuals who have some fight in them and won't back down from a challenge.

Today's candidate, Bernard Loomis, fits the bill. He's a big man, with lots of dark hair and the face of a bulldog, with heavy jowls and drooping eyes. He's sharp and speaks with a thick New York accent.

"Call me Bernie," he says, shaking both their hands. Bernie is interviewing for the position of vice president of sales and marketing, and after teasing them about their fancy offices, he shares a host of marketing ideas for Barbie. "Why not do a Barbie comic book? What about a Barbie radio show?" His ideas seem endless, and when he suggests creating a viewfinder reel with photos of Barbie in various outfits, they're convinced they've found their man. His personality is gruff, but his business savvy is impeccable.

The next candidate, Steven Lewis, is also Mattel Material and will become their new head toy sculptor. For a man so tall and lanky, he is thick-skinned and unflappable. He's not afraid of criticism and is unyielding when trying to make his point.

When all is said and done, Ruth and Jack will end up hiring two hundred new employees just to work on Barbie alone.

Thanks to Jack's patent on Barbie's construction and his royalty agreement with Mattel that pays him for every doll sold, he is now a rich man. Richer than he ever imagined. During his

negotiations when he started at Mattel, he agreed to take a modest
salary in exchange for a percentage of Mattel's revenues on any
products he helped develop. Now he's reaping the rewards. He recently bought a dozen custom-made Mr. Guy suits; he's bought art,
favoring abstract expressionists like de Kooning and Rothko. His
daughters are now in private school, and he bought three new cars,
including the royal blue Corvette convertible he's driving today.

"Where are we going?" his wife asks from the passenger's seat.

"It's a surprise."

"I don't like surprises," Barbara tells him, knotting her silk Vera
scarf beneath her chin. It's a beautiful poppy-inspired orange, red
and pink scarf that she designed herself when she worked for Vera
Neumann back in New York, before Jack uprooted her world and
moved them out to Los Angeles. "I mean it," she says. "Just tell me
where we're going."

"But that'll spoil the surprise."

"I don't care. I don't want to be surprised. Especially not by you."

He fiddles with the radio, going from station to station.

She leans over and snaps it off. "How long are we going to be
gone? I left chicken out on the counter to defrost. I don't want it to
spoil."

"I'll buy you a new chicken." He smiles until he glances over at
his wife. She's all scrunched down in her seat, refusing to enjoy a
ride in his new convertible. Any other woman would be tickled.
"Okay, you want me to tell you what it is?"

"What? And ruin your *big* surprise?"

"You know what, it *is* a big surprise. It's a big fucking surprise."
He turns the radio back on. Elvis is singing "It's Now or Never."

They're both quiet, lost in their own thoughts. Jack is wondering
when she got to be such a drag and Barbara is worrying about her
chicken, thinking what else she can make for dinner if it goes bad.

After a long stretch of silence, they enter Bel Air, where the mansions grow larger by the block. Jack points out Howard Hughes's place and where Jerry Lewis lives, along with a number of other movie stars.

Barbara gives him a few murmurs: "Uh-huh . . . Hmmm . . . Uh-huh . . ."

Moments later they pull into a long tree-flanked drive at 688 Nimes Road. It seems to go on forever until a three-story Tudor mansion comes into view.

"Well," he says with a carnival barker's flair, "here we are."

"What's this?" Barbara twists around in her seat, taking in the majestic sloping lawns, the fig and lemon trees, the giant palms and oak trees, the sheer magnitude of the property. "Where are we?"

"Surprise. I bought you a new house."

Her mouth hangs open.

"Aren't you gonna say something?"

"You bought a house—*this house*—without even showing it to me first?"

"Well, I'm showing it to you now."

"What do you expect me to say, Jack?"

"How about 'Gee, thank you, honey. I love it'?"

"You should have told me about this. You should have let me see it first."

"I wanted to surprise you, for fuck's sake."

"Well, I'm surprised all right. Can we get out of it?"

"Don't tell me you don't like it. I shelled out $235,000 for this."

The house, a mansion really, would have been out of reach before Barbie took off. But thanks to the deal he cut with Ruth and Elliot when they hired him, Jack could have bought half the homes on his block.

Jack gets out of the car, comes around to her side and opens her door. "C'mon, let me at least show you around before you tell me how much you hate it."

S tevie's new apartment isn't quite as grandiose as Jack's Bel Air mansion, but thanks to the generous raise she received for her work on Barbie, she can easily afford her own place now at Ogden Arms. It's another dingbat structure, the color of sun-bleached salmon, but it's more spacious than Casa Bella.

Along with her raise, Stevie's discovered that she enjoys soaking in a hot bath, the water scented with pricey bath oils. She treated herself to a set of satiny percale bed linens and plush bath towels. Though she still shops at places like Zodys, she's not afraid to splurge on something special at I. Magnin or Bullock's. Her father warns her to start saving for a rainy day. "Remember to pay yourself first," he likes to say. But the extra money in her paycheck is seductive and swirls about her like fresh cream added to a cup of black coffee.

A year ago, when Stevie thought Barbie was a no-go, she figured it was finally safe to show her parents and Vivian what she'd been secretly working on at Mattel.

"Is this what dolls look like nowadays?" her mother asked, holding Barbie.

"They've been paying you *that* kind of money to make clothes for *that*?" her father said. "Do they know you don't have a degree?"

But at least Vivian got it. She was impressed. "Wow," she said, working the back zipper on *Golden Girl* from the 900 series. "My God, Stevie, these are spectacular." She continued sorting through Barbie's outfits. "So you designed this one, too?" she asked, her voice pitching an octave higher.

"Yeah, along with Charlotte."

"And even the hat?" Vivian was enthralled. "These are incredible. Do you know what I do all day long at Rudi's? Swimsuits. One-piece swimsuits. That's all I've been working on for months and months. Every day it's exactly the same."

Stevie had never heard Vivian talk like that before. Usually she was so boastful about the fashion editors dropping by the shop, all the new fabrics she was working with, the great fashion shows she was attending. Her fancy lunches with Bob Mackie, Marta Krass and other classmates who no longer—not even now—invite Stevie along. In their eyes, she's not a real designer, and yet Stevie's done more actual design work with Barbie than any of them.

My Barbie's Lonely

Week by week Ruth watches Barbie's sales numbers increase. This success only makes her crave more, recalibrating her expectations. Not that long ago, she would have turned cartwheels if they moved 30,000 units a month; now she's not satisfied with anything short of 65,000.

Together with Loomis, they visit stores, checking the girls' toy aisles, where some have life-size cutouts of Barbie and everywhere you look there are Barbie clothes and accessories. Ruth tracks each style number and knows, for example, that #964 is lagging a bit behind #971 but that #911, #961 and #972 are flying off the shelves.

In light of Barbie's sudden popularity, everyone wants to do business with her. Loomis has secured dozens of lucrative licensing agreements, and now there's a series of Barbie lunch boxes and thermoses, wristwatches, hairbrushes, combs and hand mirrors, jewelry boxes, pajamas and even Barbie Halloween costumes. Each week Ruth sits through dozens of pitches.

Right now two bright-eyed, bow-tied salesmen from the Hoover

Vacuum Company are in her office. The men are hoping to partner with Mattel, wanting to create a Barbie-sized vacuum cleaner.

At the mere mention of housekeeping, Ruth cuts them off. "And what exactly do you expect Barbie to do with a vacuum cleaner?"

"Well," the first bow-tie chuckles, "now little girls can pretend their dolls are helping their mothers clean the house."

"Doesn't that sound like fun," she says, running the pad of her thumb across her perfect red nails. "Listen, fellas, I'm not gonna waste your time and I prefer you don't waste mine."

"With all due respect, Mrs. Handler," says the other man, "this is a terrific opportunity."

"With *all due respect*," she fires back, "Barbie doesn't vacuum. She doesn't do rough housework. Ever."

Moments after they leave, Jack comes to her office holding what she thinks is an oversized Bild Lilli doll. "Looks like we got competition," he says.

"What are you talking about?" She sets her pen down on her desk blotter. "And what's up with that Bild Lilli? She looks different."

"That's because this isn't Bild Lilli. Louis Marx bought the licensing rights to her. This is their own knockoff—Miss Seventeen. And she's going to go toe-to-toe with Barbie."

The mail boy heads to the secretarial pool carrying yet another canvas bag with U.S. *Post Office* stenciled in gray letters down the front. It's overflowing with mail for Barbie, who now has fan clubs springing up across the country. *Actual fan clubs*. Ruth still can't get over the number of girls who write to Barbie, asking her for advice, sharing their deepest secrets, extolling their love for her.

Ruth has the secretaries go through and answer the letters, but occasionally, when she has time, Ruth likes to read what Barbie's fans have to say.

One day, a letter addressed to Barbara Millicent Roberts—the full name they cooked up for Barbie along with the fictitious hometown of Willows, Wisconsin—takes Ruth by surprise. It's from a young girl in Barberton, Ohio, saying that her Barbie's lonely and *really, really, really* wants a boyfriend.

A boyfriend? A boyfriend for Barbie? Ruth sits with this for a moment. On the one hand, it seems so obvious, but on the other, boy dolls are taboo. But then again, so was a doll with breasts. She reads the letter again. Could it work? Would little girls play with a boy doll? With Miss Seventeen nipping at Barbie's high heels, Ruth has been contemplating ways to expand the line, and it looks like the answer just fell in her lap.

Tucking the letter back inside the envelope, she heads into Elliot's office. He's tinkering with an idea he's calling V-RROOM, a battery-operated device that imitates a race car engine and fits on a tricycle. He checks the speed sounds, ramping it up from a rumble to a full-throttle roar. While he makes notations on a legal pad, Ruth waits patiently, watching the tropical zebra fish, mountain minnows, pea puffers and guppies swimming in his aquarium. Finally, Elliot looks up at her.

"I have an idea for a second doll in the Barbie line."

"Okay, great." He makes another notation and eyes something on the bottom of the device. "Let's hear it."

"Take a look—" She hands him the letter, and as he reads, she says, "I think it's time we give Barbie a boyfriend."

"A boyfriend? For Barbie?" He leans back in his chair, letting it sink in. It's risky, but if it works, well . . . He taps the envelope to his palm, pondering, and eventually smiles as he pushes the intercom button on his desk. "Jack? You got a minute?"

Jack has barely stepped inside when Elliot says, "Ruth just came up with a brilliant idea—we're gonna give Barbie a boyfriend."

"A *boy* doll?" Jack squints like he's staring into a beam of sunlight.

"Here"—Ruth hands Jack the letter.

He glances at the handwritten words turning into symbols, all jumping around on the page. Nothing is staying within the lines. He gives the letter another penetrating look—faking it—before handing it back. "I'm still confused," he says, which is an understatement. "We know boys won't play with dolls."

"It's not a doll for boys," says Ruth. "It's for girls."

"What makes you think girls will play with a boy doll?"

"If he's Barbie's boyfriend, they'll play with him. Oh, and I already have the perfect name." She looks at Elliot and winks. "Let's call him Ken."

Ever since they started working on Barbie, Ruth and Elliot have wanted to create a toy they could name after their son. It's only fair, and they sense that Ken feels left out of all the Barbie fanfare. His sister gets all the attention—not that Barbara wants it. God no. She hates when her girlfriends tease her, and anyone who dares to call her Barbie had best take cover.

Ruth and Elliot agree that naming the new doll Ken is a terrific idea, although when they share the news with their children, Barbara is mortified.

"Why would you do that?" Barbara lets her fork clank against her plate, calling attention to their table at the Hillcrest Country

Club. "Now everybody's gonna think I'm dating my brother—that's gross."

Ruth looks at her daughter. Barbara may have cut her long hair and traded in her saddle shoes for high heels, trying to look like a sophisticated married woman, but she still sounds like a child. "Don't be silly," says Ruth, offering a wave to friends across the room. "No one's going to think that."

"Yeah," says Allen. "Only *you* would think like that, Barbara. They could name him Allen. I wouldn't care."

Barbara glares at him. "Whose side are you on?"

"I'm just saying, it's no big deal." Allen has become more assertive since the couple married. Whereas once he was silent, letting Barbara do all the talking, he now feels the need to voice his opinions, which often contradict his wife's.

"The Ken doll is not your brother and you're not Barbie," says Elliot. "They're just names."

"But they're *our* names," Barbara hisses.

"Ken, honey?" Ruth turns to her son. "Would it bother you if we named the doll Ken?"

He shrugs, more concerned by the people nearby staring at their table.

Barbara cannot accept her brother's nonchalance. "You really don't care if they name a *doll* after you?"

"Why would I care?" says Ken. "Nobody I know plays with dolls."

He really doesn't care. He's aware of the phenomenon with this doll that bears his sister's name, but Ken thinks Barbie is stupid and vapid. He's much more focused on the piano, the downy fuzz that's begun sprouting on his upper lip, and his new car. He recently turned sixteen and Ruth and Elliot surprised him with a brand-new Plymouth XNR 500. Ken hasn't yet fully grasped that Barbie is really the one who bought him that car.

———

They have agreed to fast-track Ken and launch him at next year's Toy Fair. Jack and Elliot are working nonstop, scrutinizing every detail: Ken's hair and eye color, debating if he should be smiling, should we see his teeth? And then there's Ken's height.

"I don't see why he has to be taller than Barbie," says Jack, leaning back in his chair, tossing a rubber ball into the air.

"Because," says Ruth, "boyfriends are supposed to be taller than their girlfriends. I can't help it if you're shorter than all the women you ogle."

"I happen to like tall women," he says, thinking of Stevie, which he's been doing a lot of lately. "I'm not intimidated by taller women," he says, giving the ball a rest and setting it on the table. "The point is that Barbie's still the star. She should stand head and shoulders above any other doll. Boy or girl."

They continue to bicker over it, and in the end, Ruth wins. Ken will stand twelve inches tall to Barbie's eleven and a half inches. The next battle is over Ken's anatomy. Or lack thereof.

"Where's his penis?" Ruth asks when they present the prototype.

"He's a boy," says Charlotte. "His groin can't look the same as Barbie's."

The roomful of men—grown men—are visibly uncomfortable now. Sure, they were happy to talk about Barbie's tits till the cows came home, but one mention of Ken's genitalia and they clam up, they even blush.

"The guy's gotta have a *schmekel*," says Ruth.

Twist, Frankie, Lewis, even Elliot fidget. They pick up their pencils and pretend to scribble down notes.

It's Jack who finally speaks up. "Look," he says, "obviously we need to address the groin area. But why can't we do it the same way we did for Barbie? We can *allude* to it."

"Fine," says Ruth. "Allude. I'm not asking for a set of balls here."

"I agree," says Charlotte. "Ken doesn't need testicles any more than Barbie needed nipples."

"But Ken still needs a penis or a bulge or *something*," says Ruth.

Jack picks up his sketchpad and begins drawing. "I'm way ahead of you," he says, adding some quick brushstrokes. "Here. Take a look."

Ruth glances at the sketch. "Jesus, Jack," she says as she bursts out laughing. "Ken's cock can't be the first thing you notice when you look at him." She remembers how large he initially made Barbie's breasts. Why should she be surprised that Jack would make Ken so well-endowed?

"Okay," says Jack. "I'll tone it down a little."

"Not a little," says Ruth. "A lot. How in the hell are Charlotte and Stevie expected to design clothes for him if he's got a goddamn salami in his pants?"

Original Creations

1961

While they're finalizing the last details for the Ken doll before he goes into production, Mattel's general counsel, Henry Pursell, calls an urgent meeting with Elliot, Ruth and Jack. Closing Ruth's office door behind him, Henry buttons his suit jacket and says, "We just received a notice from Louis Marx and Company."

Ruth shakes her head. "What the hell does that *shtoonk* want this time?"

"They're suing Mattel."

"For what?"

"Well," says Henry, "Louis Marx now owns the license to Bild Lilli and they're suing us for copyright infringement."

"That's a load of crap," she says, reaching for a cigarette. Despite her bluster, Ruth's instantly rattled. Her stomach twists as her mind flashes back to the night she was in Barbara's bedroom, looking at her daughter's doll collection, and how shocked she'd been by the similarities between the two dolls. Something like this could put Barbie out of business, and that's the same as putting Mattel out of business.

"That is total bullshit," Jack says, backing Ruth up. "It's just sour grapes because Miss Seventeen flopped." Their doll is still sitting on the toy store shelves collecting dust.

"That may be true, but according to the suit"—Henry pauses here to consult his notes—"it comes down to the hip joint. They're claiming you used their construction for Barbie."

"That's absolute nonsense," says Ruth, noticing that Elliot hasn't said a word. "Jack worked around all their patents. He *owns* his own Barbie patents."

Henry holds up his hand and continues. "They claim that Barbie isn't an original creation. They're basically just coming right out and saying you stole the idea from G and H."

"Oh, that's absurd," says Ruth.

Henry looks at her. "So are you saying you want to dispute it?"

"You bet your ass I do," she says.

"Okay," says Henry. "Do we *have* grounds to dispute it?"

"Hell yes." She thumps her fist to her desk. "In fact, you know what—I want to countersue."

"On what basis?"

"Louis Marx copied us."

"She has a point," says Elliot. "You've seen Miss Seventeen. They only issued that doll in direct response to Barbie."

"And Miss Seventeen's not half the doll ours is," adds Jack. "If girls buy Miss Seventeen, thinking it's a Barbie, that's going to hurt our sales."

The more they talk, the more they convince themselves of this.

"The main thing," says Elliot, "is we have to keep this out of the press. Can we do that?"

Henry shrugs. "We'll do our best."

"Elliot's right," says Ruth. "We're trying to downplay Barbie being too sexy, and if word gets out that there's any association between Barbie and a German prostitute, it'll be the end of her."

And so Mattel countersues Louis Marx, who retaliates with a countersuit to Mattel's countersuit. Round and round it goes. Meanwhile, Ruth tells herself that Barbie has no relationship to Bild Lilli. And besides, isn't everything derived from something else? She could argue that there's no such thing as a truly original *anything*. Something always exists before the next, better thing comes along. Isn't that the whole point of inspiration? Imagination? Creativity? Where would artists be without other paintings to study? Or writers without other books to read? Musicians without someone else's music to listen to, filmmakers without other movies to see? How else are you supposed to unlock what's never been done before? That initial spark has to come from somewhere, doesn't it? Barbie may have been *inspired* by Bild Lilli, but they made so many changes to the doll that Ruth would swear on her sister's grave that Barbie is Mattel's original creation.

But just to be sure, as a precaution, they make some modifications to Barbie. They soften the extreme arch of her eyebrows and lighten her eyeliner, change the glint in her pupil from white to blue. They fill in the holes in the balls of Barbie's feet and give her a different stand. They're looking for anything that won't be too costly that can put some distance between Bild Lilli and Barbie.

Ruth and Elliot are eager to capitalize on Barbie's success, and now that Ken is in the works, they're looking for additional ways to keep expanding the doll line. They want more outfits, more accessories and more projective play ideas—more, more, more. They have Barbie meetings every day, and every day there are more people joining the team. But no matter how many engineers, developers and sample makers come on board, the core Barbie team under Ruth is still Charlotte, Jack and Stevie. If Stevie's not in Charlotte's office, she's in Jack's.

For the past two weeks, however, Charlotte's been in Japan, working with the seamstresses there on Ken's new wardrobe: red swimming trunks, sandals and a little terry cloth towel. In her absence, Stevie's taken the lead and lately has been spending more time with Jack than anyone else, including Vivian, Patsy or her parents.

One evening, the third or fourth late night that week, it's Stevie and Jack again. Jack is sprawled out on his bearskin rug, ankles crossed, his fingers laced behind his head. Stevie is across the room sitting at his drafting table, where so much magic has been born. It feels a little like sitting down at Hemingway's typewriter or trying to play Paganini's Stradivarius. Jack is a master in his own right; his creativity and ingenuity seem boundless.

Stevie, on the other hand, feels tapped out at the moment. She's just finished working with Charlotte on *Winter Holiday* for the 900 series and is convinced she'll never have another decent idea. So for now she's stuck and sketching—doodling, really—hoping it will free up some inspiration. She knows that what she's drawing will never make it into production. It's a long strapless dress that flares at the bottom, almost like a mermaid's tail. She's lost in concentration and doesn't notice that Jack is now looking over her shoulder.

"What is that?"

She jumps with a start, pulling the sketchpad to her chest. "It's nothing. I'm just fooling around."

"C'mon, let me see." He reaches for the pad, his hand brushing against hers.

That simple touch of his is enough to send a current through her body. These bursts of attraction she feels for Jack always take her by surprise, though really, they shouldn't. Stevie's always been drawn to older men. Even Russell was twelve years her senior. Each time she's close to Jack like this, she's reminded of what Patsy said, about him giving her an orgasm. She's curious about him, but he's married and he's her boss. But he also smells good, and so she releases the sketchpad.

"Very sexy gown," he says, squeezing in closer, adding to the heat coursing through her.

"But it's not practical," she says, forcing her eyes from his lips back to the page. "It would never work for Barbie."

"May I?" He gestures for her pencil, and she hands it to him, feeling another spark. "You just need to trim back some of this hem . . . Gotta be careful, though, you don't want to spoil the drama." He adds some strokes to her sketch. "Open it up, so it blooms like this—" He adds a few more details.

She's watching, amazed by how he's transforming her concept.

"Now picture this dress in black. All sequins, top to bottom."

What he's just done unlocks her own ideas. "And what about black satin opera gloves?"

"Love it." He sketches them out. "Let's not stop there. What about adding just a burst of color. Maybe a single flower on the dress?"

"Or a scarf."

"A scarf. Yes, something long and silky." He nods, his hands working so fast it's mesmerizing, especially when he adds the final touch, a microphone on a tall slender stand. "Now you've got that torch singer, nightclub feel."

Stevie brings her hands to her face. "I can't believe what you just did."

"*We*—what *we* just did," he says. "We're a hell of a team, you and me."

Their eyes lock. There's an exhilarated energy pulsing in the air. It's coming from him, from her, and together they just made something incredible and now he's looking at her like he wants to kiss her. And just as he leans in, his lips mere inches from hers, she places her hand on his chest. "Hey." She gently pushes him back.

His eyes grow limpid. "Shit, I'm sorry," he says, stepping away, running his hands back through his hair. "I just . . . It won't happen again. I promise."

Stevie doesn't say anything. She's still a little stunned that they came so close to kissing, and they would have kissed, too, if she hadn't stopped him, and for that, there's a kernel of something in the pit of her stomach. It feels a little like regret.

It's All about the Breasts

R uth's up before her alarm goes off. She's always up early and isn't sure why she even bothers to set an alarm at all. She stands in the shower, her washcloth full of suds, the spray of the water tapping off her shower cap like rain on a tin roof. While the steam fogs up the glass, her mind wanders to the day ahead: a status meeting with the Barbie team, a meeting with their accountant, another one with the bankers and one with her advertising agency at the end of the day. Meetings, meetings and more meetings. Every minute has been planned out, but the one thing she hasn't allotted time for, what she has not been anticipating, what has not even entered her mind, is what she's about to discover in the shower.

As her soapy hand rides up and over her rib cage, her fingers head north, gliding over her right breast until—*What?*—she stops. She backs up, feeling for it again. *It can't be.* She feels for her breast again. It's there all right. A lump. She runs her fingers over it, around it. Does it hurt? *No.* But it wasn't there yesterday or the day before. *Was it?* Her skin turns to ice beneath the spray of hot water and she reaches for the wall as her legs go weak.

Sarah died of cancer. She was just fifty-five; Ruth is forty-three. She remembers scouring the country, finding doctors and experimental treatments, doing everything in her power to save Sarah's life. But despite it all, Sarah didn't make it; her body was consumed by cancer. It's in their family. And now it's in her, too. All she can think is, *No, not now. I don't have time for cancer.*

It's been almost a week since Ruth discovered the lump, and on that Saturday, she's offered to take Barbara shopping. Really, it's a bribe so her daughter will spend time with her. Now that Barbara's married, Ruth hardly sees her anymore, and oh, how she misses her. The house is so quiet now. Ruth even misses the slamming doors, the stomping around, the bickering that was background music for them. When Barbara was younger, the two of them loved to spend the day shopping, and she knows Barbara can't afford anything new on Allen's salary, so Ruth will take her to Giorgio's, which just opened on Rodeo Drive, and let her pick out whatever she wants.

Before she swings by to get Barbara, Ruth needs to stop at the office to check on a few things. It won't take long, fifteen minutes, maybe an hour tops. Ruth delegates as much as she can; refinancing the building, bringing on a new trucking company, ordering new boxes, deciding the best time to have the parking lot repaved—all that is off her plate. But she's the only one who can handle the forecasting or structure a marketing strategy for the new toys they're bringing out.

As she pulls into the Mattel lot, she sees Jack's car and a few others, which is not surprising—someone's always working. She says good morning to the weekend security guard and pushes through the turnstile. Twist, Frankie, Sid and a handful of others

are milling about, and she bumps into Stevie coming out of the
kitchen, carrying two mugs of coffee. When Ruth sees Jack on Mahogany Row, he asks if she's okay.

"Yeah, yeah," she says. "Just tired is all."

They each say something else, but neither one is really listening
to the other, and they both head into their offices. His door closes
first, then she shuts hers.

Before she even sits down, Ruth fishes out a cigarette from her
desk drawer. She's smoking too much. She knows this, but what
difference does it make now that she already has cancer? And she
just knows she has it. She checks the lump every chance she can,
and it's still there. A reminder of her mortality and the horrible road
that lies ahead. Like a phantom limb, the painful memories of
Sarah's illness come rushing back. Ruth can smell that sour, anti-
septic hospital fetor, hear the endless beeping of the heart and
blood pressure machines monitoring her sister's vitals. Is this what's
in store for her? Even when she's not touching the lump, Ruth can
still feel it: a throbbing sensation caused by all her nervous energy
pooling in that one spot.

She's doing her best to ignore it, hoping to bury her burden beneath the stack of work on her desk. But after a few moments of
shuffling papers, it's obvious she can't concentrate. She looks at the
pink memo slip on her desk, beating like a heart. In her secretary's
loopy script it says, *Dr. Rekers. Please call right away.* There are two
telephone numbers: *office* and *home.* This message has been sitting
there since Friday afternoon, but she couldn't bring herself to return the call, wanting to prolong the inevitable. It's the *call right
away* that frightens her. Urgency is never a good thing when it
comes to cancer. She knows that from Sarah. Ruth hasn't said a
word to Elliot about the lump. He has no idea that she went to Dr.

Rekers's office earlier that week for a needle biopsy, where they drew fluid from the lump.

As an adult she's always taken her breasts for granted. It's only now that she's in danger of losing them that she remembers how much she wanted breasts when she was growing up. She would lock the bathroom door and study her prepubescent chest in the mirror, desperately looking for any signs of womanhood. All the popular girls had already begun to develop, and, being as short as she was, she felt like a child in comparison. She'd been so fascinated and preoccupied with the whole idea of breasts. She'd studied her classmates, hoping they wouldn't notice as she sized them up to see who had them, who didn't, how large or small they were. Who wore a bra, who didn't? Who jiggled when they walked, whose nipples protruded beneath their sweaters? And what about her own breasts? What kind would she have and where were they? When those breasts she'd longed for did arrive, Sarah had taken her shopping for her first brassiere, showing Ruth how to adjust the shoulder straps, how to *get herself down in there*. Ruth had been both proud and self-conscious about wearing that bra. She'd seen the way the boys snapped girls' bra straps—a sign that they liked them—and she'd hoped someone would snap hers, too.

Until Barbie, Ruth had forgotten what a goddamn big deal breasts are—for little girls, big girls, for mothers, for men. They are the ultimate symbol of femininity, a source of female power and even sustenance for a newborn. If she loses her breast, how will Elliot react? Will he still think she's beautiful? Will he ever want to touch her again? Make love to her again? Will she live long enough to find out?

She can't put this off any longer. She looks at the two telephone numbers on the message slip. It's a Saturday, so while she lights another cigarette, she tries the home number. Her heart is doing double time while she hears Dr. Rekers's wife calling out, "Paul, it's Ruth Handler." In the background she hears a dog barking, hears a cupboard shutting, hears something else she can't decipher.

"Oh, Ruth, finally," Dr. Rekers says, sounding a little out of breath, like she's called him in from the yard, maybe the swimming pool. She pictures him standing there, dripping onto the kitchen floor, a trail of footprints leading from the door. "I'm glad you called. I've been trying to reach you."

"Well? Just tell me." Ruth grips the phone with one hand, holds her cigarette in the other. Blood is thrumming up inside her head so loud she can hardly hear her own voice. "Do I have it?"

"Have what? Cancer?" he asks, as if it could be anything else. "No. You don't have cancer, Ruth. Your biopsy came back benign."

"What?"

"That's why I called yesterday. It's just fibrous tissue. Very common. Especially in women with large breasts."

"You mean it? I don't have cancer? You won't have to take my breast?"

"It was totally benign. But—and I'm serious about this, Ruth—you have a history of cancer in your family, and you need to quit smoking."

She looks at the cigarette scissored between her fingers.

Before hanging up the phone she promises Dr. Rekers she'll quit. Just as soon as she gets through the Ken doll launch. And she'll make all kinds of other positive changes, too. She'll spend more time with the children. She and Elliot will take them all on that vacation to Hawaii they ended up canceling. She will slow down. She'll get back to playing tennis . . .

"Did you forget about me?"

She looks up and sees Barbara standing in the doorway, arms folded and fury in her eyes.

"You did, didn't you? You forgot we were going shopping today."

"No, of course I didn't." But heaven help her, just then, she did. The guilt just about clobbers her and she has no choice now but to sit there and take the beating from her daughter.

"You said you'd pick me up at eleven. I've been sitting at home waiting for you. And I knew it! I just knew I'd find you down here working . . ."

Ruth lets her rant and rave, because what is the alternative? Scaring the living daylights out of Barbara by telling her that she was on the phone with her doctor? That she thought she had breast cancer? That she thought she might die just like her aunt Sarah did? Ruth can't do that.

". . . Work always comes first with you. Always has, always will," Barbara is saying now. "How do you think that makes me feel, to be an item you have to check off on your to-do list?"

Next door, Stevie and Jack are in his office, working. This is the third weekend in a row she's gone into the office. Today they're working out the final details on a Barbie concept that Charlotte's calling *Busy Gal*. So far all Stevie's got is a red linen pencil skirt and jacket. Charlotte wants the red-and-white-striped blouse to match the jacket lining. Jack wants to plus it up, and since Barbie is a fashion model, why not add a portfolio with some sketches inside? Stevie argues they should be photographs of Barbie instead. They're going back and forth on all this when they hear Ruth's daughter pitching a fit, her voice carrying right through the wall.

It feels like Stevie's eavesdropping, and she can't believe what she's hearing. Barbara clearly resents Ruth, but can the girl not appreciate what her mother's doing? My God, here is a woman practically running this entire company. Stevie's mother only held one job. Ever. Modeling cars. Buicks, to be specific. It's how her parents met. Stanley Klein stood off to the side watching the pretty brunette on the revolving platform pointing to the adjustable wire-spoke wheels, the chrome hubcaps and luggage racks. The story goes that her father was instantly smitten, and Stevie takes solace in thinking her parents were happy together once upon a time. That is, before she came along and spoiled all their fun. She wonders what might have become of her mother had she not gotten pregnant so young.

Stevie looks at Jack, assessing him as he bends over his drafting table, working out the intricate details of the fashion portfolio. She's never noticed before what a lovely profile he has—straight nose, strong jaw, sexy Adam's apple. Her mind begins to drift, and she thinks about how Jack is kind and caring, recalling how he rolled up his sleeves to get her old clunker going when the spark plugs and alternator died, and how he cosigned for her car loan. One day, when her coffee went down the wrong pipe and she fell into a coughing fit, it was Jack who ran and got her a glass of water. And—she catches herself. *Oh whoopty-fucking-doo.* The whole thing is ridiculous. Other than the one time when he tried to kiss her, he hasn't made another pass at her, and given his reputation, she sometimes wonders why he hasn't tried again. Has he given up? Does he not find her attractive? Has he put her in the same camp as Ginger? And even if he has, why does this bother her? It's not that she wants him to kiss her. Does she? No, definitely not. But still, she does catch herself from time to time looking at his soft pillowy lips and wondering, just wondering . . .

Stevie is still wondering when another burst of shouting comes from Ruth's office. "I swear to God, sometimes I wish we never went to Europe. I wish you never saw that doll."

Someone Else's Toothbrush

t's another late night. Charlotte is back in Japan, and Stevie and Jack are in a crunch, putting the finishing touches on a new out-fit for Ken's 700 series. For *Terry Togs* they've already worked out the monograms on the blue terry cloth robe and bath towel. They've added slippers and even a pair of tighty-whities, but Jack wants more accessories.

"What if we give him, I don't know"—he shrugs—"a bar of soap. A shaver. Yeah, a shaver. And a comb. Now, *that* would make this perfect."

"Haven't you ever heard the expression 'Perfect is the enemy of the good'?"

"Who was it who said that? Shakespeare?"

"Voltaire."

"I thought it was Shakespeare."

"He may have said it, too. The point is," she says, "there's no such thing as perfect, but there *is* such a thing as ruining a great concept because you can't leave well enough alone in your quest for perfection."

"Very true," he admits, but still, the engineer in him will never be satisfied. "Let's take a break. We need food. What time is it, anyway?"

"I don't know." She checks her watch, stunned when she sees it's almost nine o'clock.

"How'd it get to be so late? We definitely need food. And a break." He goes over to the couch and collects all the blueprints resting on the cushions. "Let me just get rid of this stuff."

"What is all that?" she asks, taking a seat, stretching her arms overhead. "Are you building something? I thought you recently bought a new place."

"I did. And now I'm turning it into a castle." He flashes an arresting smile her way.

She looks at him and doesn't blink. Instead, her eyes open wider, and wider still. Something in his smile has captivated her. "You're turning your home into a *castle*?" she asks. "What kind of castle?"

"A *castle* castle." Jack grins boastfully. "Picture a magnificent castle—I'm talking with a moat, turrets, a drawbridge, the whole bit—*that's* what I'm building." He sits down beside her. It's a small couch and they're practically on top of each other.

Coming from anyone else, building a castle would be preposterous—but Jack's enthusiasm is infectious, and Stevie is unexpectedly pulled in, enchanted by the very thought of it. She wants more details. She's ready to ask if he's going to have a tower, too, but is brought up short by the way he's looking at her. The energy starts to shift, the boundaries start to blur. She's suddenly aware of the heat of his leg pressed to her thigh. It's growing hotter, reaching a fever pitch.

He feels it too, because that's when he leans over, the back of his hand brushing her cheek as he pushes a strand of hair from her face.

"You've always been building castles, haven't you?" she says, a little breathy.

"Have I?" His mouth is closer to hers now.

"The day I met you at the diner, you built a castle out of sugar cubes."

"Ah, yeah." He smiles. "You didn't like me then."

She laughs. "No, I really didn't."

"And now? Do you like me? Even just a little?"

"What do you think?" She looks first into his blue eyes and then lets her gaze drop to his mouth, and before she can say another word, Jack closes that space between them and kisses her with his soft full lips, even softer than she's imagined.

She's lost in that kiss and so it happens. It just does. Right there in his office, on his bearskin rug. Jack Ryan, the world's greatest kisser and office Casanova, delivers one doozy of an orgasm Stevie's way. And then another one.

Stevie is still lying on the bearskin rug next to him, both of them quiet as the sun begins to rise, shifting the shadows and changing the light inside his office. She didn't plan for any of this and can't remember if she even shaved her legs that morning—now officially yesterday morning. *What have we done? What have I done? I couldn't possibly get pregnant again, could I? Good God, how are we supposed to go on working together after this? We've seen each other naked.* But then she reminds herself that Jack still works with Patsy, and with Wendy in personnel, whom she's heard he had an affair with.

She gets up, a little lightheaded and starving, because they never did end up eating dinner last night. As she begins collecting her clothes off the floor, she thinks about last night and has to suppress the urge to giggle, and she's not a giggly girl.

"This was just a fling, you know," she says, clasping her bra.

"A fun fling," he says, stepping into his trousers.

"Yeah, but it was just a onetime thing. It's never gonna happen again."

"Whatever you say." He grins. "You're the boss here."

Two days later, it does happen again. There they are that night, on his tiny office couch, with their limbs wrapped around each other. So much for a onetime fling. Stevie hasn't been able to stop thinking about him, and the heat between them could melt glass.

"I could get used to this," he says, stroking her face.

And the thing is, so could she.

"What do you think about letting me take you out on a real date?"

She smiles, and when he starts kissing her again, she pulls away.

"What's wrong?"

Scooting out from underneath him, she smooths her hair and says, "Before we take this any further, I have two stipulations."

"Only two?" He gives her a disarming smile.

"I'm serious. First, I have to be the only one."

"The only one?" He looks at her like she's speaking a foreign language.

"You have to stop seeing other women. I don't want to feel like I'm using someone else's toothbrush."

He laughs, rolls his eyes. "Done."

"You mean it?"

"Of course." His jaw goes tight, but his lips still look so soft. "Okay, so what's the second stipulation?"

"The second is"—she reaches for his face and makes him look her in the eye—"you have to wear a rubber. Every time."

Jack bursts into laughter. "You've got to be joking."

"I'm dead serious. You don't get in without one," she says. The only thing men hate more than wearing a rubber is finding out they've gotten a woman knocked up. Russell was proof of that.

"Silly girl," says Jack. "You don't have to worry about babies with me. I've been snipped." He makes a scissorlike gesture with his fingers. "I have two children. I don't need any more."

"You don't have, like, syphilis or anything, do you?"

He doubles over, howling. "Oh, this is all so very sexy. And no." He wipes his eyes. "I'm clean as a whistle."

"And you're positive that you and Barbara have an *understanding*?"

"Cross my heart."

S tevie wakes two weeks later to find Jack propped up on a pillow, staring down at her, smiling. Still blinking awake, she's not sure if she's in her bed or his. They alternate staying one night at her place, the next at the Castle. She's also not sure what time or day it is. She flings off the heavy quilt, thinking she might be late for work, but he stops her.

"Hey, where you going?"

Before she can speak, Jack is kissing and stroking her, and she remembers last night, which means today is Saturday and they are in his bed and who cares what time it is. They are in the best stage of something new. There's so much to discover about each other. Intimate things like the strawberry birthmark above her navel, the ticklish spot behind his knees, the way she sometimes talks in her sleep and how he can recall every single detail of his dreams. They can linger in bed for hours swapping childhood stories, sharing kisses and sharing their bodies.

She remembers the first time he took her to the Castle. She was worried about running into his wife, but he assured her that wouldn't happen because Barbara and the girls have a separate wing. He wanted to show her around and led her through the 16,000-square-foot interior, filled with archways and tunnels and a maze of rooms that lead to more rooms. Parts of it were, and still are, under construction, and just like the home he grew up in, there is scaffolding, paint-splattered tarps and ladders everywhere.

"Can you keep a secret?" he asked.

"That depends."

"This wall"—he knocked against the stone, creating a hollow reverberation—"it's not real."

She tried it for herself, surprised.

"I'm working with a Hollywood set designer. All the archways and turrets, even the drawbridge, are made out of prop materials. They look real but they're not, and they're saving me a ton of dough."

"Well, they look authentic, so don't worry. Your secret's safe with me."

Walking her through the first floor, he said, "By the time this place is finished, I'm going to put a telephone in every room."

"Why?"

"Because I can." He bit his bottom lip and winked. "And get a load of this—" He escorted her into a dark room and threw a switch, illuminating an antique throne fit for a king.

"Where did that come from?"

"It belonged to the prince of Parma. I got it for a steal at an auction."

"How much?"

"Only $575 and—"

"Oh, only $575," she mocked.

"They wanted $1,800. I was gonna put it in the master bathroom. Over the toilet. Get it? A royal *bathroom throne*. But it won't fit."

Stevie sat down and wrapped her hands along the curved, gilded armrests on the throne. "What does your wife think of all this?"

"Oh God, Barbara hates it. Thinks the whole place looks like a dungeon."

Stevie agreed, taking in the heavy dark paneling on the walls, the candelabras in the corners, the cold wooden floors, and the stained-glass windows in the shadowy alcoves.

Later that night, after they'd thrilled each other in his four-poster bed, Jack went to the kitchen and came back with a pint of ice cream, and when he fed her a spoonful, she squealed with surprise. "Black licorice? I *love* black licorice ice cream."

"We must be the only two people on the planet who do. They're discontinuing it." He leaned over to feed her another spoonful. "I think you're my soulmate," he said.

"Oh my God." She looked at him with wonderment. "I was just thinking that. I swear to God I was."

But the minute after they said this, they had both cracked up, laughing so hard that Stevie snorted. Jack has had dozens of so-called soulmates. And Stevie, who's not even sure she believes in such a thing as soulmates, has yet to meet hers. They both see this affair of theirs for what it is, but that doesn't stop them from delighting in each other's company.

Jack gives great thought to planning their dates and thinking of where he'll take her, which flowers he'll send her. He feels like a 1950s suitor, and it reminds him of his younger years when he started seeing Barbara. Stevie feels like they're a couple of movie stars when they walk into a restaurant like Perino's and are seated at the best table. Jack's teaching her about wine and showed her how to eat her first lobster. One night as they sit side by side in a fancy banquette at the Arsenal, Stevie tries not to gasp when Jack slips his fingers inside her panties. As soon as the valet brings Jack's car around, she practically ravishes him.

In private, they spend a lot of time beneath the covers talking about work. They bounce ideas off each other, and when Stevie needs help with Ken's wardrobe, she goes through Jack's closets seeking inspiration. He in turn keeps a sketchpad on the bedside floor. She loves watching him work, loves getting this private glimpse inside the genius that is Jack Ryan.

Each time Jack thinks about Stevie he can't stop smiling. The woman's legs could hold him in a vise, squeeze the life out of him, and he'd die a happy man. Driving down Sepulveda on his way from the Castle to Mattel, he's on top of the world. Nothing escapes his awe and wonder. The sky has never been so blue, the flowers never more fragrant. He listens to the purr of his car's engine sounding so powerful, the leather on his steering wheel supple beneath his fingers. It's like a drug has kicked in, or that much-needed second drink. Right now, everything—every single thing—in his world is simply glorious.

As soon as he gets to the office, he feels the urge to go see Stevie. Trying to exercise some restraint, he reaches into his pocket for his tape recorder and turns it on, hoping the gesture will spark an idea. The tape hisses, the little red light blinks and he says nothing. All he can think about is Stevie.

He turns off the tape recorder, stuffs it back in his pocket, picks up his phone and buzzes her workstation. "Meet me in my office. Now."

"Am I in trouble?" she teases.

"You might be if you don't get your gorgeous ass down here."

Stevie hangs up and starts walking down the hallway, passing rows of cubicles. Some have plastic squirt guns, loaded and ready for action; others have found creative, suggestive ways to display Barbie and the Ken prototypes. Twist has them screwing, and Loomis has Barbie in a garter and fishnets, engaged in a sixty-nine position with Ken. Lately it's become a competition to see who can come up with the most shocking poses for plastic orgies and such.

When Stevie gets to Jack's office, he locks his door.

"C'mon, not here, Short Stuff."

He laughs at the use of her nickname for him, inspired by their first meeting at the diner on Pico Boulevard. Other times, in reference to his being so well-endowed, she refers to him as My Little Jumbo Shrimp.

"We can't," she says as he kisses her neck.

"Why not?" He keeps kissing her as he undoes the top button on her blouse, and the next one, and by then she can't think of a reason to stop him.

Salt and Pepper

The Ken doll is a bigger hit at Toy Fair than Mattel could have predicted. Buyers think Barbie's boyfriend is a stroke of genius, and mothers feel that Ken makes Barbie less scandalous since she's no longer a lone woman on the prowl.

Back at Mattel, Stevie worries that Jack may be the one on the prowl thanks to a new secretary, a pretty statuesque brunette. He's gone out of his way to welcome the long-legged typist and make her feel at home. One afternoon Stevie finds him perched on the secretary's desk, charming her with some story about his travels to Japan. Stevie feels nauseous watching how Jack's eyes are trained on the typist's breasts.

Stevie knows that for now, she's the only one. But monogamy in Jack's world has a shelf life, and she can tell they're coming to the end of theirs. Jack loves women; he cannot help himself. He's drawn to them, and they're drawn to him. Where there are women, there is Jack.

Stevie can't shake the sense that he already has his next conquest in his sights and fears that it's just a matter of time before he woos the secretary away from her typewriter and into his arms.

And then where does that leave Stevie? She won't share him, but she also knows she's not quite ready to give him up yet.

Being with Jack is intoxicating. He puts her in the center of a fantasy that he's created for her. When she's with him she feels sophisticated and daring, and the past three months have been magical. But at some point, she'll have to face the fact that being with a womanizer is a little like being on a sinking boat. You plug your finger in one hole only to find another leak has sprouted. Stevie knows she doesn't have enough fingers to keep from going under.

Not long after the Ken doll is released, Ruth comes home one day to find Elliot up in their son's room, the door closed. She stares into an Italian movie poster taped up and gently knocks. "Boys?" She hears a soft murmuring through the door. "Ken? Elliot?"

"Ah, give us a minute," says Elliot. "I'll—I'll be right out."

"Is everything okay?" she asks. "Ken, honey, are you sick?"

"I'm fine," he says, not sounding fine at all.

Ruth can't stand being shut out like this. She turns the doorknob, steps inside, and before Ken hides his face in shame, she's already seen the tears.

"Ruth," Elliot snaps, disappointed that she couldn't leave it alone and had to barge in. "Give me a minute with him, would you, please?"

She backs away, wounded that her son doesn't want her there, that he would rather confide in Elliot than in her. But both her children have a different relationship with their father—dare she say, a *better* relationship with him. While she's grateful that Elliot has such a strong bond with the kids, she's also envious. And yet she understands it. Elliot is more patient, more nurturing. He's more available to them, too. She's always on her way to a meeting, getting on an important telephone call or generally just too preoccupied with work.

While waiting for Elliot to come downstairs, she smokes a cigarette, fixes a drink and berates herself for being a lousy mother. As much as she wants to, Ruth knows she can't change her ways. She's tried, sometimes taking a sudden and overzealous interest in her children. She'll be overly solicitous of them, feigning interest in a piece of music or some foreign film Ken went to see, mooning over Barbara's new dining room table or the kitchen blender she just bought. She comes at them like a tidal wave, drowning them with attention for as long as she can sustain it. And that's the problem—she never can sustain it. It's like all her attempts to quit smoking. She can't keep it up.

Ruth hears footsteps overhead. "What's going on with him?" she asks Elliot even before he reaches the staircase landing. "Is he okay?"

"He will be." Elliot squeezes the tension in his neck before coming over to her, his hand extended for her drink. He takes a sip and passes the glass back before sinking onto the sofa. "We *really* screwed up this time, Ruthie. We never should have named that doll after Ken."

"But I thought he was fine with the name."

"That was before the doll turned out to be such a big deal. Barbie and Ken. It's like salt and pepper. You can't say one without the other. And now the kids at school are ribbing him. Saying he's dating his sister. They called him a fairy, even roughed him up a little—"

"Is he hurt?"

"Just his pride. You know how kids are. They're saying he

doesn't have a penis—you know, kid stuff. But it stings. We should have listened to Barbara."

Ruth sits beside him, her gin sloshing in her glass. She thought they were doing a good thing, that her children would be flattered and see the dolls as a tribute. She knows how Barbie has affected her daughter—the teasing from friends; the occasional request for an autograph, which Barbara hates—but Ruth never anticipated the Ken doll having any impact at all on her son. "Well, what the hell do we do now? We can't change the name."

"Hopefully this'll pass, and he'll be able to block it all out or else find a way to make them cut it out."

And he does. By the fall of 1961, Ken finds himself a girlfriend. He's seventeen years old and Suzie is the first girl he's ever shown any interest in. Ken has always been shy and awkward, and though the girl is lovely and quite pretty, Ruth can tell something's bothering her son. He's grown moody and spends more and more time in his bedroom. A kid who once played piano for hours a day, he's suddenly abandoned the one thing that brought him true joy.

As a boyfriend, Ken is going through the motions, doing what is expected. He sends Suzie flowers, buys her a charm bracelet and a necklace. He takes her to the movies and school dances, but his heart's not in it. It's like he's wearing someone else's clothes. Ruth can't put her finger on it. Maybe Suzie's not the right girl. Maybe they don't have enough in common. Maybe they're not compatible, although they seem to get along just fine and never argue.

Ken can't tell his mother or Suzie what the problem is. But the truth is that he doesn't want a girlfriend. At all. And what he does want terrifies him as much as it thrills him. He steals glances at the other boys in class, admiring their muscular physiques, their strong jaws. When he's alone at night in his room, his innocent body aches for something he fears isn't normal. Some would even say it's disgusting. He scolds himself, denies himself and tries to change himself. But it's of no use. He knows what he is, and to make certain that no one else knows, he keeps it all hidden behind a forced smile and a girlfriend.

Finding the Muse

t's a Saturday morning and Stevie is seated at a booth in Norms on La Cienega, waiting for Jack. He had a tennis game earlier and was going to swing by afterward and meet her for lunch. He was vague about his tennis partner. "Just a friend," he said.

He's already fifteen minutes late when she spots Marta Krass, a former classmate from Chouinard, heading her way. Marta keeps her oversized sunglasses on and wears frosted white lipstick and big dangling earrings. She's meeting Bob Mackie for lunch and is eager to tell Stevie that she's working with Sally Hanson at Jax. Stevie wants to tell her she's working with Jack Ryan, but outside of Mattel, that means nothing.

"I love it there," Marta says. "I can't believe how much I'm learning. I'm not actually executing any of my own designs yet, but Sally said she'd at least look at them . . ."

The envy is instantaneous. It rises up in her like acid reflux. Stevie can't help it. Jax is one of the most exciting new designers on the fashion scene. Sally and her husband have created a line of fashionable women's slacks with zippers in the back that accentuate the waistline and hips. They're in Beverly Hills and everyone from Natalie Wood to Marilyn Monroe is a client.

"And what about you?" asks Marta, removing her sunglasses, patting her hair into place. "Where'd you land?"

Stevie feels like she's about to confess to a crime. "I'm at Mattel," she says, quickly looking away, eyeing the door for Jack.

"Mattel? Wait"—Marta contorts her white frosted lips as if she's trying to solve a calculus equation—"isn't Mattel that *toy* company?"

"I'm still a fashion designer, though." Stevie immediately goes on the defensive, hating that she felt the need to tack on that *though* as a qualifier. "I'm working on the Barbie doll."

Marta laughs and then sees that Stevie is serious. "Really? You're designing doll clothes?"

Stevie's cheeks flame. "Charlotte's working there, too. Remember Charlotte Johnson?"

"Oh yeah." Marta starts searching around the diner for Bob. "I heard something about that. I can't believe she threw her career away like that." Realizing she's just insulted Stevie, Marta waves her hand in a *silly me* gesture and adds, "I didn't mean that the way it sounded. It's just"—she raises one shoulder, bewildered—"why would you both want to work on *that* doll?"

That doll? Stevie wants to ask what Marta means by *that* when Bob arrives, looking dapper and handsome as ever. She always liked him, they got along well in school, and after a quick hello, he tells her he's now Ray Aghayan's assistant. Stevie smiles and congratulates him, despite another rush of acid.

"And what about you?" he asks. "I heard you're working with Charlotte at some"—he searches for it—"what is it? A *toy* company?"

Stevie goes through the humiliation for a second time, and after he and Marta make their exit, she glances at her watch. Jack is almost thirty minutes late. She signals the waitress, pays for her coffee and leaves.

At home she sits in the living room and studies her thimbles in the shadow boxes on the wall. She's been collecting them since she was a young girl and now has hundreds, made of brass, silver, nickel, hand-painted porcelain and china. She glances away and stares at her sewing machine.

If Marta is laughing at her for designing Barbie's clothes, no designer will take her seriously. It's time to face the facts. Stevie can no longer pretend that Mattel is her ticket into the fashion world. Her classmates are moving up in the industry while the gap between where they all started continues to widen.

She thought she'd made peace with working on Barbie, but if she had, she wouldn't be feeling like such a failure right now. Clearly, the money's not enough. The dream—the dream she's had since high school—is still there inside her. It may have cooled to an ember, but seeing Marta and Bob just reignited the fire. She can't go on denying that she still wants to be a fashion designer. *A real fashion designer.*

This declaration reminds her of that conversation she had with Ruth about learning to bounce back from disappointments and false starts. *Change your plan, change your approach, but don't you dare ever give up.* Stevie needs to muster up that bounce-back quality. But how?

She's putting this all together in her mind when Jack calls, full of apologies. *They*—she's too proud to ask who *they* is—went for drinks after tennis and he lost all track of time. He doesn't say anything about coming over later and she's surprisingly okay with this, maybe even a little relieved. She needs this time to herself to learn how to bounce back, to figure out a new plan and make this a turning point for her career.

She has the weekend—the rest of Saturday and all day Sunday—to do nothing but create. She'll stay up all night like she used to when she was in school. She'll start from scratch and design an entirely new portfolio. She'll create classic, tailored dresses and slacks and beautiful silk blouses and tweed overcoats. She'll do dramatic, formal pieces, too.

From now on, instead of going to the beach after hours, she'll come straight home and get to work. She'll stop spending so much time with Jack and will focus more on creating a portfolio so spectacular that no one will be able to turn her away. She'll do the kind of designs that will get her hired in a real fashion house.

She sequesters herself in her apartment with a pile of fashion magazines, a stack of sketchpads and jars of pencils and markers. She can't remember the last time she worked on anything that wasn't for Barbie, and that one-sixth scale is so ingrained in her that she's restricted, thinking only of ideas that will work for Barbie. Before she's even put pencil to paper, she's censoring herself. She sits like that for the better part of an hour, sketching something only to crumple it up, add it to the crinkled balls of paper at her feet. She knows this sort of thing can't be forced and yet she's willing it to happen, trying to squeeze the artistry from her pores. She simply must make something amazing happen on the page. There is such heaviness and desperation in every stroke of her pencil, and everything is shit—derivative of what's already been done, already photographed in that stack of glossy magazines.

The late-afternoon sun is streaming in from the window, making her drowsy. Eventually she dozes off, waking only when she feels her sketchpad slip from her hands. She gets up, makes a cup of tea. Her left arm, from her pinky to her elbow, is smudged with pencil lead. Waiting for the tea to steep, she wonders why it is that everyone always compares up, never down. At least she's working in a related design field with fabrics, with fashions *and* with Charlotte Johnson, no less. Plus, she's getting paid for it and is probably making more money than Marta, Bob or Vivian. Some of their classmates aren't even in the field. Lucy Troy is now working as a dental hygienist; Perry White is moving furniture; Sandra Hinks is still living at home, working in a grocery store. It could be so much worse.

And the ironic part is that while people like Vivian, Marta and Bob are working with top designers, they're not executing their own ideas. Stevie is actually doing more of that at Mattel. None of them have seen their own designs finished, in the stores. Let alone featured in a television commercial. Her colleagues are still pinning fabrics and cutting out patterns for other people's designs. Stevie's not just a wrist—she's creating some of the top fashion looks. She attends fashion shows, she's meeting with fabric vendors and notions suppliers. She's right in the thick of it; the only difference is the scale she's working in.

This shifts something inside Stevie and makes her appreciate the true opportunity before her. And as that takes hold, so does a new idea for Barbie. She leaves her tea on the counter and rushes back to her sketchpad. With a sense of ease and command, she conjures up a sophisticated black-and-white double-breasted dress with a full skirt. She goes bold with the white shawl collar and tops it off with a dramatic wide-brimmed white and black hat. In less time than she spent littering her floor with dreck, she's created a smashing outfit, one she'd wear herself. And in this moment, she feels so light, so alive and proud. She's happy. Genuinely happy. And best of all, it's a happiness that's not on loan from Jack or any other man. No one can take this from her. It's hers and hers alone. She wants to capture this glorious feeling and bottle it up.

It dawns on her that Barbie rescued her from that diner on Pico Boulevard, brought her back into the fold of fashion design and gave her a license to create. All day long she's been straining her brain to come up with something when her muse, Barbie, has been here all along.

The following week, on her way to the Castle, Stevie's stopped at a red light on Rochester Avenue and takes advantage of this moment to close her eyes. She could have easily nodded off had the car behind her not honked. She was up late the night before, working up a new ensemble for Barbie. Ruth wants the team to focus more on Barbie's careers, and after brainstorming with Charlotte, they came up with the idea of Barbie the airline stewardess. Loomis is trying to secure a licensing agreement that would let them use the American Airlines logo.

Having recommitted herself to her career and Barbie, Stevie's been so busy and preoccupied that lately she hasn't spent much time with Jack outside of the office. She hasn't really missed him, either. He's aware that she's pulling away and it's making him cling to her all the more. He's already lost whatever interest he had in the new secretary and is again focused on Stevie, doing his level best to reel her back in. When she doesn't invite him along for dinner with her parents, when she opts to spend time with Vivian instead of lounging by the pool at the Castle, he sulks, he drinks. Once, when she was too tired to stay the night, he called and woke her up, begging her to let him come over. Lately, being with Jack isn't much fun. Now it feels like work, and she has enough of that with Barbie.

As she pulls up to the Castle, Brenda Lee starts belting out "Sweet Nothin's" over the radio, giving Stevie a second wind. Stepping out of the car, she sees the door to the family's private entranceway open. Two young girls—Ann, age six, and Diana, age four—drift out onto the walkway in matching sailor dresses. Stevie's never seen Jack's daughters before. Or Barbara, who has now joined them, along with an Irish setter, straining against its leash. A *dog*? Jack's never mentioned them having a pet. They don't see Stevie, or if they do, they don't acknowledge her—*Just another one of Jack's girls*. But Stevie is watching them, mesmerized. Barbara Ryan has soft, warm eyes and lots of dark hair that bounces upon her shoulders. The younger girl looks like her mother, the older one like Jack.

Despite the day's heat, Stevie feels a chill. Aside from her first visit to the Castle, Stevie has conveniently forgotten that Jack is a father and someone's husband. Even if Barbara is willing to look the other way, Stevie sees the truth right before her. Barbara wrangles the dog and her daughters into the car. They drive off and disappear, but the ghost of them remains, and it's haunting.

Stevie feels like a trespasser, slipping through the side door of the Castle. She hears Jack down the hall, talking on one of his many telephones, and she darts into the powder room and closes the door. She doesn't want to be there, doesn't want to see Jack. The switch has been thrown; all that delicious electricity that once flowed through her at just the thought of him has now been cut off. She knows that she'll never kiss him again, never feel their bodies moving together in that intense dance where he leads, having taught her all the steps. She'll never again wake in the middle of the night to find his head on her pillow and his body pressed as close to hers as he can get. None of that, she knows, will ever happen again.

That night, after Stevie breaks up with Jack, she goes home, has a good cry and pours herself a glass of wine from an expensive bottle he gave her—mostly so he'd have something decent to drink at her place. How could an affair that started out so light, so fun and easy have turned so heavy and guilt-ridden? And it's not so much because of his wife but because of Jack. She never expected him to take it so hard. How could he have not seen this coming? He'd been a mess when she left the Castle, already drunk and begging her to stay. She's still baffled by this. As her heart uncoils and goes flat, she knows she did the right thing, but still it hurts.

It's times like these when Stevie envies those little girls who can escape into Barbie's perfect world where nothing ever goes wrong. Barbie never gets a headache, never comes down with a cold or the flu. She doesn't worry about balancing her checkbook or paying her bills. She never has insomnia or gets the hiccups. Never breaks a fingernail or gets a blister from her high heels. She never gets involved with the wrong guy and never has to break up with anyone. Stevie decides that grown-ups need their own Barbie dream world every bit as much as children do.

New Projects in the Works

R uth and Elliot have just purchased a new home in Holmby Hills, an ultra-exclusive area where they can wave to Lauren Bacall, Lloyd Bridges and their other famous neighbors. It's while they're getting the Beverlywood house ready to go on the market that Ruth has an idea for Barbie and calls a meeting.

Jack, per usual, is the last to arrive in the conference room and takes the only empty seat at the table, which happens to be next to Stevie. This is the first meeting they've been in together since she ended their affair a week and a half ago. They used to always sit next to each other, sometimes letting their feet mingle beneath the table, their thighs secretly pressed against each other's. Now the proximity is too much, for both of them. It's like a vapor swelling up that only they can see. Stevie hasn't heard a word anyone's said since Jack walked in. She has no idea how she's supposed to act around him now. Without looking at him, she's aware of his every move as she nervously taps her pencil against her legal pad, stops and then starts tapping again.

Jack's been avoiding Stevie as best he can. It all feels very juvenile and out of character for him. He's always made it a point to stay friends with his ex-girlfriends and mistresses; otherwise he couldn't walk down the street without getting pelted. But this is different. Stevie's the one who ended it, and usually that's what he does. Other than his wife, he can't remember the last time a woman rejected him, and he can't get past it just yet.

He feels self-conscious and a little desperate. Sitting this close to Stevie in this meeting, stealing glances at her lips, her blue eyes and Jesus Christ, those legs—it's torture. It's like he's back at the beginning with her, when she started working here. But now he knows what he's missing, what's there, waiting for someone else.

"If Barbie's truly going to be an independent, modern girl," Ruth is saying now, "then I think she should have her own house. She can't go on living at home with her invisible parents forever."

"I like that idea," says Charlotte. "Barbie needs a home of her own. She deserves a spiffy Barbie bachelorette pad."

Stevie nods, hoping it looks like she's tracking everything being said.

"C'mon, now," says Loomis, scratching at his heavy jowls, "the whole idea sounds a little far-fetched. A woman could never even qualify for a mortgage. Barbie having her own home isn't realistic."

"Yeah," says Twist, already cracking himself up, "Ken would have to cosign her loan."

Jack is the only man in the room who doesn't find this funny, because he's reminded of the time he cosigned for Stevie's car loan. She's remembering this, too. For a split second they dare to look at each other and immediately turn away.

"Whenever you're done laughing," says Ruth, "I'd like to remind you that Barbie is not going to be limited by what society—a society controlled by men—thinks is achievable. And if that makes you nervous, too bad. Now open a goddamn job ticket and get working on Barbie's fucking dream house."

And going forward that's how they refer to it: Barbie's Dream House—minus the expletive.

Dr. Klemes, Jack's new psychiatrist, consults his notes while Jack reclines on his couch. "Are you still taking the Obetrol?" he asks.

"Can't you tell?" Jack pats his flat stomach. A month ago, right after he lost Stevie, he gained five pounds and had his doctor prescribe some diet pills. They kill his appetite but also his need for sleep. "I could use a refill."

"Already?" Dr. Klemes makes a notation in Jack's file and moves on. "Now, in our last session you said things at work were awkward?" Though it's a statement, he phrases it as a question, hoping Jack will elaborate.

"Everything's peachy. Never better," he lies, realizing that lying to his psychiatrist negates the reason for going to him in the first place. But Jack doesn't feel like getting into it. The truth is, he's obsessing about Stevie. Fits of jealousy fire off inside him when he sees her talking to one of the guys. Suddenly Jack is acutely aware of just how many young, handsome men work at Mattel. Twist is a good-looking dude, tall and muscular, and Jack wonders what Stevie was doing in his office the day before. There's Gary in shipping with his chiseled chin, and Marcus in sales with the thick wavy hair. If Jack's noticed these guys, no doubt Stevie has, too. And holy hell, just that morning Jack felt his blood pressure rise when he saw her talking to Loomis in the kitchen. How can he possibly be jealous of Loomis?

"You said last time that you were feeling restless?" Again, the doctor is making this a question, hoping Jack will provide some insights.

He shrugs but says nothing. He's working on the Dream House project but it's not going very well. He's stuck. Frankly, he could use Stevie's help, but he's not ready to pretend that everything's normal between them. They've barely said five words to each other since she dumped him.

And suddenly it occurs to Jack that this restlessness, this void in his life left by Stevie, might explain his growing interest in Ginger. Or, more specifically, his interest in *helping* Ginger. He knows she's in love with him, or she *thinks* she is, but Jack's never had the slightest romantic feelings toward her. Just as he's drawn to beautiful women, he's also drawn to exceptional intelligence. He seeks out women who can challenge him, stimulate his mind as much as his loins. The ones who hold his interest are the creative ones, intuitive and curious about the world around them.

Poor Ginger possesses few of those qualities. She's kind and overly solicitous of him, which he doesn't mind. Not in the least. But aside from that, she's not a great conversationalist, not terribly witty or clever. Many of his jokes go over her head, and oftentimes he has to point out when he's being sarcastic. She has no interesting hobbies or passions besides Jack, and that gets tiresome, even for him.

Right after Stevie ended things with them, Jack caught Ginger sobbing at her desk, and it touched him. Maybe it's because he's suffered with his own demons that he cannot stand to see anyone unhappy. Anger is different. He can handle his daughters' temper tantrums, Ruth's tirades, even his father's rants. But when someone is hurting and in distress, he wants to fix whatever ails them. Maybe this is why he likes making toys. They make children happy, and Jack therefore considers himself to be the happiness maker and will go to great lengths to instigate smiles and laughter. And so that day when he found Ginger weeping into her soggy fisted tissue, he brought her into his office for what turned out to be a lengthy confessional.

"My younger sister is getting married in two weeks," she said. "And I'm terrified that I won't be able to fit into my bridesmaid's dress."

Well, that was an easy fix. "If you want to lose weight fast, get off those stupid caramels and try some of these." He gave her a dozen or so Obetrols, with the promise to get her a prescription.

"And I don't have a boyfriend, or even a date for the wedding," Ginger went on to say, spilling more tears. "Everyone's going to pity me. I'll have no one to dance with. I'll be the unmarried older sister, the spinster."

Seeing her cry like that was too much. He had to do something to make it better, make her stop. "How about if I take you to your sister's wedding?"

"Oh, Jack." She looked up, blinking, a smile forming through her tears, a rainbow after a storm. "Would you?" She dried her eyes, thanked him and hugged him a little too tight and a little too long.

Since then and with the help of Obetrol, Ginger's lost some weight, and it turns out, the girl has potential. Another fifteen or twenty pounds and she'd have a decent figure. And a helluva pair of legs. She's lightened her hair again, too, which is an improvement. Now he just needs to work on her wardrobe. It's not like he's a fashion expert, but he does have good taste and a sense of style. Even Barbara seeks his advice when she goes shopping. Frankly, Ginger dresses like an old maid. Honestly, with just a few tweaks— lighten her hair even more, maybe fix that bump in her nose—he knows he could turn her into something truly spectacular and . . . He stops himself, lifts his hands and squeezes both sides of his head.

"Something wrong, Jack?" asks Dr. Klemes.

Jack shakes his head, reminding himself that Ginger is a woman, not his new design project.

On a Sunday afternoon, in between having coffee with her mother and meeting Vivian for a matinee showing of *Splendor in the Grass* with Natalie Wood and Warren Beatty, Stevie stops by the office. She's just started working on a new project, Barbie's new best friend—Madge or Midge; they haven't finalized the name yet. They're still in the early stages, but between this new doll and Ken, on top of everything needed to keep expanding Barbie's wardrobe, she wants to get a jump start on the week ahead.

As she pulls into the parking lot, she can tell by the cars that the usual suspects are there: Ruth, Charlotte, Loomis, Lewis, Twist, Sid and, of course, Jack. She used to be so happy to see him and now she dreads it. Now it's all awkward and strained. It's like she's back in high school. He walks past her in the hallway, refusing to look at her or say hello. Still, she has work to do, so she figures she'll just slip inside, head to her desk, do what she needs to do before she ducks out to meet Vivian at the theater.

That's her plan, but as she steps inside the building, she hears Jack clowning around with Eddie, the weekend security guard. They're laughing, joking about the illustration of Alfred E. Neuman and John F. Kennedy on the cover of *Mad* magazine. Stevie draws a deep breath as she turns the corner. Jack sees her and clams up, pressing his lips together in a tight, rigid line.

"Hey, Miss Stevie," says Eddie. "Looks like we're gonna have us a full house in here today."

"Hi, Eddie," she says, robotically opening her pocketbook for inspection. She looks at Jack; his eyes are puppy-dog sad and heavy-lidded. "Hi," she says.

"Catch you later, Eddie." Jack's already turned his back to her and is moving toward the turnstile.

"Jack. Jack? Hel-lo?" Stevie watches him walking quickly, practically sprinting to get away from her, and she snaps. She pushes through the turnstile and goes after him. "Hey, Jack, wait up—"

But he keeps walking. When he closes his office door, she barges in behind him.

"What do you want, Stevie?"

"I want us to get past this. This is ridiculous. We have to find a way to work together. My God, you're able to still work just fine with Patsy. And Wendy, too. Why not me?"

"Because—because you broke my heart," he says, realizing this sounds completely melodramatic. They were lovers, but they were not in love. Even after momentarily declaring themselves soulmates, they knew it wasn't true love.

"Oh, please, I did not break your heart," she says, calling him on this. "Your ego is what's broken, not your heart."

His eyebrows scrunch together tightly and ease apart as he squeezes his eyes shut and his shoulders start to shake. Uh-oh, she went too far. She's made him cry. This is what she's thinking until she sees that he's not crying at all. He's laughing.

"You are such a smart-ass," he says, mopping tears from his eyes. "God, I've missed you."

She chortles. "I've missed you, too, you big jerk."

And this is what it takes to get them to the other side of their affair. There they are, both of them laughing, even hugging, confessing how nervous they've been around each other, sharing all the stupid, silly things that have happened over the past few weeks that they've wanted to tell each other. They hug some more and laugh in a way that leaves them gasping for air.

After they've recovered, she asks how things are going with the Dream House project.

"Not well," he says. "I'm so behind schedule on this. I got nothing."

"Maybe I can help?" She does a little shoulder roll. "I have a few ideas. That is, if you want to hear them?"

Several weeks later, Jack and Stevie are holed up in his office late one night, just like old times, working on Barbie's Dream House. Stevie brings a unique sense of fashion and style that Jack needs and he brings the energy and his sheer genius. He's constructed the house and the furniture out of sturdy cardboard, thinking through every fold as if it were origami, already seeing the completed assembly inside his head. He doesn't even need to create a pattern first. He has pictured in his mind how the entire dollhouse will fold up into a lightweight carrying case. Meanwhile, Stevie's working out more color schemes and sleek designs for the furniture, basing the sofa on a Herman Miller design; the thin-edge bed is also a nod to Herman Miller. Jack's office floor is covered in color swatches, sketches and home decorating magazines.

Somehow it gets to be ten o'clock. They haven't eaten, too caught up in their work to realize they're both starving. Jack orders a pizza topped with pineapple—because it's her favorite and he can pick it off. He also opens a bottle of wine stored in his credenza.

"Want my crust?" she offers, knowing he likes that better than the fixings on top.

"Trade you for my pineapple."

"Deal."

Now that the breakup is behind them, they've learned to

become friends. Just friends. In many ways they make better friends than lovers. After having ravished each other's bodies, hurt each other deeply and cried in each other's arms, they've come out the other side with something stronger, even sweeter, and certainly more honest. He even tells her about the other women he's seeing. Maybe he does this to get a rise out of her, but Stevie's not fazed by Sheri with one *r*, one *i*, or Kimberly or Monica, or any of the others. Every Saturday she and Jack have a ten o'clock court time at his ritzy L.A. Country Club. Last week they saw Lenny Bruce at the Troubadour, and Jack gave Stevie two front-row tickets to a Frank Sinatra concert that he couldn't use. Things between them are clean, simple, easier now.

After they finish the pizza, Jack can see that he's pushed Stevie long past exhaustion. She's lying on his couch, her heels kicked off, her legs crossed at the ankles, her eyes heavy-lidded. He brings the wine over to her. She waves him off, but he refills her glass anyway. She's fighting to stay awake, while Jack, on the other hand, is just getting started. He's invigorated.

"C'mon," he says. "Get up, get up!" He grabs a bottle of pills from his desk and shakes out two tablets, washing one down with a gulp of wine.

"What's that you're taking?" she asks.

"Just some diet pills. They're great energy boosters. Here—" He hands her the other pill.

"Are you saying I'm fat?"

"I'm saying you're tired. These will give you some pep."

"No, thanks." She's tried pep pills before, and they made her queasy and edgy. Instead, she gets up and fixes a cup of coffee.

Forty-five minutes later, Jack is pacing. "What about crown molding? In white? Or maybe gold?"

She shakes her head. "Too formal."

"What about beams?"

"Too masculine," she says. "This isn't your castle, remember?"

"Good point." He pivots on his heel and walks the length of his office again.

"So here's a question," she says. "We have a double closet for Barbie's wardrobe, we have a hi-fi, a TV console, a bed—we gave her everything but a kitchen. Who has a house without a kitchen?"

"Ah, Barbie does."

"Yeah, but—"

"Do you cook?"

"Not if I can help it."

"Well, neither does Barbie."

Babies Having Babies

1962

One Sunday afternoon while Elliot is playing golf, Barbara stops by the Holmby Hills house. With her pocketbook still looped about her wrist, she stands in the kitchen, striking a defiant pose with one hand on her hip. Ruth's not sure what's coming. The last time Barbara unexpectedly turned up at the house, she and Allen had had a big argument. Over beef stroganoff. Apparently, he'd told her he didn't want it for dinner, but she'd gone ahead and made it anyway. That's the sort of thing—all it takes to poke a hole in the thin membrane of their marriage.

"I thought you might like to know," says Barbara, still in her fighter stance, "that Allen and I are having a baby."

Ruth looks at Barbara. She blinks. She lets out a soft jut of air as a marvelous thought comes to her: *My baby is having a baby.* It's ninety degrees outside, and despite all those misgivings about her son-in-law, Ruth's covered in goose bumps. Her eyes are misting over, too. For once, without having to make a conscious effort, she says and does all the right things. She embraces her daughter, congratulates her, asks how far along she is.

"I didn't think you'd be this happy," says Barbara, her voice suggesting she's walking into a trap.

"Why wouldn't I be happy? A baby's a wonderful thing," says Ruth, still smiling. "How are you feeling? Have you had any morning sickness?"

"Not a bit," says Barbara.

Ruth gets the impression that even if Barbara was sick as a dog, she wouldn't let on. "Well, be grateful. That's miserable. And I don't know why they call it *morning* sickness—it can hit you morning, noon or night."

"Well, I've never felt better," says Barbara.

Ruth doesn't want this to become a battle of wills, so she tries a different approach, one of nostalgia. "I remember when I was pregnant with you. Your father and I were so excited. We couldn't wait to meet you. And I just knew—I had a feeling—that you were a girl."

"Was I an easy baby?"

"You?" Ruth laughs. "Hardly. Even before you were born, you started giving me a hard time," she says teasingly. "And at one point you gave us a real scare."

"What kind of scare?"

Ruth takes a breath, takes herself back to one of the most terrifying times of her life. "I was already pretty far along. It started with horrible cramps. And these weren't like ordinary cramps. They were sharp, debilitating. And then I started bleeding. We couldn't stop it." She sees Barbara's eyes grow wide. "My doctor put me on strict bed rest. All I could do was stay in bed for eight whole weeks, just waiting for you to arrive. So see"—Ruth laughs—"even back then you didn't want me working."

Barbara cracks a tight smile. "Were you on bed rest with Ken, too?"

"No, no. He was a different story. I should have known from the start how opposite you two would be. Ken was late. My belly was out to here"—she stretches her arms out as far as they will go. "You should have seen me waddling around, trying to get on the bus—"

"*You* took a bus?" Barbara is incredulous.

"All the time back then. You'd ride it with me."

Barbara goes quiet, reflective. So many things about her mother she didn't know. After a moment she asks, "Do you think I'll be a good mother?"

"You kidding me? You're a natural, kiddo."

"How can you be so sure?"

"I've already seen you in action with Ken. You couldn't wait to have a baby brother. You were good with him, too. Better than I was. You always wanted to hold him, give him his bottle. You even wanted to burp him. You weren't too crazy about changing his diaper, though."

Barbara is laughing now, her fingers delicately covering her mouth. It's the first time Ruth's seen her this relaxed in months. It's like she's forgotten that she's supposed to be at odds with her mother, and Ruth is reminded of the sweet, loving Barbara she used to know.

The Sisterhood

1963

First thing on a Monday morning, Charlotte escorts a trio of young ladies around the office, giving them the grand tour, pausing here and there to make introductions. Stevie sees them and thinks, *There they are—the new Barbie fashion designers.*

She's known this day was coming. With Barbie, plus the Ken doll, the Dream House and now Midge, the workload is too much for just her and Charlotte. So now, in addition to Stevie, there's Dee Pryor, Ellen Watson and Carol Spencer. They're all young, about Stevie's age. Dee is soft-spoken and has a little cherub's face that fits her angelic personality. She doesn't swear, doesn't drink or smoke. She seems frail and delicate, hardly someone who could stand up to Ruth, and yet here she is. Ellen appears to be just the opposite. Like Stevie's former classmate Bob Mackie, Ellen got her start in costume design. She wears heavy dramatic makeup with thick eyeliner winged out at the sides. Carol is the youngest among them and has a terrific head of reddish-brown curls. Fresh out of the Minneapolis School of Fine Arts, she is every bit as friendly as she is talented.

After the introductions are made, Charlotte calls all of them into her office, which is small to begin with. The surface of her desk is flooded with pattern books, fabric swatches, pincushions, fitting dolls and dozens of fashion magazines. There are only three chairs and Stevie opts for perching on the window ledge, letting the new girls sit. Out of seniority, she feels it's her place to do this.

"Okay," says Charlotte, her hands splayed out before her on her desk, "let me be very blunt—" As if she knows how to be any other way. The only person more direct than Charlotte is Ruth. "We're entering a new phase with Barbie. You're all wonderfully talented, but only the best of the best designs will make it into production. That means you'll be competing against each other. But don't worry," she says with a good-natured laugh, "a little friendly competition is healthy."

Is it? Suddenly Stevie and the other designers are eyeing each other through a different lens. Now they aren't just coworkers; they're rivals. Not the best environment for promoting creativity and risk-taking, which are what have led to some of Barbie's most exciting outfits and accessories. In the 900 series, for example, they created that charming straw cartwheel hat, and there was the matching tote bag in *Suburban Shopper*. And what about the red hat and teeny-tiny gold compact mirror with the pink powder puff and a *B* for Barbie embossed on the top for *Roman Holiday*?

"And, of course," says Charlotte, "Stevie and I will be here to help if you have any questions or need assistance with something."

It doesn't take long for Charlotte's so-called friendly competition to become a breeding ground for jealousy and paranoia. If one of them sees that another designer is in a meeting with Charlotte or Jack—or, God forbid, Ruth—they'll start to worry. Dee hides her sketchpads inside her locked desk drawer. Ellen keeps her fitting dolls out of sight, and Stevie and Carol make Mia and the other sample makers promise not to share their ideas with the others.

And yet somehow the four of them get along beautifully. After just a few weeks, they form a sisterhood of sorts. They all sit together at lunch in the cafeteria. They wait for one another after work so they can all pile into someone's car and head over to the beach. They attend fashion shows together, and on the weekends they all go scouting for fabrics and do some window-shopping, hoping for inspiration. When Ruth snaps at Ellen one day, the others circle around her in the bathroom while she cries off all her eyeliner. When Dee finds Barbie and Ken on her desk, naked and posed in a compromising position, Stevie goes after the culprits— Twist and Frankie—and tells them to knock it off. And they all take Carol out to celebrate when she dazzles Charlotte and Ruth with her very first design—*Crisp 'n Cool*—inspired by First Lady Jackie Kennedy.

Not that she's proud of this, but Stevie can't help but feel a bit threatened by the newcomers. With each victory scored by the other designers, she finds little ways to solidify her place in the Barbie team. She plays big sister to these girls, showing them the ropes and at the same time letting them know her place in the Mattel pecking order. She tells Ellen why one of her designs wouldn't work because of Barbie's arm length—something Stevie learned early on. She is also quick to point out to Dee that her step-and-repeat pattern is still too large, too busy for Barbie's frame. In her own way, Stevie lets the others know that while she's here to help them, she's also the elder statesman.

Tweaks and Transformations

Ginger is out of the office for two weeks due to an "unspecified medical procedure," which Jack has sponsored. The poor girl had been suffering from a sinus infection, which led to the detection of a deviated septum, which led to a discussion about having the bump in her nose removed along with the internal blockage. Such a sweet girl, and so loyal and invaluable to him, and she'd been unhappy and self-conscious about her nose all her life. He couldn't bear for her to be so miserable, not if he could help it. So before he knew it, Jack was calling around to plastic surgeons. She couldn't afford to have it fixed, so he told her he'd pay for it. No big deal.

But in Ginger's absence, despite the attractive Kelly Girl temporarily filling in for her, Jack is lost. And it's only been one day. How is he going to manage without Ginger for two whole weeks? He's unable to make sense of his mail, all the office memos or updates on the Ken crisis. They used a new special flocking material for his hair and customers are complaining that it's rubbing off. Technically Twist is overseeing this, but Jack oversees Twist. He has to be on top of things. And even though the Kelly Girl has signed all of Mattel's required confidentiality agreements, neither Jack nor Ruth is comfortable sharing information with an outsider. For all they know, she's a plant, someone Louis Marx put in place to spy on them.

As Jack stretches out on his bearskin rug, staring at the ceiling, he realizes how much he's come to depend on Ginger for everything from his morning coffee to doing all his reading to stroking his bruised ego after a rough meeting or project setback.

There's a tentative knock on his door and Stevie steps inside. "You weren't in the status meeting this morning. You okay?"

"I'm better now." He sits up, cross-legged, on the rug.

"What's going on?" she asks.

Jack would like to confide in her, ask for her help in Ginger's absence, but his shame is too great. "Do me a favor," he says, knowing his request is going to sound odd. "Would you just read this one thing for me?" He gets up and hands her the package with the Ken updates. "Just tell me if there's anything I need to do. My mind's on a million other things. I can't focus on that piddly shit right now."

Stevie opens the packet. "Let's see here." She shuffles through the pages. "Looks like all three Ken dolls—the blond, the brown and the darker-haired Kens"—she turns the page—"yep, looks like they're all having hair issues." She sorts through more pages. "I never understood why you used flocking for Ken's hair in the first place. Why didn't you just root his hair like you did for Barbie?"

"It would have taken too long, and it was too expensive."

She is still going through the packet when Jack's phone buzzes. The Kelly Girl's voice crackles over the intercom. "I have a Dr. Geoffries's office on line two for you?"

Jack jogs over to his desk and picks up to get her off the loudspeaker. "She's out of surgery," says Dr. Geoffries's nurse. "Everything went very well. No complications."

———

Two weeks later, when Ginger returns to work, she looks like hell. Her nose is bandaged in a splint and there's a wad of gauze secured beneath her nostrils. Her eyes are swollen with purple and yellowish bruises. Rumors immediately begin to circulate—she was in a car accident, she was mugged, she walked into a door, she had a nose job.

"I had a deviated septum," Ginger corrects anyone who asks. "I needed surgery to have it fixed so I could breathe."

She heals rather quickly, and by the end of the month the bruising is almost completely gone. And so is the bump in her nose.

"Deviated septum my ass," says Frankie. "She had a nose job."

"Looks a helluva lot better than she did before," says Twist.

And Ginger's transformation doesn't stop there.

A few days later, she joins Stevie and the others in the cafeteria, and Stevie notices the only thing on Ginger's tray is a bowl of chicken tortilla soup.

"That's all you're having for lunch?" she asks.

"Oh, I'm reducing," Ginger says, her soup spoon paused above her bowl. "I've already lost twenty-three pounds. Those pills Jack gave me are really working. He told me today that I'm 'looking good.'"

Poor Ginger. The smile on her face is enough to break Stevie's heart. For years now Ginger's been trying to catch Jack's eye. Poor, poor Ginger. She's one of those girls cursed with a beautiful sister, one of those girls who never had a date to the prom, was never asked to play Spin the Bottle. She thinks that winning Jack's love will erase a lifetime of romantic disappointments. He is her first thought when she wakes each morning, her last thought as she drifts off to sleep each night. She will do anything to catch his attention and affection.

It's not until she gets bangs, lightens her hair yet again and starts wearing it pulled back in a high ponytail that it dawns on everyone, including Jack, that Ginger is trying to look like Barbie.

Welcome to the Castle

A few months after Ginger's surgery, Jack enlists her help in throwing a housewarming party, despite the Castle perpetually being under construction and his having a bulldozer parked on the front lawn. He's envisioning a luau, complete with a pig on a spit, an apple in its mouth, its skin as tan and glossy as polished leather. He invites people from the office and a handful of Hollywood celebrities, like Burt Lancaster and his next-door neighbor, Zsa Zsa Gabor. The party is a great success and Jack discovers that he loves entertaining. *Who can be lonely when you have a houseful of people?*

The following week he throws a barbecue, and the week after that it's a pool party where he brings in sand—lots and lots of sand—for beach volleyball in the backyard. Before long he's hosting two and three blowout bashes a week. Soon word on the street is that no one throws a party like Jack Ryan. People line up to get in, and no one balks at having to pay at the door. A hefty $20 covers their food, their booze and the occasional live entertainment. The drugs—mostly marijuana—cost extra and aren't offered until after dark.

There's a Gatsby-like quality to a Jack Ryan party. He's never met some of his guests, and as he snakes through the crowd, he'll hear his name tossed about: "Jack Ryan comes from oil money down in Texas." "I hear he's considering a run for the White House." "You know, his first wife was Rita Hayworth . . ."

Jack has also recently amassed a group of young college boys from UCLA. A handful of them—surfer types, muscular and bronzed—had crashed one of his parties and simply never left. Now they live at the Castle, and in exchange for room and board, they park cars and serve food and drinks. They keep up the maintenance on the yard, the tennis courts, the swimming pool, and clean up after the never-ending parties and construction work. At last count there were six of them living at the Castle, and Jack doesn't mind at all. It assures him that he'll never be alone.

While the UCLA boys help out, the bulk of the party planning comes down to Ginger. Jack's wife never attends his bashes. She and the girls stay sequestered in their wing of the estate with its own entrance and a sign out front that reads: *Private. Do Not Enter.* In Barbara's absence, Ginger gladly plays the role of hostess. She doesn't mind that in addition to her daily responsibilities at Mattel, she now also arranges for all the food, which can be anything from ribs and hot dogs on giant grills in the yard to filet mignon and lobsters. Ginger also makes sure all the bars are well stocked with scotch, vodka, bourbon, gin—all of it top-shelf—along with cases of his favorite wines. Ginger prances about like she's the queen of the Castle and goes out of her way to let all the other women know this is her turf. If any of them so much as reaches into a cupboard for a glass, Ginger is there, saying, "I'll get that for you."

Jack throws so many parties, they all start to blur together in his mind. One evening he makes the hour drive from Mattel to Bel Air. Pulling up to the Castle, he sees another party—which he forgot was on the calendar—is underway. *Peachy!* He'd been dreading the thought of walking into a quiet house.

He gets out of his car, tosses the keys to one of his UCLA boys to park and heads inside, delighted to be greeted by the chaos, the loud music, the clouds of smoke and drunken guests. He spots Joan Fontaine and Dennis Hopper in his living room. Ginger hands him a glass of J&B and a beautiful redhead passes him a joint. He's in heaven; his entire body is levitating.

Jack's always been a big drinker, but lately he has no shut-off valve. There's no such thing as too much in his world. People are dancing, spilling drinks on the floor, putting cigarettes out on end tables. Someone has helped themself to a bubble bath in his sunken bathtub. In the morning Jack will have the UCLA boys clean and he'll replace whatever gets damaged. It's a small price to pay for having a houseful of friends and people who adore him.

The hour grows later, and as the crowd thins out, Jack wanders outside, where, to his delight, more guests are hanging out by the swimming pool. Lit from underneath, the water shimmers as it laps against the tiled walls. People are relaxing on the chaise longues. Ginger appears to be passed out in one of them. The UCLA boys are gathering empty glasses, folding up the lawn tables and chairs.

Another woman in very tall, very slender heels is tottering at the edge of the pool, a drink in one hand, a cigarette in the other. She calls over to Jack, "Looks like the party's over." She laughs, takes one step backward and—*Splash!*

Water sprays all over Jack. The woman is in the pool, windmilling her arms. There's a second splash, a third and fourth, and suddenly people are stripping off their clothes and getting down to their underwear or nothing at all before plunging into the water.

Jack kicks off his elevator shoes, shimmies out of his shirt and trousers. "Looks to me like this party's just getting started."

Don't You Do What Your Big Sister Done

Weddings and babies. Ruth is consumed with both. At the age of forty-seven, she's now a grandmother. Barbara has a little girl, Cheryl, and while Ruth adores her granddaughter, she doesn't envy the road ahead for Barbara. After having her children, Ruth was miserable being stuck at home and couldn't wait to get back to work. Just as Sarah had done with her, Ruth shlepped Barbara to the office and along on sales calls. When Ken was born, she could thankfully afford a sitter while she went back to work.

Barbara is up four and five times a night for feedings, and there's the diaper changing, the bottles, the endless loads of laundry. And Allen is of no help. He can't reconcile what's happened to the Barbara he married versus Barbara the mother. They argue over the baby stroller left in the doorway, and why dinner isn't ready when he gets home from his job at the insurance company—the one he only took because he now has a wife and child to support. He hates the dirty diapers left in the tub, the baby bottles and pacifiers scattered everywhere, along with blankets that smell of sour spit-up.

Ruth can see it in Barbara's eyes—after four years, the reality of marriage, not to mention motherhood, is nothing like what she expected. Barbara will never come out and say it, but Ruth knows she's feeling chained to the house; all that freedom she took for granted is now gone. She's drowning and depressed. Ruth has offered to pay for a housekeeper or even a sitter, but Barbara doesn't want her daughter raised the way she was. She feels it's her duty to do this all herself. Ruth offers to help but is never available when Barbara decides she needs her mother: *Oh, honey, I have a meeting that day. Oh, I'd love to but I'm going to be out of town. I'll try but you should get a backup in case my appointment runs late. Let me see if I can juggle my schedule*, which, of course, she never can.

On top of this, Ken is now married, too. Two years ago, right after his high school graduation, just like his sister, Ken proposed to Suzie. He was tired of all the doll jokes and sick innuendo about him sleeping with his sister and not having a penis. He figured the quickest way to shut everyone up was to get married.

But he's only nineteen. He's a talented musician and every bit as creative as his father. He has his whole life ahead of him, and Ruth's bewildered by his choice. She doesn't know how *her* children—of all children—could have chosen to follow such traditional paths.

Marriage and babies. It's all she hears about. Even at work. A steady flood of fan mail arrives every day from little girls asking when Barbie and Ken are getting married. On top of that, they want Barbie to have a baby. More than a few letters have even suggested that Barbie is selfish for not marrying Ken, for not giving him a family.

Tucking another letter back into its envelope, Ruth stabs out a cigarette and wonders why marriage and babies are the end goal for these young girls. Her own daughter is proof that a husband and child don't guarantee happiness. Ruth wants Barbie to set a new example. Show them a different road they can walk down, one where marriage and children could be a stop along the way rather than a foregone conclusion, and definitely not the end of their journey.

Ruth's already formed a new department just to manage the Barbie fan mail and instructs the secretaries to respond to each of those letters by saying: *Having a boyfriend is swell, but Barbie is not ready to settle down and get married. She's not ready to have a baby yet when there's so much more for her to do.*

And while her staff is writing letters, Ruth gives Barbie more careers. So now in addition to Barbie the fashion designer, Barbie the nightclub singer, Barbie the airline stewardess, there'll be Barbie the ballerina, Barbie the nurse—anything but Barbie the wife and mother.

"But c'mon, Ruth," says Loomis, always looking to challenge her, "you can't have Barbie stay single forever."

"And why not?"

"It's only natural that Barbie would marry Ken and have a kid," he says, unwrapping a stick of Juicy Fruit and folding it in half before popping it in his mouth. "There's a lot to be said for traditional play models. You see what's happening with Kenner's Easy-Bake Oven."

"Big whoop," says Jack. "It's a hundred-watt light bulb. That's what cooks the little cakes. That's their big fucking idea."

"Yeah, but it's selling like hotcakes—no pun intended," says Loomis, rolling the foiled gum wrapper into a BB of a ball. "I think we need to follow a more traditional course for Barbie."

"Jesus! Do any of you remember why I created her in the first place?" says Ruth. "Look how she's changed the marketplace. We practically built Mattel on Barbie's back. You all have jobs because of Barbie. If you turn her into a housewife and mother—where do we go from there?"

"We can grow the line over time by introducing a second baby, and then a third—at some point, hell, we could even give her twins," says Loomis. "What's wrong with that?"

"For starters," says Ruth, "it puts us in the baby doll category, where we never wanted Barbie to be in the first place. On top of that, those baby dolls would be the size of a thimble. You wanna play with a thimble? You say you'll grow the line by adding more babies, but what do you do with the babies she's already got? They never grow up. They don't age. You can't just keep adding more infants—she'll end up with a litter. And then there's Barbie's wardrobe. Right now seventy-six percent of Barbie's revenue comes from her wardrobe. She's a fashion doll, not a mother. We can't dress her in aprons and housecoats. It's a step backward and it'll cut off future revenue streams. Independent Barbie, single Barbie, can do anything. She can take on new careers, new fashions. She can keep up with the times. Reflect the way women are changing. The way society's changing, too. I don't want little girls to think conventionally and see themselves as just wives and mothers. That's what baby dolls are for. Not Barbie." She sits back, exhausted, exhilarated and oddly surprised by her own words and what Barbie really means to her. Yes, Barbie is lucrative, but—and Ruth loathes being overly sentimental—she recognizes that her doll has also come to symbolize something far greater than their paychecks.

The men shift in their chairs, and after an uncomfortable silence, Jack speaks up. "She's right, guys."

"Of course I'm right. I've been right about Barbie all along. You'd think by now you'd trust my instincts."

"But we still have to address the whole nurturing issue," says Lewis. "We can't ignore that people think Barbie's selfish."

"Well," says Ruth, tossing her pen onto the table, "we're not going to fix that by giving her a husband and baby. We have to find another way."

Stevie is in a design rut and stays late one night to read through the latest flood of fan mail, hoping for inspiration. She's looking for clues about how little girls want to play with their Barbies, especially when it includes Ken.

Ruth is about to leave for the day when she notices Stevie in the conference room, sitting before a pile of letters. "Anything intriguing in there?" she asks.

"Just more girls wanting Barbie to marry Ken and have a baby." Stevie shakes her head. "I just don't get it."

"You shouldn't be surprised," says Ruth, taking a seat and shrugging off her jacket.

She pulls out a cigarette and Stevie realizes she intends on staying for a bit. This isn't one of her pass-throughs. Stevie feels a little honored. It's not every day that a designer gets time like this with Ruth, outside of a meeting, just one-on-one.

Ruth picks up a letter, reads a few lines and sets it back down, nudging it away as if to distance herself from it. All this nonsense about Barbie being selfish. She has no idea how to change that perception. "I blame society. Just look at the magazines and what's on television. You've got programs like *The Donna Reed Show* and *I Love Lucy*. The women on those shows are always stuck in the home."

"I would go stir-crazy. I don't get how my mother does it," says Stevie. "She has zero interests of her own—I mean, not even a hobby. She doesn't do anything all day long other than wait on my father. And when he's at work, she's *waiting* for him to come home so she can *wait* on him some more. If that's what marriage is supposed to be like, I would rather stay single the rest of my life."

Ruth laughs, reaching for an ashtray. "I assure you, not all marriages are like that."

"Well, obviously yours isn't."

"Thankfully, I have a very modern husband. Keep looking. There's some good ones out there."

"I'm not in any hurry." She picks up another letter.

"Good for you."

"Listen to this," Stevie says, reading from the letter. "*My Barbie can't wait to marry Ken and learn to keep house.* It's like they're trying to imitate their mothers or something."

"Well of course they are," says Ruth. "That's what little girls do. They imitate the women in their lives. They're influenced by what they see around them."

"Well, your mother must not have been very conventional."

Ruth nearly coughs. "You can say that again. But I take after my sister, not my mother. My big sister was the one who raised me. And there wasn't anything conventional about her."

Stevie wonders what happened to Ruth's mother, but she doesn't dare ask.

"Sarah was a woman ahead of her time," Ruth continues. "She owned a drugstore, and I watched her deal with bill collectors, bankers, hustlers. I saw her chase thugs out of her store who were trying to shoplift." Ruth smiles, takes a long, luxurious drag off her cigarette, lost in her own reverie. "Sarah was very wise. She was married, but Louie"—Ruth shakes her head—"he wasn't much help. She never expected him to take care of her. She taught me not to depend on a man or on anyone but myself."

Stevie has never seen this side of Ruth before, and she is a sponge, taking in every word. Little does she know that as Ruth speaks, a new idea is beginning to crackle alive inside her. For days now, she's been stewing about those claims that Barbie is selfish and wondering how she's going to remedy it. And now she realizes she has the perfect solution: Barbie can be like Sarah.

And so it's because of Ruth's big sister that Skipper is born.

Going Public

t's November and it's cold in New York City, which gives Ruth an excuse to wear the fur coat Elliot bought her for her forty-sixth birthday last year. She and Elliot flew into town with Henry Pursell, Mattel's general counsel. In addition to overseeing the never-ending lawsuit with Louis Marx, he's helping them take Mattel public, putting them on the New York Stock Exchange. Henry's there with Ruth and Elliot for a meeting with a group of underwriters representing some of Wall Street's biggest investment banks. The whole thing is so heady. Who would have ever guessed all those years ago, when Elliot and Matt were working out of the garage and Ruth was hawking their wares, that they were building a company that would one day go public? Ruth still can't get over it, and God, how she wishes Sarah were alive to see this.

Their meeting is at the Harrington, one of those stately, dark-paneled old-money clubs that smell of aftershave, along with pipe and cigar smoke. Chilled to the bone, Ruth rubs her gloved hands together as the three of them enter the foyer, the clacking of cue balls coming from the billiards room off to the side. Everywhere

Ruth looks she sees tuxedoed men eyeing her askance, as if she's done something wrong.

And apparently she has. An older man with a few gray hairs streaked across his pink pate comes rushing up. "Ah, excuse me? May I help you?"

"We're from Mattel," says Elliot. "We have a meeting with Goldman Sachs, Lehman Brothers and—"

"Oh, of course, of course. Mr. Handler. Mr. Pursell, I presume." He smiles, bows. "Welcome. We've been expecting you."

Ruth looks at Elliot and Henry and cocks an eyebrow as if to say, *What am I, chopped liver?*

"The other gentlemen are already here, upstairs." The bald man snaps his fingers, and a younger tuxedoed man appears at his side. "Please show Mr. Handler and Mr. Pursell to the Franklin Room." He smiles and gestures toward a bank of elevators.

As Ruth starts to follow them, the older man places his hand on her shoulder. "Ah, excuse me, miss—I'm afraid this is a gentlemen's club." He tilts his head and smiles as if the rest is implied.

She smiles back. "Well, then, if this is a *gentlemen's* club, I suggest you behave like one and take your goddamn hands off me." She brushes him aside and keeps going.

The older man leaps in front of her. "I'm—I'm very sorry, madam," he stammers, "but we do not allow women here inside the Harrington."

Elliot and Henry backtrack to her side.

"My apologies, Mr. Pursell, Mr. Handler. But those are the club rules."

She laughs. "Well, you're gonna have to bend your rules, buddy. I have a meeting to get to."

"This meeting can't take place without her," says Elliot.

The man is unsettled, thinking. "Very well, then," he says eventually, turning to his lackey. "Timothy will take you gentlemen to the Franklin Room and I'll see to it that the young lady joins you in there as well."

Young lady? Ruth rolls her eyes. "Go on"—she motions to Elliot and Henry—"I'll meet you up there."

"Now, if you'll follow me," says the older man. "I believe you'll be more comfortable coming this way."

Ruth laughs. "What are you gonna do, take me up the service elevator?" The man's face turns as pink as his scalp. "I was joking," she says.

"Well, we could take the stairs, but—"

"The service elevator it is." She's not willing to give him the benefit of seeing her humiliated. She squares her shoulders and follows him back through the kitchen and down a long bare hallway. They step into the service elevator, and she stares the older man down. By the time they reach the Franklin Room she sees pinpricks of sweat sprouting on his brow. Good.

Elliot and Henry are seated around a shiny conference room table along with representatives from Goldman Sachs, Lehman Brothers, Chemical Bank and Chase Manhattan Bank. It's clear when she enters the room that the bankers regard her as Elliot's wife, assuming she's tagged along to New York for the shopping and theater. Ruth makes her way around the table, firmly shaking one suit's hand after another before settling into the empty chair next to Elliot's.

"Ah, Mrs. Handler," says the man from Goldman Sachs, "we'll get you another chair. That seat is actually for Mattel's head of finance."

"Good," she says, "because I *am* Mattel's head of finance."

She's flustered him, and the others, too. It's so easy to knock them off their game. If only she'd known how to deal with men like this in her twenties and thirties. When she was younger, she played a room like this differently. Following her sister's advice about balancing her toughness with a feminine ruffle, she came into business meetings armed in a low-cut dress, high heels, red lipstick and an extra dab of perfume. But now she's found her own balance; she's still feminine, but she's not about to give another man a cheap shot down her blouse or strategically cross her legs. She's earned her place at the table—this is her goddamn company they're discussing—and she can hold her own, on her own terms.

One of the bankers begins passing out packets in neat folders that have been meticulously prepared. They're still directing the conversation toward Elliot and Henry when they discuss the size of the float—how many shares would be newly issued by Mattel and how many shares would be sold by Elliot and other insiders.

Ruth listens, and when they're done speaking, she takes over. "And now, gentlemen," she says, "I have a few questions for you." In rapid fire, she asks: "What's the underwriting fee? What do you propose for the road show? What's your time frame? How many cities are we talking about? When can I expect to see the order book? And lastly, gentlemen, what will the price range be on the offering?"

By the end of the meeting, no one has any doubt as to who's in charge. When they emerge from the Franklin Room, she boldly steps into the elevator with the men. No one says a word, not even the elevator operator, whose skin goes ashen.

They step into the lobby and the quiet is unsettling, especially since it's full of men gathered around a television set, their heads hung low, a few of them openly sobbing—so engulfed with despair, they don't notice the woman in their midst.

Ruth turns to Elliot and Henry. "What's going on? Did somebody die or something?"

One of the men overhears her and says, "Yes. It's the president. President Kennedy is dead."

Points of Articulation

1964

Kennedy's assassination throws the country into a state of grief and uncertainty. A collective innocence has been shattered. It isn't just a turbulent time for the nation; the start of 1964 is equally challenging for Ruth. Even though Mattel's initial public offering exceeded everyone's expectations, it was followed by an upset. After years of back-and-forth, the lawsuit with Louis Marx and Mattel's countersuit are both dismissed. The judge has awarded no damages, and both sides must cover their own legal fees. Ruth wants to appeal, but according to the lawyers, they can't reintroduce the suit. It's over and done with. Elliot tells her she should be relieved, that it could have gone the other way. At least now Barbie is out from under the cloud of Bild Lilli and no one is the wiser.

But Ruth doesn't even have time to appreciate that, because she's recently discovered another lump in her breast. After the biopsy proves benign, Elliot pleads with her to quit smoking. She's tried before. Most efforts only last a matter of days, sometimes only hours. Once she did manage to go three and a half weeks without a cigarette, but when she stepped on the scale and saw that she'd gained five pounds, she went back to smoking. This time, though, after her latest health scare, her doctor recommended a hypnotist who's had success with other smokers.

So now Ruth sits in the waiting room at Dr. Mandry's office, hypnotist to the stars, claiming such clients as Montgomery Clift and Kim Novak. When the nurse slides back the glass window to say that the doctor is running behind schedule, Ruth doesn't mind a bit. She's not quite ready to quit smoking. What is she going to do with her gold cigarette case, the one with her initials engraved on top? Not to mention the matching lighter. Just thinking of all she's being asked to give up makes her anxious, makes her want a cigarette.

She's brought some work with her, hoping it will take her mind off things. She starts by checking the *Wall Street Journal* to see how Mattel's stock is doing. Yesterday's close was at an all-time high of $36.47. She and Elliot always said if it ever hit $40 a share, they'd buy his-and-hers Rolls-Royces. It seemed absurd at the time, but now it's a real possibility. Hopefully Skipper's upcoming launch will give their stock another boost and send them car shopping.

Ruth sets her newspaper aside and begins reviewing the weekly W Report. This is a comprehensive list of each toy Mattel sells—capturing the production status, shipping and sales data dating back to the product's launch. To her this is the most important document to cross her desk. She's pleased to see that the new Midge doll is performing so well. As she should have expected, after Midge came out last year, the mail flooded in: *Poor Midge, she's all alone. A third wheel* . . . So they created a boyfriend for Midge: the Allan doll, purposely spelled with an *a* to somewhat pacify Barbara's objections.

"Mother, can you please just leave my family out of this," she said when Ruth first told her.

Barbara was furious, but Allen was flattered. He loved the idea and felt like for the first time he was an accepted member of the Handler clan.

And the Handler extended family is growing in all directions. Not only is Barbara pregnant again, but Ken's wife is also expecting. After this last cancer scare, Ruth just wants to live long enough to watch her grandchildren grow up and is determined to quit smoking.

Finally, Ruth's called into the doctor's office. She's trying to remain open-minded and hopeful about this process. There's a comfortable recliner, dim lighting, lots of breathing, lots of counting backward, lots of closing her eyes, picturing black smoke with each imaginary puff she takes. The doctor's voice is flat, monotone and frankly monotonous. He could put her to sleep faster than he could hypnotize her. Still she tries, breathing, counting, picturing . . . This goes on for the better part of forty minutes and all Ruth can think about is work and how soon she can get the hell out of here and have her next cigarette.

"Hey, come here." Jack pulls Stevie into his office just as she's getting ready to leave for the day. "I want to show you something. Look at this—" He holds out a twelve-inch plastic male doll with bulky shoulders, arms, and legs, dressed in army fatigues.

"Has Ken been working out? Or did he get drafted?"

"That's not Ken. That, my dear, is a prototype of G.I. Joe— *America's Movable Fighting Man.*"

Stevie sets her pocketbook on his desk and drapes her raincoat over his chair. Picking up G.I. Joe, she fiddles with his arms and legs.

"Would you look at the way he's constructed?" Jack says

excitedly. "We're talking nineteen points of articulation. Everything on this guy moves. The head, the neck—" Jack takes G.I. Joe from Stevie to demonstrate, twisting limbs and joints. "Look at the shoulders, the biceps—even the ankles. Un-fucking-believable. We need to do something like this for Barbie."

She arches an eyebrow. "You want to give Barbie biceps?"

"I want her to move. To come alive like this."

"Where did he even come from?"

"Hasbro."

"Really? How'd you get your hands on their prototype?"

"Oh, I have my sources."

"I'm afraid to ask what that means."

He laughs, rippling his eyebrows suggestively.

"Be careful. Remember, you're sleeping with the enemy."

"Oh, I'd hardly call her the enemy." Jack glances again at G.I. Joe. Reaching for his pocket recorder, he pushes the button and says: "More points of articulation needed for Barbie. Per Hasbro's fighting man." He clicks off the tape recorder.

"Well," she says, "just don't go giving away any trade secrets during pillow talk."

"Never." He smiles, realizing for the first time that she's got her coat and pocketbook with her, that she was on her way out. "Where are you rushing off to?" he asks.

"The Ferus," she says, slipping into her raincoat and smoothing down her collar. "There's a John Altoon exhibit opening tonight."

"Sounds fun," he says, feeling a prickle of residual jealousy surfacing. It just happens from time to time of its own accord, something he can't control any more than he can control the weather. "So," he says as casually as he can make it sound, "who ya going with?"

"No one."

"No one? You're going alone? By yourself?" He's both relieved and impressed. He could never do something like that, take himself to a museum or an art gallery. Never in a million years.

The Ferus Gallery is crowded, and Stevie's as fascinated by the people as she is the artwork. There are lots of shaggy-haired men, and women with exotic eye makeup and jewelry, clustered together in circles that seem to be by invite only. It's easy to spot the artists in the room, the ones who possess an effortless cool. They're highly stylized with expensive shoes, the right eyewear, cigarette in one hand, drink in the other. Then there are the couples like the pair across the way who are not entirely comfortable with each other or with the room. Stevie assumes this is their first—and probably their last—date, whereas another couple standing in the back are just as enraptured with each other as they are the paintings. The woman stands in front of the man, leaning into his chest as he wraps his arms about her waist, his chin propped on her shoulder. Couples like that send a deep ache to Stevie's heart. They're the ones who make her want to be in love. In *real* love, and with the right person—if such a person even exists.

She shifts her attention back to the art. She's a novice and doesn't really know exactly what she's looking at. If asked, she'd say Altoon's work is kinetic, crackling with color and extreme brushstrokes. They might laugh, consider her a fraud, but she's not pretending to be part of the West Coast art scene. Far as she can tell, she's the only woman there by herself. She doesn't care. No one's paying attention to her anyway, and she didn't want to deprive herself of an abstract expressionist opening just because she's not part of the in crowd and not part of a couple, either.

Your Girl's in Trouble

Ruth and Elliot are having dinner at Musso & Frank Grill on Hollywood Boulevard with their financial advisor, Bob Mitchell. Bob's a trusted friend and has been with them since the early Burp Gun days.

Over grenadine of beef with béarnaise sauce, he launches into a recap of Mattel's success. "You're the undisputed king and queen of the toy industry," he says. "Your sales have doubled in the past three years. Incredible." Bob dabs his mouth, sets his napkin aside and consults his files. "Thanks to Barbie, you currently have"—he licks his thumb and flips through the pages—"more than twelve percent market share. This is fantastic, but"—he pauses for emphasis—"we need to look to the future. Your stockholders are going to expect you to sustain and even exceed this kind of growth."

Elliot blows out a deep, doubtful breath. "How?"

"The easiest thing to do is start acquiring other toy companies. That'll give Mattel more bulk and keep the profits growing at a steady rate."

"But we can't just buy other toy companies and turn them into little Mattels," says Ruth.

"Actually," says Bob, taking a sip of wine, "I think you can. I want to introduce you to someone who's an ace with acquisitions. His name is Seymour Rosenberg. Used to be a patent attorney. Worked for Howard Hughes before he joined Litton Industries. He's looking for the right opportunity, and I think Mattel could be it. They say Rosenberg's a true maestro when it comes to M and A." Bob signals for the check. "I think he's just the guy to guide you all the way to the top."

The following week they meet with Seymour Rosenberg. He arrives at Mattel with all the Wall Street swagger Ruth's expecting. He's short and stocky and wears an expensive tailored suit, a silk tie and a chunky Rolex watch. As they give him a tour of the offices, he comments on all the attractive women who work there. They introduce him to Jack and Charlotte and to all the department heads. No one knows exactly why he's there.

Later that night over dinner at the Dresden, Rosenberg closes his menu, shakes a Cartier cuff link out from his jacket sleeve and says, "I'm not gonna mince words here—your girl's in trouble."

"What?" Ruth and Elliot say in unison.

"I hate to say it, but I'm afraid Barbie's in for some rough times." He tells them that the women's liberation movement has their claws out and they're coming for Barbie. "They want to take her down."

Ruth finds this hard to believe. Despite all the naysayers—who have been in Barbie's orbit since the very beginning—the average ten-year-old girl owns four Barbies, and Mattel is issuing more merchandise each quarter. Barbie was on the *Dean Martin Show*, for God's sake. And besides, they're planning to introduce two exciting new Barbies.

Earlier that month, Jack rushed into Ruth's office holding a prototype of a new doll he's been working on. "I'd like to see G.I. Joe do this," he said, demonstrating his latest Barbie innovation, Twist 'n Turn Barbie. And that was right on the heels of Jack developing a Barbie with bendable legs. Thanks to Jack, Barbie can now cross her legs and strike different poses. These are the first dramatic changes they've made to Barbie in years. Both are costly redesigns, involving new molds and plastics, but they have no doubt that these dolls will more than pay for their up-front investments.

"If you stick with me," Rosenberg is saying now, pausing to swirl his wine, "I promise you I can help you navigate whenever hard times come down on Barbie. And more importantly"—he takes a sip—"I can take Mattel to the next level."

Ruth and Elliot find themselves at a crossroads. They think Seymour Rosenberg will be an asset, and yes, there is considerable pressure from the board of directors and their shareholders to grow, which Seymour knows how to do. But this is their company. Ruth and Elliot started it from nothing, and bringing in Rosenberg will change everything. Maybe for the better—they'll all get richer, but is that all that matters?

"What should we do?" Ruth asks. She and Elliot are sitting side by side on the sofa in the living room; all the lights are out but one. It casts a strange shadow across the floor, like there's a ghoul watching over them.

Elliot makes a sound, part laugh, part sigh, as the lines deepen in his forehead and at the corners of his soft brown eyes. "I was hoping you'd know," he says, reaching for her feet and planting them in his lap, gently massaging one and then the other.

She gives herself over to his touch, the way his thumb works the ball of her foot, his fingers rubbing the arch where she didn't even know it ached until now. "Let me ask you something, Elliot—what do you want to be remembered for? I mean besides being a good husband, a good father and grandfather. For being a mensch."

"Sounds pretty good to me. We have two grown children and we have grandchildren now. Isn't that enough?"

She goes quiet and contemplates. Barbara and Ken have their own lives, their own families. What's left for her? Seymour's saying Barbie's in trouble, and without Barbie, what have they got? If they don't bring in someone like a Seymour Rosenberg, Mattel could still grow, but not at a rate that will satisfy their board of directors and stockholders. The value of the company will drop, followed by rounds of layoffs. They'll be forced to close one plant after another. They'll discontinue various toys, and soon Mattel will be just another company that showed great promise before it fizzled out.

And what if she dies young like Sarah? Ruth wants to be remembered for something. She wants to leave her mark on this world. If they hire Rosenberg, they could build a legacy. Their toys, their names, could live on forever, long after she and Elliot are gone. Why stop now, halfway up the ladder? Why not climb to the very top?

"Think about it," she says. "You and me—we're the American dream. A rags to riches story. This is a chance to take our place in history. We could be right up there with General Motors, IBM, AT&T."

Elliot squeezes her toes gently and laughs. "Now you're dreaming."

"But that's what we've always done, isn't it? We dream. This could be our shot. We could make Mattel one of the greatest companies that ever existed."

It's this conversation and her vision that decides it. They bring on Seymour Rosenberg as their executive vice president, head financial advisor. To sweeten the deal, they even give him a seat on their board. Elliot becomes Mattel's new chairman and Ruth is now president.

PART THREE

———

Buckle Up

Anatomically Impossible

1968

Mattel sent Barbie to the moon back in 1965, leaving the USSR and the U.S. in her wake. As an astronaut, Barbie's sales continue to soar through the stratosphere. Little girls everywhere are orbiting the planets and letting their imaginations take them to the farthest galaxies of their minds. Meanwhile, back on Earth, there's pandemonium all around. Boys are growing their hair longer while girls are wearing their skirts shorter. Hundreds of thousands gather to protest the Vietnam War. Young men are burning their draft cards while the civil rights movement and the women's movement steadily churn, picking up speed like hurricanes looking to make landfall.

It's around this time that Stevie tags along with Vivian to her first consciousness-raising session. She has no idea what to expect. All Vivian's told her is that it's a group of women who get together and talk about all kinds of things, which is somehow supposed to be empowering. They arrive at a bungalow in Silver Lake. The smell of patchouli incense greets them at the door. There are about fifteen women, most of them around Stevie and Vivian's age. The living room is small. All the seats are taken, women are sitting knee against knee on the couch, others perch on the armrests while some take the oversized pillows on the floor. Stevie and Vivian opt for a space on the rug, next to some other late arrivals.

Everyone is friendly, welcoming. There's a safe, open feeling in the air as they take turns sharing the most intimate aspects of their lives, and before the night is over, Stevie will know more about these strangers than some of her girlfriends whom she's known since grade school. Some confess to having had abortions and others sob for friends who died that way. One woman talks about being raped and how the police officer said it was because she dressed like a tease. A twenty-nine-year-old doctor claims she can't find a job because the male surgeons say she's too emotional and can't operate when she has her period. A young mother cries because she feels like a slave to her husband and children. She went to graduate school and holds a master's in journalism. She has no idea what happened to her life. A single mother complains there's no childcare available. How can she go to work and support her family if there's no one to take care of her children during the day? Like Stevie, many of them reject the status quo of their mothers' generation, which prompts Stevie to talk about her own mother. She surprises herself when she begins telling them about her fears of ending up like her and how close she came to repeating the same mistake.

That night, they cry, they laugh, they reassure one another that *No, it's not just you.* They want to open credit cards in their own names. They're tired of being discounted, underappreciated and, above all, sexualized. They are more than tits and ass. They have brains and their own brand of brawn. They embolden one another and are calling for revolution. A surge of strength and unity overcomes them all.

Stevie feels a connection with these women. At least she does until the evening takes a turn. She doesn't even remember who brought up Barbie, but in no time, the others are joining in.

"That damn doll embodies everything we're against," says one woman.

"Personally," says their hostess, "I'd like to wipe that smile off her face."

"Her body's completely distorted," another one says. "She's an anatomical impossibility . . ."

"And what about her diet book?" says another. "Did you guys hear about that?"

Stevie shifts on the floor, keeping her eyes low. Aside from Vivian, no one knows she works for Mattel and had a hand in creating Barbie's diet book. It was sold with Barbie's *Slumber Party* ensemble in the 1600 series: a sweet pink silk pajama set with a matching robe and slippers. The problem is it includes a bathroom scale set at 110 pounds and a diet book. At the time, Stevie thought they were so clever by putting *How to Lose Weight* on the front cover and *Don't Eat* on the back. *Isn't that cute? Won't that be fun?* They got more hate mail than ever before.

Stevie wanted to scream, *We didn't mean "Don't Eat" literally!* Still, she blames herself. She should have known better. She sees what's happening with Ginger. Right before her eyes she's witnessing a grown woman trying to turn herself into a Barbie doll. And why? Just to get the attention of a man? Barbie is supposed to be aspirational and remind girls of all the choices they have, not make them feel bad about their bodies.

The others are still going on and on about Barbie, and Stevie is feeling defensive. They're attacking not just her doll but Ruth and Charlotte. And Jack. She wants to set them straight, explain the reason why Barbie's waist is so small, why her feet are so tiny.

Someone else chimes in: "Barbie's a dangerous role model for young girls. She's destroying their innocence. Confusing them. Barbie is not what a woman's body is supposed to look like."

"Oh, for God's sake," Stevie explodes. "She's a doll—a plastic toy. No one's asking anyone to look like her." They're all staring at her now. "You know," she says, unable to pull herself back, "I was on board with everything I heard here tonight, right up until you started in on Barbie. She's not the problem. You're blaming Barbie because it's easier than taking on the real culprits—society, the government, the men in our lives."

That moves them off Barbie, and for the next hour they take on the chauvinists.

The Happiness Maker Is Back

Goldman Sachs is hosting an analysis conference where they've invited leaders within the toy industry to present trends and new product launches. Ruth and Elliot were asked to participate, and they agreed that it made sense to have Jack there, too, a nice way to round out their portion of the program. They especially want Jack to talk about his latest innovation, Talking Barbie, which will be coming out later that year.

Jack flew in two days early so he could have dinner and spend some time with Sheila, an old girlfriend who was at Vassar when he was at Yale. He's sitting at the bar at the St. Regis, waiting for her to arrive. It's been years since he's seen her, and when she steps into the King Cole Bar, Jack almost doesn't recognize her. And not just because she's changed her hairstyle, wearing it shorter now with a wisp of bangs, but because she's got a fella with her. Sheila is the executive secretary to the publisher of the *New York Times*, and the guy is a reporter who wants to interview Jack.

Jack's flattered when the reporter says, "Sheila's told me what a genius you are. She says you're Mattel's secret weapon—the man who invented Barbie."

"Well, I wouldn't go that far," says Jack, sounding surprisingly humble, even to his own ears. "Ruth—that's Ruth Handler, one of the owners—we worked together on Barbie and had a whole team helping us. The Handlers—Ruth and Elliot—have built a great organization. There's lots of top-notch talent there . . ." As he gushes about Mattel, he feels something akin to a father's pride. Aside from Rosenberg, whom he's been butting heads with from the start, Jack loves the company. He eats, sleeps and breathes Mattel, and he wouldn't trade his time there for anything in the world.

They talk some more over another round of drinks and a heap of oysters.

Slurping a Blue Point, the reporter flips through his notebook to a clean page. "So let's talk about what Mattel is up to now."

Jack takes this opportunity to plug their newest doll in the Barbie line: the Christie doll. Christie is Mattel's second attempt to show their support for the civil rights movement. Their first effort was the Francie doll, a new Barbie friend that Negro girls could relate to. Good intentions but without nearly enough planning. Instead of designing the doll as a whole, they took shortcuts. They relied on the existing molds for the white Francie doll and merely used a darker shade of plastic. As soon as the dolls arrived, even those at Mattel had misgivings, and yet they put it on the market, offending countless customers and garnering so much hate mail that they discontinued the doll and went back to the drawing board. This time they did it right, giving the Christie doll her own molds, her own features, and her own hairstyle.

They just shipped the new dolls to retailers two weeks ago and the advertising is starting on Monday. Jack knows that Ruth and Elliot will be thrilled that he's not only getting all this press for Mattel but also getting them free publicity for Christie.

———

Ruth and Elliot take a late-night flight, arriving the day before the conference so they'll have time to visit with Ken and Suzie, who relocated to New York after the baby was born. That morning Ruth has ordered room service and is relaxing, enjoying her coffee while reading the *New York Times*. She sees that Robert Kennedy has just announced his bid for the presidency . . . Martin Luther King Jr. is preparing to lead a march in Memphis next week . . . More bloody accounts coming out of Vietnam . . .

When she turns to the business section, she's stunned to see the headline above the fold: THE BRAINS BEHIND BARBIE. Next to that she is even more shocked to see Jack's headshot, the one taken for their company brochure. She's confused as she continues reading about the *brilliant, stupendous, charismatic*—and every other buttery adjective—Jack Ryan, the boy wonder who attended Yale, worked at Raytheon, and created Mattel's most successful toy, the Barbie doll, named after his wife. *What?*

Ruth drops the newspaper to her lap. She doesn't know what to make of this article. This isn't like Jack. He's always given credit where credit is due. He has a big ego, but he's fair. The problem is, Ruth also has a big ego, and creating this doll, being able to put her name on it, gives her legitimacy as a toymaker, and Jack's just taken that away. It doesn't matter that conference attendees will be impressed, that the timing in some ways is perfect; she feels slighted. Left out and left behind, just like she felt as a child whose mother didn't want her. Even though Ruth knows the truth, that Barbie is as much her creation as, if not more so than, Jack's. *Hers versus Jack's.* The idea of ownership has never factored in before. Yes, she owns Mattel, but who owns Barbie?

She hears the shower turn on and calls to Elliot, saying she'll be right back. With the *Times* in hand, she heads down to Jack's room. Two knocks, three knocks, and he calls out, "Go away. I'm sleeping."

"Jack, it's me. Open up."

He answers the door, wearing a black velvet monogrammed robe and a satin eye mask pushed up onto his forehead. "This better be important," he says, gesturing her inside.

To her great relief, Jack doesn't have a woman in his bed—a possibility that hadn't occurred to her until that moment. She holds up the *New York Times*. "Since when did you create Barbie? She was my idea. She's named after my daughter, too. Not just your wife."

"What are you talking about? I didn't say that."

"It's right here. See for yourself." She thrusts the paper at him.

Even if he were wide awake, he wouldn't be able to read it. Jack has never read a newspaper in his life. Pulling the sleep mask off his forehead, flinging it onto the bed, he tries to recall what he told the reporter, wishing he knew what ended up in print. "I'm sorry, Ruth. He twisted my words. We were talking about the Christie doll. I swear, I hardly even mentioned Barbie."

"Well, you sure as hell said enough."

"Oh, c'mon, why would I do something like that?"

"I don't know, Jack. You tell me." She tosses the paper onto the bed and storms out.

Jack is shrinking, not only because Ruth thinks he wronged her but because he can't read what they wrote about him. He wonders how quickly Ginger can get her hands on a copy of the *Times*. He tries to reach her but forgot that he's given her a few days off while he's out of town. He can't get a hold of her at home, either. He's on his own. All the words jump about the newsprint, a few familiar ones leaping out at him: *Mattel. Jack Ryan. Yale. Raytheon.*

Missile. Barbie . . . Why can't you just read like a normal person? His word blindness is a curse. It makes him hate himself, makes him revert to the dumb, short kid from elementary school. All he wants is to prove to the world that he's good enough—better than good enough. He wants to be seen as a sublime engineer, a celebrated inventor. Instead, he's staring at a bunch of words that are making him feel stupid. And if there's one thing Jack can't stand, it's feeling stupid.

He sulks in his room for much of the afternoon, turning house-keeping away twice. Finally, he drags himself into the shower. There's a cocktail reception for the conference starting soon, but he can't bear to face Ruth and Elliot. Or anyone else. The only thing that will make him feel whole, make him feel like less of a loser, is a stiff drink and the attention of an attractive woman.

He heads downstairs and enters the hotel lounge, where he sees a pretty young woman sitting by herself at the end of the bar. The satin strap on her dark blue dress has slipped off her shoulder and she can't be bothered to right it. Her blond hair looks professionally coiffed, done up in meticulous twists and complicated coils. He helps himself to the empty stool beside her and makes a little small talk. This one is a talker, all right. He buys her a drink and she opens up in the way only a stranger in a bar already two drinks in will do. Her name is Shelley. She's twenty-six, from New Rochelle. She's in the city for a friend's wedding being held in the hotel.

"I snuck out before the reception started," she says. "My ex-boyfriend is in there with his new girlfriend."

"Ah, that's tough," says Jack sympathetically.

"No one told me he was bringing a date. I didn't even know he had a new girlfriend."

"And I thought I had a bad day," he says. This girl's misery supersedes his own. He needs to make this better. And he can.

Shelley continues, "I feel like such a fool. I thought he was coming alone. I thought we'd get back together tonight." Tears collect in her eyes, but she blinks them away. "I spent all this money on this stupid dress, I got my hair done, my nails done. I'm such an idiot . . ."

"Well," says Jack, "if it's any consolation, I think you look ravishing."

"You do?"

"I do. I noticed you as soon as I walked into the bar."

They finish their drinks, he takes her to dinner and by the time he invites her up to his room, he's not thinking about that newspaper article anymore. His only focus now is Shelley. He is tender with this girl as he slips off the dress she bought for her ex-boyfriend. He unpins her lustrous hair, stiff from too much hair spray. He goes slowly and takes his time with her. He doesn't care about his own satisfaction. Tonight it's all about her, about Shelley.

And as he is pleasing her, watching her back arch, seeing how she grips a fistful of sheets and takes in all that intensity, he feels his power coming back to him. Jack Ryan, the brilliant engineer, the premier toymaker, the happiness maker, is back. *Outta sight, man, outta sight.*

The Difference between
the Men and the Boys

1969

The UCLA boys have been working all day to transform the Castle's dining room into a medieval cave for one of Jack's Tom Jones parties, inspired by his favorite movie of the same name. The movie came out years ago, but Jack manages to find every theater in town still showing it. He's seen that picture at least a dozen times.

So while the muscular tawny boys are positioning the prince of Parma throne, which weighs at least 300 pounds, at the head of the long table, Jack's personal chef is busy preparing lamb chops and a watercress salad, green beans and corn on the cob. At half past six, the harpsichordist who will serenade them all throughout the evening arrives. The four-foot-tall candles are lit, the goblets of wine are set out on the table and Jack is ready for his dinner guests.

He's invited Stevie and Patsy from the office, along with an art dealer and his long-legged wife. Also in attendance is a Hollywood producer with a young blond starlet whom no one's ever heard of and Zsa Zsa Gabor. Zsa Zsa is accompanied by her Yorkshire terrier and a journalist from *Life* magazine, because wherever Zsa Zsa goes, the press follows. The journalist has a pointy goatee—which may or may not be part of his costume—and has a Nikon camera looped about his neck, hanging down over his ruff collar.

Jack requested that everyone come in costume and asked Stevie to design a green velvet hooded cloak for him. He insists on carrying a genuine sword, which he slices through the air every now and again. After too many drinks, Stevie and Patsy convince him to set the sword aside before he beheads someone.

Jack seats Zsa Zsa at the head of the table, on the throne, and then places a bejeweled crown upon her platinum updo. Like much of the ornamentations in the Castle, the crown is a fake loaded up with rhinestones. Zsa Zsa is delighted to be the focal point of the evening. Stevie is less amused. She's not a fan of Zsa Zsa's, mostly finding her to be boring and self-absorbed. Before the first course comes out, it's fairly obvious that the starlet, dressed in a country maid outfit that laces up the front and gives her breasts an added boost, has caught Jack's eye. Even the Hollywood producer takes note of the way Jack is glancing at her, and she at him.

As the UCLA boys bring out the food, Jack's guests search the table for silverware. There is none. And there will be none.

"It's a Tom Jones party," Jacks says, laughing. "You have to eat with your hands."

And so they do. But the lamb is fatty and slippery. There's no way to do this gracefully, and after several rounds of cocktails and bottles of wine, it doesn't much seem to matter. The art dealer's once very proper wife is now gnawing on a bone; Zsa Zsa's dog has his paws on the table, lapping up the juices off her fingertips; Patsy can't seem to hold on to her ear of corn; the starlet has lamb juice dribbling down her chin and onto her very ample cleavage. When Stevie sees Jack refill his wineglass again, she nudges his water glass closer, which he ignores.

After dinner, the college boys escort the ladies—and the art dealer, who is too drunk to walk a straight line—out of the Castle and into Jack's latest purchase, a 1935 fire truck with a ladder, booster tank and hose reel. The once bright red body is now faded from years of baking in the hot California sun.

After all his guests are on board, Jack revs up the engine, laughing as he proclaims, "You know what they say: 'The difference between the men and the boys is the price of their toys.'"

And with the bells a-clanging, they speed down Sunset Boulevard, where Jack parks his fire truck outside the Pandora's Box nightclub. There they dance and drink and dance some more. The reporter is scribbling notes all the while, as his Nikon captures the evening's highlights.

It's getting late, and one by one, Jack's guests, including Stevie and Patsy, say their goodbyes and head home. When they announce last call, the only ones left standing are Jack, Zsa Zsa and the reporter.

As they're driving back to Bel Air in the fire truck, the reporter turns to Jack and says, "So is it true, man? You're the cat who invented the Barbie doll?"

Executives and Pishers

Three months later, Ruth and Elliot get together with two other couples to play poker. It's their standing game, a nickel ante; the minimum bet is a dime, and the maximum is a quarter. This is the last vestige of their ever-shrinking social life, because Ruth can never pry herself away from work long enough for dinner parties, round robins at the club, even a simple Sunday afternoon barbecue. But poker night is different—that, she makes time for.

These three couples have been friends for as long as Ruth and Elliot can remember. They, along with another couple, formed a stock club years ago when they were all just starting out. Each couple put in $500, and they took turns being president, secretary, treasurer. They named the club E&P Investments, which stands for Executives and Pishers, because two of the men are professionals and the other two are more entrepreneurial. As soon as Mattel went public back in 1963, they all invested, modestly at first. But when they saw how well the company was performing, they increased their positions.

Tonight, their friends Natalie and Doug Grossinger are hosting the game. Natalie fancies herself an interior designer, and the two of them—Ruth and Natalie—nearly had a falling-out over an end table in Ruth's Holmby Hills house. Ruth doesn't always care for Natalie's tastes and finds her opinions to be as sharp as the clavicle bones protruding from her rail-thin frame. *She's a maven, a know-it-all*, she often says to Elliot. *But only when she's drinking*, is his excuse for Natalie. Elliot likes Natalie. He gets a kick out of her even though the woman can't hold her liquor. That night Natalie serves gin and tonics and has set out potato chips and French onion dip. Doug is a dentist and likes to tell stories about the movie stars whose teeth he's capped.

"I'm serious," says Doug, speaking of Rita Hayworth. "Look at her teeth in *Circus World* and then look at her teeth in *The Happy Thieves*."

"Isn't there some sort of privacy between patient and dentist?" asks Elliot, which is the same question he asked the time Doug told them about John Wayne swallowing one of his front teeth on a taffy apple.

"Ah, c'mon, I'm a dentist, not a shrink. Besides, why let ethics get in the way of a great story?"

The other couple that night is Trudy and Marvin Silver. Marvin owned a bowling alley until about ten or twelve years ago, when he invested in a newfangled restaurant franchise called McDonald's. Trudy and Ruth used to play tennis at the club, but because Ruth works so much, it's been ages since she even held a racket.

Doug is shuffling the cards and about to deal the first hand when Natalie starts talking about an article she saw in *Life* magazine.

Ruth braces herself for what's coming next.

". . . and you'll never guess what," says Natalie. "It was all about Jack Ryan. *Your* Jack Ryan."

"Did everybody ante up?" asks Elliot.

"What a character he is," Natalie says, pointing to Ruth with her near-empty glass. "Jeez Louise." She shakes her head. "It was all about these crazy parties he throws. Did you know about those parties, Ruth? They say really wild stuff goes on there. Is it true? Do you know about them?"

"We haven't been to one of his parties in years," says Ruth.

"That's because you work too much," says Marvin, wagging his finger at her.

"I hear they're crazy parties," says Natalie. "Booze and drugs. And sex. I'm talking *really* crazy stuff."

Ruth lights a cigarette, shooting the smoke toward the ceiling.

"Are we gonna play some poker here or what?" asks Elliot. He can tell Ruth is getting annoyed and he doesn't want anything to spoil their one night out.

"Yeah," says Marvin, "let's deal those cards."

Natalie squeezes what's left of her lime into her glass and throws in a splash of gin. "Who needs a refill?"

"I'll take another," says Elliot, draining the dregs of his glass.

"So about those Jack Ryan parties," Natalie says as she fixes Elliot's drink, knocking a handful of ice cubes onto the floor. "Is it true that he has waterfalls and a tree house?"

"We wouldn't know," says Elliot. "We don't go to Jack's parties. We're too old. Bunch of kids. Not our scene."

"Deal," says Marvin, slapping the table.

Doug shuffles again and starts doling out the cards.

Natalie slides Elliot's drink over to him. "In that article," she presses on, "they said something about how Jack Ryan invented that Barbie doll of yours."

"He did?" asks Trudy. "But Ruthie, I thought *you* invented it."

"I did," says Ruth, setting her cigarette in the ashtray while she picks up her hand, arranging the cards. Her nerves are blistering up just like they did the morning she flipped through her copy of *Life*. When she saw the photo of Jack hanging off the side of an antique fire engine and the headline: MEET JACK RYAN, THE MAN WHO INVENTED THE BARBIE DOLL, she nearly spilled her coffee.

Natalie harps on, "But it said Jack Ryan was the one who invented your doll."

"Everyone knows Ruthie created Barbie," says Elliot.

Ruth sets down her drink and picks up her cigarette. "Who dealt—Doug?" She turns to Trudy on his left. "C'mon, Trudy, what's it gonna be? Bet or pass?"

"But Ruth," says Natalie, having crossed from slurry to sloppy, "why would they say he made your doll?"

Doug turns to his wife. "Natalie, did you eat lunch today? Eat something, would you?" He reaches for the bowl of potato chips.

Natalie swats his hand away, sending a few chips overboard and onto the table. "But this is *Life* magazine we're talking about," she says. "Millions of people read *Life*. And now they're all going to think Jack Ryan made your doll instead of you."

"You should set the record straight," says Marvin.

"I don't need to set the record straight," says Ruth. Or does she? She stubs out her cigarette, feeling her blood pressure spike, her cheeks beginning to flush. This is the second time Jack's done this to her. Last year, when the *New York Times* said Jack created Barbie, he apologized, swearing up and down that it had been unintentional, that the reporter had put words in his mouth. She had been furious at first, but after cooling off, she decided to give him the benefit of the doubt. It's harder to do that this time, especially when after she confronted Jack about the article, his only defense was: "I can't help what they print about me in the press." She doesn't know if he's deliberately trying to get under her skin—which really isn't like him—or if he's so pickled from all the booze that he doesn't know what he's saying.

Either way she finds it hard to stay mad at him for very long, partly because he's so damn talented. When they thought he'd never be able to top his bendable-legs Barbie, he created Twist 'n Turn Barbie and then Talking Barbie. And now, thanks to Jack, they're already moving into production on a new Living Barbie, who bends not only her knees but also her ankles, elbows and waist. Plus, they're getting ready to launch yet another one of Jack's inventions for their toy car line—Hot Wheels. Technically, he created it with Elliot, but Jack was instrumental in the development. So while yes, he can be a pain in the ass, and yes, he drinks too much and shoots off his mouth to the press, Mattel wouldn't be where it is today without him.

"Speaking of Barbie," says Marvin, "did you see what your stock did today? Forty-eight-fifty a share."

"I remember when all you had was that little plastic ukulele," says Trudy.

"We can say we knew you when," says Marvin. "Here's to Ruthie and Elliot." He raises his glass.

"And to Mattel," says Doug.

"May the stock hit $50 a share," says Marvin as they all clink glasses.

What's My Line?

Jack is on fire. The man is unstoppable, outdoing himself at every turn. Everything he touches turns to gold. Frankly, he's done more to grow Mattel than Seymour Rosenberg has with all his bluster about acquisitions, all his warnings about Barbie being in trouble. He couldn't have been more wrong about that.

Barbie's sales are stronger than ever, and now, on top of all his previous successes, Jack is going to be on television. He's a contestant on the popular show *What's My Line?*, where a star-studded panel of actors and entertainers will ask him a series of questions and try to guess his occupation. Ruth and Elliot are so thrilled about this added publicity for Mattel, they've insisted on paying for Jack's flight to New York and his suite at the Plaza Hotel.

The show airs live on Sunday night at ten thirty, and when Jack arrives at Studio 50 an hour earlier, the live television audience is already lined up on 53rd Street, waiting to be let into the auditorium. Jack is greeted by the producers and says a quick hello to the host, John Daly, before he's ushered into hair and makeup. Since they're going to be broadcasting in color, Jack is wearing a double-breasted yellow and blue plaid jacket with a blue turtleneck and has a peace sign hanging from a gold chain about his neck.

One of the producers, a man with bushy eyebrows and a clipboard, sidles up beside him at the makeup mirror. "Now, I just want to go over a few things." They review the game rules and confirm the spelling of his name. "And let's make sure we have the correct job description for the caption." He consults the clipboard again. "We have your occupation as *Toymaker for Mattel*."

Jack steals a glance at himself in the mirror. Framed in light bulbs all around, he looks like a movie star. Who would have ever imagined that he—Jack Ryan, miserable lonely kid from Riverdale—would appear on television? And on *What's My Line?* no less. He assesses himself in the mirror again. He's not just a toymaker; he's a star. He's also Mr. Im-pul-siv-i-ty and there's no time for consequences. "Tell you what," he says to the producer, "let's just make one small change to that caption."

After they pancake his face and spray his hair in place, Jack is led into the greenroom, where he meets the other contestants—a whale trainer and Lyndon Johnson's speechwriter, along with this week's mystery guest, Raquel Welch. The celebrity panelists—Arlene Francis, Dorothy Kilgallen, Tony Randall and Steve Allen—are in a separate greenroom, away from the contestants, to ensure there's no cheating. And, of course, they'll be blindfolded when it's time to question Raquel Welch, who seems quite charmed by Jack. He's thinking of taking her out for a late supper afterward. *Why not?* He's an up-and-coming famous inventor. She's not out of his league.

Showtime is drawing nearer, and they can hear the producers warming up the studio audience with rounds of applause and instruction. Jack's heart begins beating wildly when the man with the bushy eyebrows and the clipboard calls for him. "You're the first one up," he says, leading Jack backstage. There are crew members rushing around, adjusting lights, tweaking microphones, preparing cue cards and the teleprompter. From the wings, Jack hears the crack of applause as he watches Arlene Francis take her place at the panelist desk. As the other panelists are introduced, the man with the bushy eyebrows rattles off last-minute instructions on where to stand, where to look. Jack's adrenaline kicks up a notch higher. He can't wait to get out there and take his place under the lights, in front of the fans and the entire nation.

Meanwhile, it's seven thirty in Los Angeles and all of Mattel is watching along with the rest of the country. The engineers are at Twist's, Stevie has gathered with Patsy and the other designers at Dee's, Charlotte is tuned in, so are the stockholders and of course Ruth and Elliot are watching with Barbara, Allen and their kids.

When they introduce the first contestant, Jack swaggers onto the stage, all smiles, looking rather dashing in a flashy sports coat. After he writes his name on the chalkboard, the host, John Daly, welcomes him, asks where he's from and invites Jack to take a seat across from the panelists.

"Before we begin," says the host, "let's show our TV audience and our viewers at home exactly what your line is."

This is the moment when *Toymaker for Mattel* will be revealed to millions of viewers. Ruth inches closer to the television set, excitement firing off inside her body. You can't buy this kind of publicity. She's shushing the kids while she squeezes Elliot's hand. But when the caption comes up on the TV screen, what they—and everyone else—see instead is *Creator of the Barbie Doll*.

Ruth may have forgiven Jack twice before for claiming he invented Barbie, but announcing it on national TV is too much. She'll be damned if she's going to let him erase her from the equation, not after the sacrifices she made, the risks she took to bring Barbie to market. She worked her tail off, and he's not going to deny her the bragging rights to Barbie.

As soon as Jack's back in the office, Ruth rips into him. "*You* created Barbie? *You* created her? How dare you!"

"Jesus, Ruth, can I at least get a cup of coffee before you—"

"Shut up. Shut up before I slice your goddamn balls off."

"Whoa—" Jack backs up, his shoulders pressed to the Mahogany Row wall. "Why are you so upset? It's not like I got up there and lied. I *am* one of the creators of Barbie."

Ruth's eyes narrow and her lips squeeze together in a tight round bud of fury.

"Oh, c'mon," he says, "it was great publicity for Barbie. And for Mattel."

"Just shut the hell up and stay out of my way."

"You're overreacting. I didn't do anything—"

"I mean it, Jack, shut your mouth and just stay the hell away from me."

And so Jack's appearance on *What's My Line?* marks a turning point in their relationship. There's no forgiving this time. No putting this behind them. The two are openly hostile. They don't even bother with a *good morning* anymore, or making eye contact when they pass each other in the hall. They speak to each other only when absolutely necessary.

Elliot is ever congenial and diplomatic, trying to make things as pleasant as possible, given the circumstances. They used to be one big happy family, and this is eating his *kishkes* out. He's sure the rest of the staff is picking up on the tension and he worries about company morale. He continues to play his marching music each day, but it's just background noise—it lifts no one's spirits. Least of all his.

Though Jack's trying to play it cool, claiming Ruth's rancor doesn't bother him, he's not doing okay. Stevie's worried about him. One morning he questions why she didn't come to his party the night before.

"I *was* there. Jesus, Jack, you need to ease up on the booze." She swears she can smell liquor on him, and it's not even nine o'clock. "Did cocktail hour start early today or are you still drunk from last night?"

"I don't even remember last night," he says. "I woke up with two women in my bed." He shakes his head and laughs. "Apparently, I had one hell of a time. Too bad I can't remember it." He laughs again, harder this time, making his shoulders shake until his laughter dissolves into a fit of tears. "Oh, Stevie." He holds out his arms to her, a child reaching for his mother. She goes to him, tries to soothe him as he sobs. "Am I losing my sex appeal?"

"You just had sex with two women last night, what do you think?" she says, trying to lighten the mood.

He sniffles pathetically. "Do *you* still find me sexy?"

She doesn't want to hurt his feelings. He looks terrible— exhausted and bloated. And he's recently started dyeing his hair shoe-polish black in an attempt to cover the sprigs of gray sprouting up around his temples. It's hard to see him this way, hard to believe there was a time when she found him so irresistible.

Look, Just Look

Ruth has officially quit smoking. Today marks three and a half months since she's had a cigarette. After Elliot begged her to try hypnosis again, she returned to Dr. Mandry, and now, after several weeks of treatments, his techniques have taken hold. This is the longest she's ever been smoke-free, and to top it off, she hasn't gained a single pound.

Now whenever Ruth thinks about a cigarette, she closes her eyes and counts backward from ten. She reminds herself, *Smoking is a choice. I have free will. I am in control. I do not want a cigarette.* And just like that, the urge goes away. She still can't get over it. She's been smoking since she was seventeen, and now she's cured.

She arrives at Mattel and settles in with a cup of coffee and looks at the weekly W Report. She's pleased to see that Barbie's *Black Magic Ensemble* in the 1600 series—inspired by one of her own favorite cocktail dresses—is gaining traction.

At nine o'clock Ruth's secretary buzzes her office, letting her know that the reporter from *Look* is here for their interview. The magazine is doing a big feature story on Mattel, and the reporter has already met with Elliot, Rosenberg and Jack. Now it's her turn. Unlike Jack, Ruth doesn't like talking to the press. While she recognizes that it's necessary from a public relations standpoint, she considers it a big distraction.

The reporter is a young man with Brylcreemed hair and a fleck of toilet paper on his chin with a rusty dot of dried blood, the vestige of a shaving nick that morning. He sits opposite Ruth and eagerly begins asking the usual questions: *What do you think is the secret of Mattel's success? Are you surprised by Barbie's sustained popularity? How has Barbie's success changed the company?* Funny that reporters never ask what it's like to be a woman running a company the size of Mattel. She's an anomaly, but that doesn't interest them.

The reporter flips through his notes, saying, "Oh, there's something else I wanted to ask you about . . ." He scans the pages until he finds what he's looking for. "Can you just clarify something Jack said about his royalty payments—"

"What?" She gives him one of her looks that could stop a train. "Jack talked to you about his royalties?"

"Well, yes . . ."

Jesus, she doesn't want Jack's financial arrangement in the press. "I'm sure you can appreciate that one's compensation is a private matter," she says, keeping her voice measured as she tries to dodge the subject, already thinking how they can kill this story.

The reporter keeps asking more questions—*What new toys does Mattel have in the works? What do you think is the most exciting toy on the market today? Where do you see Barbie going in the future?* . . . She answers, but it's a genuine struggle to get through the rest of the interview. The rage is festering inside her head, and she would kill for a cigarette.

When the interview is finally over, Ruth sits at her desk, taking deep breaths, unable to count as she's been taught, because she can't believe Jack could be so stupid as to discuss his royalties with a reporter. She remembers their negotiations with Jack when they offered him the job. He had the gall to ask for a starting salary of $25,000.

"C'mon, Jack," Elliot had said. "We're a small company. We might be able to get you there in a few years, but now . . ." He shook his head. "There's no way."

Jack nodded, scrubbed a hand across his face. "Tell you what— I like you two. I think we could work well together. Let's start me off at a modest salary—you decide what you can swing, and in addition, give me a cut of revenues on products I help develop. Let's say 5 percent."

Ruth had laughed. "Let's say 1 percent."

They eventually agreed on 1.5 percent. Since then, his salary hasn't increased much, but thanks to Barbie's success, he's done just fine for himself.

She tries to move on to some marketing reports, but something about Jack's royalties keeps tugging at her. When she can't shake it, she fishes out Jack's contract. It's dated February 3, 1955, and is now yellowed around the edges. She assumed he only got royalties on the sale of patented products, but the contract says he's entitled to a royalty on sales of *any products* he's developed. *Patented or not? Jesus Christ*—that could apply to just about every toy they've made. Numbers are flashing through her head as the knots in her gut tighten. She moves on to the bank statements, looking at the checks they've cut Jack, dating back to Barbie's launch and before. Her phone is buzzing but she doesn't answer it. She's too engrossed. Too busy punching numbers into the adding machine with a force that nearly breaks her fingernails.

An hour later, she takes a look at the total. Now she wants a cigarette. She wants a cigarette so badly she's practically twitching.

Breathe, she thinks. *Count backward from ten. Smoking is a choice. I am in control* . . . She tries all the tricks the hypnotist has given her. She tells herself the urge will pass. It always does. But today it's not.

Grabbing her pocketbook and car keys, she heads to her Rolls-Royce, parked right next to Elliot's Rolls-Royce. She glances down at the closed ashtray, wondering if there might be a butt left in there. There isn't. She pulls out of the parking lot, furious with herself for not staying on top of Jack's royalties. She used to handle all the payroll herself even though, back then, as a woman she couldn't sign the paychecks. It was always Elliot's signature. But they've gotten too large. Now there's a separate payroll department that handles all that. Ruth doesn't even have time to look at the payroll anymore.

She makes a sharp turn—the car behind her honks as she pulls into a Thrifty on Jefferson Boulevard. Ignoring the alarms going off in her, she briskly walks into the store and buys a package of cigarettes. She has the cellophane wrapper already off before she's back in the car and pushing the cigarette lighter in, waiting anxiously for it to pop. Those red-hot coils are such a welcome sight as she inhales deeply. God, how can something so terrible for her make her feel so much better? It's just one cigarette. One cigarette doesn't mean she's going back to smoking.

Two cigarettes and twenty minutes later, Ruth returns to Mattel, where she finds Elliot waiting for her in her office. "Where have you been?" he asks.

She doesn't dare answer and instead reaches for the curling strip of paper she'd torn off the adding machine feed earlier. "Look, just look at this—we have to kill the *Look* story. Jack was blabbing to that reporter about his royalties."

"What? Jack wouldn't—"

"Oh, yes, he would. And just look at what we've paid him over the past five years alone."

Elliot glances at the strip of numbers. He blinks and checks again. "That can't be right. Are you sure?"

"Oh, I'm sure."

"Jesus." He brings his hand to his mouth. "Christ, that's a lot of money."

"How could we have been so stupid?"

"We weren't stupid, Ruthie. It seemed like the right move at the time. When we hired Jack, the agreement made sense. How could we have predicted that we'd ever be this successful?"

"We're paying him over a million dollars a year in royalties and you know damn well that total's only going to rise. We can't keep paying him that kind of money. We just can't."

He gets up, loosens his necktie and drops down onto the pink sofa. It is a hell of a lot of money, but they have a contract with Jack. They can't break it. He'll leave the company. Even worse, they could get sued, and Elliot doesn't have the stomach for another lawsuit, especially not one with Jack. Elliot and Ruth are making more money than he ever dreamed possible. They own a beautiful home, two Rolls-Royces and they just put an offer in on a beach house in Malibu. They want for nothing. The way Elliot sees it, Jack's worth every penny they're paying him. So why not let Jack make his money and he and Ruth make theirs? Besides, whatever Jack makes, they'll still be making that much more.

But Ruth sees it differently. For her it's not just the money. It's the principle of the thing. It's about her knocking Jack down a peg or two. Ever since his appearance on *What's My Line?*, he's been masquerading as some sort of minor celebrity. He even managed to get himself on *The Merv Griffin Show*, where he once again bragged

about creating Barbie and jabbered on about his disgusting sex parties. Ruth is convinced that Jack—more so than the women's
movement—is going to ruin Barbie's reputation. "We need to do
something about this, Elliot."

"Like what?"

"I don't know. Get Rosenberg in here."

When Rosenberg joins them, Ruth explains what she's just uncovered and says, "You're the head of finance now. You gotta get us
out of this mess. There's gotta be something we can do about this."

"Don't worry," Rosenberg assures them both. "We can fix this."

"But how?" asks Ruth. "We have a contract. What can we do?"

Rosenberg smiles. "We can start phasing him out."

"What?" Ruth can't believe the panic this invokes in her.

"We *need* Jack," Elliot insists.

"Correction," says Rosenberg. "You *needed* Jack. He served you
well. Got you from A to B. Now it's time to move on."

"But getting rid of Jack doesn't solve the problem," says Elliot.
"According to his contract, he's still entitled to royalties on all his
patented products."

"Not if we find ways to work around his patents," says Rosenberg with a wink. "You think Jack Ryan's the only engineer out
there who can design a doll? A toy gun? Please." He laughs. "We'll
find someone else who can redesign, reengineer the dolls so you
don't have to go on paying Jack."

"Is that ethical?" asks Elliot.

"Perfectly ethical. It's not nice, but it's done all the time.
Trust me."

After Rosenberg leaves, Elliot says, "Are we sure about doing
this? I want to rein Jack in, not get rid of him."

"But I don't think we can do one without the other." Ruth gets up from her desk and joins him on the sofa. "I know it's hard, but we have to cut the emotion. This is a business decision."

Elliot looks at her, his eyebrows knitting together as his expression changes to one of alarm.

"What is it?" she asks. "What's wrong?"

"Have you—Jesus, Ruthie, are you smoking again?"

The Two Jacks

Ever since Rosenberg came on board, Jack hardly recognizes Mattel. Neither does Stevie. There are so many new hires, including a young lawyer with movie star looks. Stevie hasn't met him yet, but she's heard all about him. Not since the early days of Jack Ryan has anyone set the women of Mattel's hearts aflutter quite like Simon Richards.

As for Rosenberg, Jack started having problems with him almost immediately, ever since that sonofabitch took over their weekly staff meetings, which Jack used to run. Plus, Jack thinks Rosenberg is stifling everyone's creativity, roaming about the office several times a day, checking up on people, making sure they're doing their jobs. Whenever anyone sees him coming, they quickly end their telephone calls, break up their conversations, put a ceasefire on squirt gun fights and other shenanigans.

"Rosenberg gives me the creeps," Stevie says to Jack. The two of them are in Jack's office, reviewing the outfit for a special, limited-edition Twiggy Barbie with short blond hair, oversized blue eyes and spiky eyelashes. "I feel like he's always staring at my breasts."

"He probably is."

Stevie's on the couch, her heels kicked off. Jack is on his bear-skin rug, stretching out his back, groaning.

"Dare I ask how you threw out your back?"

"You don't want to know." He groans again, louder this time.

"Jesus, Jack, you sound like you're having sex."

"Honey, you better than anyone know that's not what I sound like when I'm in the throes of passion."

She laughs, giving him a playful nudge with her foot.

T he next day, Rosenberg comes into Jack's office with a man Jack's never seen before. The guy's tall, taller than Rosenberg and almost half a foot taller than Jack. He's square-looking, with an outdated hairstyle, and wears a boring white shirt and skinny dark tie.

"Jack Ryan"—Rosenberg holds out his hand like a presenter—"say hello to Mattel's *other Jack*—Jack Barcus."

After the two shake hands, Rosenberg attempts to clasp them both around their shoulders but can't reach Barcus with grace, so he ends up slipping one arm about the man's waist. "My two Jacks," he says with an uneasy smile. "The future of Mattel's research and design is in your hands."

"Excuse me?" Jack looks at Rosenberg first and then at Barcus, who eyes him sharply.

"We're starting up a second design group," says Rosenberg. "So now we'll have two design teams, the Ryan Group and the Barcus Group."

Mr. Square has suddenly gone from being a dweeby schlub to being a contender. This is going to be an outright competition.

B arcus?" Jack corners Ruth and Elliot, finding them both in Elliot's office. "Who the hell is this Barcus guy?"

"Come in, Jack." Elliot rises from his desk, an apologetic look on his face. "I'm afraid Rosenberg jumped the gun on things."

"We wanted to tell you first," says Ruth.

"Tell me *what*? That you're bringing in another engineering group?"

"We have to," says Elliot. His expression is one of bewilderment, as if there's no other choice. "The company is growing. Think of it as a good thing."

"How in the hell is this a good thing? What kind of message does this send to my entire team?"

"Your department isn't the only one that's being restructured," says Ruth, unable to look at him, focusing instead on Elliot's lava lamp. "We have to bring on more manpower," she adds, staring at the red globules oozing about.

"And you didn't think this was worthy of a conversation first? Ruth, I know things haven't been exactly great between us lately, but I thought we were in this together. I helped grow this company and this is the thanks I get?" He senses the pressure building up behind his eyes and—*Jesus Christ*—he feels like he's about to cry. No, fuck no, he can't. He won't give them the satisfaction of seeing him break. He has to get the hell out of there. Shaking his head, he walks out, slamming the door behind him.

Ruth looks up at Elliot, who reaches for the Maalox in his top drawer, unscrews the cap and takes a swig straight from the bottle.

"Why the hell did Rosenberg go ahead and introduce Jack to Barcus?" he says. "That wasn't what we agreed to. He loused this whole thing up. I can't blame Jack for being upset."

Ruth feels a dull headache forming across the back of her skull and all she can think is: *What have we set in motion?*

Who's Pulling the Strings?

Despite their plan to squeeze Jack out, Ruth and even Seymour Rosenberg can't deny the man's superior engineering skills. In rapid succession, Jack has been awarded patents for the hip and ankle joints for Living Barbie, the movable waist for Twist 'n Turn Barbie and of course the voice box for Talking Barbie. And there's not a damn thing they can do about it.

Jack's past winning streak has Barcus shaken up. "Got a second, Ruth?" he says one day, hovering in her doorway, beads of perspiration on his forehead.

"What is it?" She's deep in concentration, reviewing the unprecedented number of orders for the new Living Barbie.

"Tell me what you think of this?" Barcus inches inside her office, holding a stack of mechanical drawings.

She sets her index finger on the line for Sears, marking her place while Barcus shows her his Blinking Barbie. "Look, you tilt her head this way and that and she blinks."

"It's been done before," says Ruth.

"But—"

"Reminds me of baby dolls."

The next week, Barcus is back with Flexing Barbie. "See," he says, "her toes flex up and down."

Ruth rolls her eyes. "And how does *that* add play value?"

With each rejection, Barcus's desperation grows while Jack's ego does the same. Striding about the office, Jack turns on the charm, endearing himself to members of the Barcus team. He examines their designs, offers suggestions for improvement, invites them to his upcoming parties.

One afternoon Barcus discovers that Jack has taken the entire Barcus team out to lunch. And at the Bistro in Beverly Hills, a restaurant none of them could afford to dine at. Barcus is livid. He storms up and down the hallway, checking his watch while looking at the empty workstations.

At half past two, unable to contain his rage, Barcus bursts into Ruth's office. "They're all gone." He's shifted from fury to full-blown panic. "My entire team is out doing *God knows what* with Jack Ryan."

By the time the Barcus team returns, it's nearly four o'clock and none of them are in any condition to work. Only Jack appears immune to the countless martinis. Barcus's top engineer is already throwing up in his wastebasket; another is moments away from passing out at his drafting table.

This is becoming a real problem with the two of them," Ruth says to Rosenberg the next day. "Jack's little luncheon cost us a day of productivity. Plus, he's got Barcus spinning out of control. And"— she hands Rosenberg an inventory sheet—"have you seen the November orders for Living Barbie? Sales are exploding," she says.

Rosenberg looks at the totals, and Ruth can tell by his expression that the numbers are even higher than he was expecting.

"The whole idea was to pay him *less*, not *more*," she says. "You were supposed to save me money in royalties, not pay Jack more and make him a hero to boot."

Jack used to relish his bouts of insomnia. No more. Setting aside all his victories over Barcus and his success with Living Barbie, he lies awake at night, disarmed by the mounting pressures at work. He hates what's happened between him and Ruth, how she won't even look at him anymore. And he blames Rosenberg for that. He's poisoned her against him.

Dr. Klemes has challenged him on this point, reminding Jack of the times he took credit for creating the doll, not to mention doing so on national television, first on the game show and then on *The Merv Griffin Show*. But Jack sees it differently. He thinks Ruth's anger and mistrust are all coming from Rosenberg, and it has Jack agitated and paranoid. And despite all the pills and all the booze, Jack still can't sleep.

The worst hours are after two a.m., when the parties wind down and all the sane people are in bed. That's when his inner demons come out. When he's surrounded by darkness, everything frightens him. His body is in a state of rot and decay. He worries that the scab on his arm isn't healing fast enough and could be cancerous. He fears that Ruth or Rosenberg will slip poison into his coffee. He makes a mental note to have his car brakes checked in case they've been tampered with. He knows this is all absurd, but he can't get a handle on his thoughts. The danger escalates, and by three or four in the morning, when he cannot take the solitude anymore, he wakes up his newest batch of UCLA boys. Word has gotten around campus, and now when one group graduates, another group moves into the Castle. The new guys—there are seven of them at last count—are up for anything. They'll join Jack at the pool for a late-night swim or sit in the gazebo and smoke grass until the sun comes up and it's time for him to escape into work.

One morning, after three nights of insomnia, Jack gets called into Elliot's office and finds that he's walked into an ambush. Ruth is there. So is Rosenberg, slurping his coffee. And Barcus, perched on the window ledge like a pigeon.

"I didn't know this was gonna be a party," says Jack. He's playing it cool, trying to keep his composure.

"I'm afraid we've got a problem," says Elliot, massaging his hands together. "I just got off the phone with Sears. They're saying customers are complaining about Talking Barbie."

"Complaining? About what?"

"Looks like the speaking device is overheating," says Elliot. "It's melting the dolls."

Jack shakes his head. "That's bullshit."

"You wanna tell that to Sears?" Rosenberg says, taking another slurp of coffee.

"It's that new plastic you used," Barcus says with glee. "The arms and legs are melting off, too."

"This is going to have tremendous repercussions," Rosenberg says, getting all wound up, making big sweeping arm gestures along with doing lots of headshaking. "It's a complete disaster. And the timing stinks. We have our end of the year stockholder meeting in two months and this is not going to land well with them. At all."

The last time Jack got a jolt like this was the '68 earthquake, which knocked him out of bed. He feels his world falling out from under him and drops into a chair. Yes, he recently changed the plastic to something more cost-effective, but he tested it. Only now he's questioning if he tested it enough. But he's Jack Ryan—he doesn't make mistakes like this. He's embarrassed, mortified, but mostly he's enraged that Ruth and Elliot didn't come to him with this privately. Why are they putting him on display, trying to publicly humiliate him?

Knowing Ruth hates it when he talks to the press, Jack seeks his revenge by arranging an interview with *Esquire* magazine. Two journalists—a reporter and a photographer—come by the Castle to get the goods on the illustrious toymaker and party thrower.

John Riley, the writer, is focused on Jack's social life, his cadre of beautiful women and his extravagant parties, but Jack's modus operandi is to throw Ruth under the bus. And unfortunately, with Ruth, so too must go Elliot. Rosenberg, well, he was already dead to Jack. And Barcus is nothing more than an annoying gnat, not even worth mentioning.

The reporter writes in his pocket notebook, asking Jack why he has so many telephones, if he really throws up to twenty parties a month, if the rumors about the UCLA boys living there are true. He asks a lot of questions, while the photographer sets up his tripod, snapping off pictures, going from room to room, posing Jack in various settings.

Jack takes them out to his tree house. From the time he was a young boy he wanted a tree house, which his mother wouldn't allow since it would ruin her home's facade.

"That's hardly what I'd call a tree house," says the reporter.

"It is so," Jack insists. "There's a tree"—he points to the giant oak—"and there's the house. Isn't it peachy?" He leads them up a circular staircase that wraps around the giant trunk and opens into a spacious, elegant room. "Voilà!"

"This is more like an apartment that happens to be up in a tree," says the photographer, taking pictures of the chandelier hanging above the dining room table.

"I had that designed in Florence," says Jack.

The reporter jots this down in his notebook.

Eventually they end up back inside, in the library, which is just another prop in Jack's Castle. He's carefully staged his library to overcompensate for his word blindness. It gives the impression of Jack as a learned man who relaxes in a leather club chair before a roaring fireplace with a classic novel in his lap and a glass of wine in his hand. The books, once belonging to a true bibliophile, were purchased from an estate sale and are authentically worn with yellowing pages, cracked spines, even some forbidden dog-eared pages.

As they linger in the library, Jack keeps waiting for the interview to shift toward Mattel, but the conversation isn't heading that way. When the reporter caps his pen and starts to close his notebook, Jack launches into a well-rehearsed tirade, referring to Ruth and Elliot only as "the Couple."

"The Couple," Jack says, "are tough folks to work for. Especially *her*. I don't like to brag or be too boastful, but Mattel wouldn't be what it is today without me. I invented Barbie, you know. That's right, I sure did. She's named after my wife, Barbara . . ."

A Change of Plans

t's early December. Tomorrow Ruth, Elliot, Seymour Rosenberg and a handful of others will head to New York for Mattel's end of the year stockholder's meeting. Ruth is somewhat out of sorts. That morning she learned that Barbara is getting divorced, which is not surprising but still upsetting. At least divorce is not the stigma it once was, not like when Charlotte got divorced. Times have changed and Barbara will be better off in the long run. But for now, her daughter is broken, and Ruth feels vindicated for her decision to have discontinued the Allan doll three years ago. Even then, she knew the marriage wouldn't last.

Ruth is in her office early that day, putting the finishing touches on her speech for the stockholders. She plans to gloss over the Talking Barbie disaster and play up the company's growth: *We have now surpassed $100 million in sales in over sixty countries . . . Achieved dominance over a $2 billion toy industry . . . New plants opening in Taiwan and Great Britain . . .*

She's still working on this when Rosenberg pokes his head into her office and asks Ruth to join him for lunch. Elliot is coming, too. She assumes it's to regroup before they leave for New York, but no. It's over pricey chef salads that Rosenberg clobbers them with a change of plans.

"I'll cut to the chase," he says. "Ruth, you're not going to New York."

"What?"

"You won't be delivering the year-end review."

"What? What are you talking about? I do it every year. I've already got my speech written."

"As do I," says Rosenberg, an open hand placed upon his chest.

"Is this some kind of joke?" asks Elliot. "*You're* going to give the end of the year report?"

"That's right. I've already discussed it with the board of directors."

Rosenberg's been talking to the board? Without Elliot? He's been doing this behind both our backs? Ruth feels like she's been stabbed in the heart. Elliot does, too.

Rosenberg wipes his mouth with his napkin. "There's no easy way to say this. And Ruth, God knows everyone appreciates all that you've done, but going forward, you just"—he shakes his head—"you can't be the face of Mattel."

"What? Are you out of your fucking mind? I built Mattel. Mattel is nothing without me."

"Trust me, Ruth"—Rosenberg offers a half-hearted shrug—"Wall Street will eat you alive."

She laughs bitterly. "If you think that, then you don't know me very well."

"Fine," says Rosenberg. "I'll just come right out and say it. You're not the right person to take Mattel into the future."

"Why the hell not?" asks Elliot.

"Give me one good reason," says Ruth.

"I'll give you three." Rosenberg starts counting off on his stubby fingers: "First, you're a woman. Second, you're Jewish—"

"Excuse me," she flares, "*you're* Jewish."

"Third," he says, not acknowledging her point, "you don't have the right temperament. You talk like a drunken sailor. You're too rough around the edges. No one knows how to deal with you. They're more comfortable dealing with a man—even a Jewish man—who knows his way around Wall Street."

"You sonofabitch." She tosses her napkin on the table and bolts out of her chair. "Go fuck yourself."

Elliot rushes after her, leaving Rosenberg at the table.

Before they get to the car, Ruth says, "I'm gonna fire that piece of shit. I swear to God, I am."

Elliot quietly, gently informs her that she can't do that.

"What do you mean I can't? Because of him, I'm president of this company. I can do whatever the hell I want."

"Ruthie, think about it. You can't fire Rosenberg. Wall Street loves him—right or wrong, they do. You saw what bringing him on board did to our stock. If we turn around and fire him, people will lose confidence in the company. It makes us look like we don't know what we're doing."

"But you heard what he said to me in there. That cocksucker owes me an apology."

Elliot is nodding. "And I plan to talk to him about that. I'll get him to apologize. But Ruthie, I'm afraid that won't change the outcome. He's already met with the board, and right now, they're the ones making the decisions, not us."

After Ruth and Elliot get back to Mattel, she walks out to the main floor. They've recently invested half a million dollars for another 35,000-square-foot addition to the building. They've rearranged departments and moved desks and workstations closer together to accommodate all the new hires, some of whom she hasn't even met because Rosenberg brought them on board. There are new engineers, new research teams. They have a new general counsel who has been beefing up their legal department. Ruth's heard the girls buzzing about Simon something or other.

She's feeling almost as nostalgic as she is raw, remembering the good old days when she knew everyone's name, the names of their wives and husbands, their children, too. She remembers the times Barbara and Ken came to the office, delighted to play with all the new toys. Now Ruth's standing in the middle of what used to be the model makers, section, which is now the customer service department, or maybe it's human resources—she can't remember. She feels disoriented. Where's Charlotte? Where are the designers? Nothing and no one is where they should be. Her chest feels a squeeze; she's perspiring and queasy. For a moment she worries that she's having a heart attack, but it's just that she knows she's losing control of her company. She's sold out Mattel to Wall Street.

PART FOUR

Fall of the
Dominoes

Im-pul-siv-i-ty Strikes Again

1970

The new decade is off to a difficult start for Jack. His father died on Christmas Day, flooding Jack with a mixture of grief and guilty liberation. With his father gone, he's free to begin divorce proceedings, despite his mother's harping about marriage vows being sacred. It's not that his mother's opinions don't matter, but they don't have the heft of his late father's expectations. Jack can deal with disappointing his mother. After all, he's been doing that all his life. And so the day after the funeral, Barbara and the girls moved out of the Castle.

Between his father's passing, his mother's nagging and the divorce, Jack had all but forgotten about the interview he gave to *Esquire* magazine several months before. But now the issue is on the newsstands. Of course, he can't read it himself, but he's seen the pictures. Utterly ridiculous photographs. *How could I have thought this was a good idea?* There's an absurd photo of him in a smoking jacket—*a smoking jacket*—lying beneath a fur blanket—*a fur blanket*—in his bed—*in my goddamn bed*—talking on the phone. Two university flags—Yale and Harvard—hang above his head. He looks like a pompous fool. A caricature of himself.

Despite the photos, he's desperate to know if the article has properly lambasted Ruth. He calls Ginger into his office and hands her the magazine.

"Wow," she says, opening to page eighty-three. "Look at you. This is so exciting."

"Just"—he makes a circular *hurry it up* gesture—"just start reading, would you?"

She clears her throat and begins. "*Class in Our Time*. And there's a caption beneath the photo. It says"—she pitches her voice up an octave higher for effect—"*That's Jack Ryan on one of his 140 telephones. Come on over for some corn on the cob.*"

"Ah, fuck!" He slaps the sides of his head. "Corn on the cob?" He moves from the couch to his bearskin rug, squirming as Ginger reads the full nine pages about *Jack Ryan the playboy, the mad scientist, the man who throws orgies at his Bel Air castle*. They hardly mention Barbie or the Couple at all. His plan to sabotage Ruth has backfired spectacularly. He's a laughingstock. He is beside himself and would like to crawl into a hole and die. This issue is out in the world now, on every newsstand, in every drugstore, landing on people's doorsteps. Everyone's reading it and he's mortified.

"Why are you so upset?" says Ginger. "You got a whole feature in a major magazine. You're famous."

"Or infamous."

"Aw, no, don't say that. That's not so. You're the life of the party, and they captured how brilliant and creative you are. And"—she smiles suggestively—"you're one of Hollywood's most eligible bachelors."

"Except for the fact that I'm still technically married."

"Well, you're *almost* unmarried, which reminds me, your lawyer dropped off some papers for you to sign."

More papers. More words. He stands up, rubs his eyes and

squeezes the back of his neck. His body's tense, and his blood feels thick, like it's not even circulating anymore. Ginger is already standing behind him, massaging his shoulders and cooing in his ear, reminding him to breathe and relax. He feels her breasts pressing against him, smells her perfume, the one he gave her for Secretaries Day—L'Air du Temps, one of Barbara's favorites. It used to drive him crazy. He dares to close his eyes and sink into Ginger's touch when he's bolted to attention.

"Am I interrupting something?" It's Ruth, standing in his office, the *Esquire* magazine in her hand. "Ginger, I need to speak with Jack. Privately."

Ginger retreats to the ladies' room, where she sobs into a fistful of paper towels, yanked from the wall dispenser. *Why did Ruth have to barge in and ruin the moment? Why doesn't Jack ever make the first move? How many times can I throw myself at him?*

She studies herself in the mirror, wondering what's wrong with her. He's said so himself: *If Barbie were real, she'd be the perfect woman.* Ginger's trying her best. People say she looks like Barbie, but Jack only tells her she's getting too thin. But she knows for a fact that Jack likes thin women, and if she could just break 110—the number on Barbie's scale, a number she's given magical powers to—then maybe he would look at her the way he looks at other women, the way she sees him looking at Patsy, at Stevie and at so many other women, but never her.

Meanwhile, Ruth is still in Jack's office, berating him. "I hope you're satisfied." She shakes the magazine in his face. "You've made a mockery out of my company and Barbie. How dare you drag Barbie's name into your disgusting, perverted lifestyle. If you hurt her sales, I swear to God, I'll sue you for damages."

"Jesus, Ruth, nobody's going to hurt her sales."

But they both know Barbie is under attack. Stevie reports back from her consciousness-raising groups and rap sessions, which she attends both to get a bead on Barbie and to air her own grievances. The National Organization for Women is looking for any excuse to blame Barbie for everything from gender inequality to low self-esteem. NOW has even gone so far as to attack Mattel for advertising *smart toys* to boys and *frilly Barbies* to girls.

Still, Ruth is in a rage, and for now, it's all Jack's fault. "I don't want Barbie's image tarnished because of your drugs and disgusting sex parties."

"Sex parties?" He forces a laugh. "I wouldn't exactly call them sex parties."

"Obviously you don't care about your reputation, but I care about Barbie's. And mine. You look like a goddamn fool in this article." She shakes the magazine like a pom-pom. "You're a clown. An idiot . . ."

Each time Ruth opens her mouth with another insult, Jack shrinks more inside his skin. He covers his ears like a child and finds that he's twelve years old again. He's just been called into the principal's office, where his mother stands, scolding him for designing a crystal radio set during English class. Like Ruth, Lily Ryan calls her son a clown, an idiot.

There's little left of Jack by the time Ruth leaves his office. If he could take back the article, he would. But it's out there now and he has to live with the consequences, another result of his im-pul-siv-i-ty. He reaches into his desk drawer and shakes a Valium tablet into his palm: the latest medication that Dr. Klemes has prescribed, and even though it's not yet noon, he washes it down with a glass of scotch.

They Got It All

R uth grinds out her cigarette, tucks her hair into her shower cap and runs her hand under the water to test the temperature. She likes to shower in the evening before bed to help her relax from the stress, of which there's no shortage.

Aside from all the ongoing tension with Rosenberg and Jack, for the past six months it's been one upset after another. Last December, a fire broke out in their Mexicali factory, killing one of their assembly-line workers. Given the destruction and devastation, they were fortunate there weren't other casualties. That facility was where all the bits and pieces—the arms and legs on Chatty Cathy, the musical scales on the xylophones, the tires on Hot Wheels, Bugs Bunny's voice box, and other toys—come together. The entire building burned to the ground, destroying all their merchandise that was about to ship for Christmas. It's June now and Ruth's still dealing with the aftermath. Rebuilding has been slow and costly. Their insurance is only covering part of what they lost. They took a significant hit on last year's Christmas sales and their first-quarter earnings were soft. Second quarter isn't looking much better. Even their Hot Wheels sales have cooled down. But at least Barbara's divorce is finalized. That's the only good thing that's happened so far this year.

The steamy water pelts down on her back and shoulders, which are knotted and tense, trying to release. Ruth's sudsy fingers glide over her skin, under her arm and across her left breast, where they stop. She presses, rubs, rinses, presses again. Her breathing turns shallow. She moves to her right breast, scarred like the left one from previous needle biopsies. She goes back to her left breast. It's there, all right. Another lump. But it feels different from the other ones. Her body is suddenly scalding. She sees little stars and feels like she's about to pass out. She turns off the shower and gropes for a towel.

Dripping wet, she studies her breasts in the mirror, raising her arms above her head, turning from side to side. She can't see the lump, but her fingertips confirm it's there. She closes the toilet lid and drops down, unable to believe this is happening again. She's never really been free of this fear, and there's never a good time for cancer, but she's not prepared for this. Not now. And heaven help her, she wants a cigarette.

She gets up, slips into her bathrobe, tightens the belt. Sitting in the chair, off in the corner of her bedroom, she smokes as she looks at Elliot. He's asleep and she doesn't wake him for this. She doesn't want to face it; she wants to make it go away and reasons that it's probably just another fibrous cyst, maybe scar tissue from a previous biopsy. The main thing is not to panic. She tells herself they'll find nothing. And yet she's terrified. Even with the cigarette in her hand, she swears she'll quit smoking. She promises she'll go back to the hypnotist. That is what she tells herself, and this time she means it, because even Ruth knows this lump feels different.

I t all happens so fast. One day Ruth and Elliot are in the doctor's office and the next, she's having exploratory surgery. Afterward they tell her she's lucky. "We got it all," says the surgeon. *All* including her breast. And her lymph nodes. She won't remember the doctor saying anything about the nerve and muscle damage because Ruth is still stuck on the fact that this was only supposed to be *exploratory* surgery. They weren't supposed to take anything.

One week later, she leaves the hospital and recuperates at their Malibu beach house. At first, nurses come and go, arriving to change her dressing, check her surgical drains. Each day there's a little less gauze, and that's when the nightmare of what she's left with sets in. She can see the stitches now, can see the red, angry, puckered flesh and how badly she's been marred.

Ken and Suzie have flown in from New York for the week, bringing their three children with them. Barbara lives close by and is there every day with Cheryl and Todd. All of them act as if this is a family reunion. During the afternoons, Ruth sits on the back porch watching her grandchildren build sandcastles and jump the ocean waves. In the evenings, big meals are prepared. One night Elliot pulls out his projector and trays of slides followed by home movies. The next night he brings out his first toy, the Uke-A-Doodle, and they have a sing-along while Ken accompanies him on the piano. There's laughter, there's reminiscing and no one mentions the word *cancer*. It's as if she had a hernia operation or an appendectomy.

Ken is the only one who comes close to acknowledging what she's been through. One night she excuses herself from the table. She's exhausted and needs to lie down. She has her arm propped up on a pile of pillows but can't get comfortable. The endless throbbing that runs from her rib cage to her armpit is relentless, and her entire left side is tingling, like half her body has fallen asleep.

Moments later her son knocks on the door. "Can I come in?" Sitting on the side of the bed, he says, "You're gonna be all right. They got it all."

There it is again. *They got it all.* She smiles, but thinks, *What if they missed even just one tiny speck? It could come back. It could be regenerating inside me right now.* She's terrified that the cancer is not done with her. The very thought is like a hot stove she can't get too close to, so she backs away and changes the subject, asking him about life in New York.

"You're so far away now. Do you think you'll ever move back?"

He shakes his head. "I'm happier in New York." He tells her about the screenplay he's writing and the director he wants to work with, Roland something or other. *Roland has a great idea for the main character. Roland wants me to consider changing the ending. Roland invited me out to his place in the Hamptons.* Ken is still talking about Roland when Ruth—sensing there's more between Ken and Roland than the screenplay—changes the subject again. "Before I forget, your father brought home some new Barbies for the girls. You can—"

"Ah, Mom." Ken shakes his head. "The girls don't play with Barbies anymore."

"What do you mean, they don't play with Barbies anymore?"

Ken makes a small gesture suggesting the reason should be obvious. "Stacey's too old, and Sam—"

"Oh, that's nonsense," she balks. "Your sister's collected dolls all her life. Some people even think those Barbies will be worth some money one day. And Samantha's certainly not too old for Barbie."

"No, but Suzie and I—well, we want the girls to understand that there's more to life than fancy clothes and pink cars."

She knows he's always thought Barbie was silly, but this feels different. Now Ruth feels she's being judged by her son. Possibly even punished. "You're not still upset about the Ken doll after all these years, are you?"

"It's not about the Ken doll," he says, though going through life as Barbie's emasculated boyfriend has done him no favors. Or his children, whose friends all know their father is Ken, which has been met with mixed reviews. They may or may not realize that Barbie is also their friends' aunt.

While Ken's still talking, Ruth's eyes grow heavy. She can't fight the exhaustion anymore and drifts off to sleep.

Elliot wakes her several hours later. The sun has set, and he turns on the lamp on her nightstand. "Why don't we get you ready for bed," he says, helping her sit up. He starts to unbutton her blouse, but she stops him, her eyes squeezed shut.

"Ruthie," he says gently, "I'm going to have to see sooner or later."

But there's no way to prepare him for what's left of her. "No, no, I can get myself undressed." But she can't. Each time she moves her arm it sends a searing pain so fierce it makes her want to retch. She gives up and sleeps in her clothes that night.

The next day Barbara encourages her to take a walk on the beach. Other than her doctor and nurse, Barbara is the only person Ruth allows to see her naked, and that's only because she's so weak and needs help bathing and getting dressed.

"I'm sorry you have to do this," she says later as Barbara helps her out of the tub because her body can't handle the water pressure from the shower.

"How many times did you give me a bath when I was little, huh? It's my turn now." She gently towels her off and opens the dusting powder. "This'll make you feel better," she says, lightly brushing the floral-smelling powder across Ruth's back and shoulders. "You've always been so tough," Barbara says. "And don't take this the wrong way—I mean, I'm not happy that you're going through all this—but I do kinda like this vulnerable side of you. I've never seen you drop your guard for anyone. I never knew how to get close to you because you never needed me. And now, whether you like it or not, you do."

I like it is what Ruth wants to say, but she can't get the words past the lump in her throat. She reaches up with her good arm and squeezes Barbara's hand. "I know I wasn't a great mother when you kids were growing up, but I did the best I could. I did for you and Ken what Aunt Sarah did for me. I didn't know any better. But now when I see you with Cheryl and Todd"—her voice begins to crack—"well, I see now what I missed out on. You're wonderful with those kids. So kind and patient, so full of love for them. You're much better at this than I ever was. I don't know how you turned out to be so good at motherhood, because you certainly didn't get it from me." And with that, even though it sends a piercing blade of pain through her, she finds a way to press a kiss onto Barbara's hand.

Another week goes by. Ken and his family are back in New York. Barbara is busy with the children now that school is out for the summer. Elliot is back at work and Ruth is struggling to fill her days. She doesn't want anyone at Mattel to know about her breast cancer, so Elliot tells anyone who asks that she's recovering from pneumonia. Breast cancer is taboo. There's a stigma associated with it. Even in her doctor's office, when she's in the waiting room, surrounded by women who also have breast cancer, who could benefit from each other's stories, comfort each other and give each other hope, they stay silent. They keep everything to themselves, barely even looking up from their magazines. But the anxiety and sadness in there, it's palpable. Along with guilt and shame, like it's their fault they got sick.

Ruth definitely blames herself. All those years of smoking. She did this to herself, a self-inflicted wound. And how can it be that after losing a breast, she'd still kill for a cigarette? The urge comes over her with an intensity as gripping as the pain. She has sessions with her hypnotist, who comes to the house twice a week. She eats celery and carrot sticks, slices of apples, and chewing gum, which she despises. Elliot has cleaned every ashtray and thrown out any cigarettes he's found, even forcing her to reveal her hiding places: the bottom drawer in her bathroom and the back of the cedar closet. It's a good thing, too, because she's emotionally fragile and would surely cave if she could get her hands on a cigarette.

Time drags on. Except for her pregnancies, she's always been in an office, surrounded by the business bustle—telephones ringing, typewriters clacking, people coming and going. This nothingness where she plans her days around what to eat for lunch is mind-numbing. She asks Elliot to bring her some paperwork from the office, but she hasn't got the attention span to review W Reports or anything else. Instead, she passes each afternoon watching *All My Children* and *General Hospital*, trying to escape into the make-believe lands of Pine Valley and Port Charles. Five weeks into this, she's about to lose her mind. After much pleading, her doctor says he'll consider letting her return to Mattel in another month or so.

In anticipation of going back to work, the big question is what she'll wear. She stands before her closet filled with racks of finely tailored dresses and business suits. She's spent a fortune on her wardrobe, has favored designers like Pierre Cardin, Givenchy, Yves Saint Laurent. Her clothes are sleek, formfitting, and she can't wear any of them now. The sight of them hanging there, mocking her, is too much. She drops to the side of the bed and begins to weep.

Barbara finds her like that, slumped over herself in a night-gown, face in her hands. When Ruth explains her predicament,

Barbara suggests they go shopping. "We'll go to Bullock's," she says. "They have a great lingerie department. They must have some sort of special bras there."

Ruth resists. She hasn't been out in public other than to walk along the beach. But Barbara insists with a force to rival Ruth's own resolve.

I can't believe this is all they have," says Ruth, holding a prosthetic breast, something akin to a beige teardrop. It doesn't look like a breast. It doesn't feel like one, either. "These are awful," she says, rooting through a bin of stiff blobs in various sizes, ranging from #1, being the smallest, to #6, the largest. "I could design a better breast than this." She thinks, *I'd do it, too, if I had the energy*. But she is depleted. It takes all she has just to make it through the day.

She and Barbara go to the fitting room, and she's reminded of the time Sarah took her to buy her first bra. It hits her like a double whammy, and she can't handle the loss of her sister along with the loss of her breast. If she's going to get through this, she has to look to the future.

"Who invented this monstrosity?" Ruth asks, hoping to shift her mood. She's holding up a thick white surgical bra, lined with built-in holders for the teardrops. "Frederick's of Hollywood's got nothing on these people."

Barbara chuckles. "Try this one." She hands Ruth a different size, but it fits no better.

"Now it looks like I stuck a sock in my bra."

"You *are* a little lopsided," Barbara agrees, laughing.

"A little?" Ruth raises an eyebrow, making Barbara laugh even harder. "This doesn't look remotely natural. Hell, even Barbie's breasts look more natural than these." She starts laughing, too. "I should go into the boob business again."

Barbara takes it up a notch higher. "These aren't prosthetics, they're *pathetics*."

This cracks them both up.

"Oh God," says Barbara, "I think I just peed myself."

Ruth doubles over, practically howling now, clutching her sides. "Oh, stop, stop," she begs. "Stop making me laugh. It hurts." But it also feels good.

The Coffee Klatch

One morning in the galley kitchen, Stevie finally meets the elusive Simon Richards. He joined Mattel's legal department almost a year ago, but they've never actually met. She's passed him in the hall, seen him out in the parking lot, but she's never been this close to him, and now she understands why her female coworkers are so taken with him. Or else she thinks it could be the power of suggestion. But no, Simon Richards is absolutely a handsome man, impossibly chiseled with a full head of dark hair and white symmetrical teeth.

He's attempting to make a pot of coffee, and while he may be an ace with contracts and negotiations, he can't quite figure out how the coffee machine works. She's impressed that he's even trying. Most of the guys just call out to the nearest female, "Pot's empty."

"Here," Stevie says, taking over. "It's a little tricky." Her hand brushes against his as she reaches for the basket, and it sets off an unexpected flutter of excitement. It's been so long that she's almost forgotten what that initial spark of attraction feels like. She's sud-

denly all girly-like, which really isn't her style, but she has to admit
it's fun, electrifying.

Simon starts making small talk, asking how long she's been at
Mattel and what exactly she does here. She's scooping coffee
grounds into the basket as she speaks, glancing up whenever she
can to study the golden flecks in his hazel eyes. He's very distract-
ing, and she loses count on the coffee.

"Do you have any idea if that was six or eight scoops?" she asks.

He laughs. "To be honest, I wasn't paying attention to the coffee."

Is he flirting with her? Her cheeks flush, and as she dumps the
coffee grounds back into the canister to start over again, Jack appears.

"What have we here? A little coffee klatch?" He leans against
the counter, sizing up the situation.

The invisible tug—or whatever it is—between Stevie and Simon goes slack.

"Hey, Simon," Jack says, "I've been meaning to ask you about a
licensing agreement . . ." Jack rambles on until he's satisfied that
whatever was brewing between Stevie and Simon is gone.

Elliot and Ruth used to make the rounds in the cafeteria. Back
in the days when it was easy to keep track of all their employees, they would take turns having lunch with different groups: the
engineers one day, the designers the next, sales the day after that.
Now Mattel's too big, and Ruth is still out sick, so Elliot looks for
familiar faces to eat with.

He sees Jack sitting at a table in the back row with Stevie, Patsy
and Ginger. Because of Ruth, things have been strained between
him and Jack, but Elliot still wants to repair the damage, put things

back the way they were, and so he heads over with his tray. When he joins them, they're all talking about the shocking news that Janis Joplin has died from a drug overdose.

"First Jimi Hendrix and now her. Those rock stars are dropping like flies," says Elliot.

"She was just twenty-seven," says Ginger. She's barely touched her soup but allows herself one plain corn tortilla, which has fewer calories than the flour ones.

"Gotta know how to handle your drugs," says Jack.

Stevie wants to say, *Remember that*. On top of whatever medications his doctor has him on, plus all the booze, Jack's recently discovered cocaine. It's a dangerous combination, and she's warned him to be careful.

Changing the subject, Stevie asks Elliot about Ruth. "We miss her around here," she says.

"She'll appreciate hearing that. She's coming back soon. She just wants to, you know"—he glances down at his untouched burrito—"she wants to make sure she's a hundred percent over *this* before she comes back." He's a bad liar and quickly shifts the subject away from Ruth's health, saying that he showed her Barbie's new *Lemon Kick* outfit from the 1400 series. "She just loved the yellow chiffon and those palazzo pants . . ."

While Elliot's talking, Stevie gets a strange, though not altogether unpleasant, feeling. It's hard to describe—it's like the sensation of thermal heat building beneath the ground. She senses she's being watched. And she is. From the other end of the cafeteria, she glances up and locks eyes with Simon. He's seated at a long table with the other lawyers. She smiles, and when she turns back, Jack's eyes are all over her. He knows that look. There was a time when she looked at him in that same way.

H ow long does it take someone to get over pneumonia, anyway?" Stevie asks Jack later that day.

They needed what Jack calls a *creative breather*, an excuse to get
out of the office and free up their imaginations. The two of them
are down by the beach. They've left their shoes on the dock and
Jack has rolled his custom-made trousers to his calves. They walk
along the surf, the water sloshing over their bare feet.

"When do you think Ruth's coming back?" she asks.

"Don't know. Don't care."

"Don't say that."

"Well, I for one don't miss the bitch."

"Hey, c'mon, cool it with the Ruth bashing."

"I know, I know, you *love* her." He makes a half-hearted jazz
hands gesture.

"I do. And I'm worried about her. She's important to me. And I
hate that you two don't get along anymore."

"It's her fault. She's a ball-breaker."

"Because she's had to be." Stevie stops and faces him. "Do you
have any idea what women in the work world are up against?"

"Oh my God. Here you go again with your women's lib stuff. I
think I liked you better before you started going to those meetings."

"You sound like a chauvinist. You know, a man can throw his
weight around and no one questions it, but if a woman exerts even
a little forcefulness, she's a ball-breaker. I happen to admire Ruth."

"I used to admire her. Before I started to despise her."

"Enough, Jack. I mean it."

"Okay, I'll shut up about her."

"Thank you."

They start walking again. There's a slight breeze and the sunlight is glinting off the ocean, sparkling like a sea of diamonds.

"So," she changes gears, trying to sound casual. "What do you think about Simon?"

"Richards? You mean Mr. Pretty Boy?"

"He's not pretty. He's handsome."

"Oh, you think so, do you?"

"And what if I do?"

"Oh God, Stevie"—he stops walking—"please don't tell me you've got a *thing* for him."

"I'm not saying a damn word."

"I'm losing you, aren't I?"

"You'll never lose me, Jack."

"Sure I will." He loops his arm around her waist. "Just don't leave me yet. I still need you, kiddo."

Not So Ruthless Anymore

1971

Helen Reddy is topping the music charts. "I am woman, hear me roar . . ." plays each time Ruth turns on the radio. *I used to roar*, she thinks. *Hell, I was roaring before Helen Reddy was even born. What's happened to me?*

Ruth's been back at work for six months now, but she doesn't feel like herself. She doesn't look like herself, either. She's fifty-four and feels ninety-four. She's gained fifteen pounds, and on her petite frame it might as well have been fifty. She diets but to no avail. Her hair seems to have gone gray overnight. She has no patience to sit in a beauty parlor, and so she leaves it.

Eventually, she and Barbara did find a prosthetic breast at the May Company. But it was heavy, stiff and pressed against her chest, taking her nerve pain to a new level, and eventually she stopped wearing it. Now there's a sunken cavity in her chest, and nothing she wears really camouflages this, not even when her blouses are a size too big and she buttons them to her chin.

She worries everyone is looking at her, at what's left of her. She feels their eyes on her even now, as she enters the boardroom for their monthly planning meeting. Almost everyone seems to have a cigarette going. She can't tell them not to smoke. They think she had pneumonia—surely she's fine by now. But oh, the smell of their cigarettes is intoxicating. It's like inhaling a favorite food.

Aside from herself and Charlotte, it's all men, several of whom Ruth doesn't get along with. Rosenberg plucks a donut from the plate in the center of the table. He's missed a button on his shirt and it leaves a pucker across his belly. His sloppiness, his lack of attention to details, even about himself, drives her crazy.

Once Rosenberg starts the meeting, she sits back, listening to his update on new acquisitions. Jack barely looks up. He seems to be as much of an outsider as she is these days. Rosenberg's been on a buying spree, gobbling up businesses—a pet food company, some sort of audio tape company, and now he's set his sights on Ringling Bros. and Barnum & Bailey Circus. *This whole place is turning into a circus*, she thinks. The meeting is all over the place. They move from topic to topic without resolving anything. When she was in charge, they followed a standard protocol, but in her absence, Rosenberg has adopted his own methods.

Elliot tried to intervene, but he's always been on the creative side and left the business logistics to Ruth. He's admittedly out of his depth when it comes to these things, plus he was too worried about Ruth's health to go to battle with Rosenberg. She hasn't been herself since the surgery and he doesn't know how to help her through this. She won't let him touch her anymore and he can't make her understand she's still beautiful to him. He doesn't love her any less—if anything, he loves her even more.

Now that she's back, Ruth doesn't like what she sees happening under Rosenberg's leadership. After all their previous success, things seem to be spiraling downward. They'd barely recovered from the Mexicali fire when another crisis hit them. In July of last year, while she was still at home recovering, the International Longshore and Warehouse Union decided to strike. All their members walked off the job. The ports along the West Coast have been abandoned, and Mattel's inventory is just sitting idle along with everyone else's. If the strike doesn't get resolved soon, they're going to be in danger of messing up another Christmas season—which would make two in a row.

Unable to keep quiet any longer, Ruth asks Rosenberg about the Toy Line Projection reports.

"We don't need the TLP reports," he says.

"How else are we supposed to know if our forecasts are right? What about ad spending? Delays in the production schedules? How are we going to—"

"Ruth," Rosenberg cuts her off with a patronizing laugh, "relax. I've got this under control."

"No, I don't think you do." She's been rather meek ever since returning to work. Just getting through her days is physically and emotionally exhausting. Even now the timbre of her voice is weak and there's perspiration breaking out along the nape of her neck and underarms. In the past, taking on a challenger, mopping the floor with them, never fazed her. And here she is sweating. "Seymour," she says, "this sounds like a disaster waiting to happen. I want—"

Rosenberg slams his hands on the table, a thunderous sound that makes everyone jump. Including her. "I'm running this meeting, Ruth. Not you. If you don't like what I have to say, then I suggest you leave."

And she does. Ruth barely makes it to her office before she starts to cry. She flings herself onto her pink sofa and muffles her sobs in one of the throw pillows. This isn't the first time she's cried in the privacy of her office. Since her surgery, she's been overly emotional. She wants a cigarette but doesn't dare. Elliot will kill her faster than the nicotine.

She's furious with Rosenberg. And herself. She's mad that she's gained all this weight, that she can't make the nerve pain stop, that she can't even brush her own hair without wincing, that somebody rearranged all the toys in the lobby display case, that she wants a cigarette and they've taken that away from her, too.

She practices her breathing and other exercises her hypnotist gave her. They never should have brought Rosenberg on board. She doesn't even recognize the company she built. Or herself. Who is she now, sitting back in meetings, letting everyone else run the show? She's lost her edge along with her breast. She never would have backed down in a boardroom before. No one would even think to call her Ruthless anymore. She needs to do something to regain the ground she's lost, the ground that's been stolen out from under her. She needs to make a move, needs to reclaim her power and let everyone—especially Rosenberg—know that she's still in charge.

A few days later, almost by accident, Ruth discovers her next play. It comes to her while doing the one tedious task Rosenberg hasn't taken away from her, which is reviewing the company contracts. That's when she realizes that Jack's contract is up for renewal.

Years ago, when they became aware of their unintentionally generous royalty arrangement with Jack, they couldn't do anything because they were legally bound to honor their agreement. Much as she wanted to, she never said a word about it to Jack. But his contract is about to expire, and this presents her with an enticing opportunity. Rosenberg—with all his Wall Street experience, even with his genius idea to bring on Barcus—couldn't fix the problem, but she sure as hell can.

She runs her plan by legal and they assure her that yes, it's within her power to restructure Jack's contract, though they doubt Jack will go for it and warn that she needs to be prepared for that. She doesn't really hear that last part because she's focused on Jack—she wants to make an example of him. She needs to let it be known that she's calling the shots again.

She's like a snowball rolling downhill, picking up speed and mass as she goes. She spends the rest of the day reworking the details of Jack's contract to her specifications. From now on Jack will receive royalties only on the products he holds patents for. It's a drastic change. It will reduce his income by almost a third. But even so, he'll still be making millions. Hopefully Barcus will eventually figure out his work-arounds on Jack's patents and they won't have to pay him for those, either.

When she gets it all set, she huddles with Elliot and Rosenberg in her office. "Look what's up for renewal," she says, waving a document.

"Is that Jack's contract?" asks Elliot.

She nods. "I want to restructure it."

"Restructure it how?" asks Rosenberg.

She explains the changes she wants to make, which makes Elliot uncomfortable. "Ruthie," he warns, "that's awfully extreme."

Rosenberg never liked Jack to begin with and is all in favor of this move.

"But if we push Jack too far," says Elliot, "he'll leave."

"Isn't that what we want?" asks Rosenberg.

"I don't know, is it?" Elliot counters. "That was the plan once upon a time, but is Barcus anywhere near as good as Jack? No. Think about Twist 'n Turn, the bendable legs, Hot Wheels—shall

I go on? Jack's been instrumental in the launch of Malibu Barbie, while Barcus is dicking around with ways to give Ken facial hair."

"I know, I know," says Rosenberg. "But the real question is this—will any product or *future* products that Jack designs be worth what you're paying him? I don't think so. And if Barcus can't get the job done, we'll hire another engineer—hell, we could hire a whole new team of engineers for a fraction of what we're paying Jack now."

Elliot looks at them both, bewildered. He's had his own differences with Jack through the years, but he wants them to hit the brakes on this. He wants cooler heads to prevail, but he hasn't got the strength to fight them.

"We have to do this, Elliot. It's time," says Rosenberg.

"I'll handle it," says Ruth. "I'll talk to Jack." She's so cold. So emotionless about it. But she has to be this way. If that soft spot she once felt for him opens up, she won't be able to go through with it.

Jack is nursing a hangover. His stomach's sour, his head's pounding. Ginger comes to the rescue with aspirin, seltzer, and a bottle of Visine. Looking into the mirror on the back of his door, he sees how bloodshot his eyes are. The drops do little to relieve the burning or the redness.

"Ruth just called," says Ginger. "She wants to see you in her office."

He groans. He really didn't miss being at Ruth's beck and call while she was out with pneumonia or the bubonic plague or whatever the hell she had. "Tell her I'm sick."

"I already did. She said, and I quote: 'Tell him to get his ass in here. Now.' End quote."

"Lovely." Before he turns back around, he catches Ginger's reflection in the mirror, observing how drawn her face is, how bony her arms are. "Are you still taking those diet pills?"

"Of course." She smiles. "Just a few more pounds to go."

"No, stop it. Don't lose any more weight," he says. "You're getting too thin. You should put back on a good ten pounds."

"But Jack—"

"I'm telling you, stop with the dieting." He takes the aspirin with a swig of seltzer and sits on his couch, slowly sipping the rest until he's drained the bottle. Then and only then, when he's good and ready, does he mosey on over to Ruth's office.

"You look like hell," Ruth says.

"I could say the same for you."

"Well, this meeting's off to a pleasant start. As long as we're having such an honest exchange, I wanted to talk to you about something. Have a seat."

He considers standing just to make a point, but that strikes him as juvenile. Besides, his back is aching. He'd be more comfortable sitting, so he obliges and takes a seat.

"Your contract is up for renewal, and we've decided to restructure your deal," she says, sliding a revised copy of the contract across the desk toward him.

Jack picks it up, and while the words are making no sense, circling and spinning before his eyes, various sets of numbers jump out at him. While he pretends to read, Ruth keeps talking.

"As you can see," she says, "this new agreement stipulates that you'll receive royalties *only* on the products you hold patents for."

His head snaps up. "What kind of horseshit is that? What about products that aren't patented?"

"What about them? You won't be entitled to royalties on those going forward. Frankly, you never should have gotten royalties for those in the first place."

"And you expect me to take this kind of a haircut?"

"That's the deal, Jack. Take it or leave it." She holds out her pen for him to sign.

"Whoa, whoa, wait a minute. Just slow down."

"This has been a long time coming. Don't act like you're surprised. It's not personal. It's business."

"Like hell it's not personal. We used to be on the same team, you and me. When did we become enemies?" He stands up, taking the contract with him. "I need to think about this," he says. But what he really needs is for Ginger to read it to him.

He leaves Ruth and motions for Ginger to follow him into his office. Closing the door, he hands her the contract. "Start at the beginning. Every word. Don't leave out so much as a period."

She sits beside him, and as she reads, Jack is mentally adding and subtracting the numbers. At one point he clasps both sides of his head and springs up off the couch. Ruth's asking him to give up almost $2 million. And that's just for this royalty period alone. "Shit. Goddammit. God. Goddammit." He paces the room while Ginger keeps reading, interrupting her every now and again with another "Motherfucker. I can't believe her. That bitch . . ."

What's he supposed to do about this? Leave the company? But Mattel has been his world. What would he do if he did quit? Redesign the Castle. Again? Be a professional party thrower? That's not enough. He's not ready to leave. He still has ideas. He feels he's just getting started. Besides, he knows Ruth wants him to quit, and he's not about to make this easy for her.

"Give me a pen," he says. Out of spite and stubbornness, he signs the contract. His signature is big and elaborate, the *J* and the *R* overly rounded. It's practiced, meant to be imposing and overcompensate for the fact that he can't read whatever he's put his name to. Handing the contract back to Ginger, he says, "Give it to her. Do it now. Let's just get this over with."

But as soon as Ginger leaves, he wants to stop her, take it all back, rip the contract to shreds. But it's done, and the walls are closing in on him. He's clammy and lightheaded, huffing with each breath. Jesus, is he having a heart attack? Is he cracking up? He calls Stevie. She's not at her desk. He takes two Valium—this is certainly a two-Valium event—and because he's out of seltzer, he chases it down with bourbon.

Fifteen minutes later, Ginger knocks gently on the door. "Are you okay?" she asks, stepping inside to check on him.

"Oh God, Ginger," he says, already feeling loopy, the booze hitting him hard on an empty stomach. He's probably never been happier to see anyone in his entire life. He cannot be alone with his thoughts. It's too dangerous. He's alternating between feeling he's been wronged and feeling he's a horrible human being who deserves this. Right now he needs someone to make him feel whole, to prop him up, and there is no better person for the job than Ginger.

"Oh God, Ginger," he says again. "What have I done?"

"You haven't done anything," she assures him. "You're brilliant. You're magical. You're *everything*, Jack. Don't you know that?"

He looks up and she's right there, so close to him. Too close. He can smell her perfume, smell the mixture of the Life Savers peppermint in her mouth along with her last cigarette. Who's to say if it's the perfume or the booze and pills taking effect, but in that moment when he looks into Ginger's eyes and takes in her emaciated body, he swears he's never seen anyone so beautiful. He can't get over the change in her. And it's not just her nose and her hair color—she is a woman transformed. Once an ugly duckling, now a beautiful, glorious swan. All this admiration for her is swirling about his mind; it's taken hold of him, and before he can get out in front of himself, he's kissing her.

R uth is still in her office, looking at Jack's signature in a state of disbelief. She wanted to regain her ground, let people, especially Rosenberg, know she's back in power. But she doesn't feel powerful at all. Just the opposite. She thought Jack would resign. She expected he'd already be packing up his office. Instead, he's staying, and she's surprised by how remorseful and guilty she feels. Yes, she's sick and tired of Jack taking advantage of her and the company, but she knows his contract cuts are brutal.

At that moment she hears something awful seeping through the wall next door in Jack's office. Is it possible? Is he actually in there crying? *Aw, shit.* Since they do still have to work together now, maybe she should try and smooth things over a bit, maybe explain again that it was a business decision and not personal? Though, of course, it is personal.

She pushes away from her desk and heads for his office. She's about to knock on Jack's door when the sounds coming from inside begin to change. It's more moaning and groaning and she can't believe it. *That sonofabitch.* He's not in there crying. He's in there balling his secretary. And on her dime.

Furious, she takes off down the hall only to find a man on all fours, camped out under one of the other secretary's desks while she's unknowingly hunched over her typewriter. Ruth knows it's Rosenberg. She recognizes his Gucci loafers. *Good God. First Jack, now Rosenberg. What a couple of cads.* How many times has she seen Rosenberg not so stealthily drop his pen or notepad in a meeting just so he could bend down and look up the girls' skirts?

A flare of anger rises up inside Ruth and she kicks him in the butt—harder than she expected to. He goes flying forward and smacks his head against the desk. Ruth wouldn't be surprised if he's seeing stars.

The secretary looks up, gasping with a start.

"Jesus, shit! Whoa—what the—" Rosenberg rubs his head.

"Get up," Ruth says. "Show's over."

The Three Way

No man has ever puzzled Stevie quite as much as Simon Richards. She can't figure him out. For months now he's smiled, said hello, occasionally asked about her weekend. But that's it. At times he seems to be on the verge of asking her for a date, but nothing ever comes of it. He's as aloof as he is handsome. He's also the first man since Jack that she's been even remotely interested in, but she's given up on Simon ever taking her out.

Because of this, she's a little aloof one afternoon when they find themselves alone in the galley kitchen. And of course, as soon as she's decided to forget about him, that's when, out of the blue, he asks if she'd like to go for a real cup of coffee sometime.

That real cup of coffee the next day turns into a four-hour conversation.

"So, let me get this straight," she says, "you waited all this time to ask me out just because we work together?"

"Haven't you ever heard the expression 'Don't shit where you eat'?"

"But this is Mattel—everyone's shitting where they eat."

"Yeah," he laughs, "I'm starting to realize that. Did you know about Frankie and Gina? And Wendy and Twist?"

"It's a very busy place," she says, laughing.

"What can I say"—he shrugs adorably—"I used to work in an uptight law firm."

She smiles, staring into his eyes. They're warm, and he has exceptionally long lashes for a man. His eyes are his best feature. Or maybe it's his mouth and those perfect teeth. She can't decide. "So," she says, forcing herself to break her gaze, "how do you like working at a toy company?"

"It's a lot more fun than a law firm. But what's with the marching music?"

She chortles. "You'll get used to it. I hardly even notice it anymore. But in the beginning—oh God—I used to hear 'Stars and Stripes Forever' in my sleep."

They fall silent, looking into each other's eyes. The attraction is strong, and with just a glance it's growing stronger. Her heart is beating a bit faster; her body is filling with a whoosh of heat.

With a sigh, he says, "I'm glad we're finally doing this." He smiles, his lovely eyes crinkling as she feels another delicious whoosh of heat course through her.

When they can't drink any more coffee but find they still have things to say, they take a walk down Third Street in Santa Monica. Each time their arms accidentally touch, they both feel a charge of excitement.

That weekend they go to the movies to see *Billy Jack*, and afterward they have dinner at the Sea Lion in Malibu. They're seated by the windows, watching the waves crashing up the shoreline, a spray of ocean mist on the windows. They're having marine salads and a glass of Chablis.

He's quiet during dinner, and when she asks if everything's okay, he drums the table and says, "Well, there is something I've been wanting to ask you about."

"Sounds serious."

"No. Not really. At least I hope it's not serious. It's about Jack Ryan. You and him. Are you two"—he stops, searching for the right word. "What exactly *are* you two, anyway?"

She takes a sip of wine. "We're friends, but"—she takes a second sip—"there was a time we were more than that."

"You and the little guy?" He gives his head an odd tilt. He's surprised.

"But now we're just friends."

"So just friends?"

"Just friends. But," she's quick to add, "Jack's important to me."

Simon takes that in, nodding. "That's fair. He's your friend. I get it."

Stevie invites Simon back to her place that night and they sit up talking, just talking. There's never a break in the conversation. They tell each other about their childhoods and discover that they're both only children. He grew up in New York and relocated to L.A. just for Mattel. He's still getting used to driving everywhere. He also wonders how everyone can breathe out here with all the smog, and she promises to get him a gas mask. They talk about their past relationships. He hasn't had a serious girlfriend since law school and, like her, has been more focused on his career than his personal life. They lose track of time as the light inside her living room changes and faint shadows appear with the dawn. She walks him out to his car just to have a few more minutes with him, and as the sun begins to rise, he finally, *finally* leans over and kisses her.

Stevie's been seeing Simon for almost three months now. One night at dinner, he smiles, reaches across the table for her hand. "I've got it bad for you, Stevie Klein. You know that, don't you?"

"I've got it bad for you, too," she says, gazing into his eyes.

He stays over for the first time that night, and in Simon she finds a lover who is tender and gentle, passionate and devoted to her, able to give his everything to her. There's no objection to using protection; in fact, he assumed he would without her having to ask. There's no one he needs to get rid of first and no one waiting in the wings to take her place. It's just the two of them and nothing before has ever felt this right.

One Saturday morning, several weeks later, Stevie and Simon are lying in her bed, a breeze blowing through the open window. She likes his scent on her pillowcases and bedsheets. She likes that bits of him have accumulated at her place: his swimming trunks, a pair of tennis shoes, an extra button-down shirt and tie. A second toothbrush, shaving cream and a razor are in her bathroom. She notices his dirty socks, T-shirts and underwear in her hamper, meaning those too are now here to stay. She encourages the over-flow happening inside her closet, in the drawer she cleared out for him in her dresser along with the shelf in her medicine cabinet.

Being with Simon feels completely natural to her. And easy. There's no struggling to carve out time for him versus time for Mat-tel. If she works late, he heats up dinner for her when she gets home. If she has a bad day, has a problem with Lewis or Twist, he'll listen while she teases it out of her system. On weekends, if she has to work, he understands. Sometimes they'll both go into the office on a Saturday and meet up later, when neither one is preoccupied. With Simon, she doesn't have to make a choice. She can have both her career and a relationship. She's just plain happy. Happier than she ever thought she could be.

"I need to tell Jack about us," she says to Simon that morning. "I'd rather he hear it from me than someone else. He's fragile right now. And he gets weird sometimes. We're just friends, but he—he still gets jealous. Possessive-like, you know what I mean? I don't want him to give you a hard time at the office."

"Well," he laughs, "I'm not afraid of Jack Ryan." He props himself up on one elbow and reaches over to tuck a lock of hair behind her ear. "He doesn't have any power over me. Really, he doesn't even have much power at Mattel anymore."

Later that day, Stevie goes to the Castle to tell Jack in person. The two of them are lounging out by the pool. Jack is in his tennis whites, a towel slung about his neck as he cools down after his match with one of the new UCLA recruits. She's in her bathing suit, a straw beach bag filled with magazines and suntan oil at her side. The lawn sprinklers are shooshing back and forth across the grass. One of the UCLA boys brings her a glass of crisp white wine. He stealthily admires Stevie's sleek, tanned body but is careful not to look too hard or linger too long for fear of igniting Jack's jealous streak. All the UCLA boys know that only one person is allowed to flirt with Stevie, and that's Jack.

Jack's telling Stevie about some wild party he went to the night before with Zsa Zsa. Afterward they took to the Sunset Strip in his fire truck, going from the Hullabaloo to Whisky a Go Go.

"It was outta sight, man."

She props her sunglasses on her head and studies his face. His eyes are bloodshot, there are dark circles beneath them, broken capillaries have recently sprung up on his cheeks. "I realize this is a dumb question to ask you of all people," she says, "but what do you see in her?"

"Zsa Zsa? Are you kidding me? She's a Hungarian beauty."

"Like I said, it was a dumb question." She laughs.

"Plus, she's sophisticated and savvy. And she's worldly."

"And she's a gold digger."

"Well, she can dig all she wants," he says. "Thanks to Ruth, I'm broke."

"You're not broke. You're far from broke."

"I'm still thinking of suing that bitch. My lawyers say I have a strong case."

She mockingly covers her ears. "I can't listen to this anymore."

Just then a beautiful strawberry blonde in a tiny little dress and very high-heeled sandals comes out of the sliding back doors and appears at Jack's side.

"Stevie, this is Marlene." He reaches for the woman's hand and pulls her down onto his lounge chair. "Marlene's my social secretary."

Stevie smiles, a little stunned. *Since when do you have a social secretary?* "Very nice to meet you."

"Nice to meet you, too," Marlene says in a French accent, laughing as she straightens the front of her dress. Prying her fingers away from Jack's grasp, she says, "You let me go—I have Swedish meatballs arriving."

"Go, go," he says. "Go get your meatballs."

After she's slipped back through the sliding doors, Stevie sits up, shaking her head. "Social secretary?"

"I need help." He shrugs. "What can I tell you, I'm a very sociable guy."

"I'll say."

Jack's parties have become almost legendary. He throws as many as four or five a week. *Time* magazine has compared Jack Ryan's parties to Hugh Hefner's at the Playboy Mansion. Marlene has been hired to amuse him and help him manage it all.

"Well, she's lovely," says Stevie.

"And smart, too. She's a foxy chick. And that accent. *Ooh la la.* Drives me crazy."

"Does Ginger know about her?"

"Ginger?" Jack winces, realizing he's been found out. "God, that is such a mess."

"Yeah, and when were you going to tell me about *that mess*?"

"How'd you find out?"

"You kidding me?" Stevie laughs sadly. "Ginger told me all about it. She thinks you're her new boyfriend now."

"Christ."

"Hey, I have an idea—why don't you have a ménage à trois with Ginger and Marlene? It's very French."

"That's not a bad idea."

"I was joking, My God, you are such a chauvinist."

"How does *that* make me a chauvinist?"

"Because you objectify women."

"I love women."

"We're going in circles here."

They laugh, and when they come to a lull in the teasing, she changes her tone. "So, there's something I've been wanting to tell you."

"Ooh, sounds serious."

"Well, it is, actually."

Jack sits up. "What is it? You're not sick, are you?"

"No, no, it's nothing like that." She adjusts her sunglasses and glances at the pool and then back at Jack. "It's just that, well, I've started seeing someone."

He laughs. "Oh, that. You're talking about you and Simon?"

She's surprised. "You know about us?"

"Well, I've had my suspicions." He twists his lips into something that's not quite a smile. "And now you've confirmed it."

"And?" She hesitates, making sure this isn't some kind of a

trick. "And you're okay with this? You won't let it interfere with our friendship?"

He's still smiling. "I knew this day would come eventually. But hey, Simon seems like a decent fella. And he is awfully pretty."

She slaps him playfully.

He leans over and cups her chin in his hand. "Does he make you happy, kiddo?"

She nods, still waiting for the other shoe to drop.

And it does, sort of.

Jack gets up from his lounge chair and plunges into the pool, still in his tennis clothes. He stays underwater so long that she fears he's trying to drown himself. She goes to the edge of the water, kneels down, shouting at him. She's about to go in after him when Jack rockets through the water's surface, running his fingers through his hair, laughing like a madman.

One week later, Ginger's waiting for Jack to return from an appointment. He was rather mysterious about it for some reason. Even though Jack has just ended their relationship, she refuses to believe it's over. She thinks if she can just lose those last three pounds, she can get him back. She has to get him back. She just has to—and so, she takes another diet pill.

She checks the clock on her desk. It's almost four. Where is he? He left over three hours ago but didn't say where he was going. Something's wrong. What if something happened to one of his daughters? What if he's sick somewhere? What if he's been in a terrible accident? She frets over this until it occurs to her that maybe he's already come back. Maybe he slipped back in when she was in the ladies' room, or getting coffee, or making copies down the hall in the Xerox room. After all, she hasn't been glued to her desk this whole time. He could have easily come through the lobby and gone straight into a meeting. This gives her a quick wash of relief as she reaches for the mirror in her top drawer to check her makeup.

She looks but doesn't see the hollowed-out cheekbones, the gaunt circles beneath her eyes. Instead, Ginger still sees a fat mousy girl with a Dick Tracy nose. Maybe it's the hair color? But she's a platinum blonde now. She can't go any lighter, and the hairdresser has warned that her hair's already damaged, full of split ends. She touches up her lipstick just in case Jack *is* back. She smiles to check her teeth for food, despite not having eaten anything since the day before, and adds a dab of perfume behind each ear.

She reviews Jack's calendar for the third or fourth time, making sure she hasn't missed something. She sees no meetings scheduled for that afternoon, and whatever hope she had is now canceled out, replaced by knurling in her stomach. A new fear sneaks up on her. Something tells her that wherever he is right now, he's not alone. He's with someone and she has a feeling she knows who it is. She gets up from her desk and goes searching, checking the main conference room, the smaller meeting rooms. She checks the archive room, the model making room, the kitchen, the cafeteria and lastly the design department. She knew it. Stevie's not at her desk.

Jack and Stevie have just visited a sanatorium that Dr. Klemes recommended and Stevie begged Jack to look into. It's half past six when they return to Mattel. The parking lot has pretty much emptied out save for Ruth's and Elliot's Rolls-Royces and a handful of other cars. Jack is quiet, somber, even a little agitated. The whole way home he told Stevie he doesn't need to check himself in somewhere. He can handle it. She's overreacting.

"I'm not Neely O'Hara. This isn't *Valley of the Dolls*, you know."

"It would just be for a little while, Jack."

"Well, it ain't happening, so forget it."

After pushing through the turnstile, Jack heads back to his office on Mahogany Row, and Stevie stops into the ladies' room, where she finds Ginger crying. After one look at Stevie, Ginger begins to bawl even harder, sinking to the tiled floor as if her spindly legs can't hold her any longer.

"Are you okay?" Stevie asks. "You look pale." She dampens a fresh paper towel and kneels down beside Ginger, placing it across her forehead. She murmurs something in return, indicating that the cool dampness feels good. Ginger's eyes start going glassy again before she drops her head to her bony hands, her shoulders quaking.

This goes on for a ridiculously long time and Stevie's thighs are aching from squatting in place. Eventually she just gives up and sits down next to Ginger. Another round of tears and Stevie glances at her watch. It's almost seven o'clock now. She has a mountain of work waiting for her.

"C'mon," she says. "It's getting late and—"

"Just go. Let me be."

"You can't stay in here all night."

And with that Ginger howls, letting out a string of spittle and a mumble of words. "Why doesn't he want me? I'd do anything for him but he still doesn't want me."

"Because," says Stevie, "you know how Jack is. He's got a million different women."

Ginger starts to sob again, and there's no way to make her see that it's not Jack she needs, and that no amount of plastic surgery or hair dye or dieting can fix what ails her. There are some places no scalpels can reach, no pills can remedy.

"Oh, Ginger, c'mon now. Get a grip on yourself."

The door opens and in walks Ruth, which is always a bit disconcerting. Shouldn't she have her own private bathroom? No one wants to pee in a stall next to Ruth Handler. The sight of Ruth is enough to make Ginger pull herself together.

Ruth's eyes go from Stevie to Ginger and back to Stevie. "What are you two still doing here? It's late. Is she sick?" Ruth asks, helping Stevie get Ginger to her feet.

"She'll be okay," says Stevie. "She's just—just a little upset is all."

"Does this have something to do with Jack?" asks Ruth.

"No, no," says Stevie even as the mention of his name makes Ginger start wailing all over again.

Who's to Blame?

The air in the conference room is thick. No one says anything at first as they all process the news. Ruth is gripping her coffee mug as if with an aim to shatter it. Elliot sits, his face grimacing. Rosenberg's pallor has gone ashen. This is all a result of Patsy presenting them with Mattel's quarterly financial statement from their accounting firm, Arthur Andersen.

Rosenberg's the one who prepared the statement, which the outside auditors reviewed prior to making huge adjustments. So, long before this meeting, he knew what was coming. He knew that statement would show a loss of $30 million after taxes.

"Well, this is unfortunate," says Ethan Clark, their new head of investor relations. He looks again at the statement.

Ruth is sick inside. She's been expecting a loss, but nothing even close to this. Since going public, she and Elliot have taken modest salaries, knowing that the bulk of their wealth is in the value of their stock. But a massive loss like this changes everything. They own a chunk of that $30 million hit, and in an ironic twist, Jack is now making more money than they are because his earnings are based on revenues rather than profits.

"We'll blame it on the dockworkers' strike," says Rosenberg, his hands thrown to his sides, as if that clears them of any responsibility.

"If you don't mind," says Ethan, gently rebuffing Rosenberg, "I'm less interested in looking for someone to blame than I am in finding ways to reassure our investors." Ethan Clark is an eloquent man, thoughtful and fair. "With no resolution on the horizon with the strike, we need to brace ourselves for another disappointing Christmas season." This is the cherry on a melted sundae.

When the meeting adjourns, Ruth is drained and feeling that this nightmare is partly her fault. The warehouse fire, the dockworkers' strike—those are all circumstances beyond her control, and intellectually she knows this, but she still feels responsible. If she hadn't gotten cancer, she would have been more on top of things. She wouldn't have relegated her workload to Rosenberg. Not that it would have necessarily changed the outcome.

She's trying to reconcile all this as she steps out of the conference room and immediately senses that something's off. It takes a moment before she realizes what it is. It's quiet. There's no marching music. Someone must have turned it off. Ruth looks down the hallway. People are huddled in clusters, murmuring; some are crying. *Could this possibly be about our financial loss? How would they even know about it?*

Her secretary rushes over to her. Her eyes are red. She's been crying, too.

"What's going on?" Ruth asks. "Is everything okay?"

"It's Ginger," her secretary says. "She didn't come into work today. And she didn't call in sick. We tried calling her all morning but she wasn't answering her phone. Finally, Jack went to check on her and"—a ripple of tears slides down her face—"he found her. In her bed. They said it was a heart attack. My God, she was only thirty-six years old and she had a heart attack. She's gone. Ginger's dead."

The funeral is a horrible and haunting scene. It's an appropriately overcast day, bearing the threat of a downpour at any moment. A minor crowd has amassed at Ginger's gravesite. Her family is clustered together, the mother barely able to stand without the help of her sons on either side of her. The father, whom Ginger was sure never really loved her, can't see his daughter's casket through the blur of his tears.

Ruth and Elliot are there, along with all of Mattel. They have closed the office for the day. It's the first time in ages that everyone has put aside their differences. Ruth and Jack even embrace, both sobbing into each other's shoulders. Ginger has been with them for sixteen years, since 1955, when Jack started. There is a shared but fleeting thought that Ginger's passing will be the bridge that connects everyone back together. But after the service, everyone goes their own way and old grievances resurface.

"Jack killed that poor girl," says Ruth when she and Elliot are in his Rolls-Royce, heading back to Mattel. Despite closing the office, the two of them can't afford to take the day off, not with everything else that's going on.

"That's not fair, Ruthie. You can't blame Jack."

"Oh, no? Who gave her those diet pills? He saw how thin she was getting. Did he do anything to stop her? To help her?" She's spouting off about this but all the while she's wondering if she's also to blame—even if just a little—for creating Barbie in the first place. What if there are others out there like Ginger, starving themselves to death, measuring themselves against a plastic figurine?

In another car, heading toward the Bel Air Castle, Stevie is driving Jack's Mercedes, listening to him complain about Ruth and Rosenberg. Jack's too upset to drive, and frankly, he's taken too many Valiums.

It was Simon who told her to drive him home, saying, "He needs you now. Go take care of him." Simon understands her relationship with Jack as best he can. He knows there's nothing to be jealous of; the guy's a mess. But Stevie's loyal to Jack, and sometimes Simon worries that she thinks she can change him, protect him, save him from himself.

"I bet Ruth's calculating how much it's going to cost her to shut down the office today," says Jack. "All she cares about is money. She's a greedy bitch."

"And you're a greedy bastard."

"Mattel's taken all my money."

"You're still plenty rich," Stevie says.

"My lawyer thinks I should sue them."

"Oh God, Jack, don't start with that again."

He half laughs, half cries. "I'll open my own damn company. I can engineer circles around Barcus . . ."

She's heard this all before. She can't listen anymore and snaps on the radio.

"And," he says, turning it off, "did you see the way Rosenberg was trying to *comfort* all the girls, trying to cop free feels . . ." Jack starts to sob all over again. "Poor Ginger. I told her to lay off those pills. I told her she was getting too thin. Didn't I? Didn't I tell her all that?"

When they get back to the Castle, Jack pours himself a drink, which is about the last thing he needs. He's been drinking for days on end, trying to drown his pain, but it's not working. He's crying again and wants her to hold him, which she does. And what begins as her trying to soothe him turns into something else altogether. He kisses her, first on the neck and then the lips.

"Jack, no." She pulls back.

"Yes." He leans in to kiss her again. He wants to feel something other than pain. He wants to lose himself in her body.

"No. I mean it. Stop it," she says, pushing him away and standing up.

He breaks down into convulsive sobs, mumbling something she can't decipher.

She looks at him, at his tearstained eyes pleading, and a horrible feeling overcomes her. She's scared. Not for herself, but for him. He's rocking back and forth, tugging on his hair; a thread of spittle is gathering in the corner of his mouth. She hardly recognizes him. This is more than just the booze and the pills. There's something else seriously wrong with him. That's when she calls for the UCLA boys.

It takes them nearly an hour to calm him down—or, more accurately, for him to wear himself out—so they can get him into bed. More than anything, Stevie wants to run. She wants to unsee the whole thing, but she can't turn away. And so she stays with her friend until he finally, thankfully, falls asleep.

Top-Heavy and Flat-Footed

1972

After Ginger's death, Jack took a leave of absence from Mattel. He could barely function. He was losing all the women in his life. First his wife, then Ginger. And Stevie—he was worried, after the funeral, that she would abandon him, too. It felt like his appendages were dropping off, vital organs withering and drying up. He'd sulked for the longest time, drowning in booze and perfume, waking up each morning with a different girl in his bed, unable to recall their names or how or where they'd met. The blackouts bothered him, but they did at least interrupt his thinking and give him a break from his mind and its many tortures.

Who knows how long he would have carried on like that had it not been for his UCLA boys. They found him one night passed out in his sunken bathtub and were unable to wake him up. Later, at the hospital, after they'd pumped his stomach, he was admitted to a psych ward.

After a little drying-out time and some new meds, Jack is back at work. But everything's changed. In his absence, Barcus has taken the lead on certain projects and has made some abysmal decisions. Jack can't believe Ruth approved them and wonders if she's lost the will to fight with these guys. Their new initiatives are the sort of things Jack would have vetoed on the spot.

Case in point: Barbie's new breasts. They've decided to enlarge them, and while Jack is a confirmed breast man himself, he never would have gone in that direction. Why on earth would you increase the very problem you've been battling against from day one? He remembers Ruth saying, *Smaller, Jack. You gotta make those tits smaller.* But by the time he returned to Mattel, Barbie's new boobs were too far down the line. Talk about top-heavy. Her breasts defy gravity, and thanks to those bigger boobs, Barbie is about to fall flat on her face.

For the first time since her "birth" in 1959, Barbie's sales are down. Women hate her now more than ever. At that year's Toy Fair, the feminists were out in full force, protesting in front of the 200 Fifth Avenue building. NOW handed out leaflets condemning Barbie—everything from her body to her bubblegum brains and her materialistic world.

Ruth is panicking, and when Ruth panics, Elliot panics, as do Charlotte and Jack. It trickles down, and eventually the whole team is riddled with anxiety. They gather in meeting after meeting, brainstorming ways to keep Barbie relevant, ways to appease the women's liberation movement while not alienating the antifeminists.

"Why don't we have a Burn Your Bra Barbie?" suggests Barcus.

"Oh yeah, that's just fucking brilliant," says Jack. "And how would you execute that? Package Barbie with a book of matches? Lots of luck selling that to mothers."

"What about if we create a Protest Barbie?" says Loomis. "We can have her marching *with* the women's libbers."

"In those heels?" says Charlotte.

"So we'll flatten her feet," says Barcus. "That's an easy fix."

Stevie, who's been taking all this in, finds she can't stay silent any longer. "It's not that simple. This isn't something that's going to be resolved in this boardroom or with a new product design. The problem isn't Barbie's feet. It isn't Barbie at all. It's society." Nobody says anything, but there's a lot of chair shifting, sighs, grunts, even some groans. "Like it or not, guys, women are fed up. They're lashing out because they're sick and tired of—"

"Of what?" asks Lewis.

"Where do you want me to start?" says Stevie. "Should we talk about pay scales? About birth control? Our right to have an abortion—"

"Okay, whoa," says Loomis, hands out like a referee. "I think we're getting off track here. We're not gonna solve the women's liberation movement gripes. We're not gonna *fix* society. What we're gonna *fix* is Barbie."

And so they try to do just that. Barbie goes flat-footed, which only flattens her sales more.

Y ou're awfully quiet today," Dr. Klemes says to Jack, who is stretched out on the leather sofa, hands laced behind his head.

"Don't really have much to talk about," Jack says, though his body is burbling with things he should be discussing with his doctor.

"You're sure, now?" Dr. Klemes asks. "Nothing's bothering you?"

"Yep. Positive." But the truth is, his head is full of nonsense. Everything has him on edge. He lost his cool with Ann the other day and slapped her. Aside from a spanking when she was little, he's never raised a hand to her. His car is making that weird rattling sound again. He has to remember to get an extension on filing his income taxes. He needs to pick up his suit at the tailor's. He doesn't like his new secretary, who questions why she needs to read everything to him. He worries that the bags and dark circles beneath his eyes are aging him. He's starting to go gray all over, too, not just at the temples. He feels old and broken. And on and on it goes. He's making himself crazy. He would give anything if, for the love of God, he could just stop thinking, just turn off the noise inside his head.

"Okay, then," says Dr. Klemes, consulting his notes. "Tell me, how are things going at work?"

"Fine. Peachy." He shifts his weight on the sofa. It makes an embarrassing impolite sound. In a company as large as Mattel, where you can go weeks and months without seeing someone, why is it that he runs into Simon every fucking day? Stevie is in love with the guy and Jack's happy for her but sad for himself. He glances at his watch, wishing their time would be up.

Dr. Klemes scratches down some notes and changes the subject. "I want to make some adjustments to your medications," he says, scratching down more comments in his file. "How's your appetite?"

"I can't eat," says Jack.

"Uh-huh." More notes are scratched down. "And are you sleeping?"

Jack shakes his head.

"I'd like to start you on phenobarbital. See how you respond. Maybe it will help regulate your sleep patterns."

Jack gives a sad laugh. If only the answer were in another pill. He either sleeps for days on end or else is wide awake, unable to shut himself down. There's never anything in between, anything resembling normal. He sees no end in sight, no relief. This is it. This is going to be him for the rest of his life. He drives his fists into his tear-soaked eyes. "I don't want to live like this anymore. I can't. It's too damn hard. I hate myself. I hate my life. I'm done . . ."

Scratch. Scratch-scratch. After Jack manages to collect himself and promises that he's not *really* thinking of killing himself, Dr. Klemes gives his pencil a rest and says, "In addition to the phenobarbital, there's a new medication I'm going to prescribe. It's showing a great deal of promise for individuals who suffer from *moodiness.*"

Jack's thankful that the good doctor remembered not to say *manic depression.* He's not crazy. He's not.

Lithium. Jack hates it. It makes him even more exhausted than he was before. It makes his hands shake and it's making him gain weight. He's not supposed to drink while he's on it, but he does anyway. But more than anything it has made his world dull, colorless, blunting everything that was once sharp, distinctive, alive. He is flattened down, no pizzazz, no flair. Everything that had been worthwhile is now gone. And sex—he no longer wakes up with a hard-on, and when he does manage to get aroused, he can't maintain it. How is he expected to function, to create anything while he's in such a placid state of mind?

People ask what's wrong with him. If he's going to have another party anytime soon. They don't like medicated Jack. He's boring. A real drag. No fun at all. Jack's not sure he even remembers how to have fun.

One month and five pounds later, he's done. Surely, being a little *moody* is far better than feeling nothing at all. The lithium goes down the toilet and Jack goes back to being the life of the party.

A Little Favor

Stevie looks forward to Sundays. It's the one day of the week when she rarely goes into the office. It's the one day she doesn't set her alarm. The one day when she and Simon can linger in bed for as long as they please. Still beneath the covers, they'll have coffee in bed and exchange newspaper sections while making plans for the day, which usually include dinner with her parents. Her folks never liked Russell, thinking he was too old for Stevie. The same was true of Jack, whom they briefly met one day at her apartment. But her parents have taken a liking to Simon. Especially her father.

Stanley Klein makes sure there's extra beer in the icebox so the two of them can watch football and basketball games together. They talk about the stock market, Nixon's reelection, and Bobby Fischer—manly subjects he would never think of discussing with his daughter. Her father even unearths a chessboard for them. Does he not know that Stevie plays chess? Her father laughs, he makes conversation, he even gives Stevie a hug when she comes through the door. This is all so illuminating to her. It took bringing Simon home, bringing another man into the picture, to understand that her father, right or wrong, has felt like the odd man out, his world surrounded by women. All this time he's been starved for male companionship.

On one particular Sunday, their morning routine is disrupted by two back-to-back telephone calls. The first is Stevie's father, calling for Simon, asking if he'll come by early to help him build a new bookcase for his encyclopedias. The other is Stevie's former classmate Marta Krass, sounding a little desperate when she asks if they can meet for lunch that day.

Two hours later, Stevie is sitting beneath an umbrellaed table on a patio in Venice Beach. Hippies, dressed in their signature sandals, tie-dyed shirts and love beads, linger on the boardwalk, handing out flowers, saying "Make love, not war." The beach is crowded with sunbathers, and the water is peppered with surfers.

"Thanks for meeting me on such short notice," says Marta, unfolding her napkin, smoothing it onto her lap.

"Well, you said it was important. Is everything okay?"

Marta sighs, chews on her lower lip. "So, I guess, yeah." She nods. "Sally Jax, well"—another sigh, another scrape of her teeth across her lip—"Sally let me go. She fired me."

"I'm so sorry."

"Yeah, well, apparently they're taking Jax in a new direction and Sally doesn't see me as"—her fingers blink—"*part of the equation. Sally said they don't think I'm*"—more finger blinking—"*cut out for a future with Jax.*"

"Ouch. That's rough. Well," says Stevie, "it's a tough business but I'm sure something will turn up. There's lots of other designers, other houses you can go to."

"But that's just the thing. I've been looking. For a while now. I've been everywhere. I even interviewed to be Bob's assistant. If your own friend won't hire you, you know you're in trouble." She sighs again, tries to laugh. "You remember when you were looking for work—you know how hard it is in this business."

Stevie nods. "But don't forget, I had zero experience *and* no degree."

"Yeah, but look where you are now." Marta's eyes widen. "My niece plays with Barbies. All. The. Time." She rolls her eyes disapprovingly. "But the clothes for that doll are just amazing."

"They really are, aren't they?" says Stevie. Marta doesn't say anything in response. Stevie can tell she has another agenda.

"It's just that I'm—I'm starting to panic a little. My rent's due and I'm almost broke."

"Well, I'll get lunch, so don't worry about that." She can tell by the way Marta is looking at her that picking up the bill isn't exactly what she had in mind. Stevie considers them friends, but not the type of friends you'd hit up for money. And yet, she's in a position to help, so she shrugs and says, "I mean, I can help you with a small loan?"

"Actually"—Marta glances out at the beach, then back at Stevie—"I was hoping you could do me a little favor. I was kinda hoping you could get me a job there."

"Where?"

"You know, at Mattel."

"*You* want to work on Barbie?"

The last time she ran into Marta, Stevie had been embarrassed to say she was designing for Barbie. Well, she definitely doesn't feel that way anymore. There's something to be said for knowing your worth, and Stevie has come to appreciate that she's landed in a coveted spot in the design world. Mattel has been good to her. Stevie's been promoted to senior designer and has gotten steady raises and some handsome bonuses along the way. She's making more money than she ever imagined. The fact that Marta just asked her for a job only proves that she's now recognized among her peers as a bona fide fashion designer.

Marta might be the first, but she won't be the last who'll come to Stevie hoping to work on Barbie. And it won't just be students and aspiring designers who want in. Soon, the biggest names in design, like Oscar de la Renta, Christian Dior and even her former classmate Bob Mackie will want to dress Barbie.

Bill and Hold

1973

It's late February and Ruth has broken out a soft pale blue cashmere sweater that day. It's the first time she's been able to wear anything formfitting since her mastectomy. Finally, after a three-year hunt, she found someone who could custom-make a prosthetic breast for her.

Peyton Massey is in Santa Monica and has earned a reputation for making prosthetic feet, arms and legs, mostly for Vietnam vets. She figured a breast couldn't be that much more difficult and convinced Massey to give it a try. Her Peyton Massey breast is more comfortable, but still far from perfect. It weighs about a pound and the nipple is too large. When she takes off her bra at night, there are deep grooves in her shoulder from where her strap has been digging into her skin. If she wears the breast for too long, it aggravates her nerve damage, and whenever she sweats, the plastic leeches a chemical smell that she tries to mask with too much perfume.

With her fake breast and her cashmere sweater, she pushes through the turnstile and heads to her office. She sees a press release on her desk. FOR IMMEDIATE RELEASE. MATTEL ANNOUNCES FOURTH QUARTER AND FULL YEAR EARNINGS . . . The press release has already gone out, so she's not sure why they even bothered giving her a copy. As she reads, she's surprised to see that the numbers are much stronger than expected. Mattel has just come off two devastating years of losses. First with the factory fire in Mexico and then the dockworkers' strike, followed by their $30 million loss—and all that was before the BBB, which is how they're referring to Barbie's Big Boob disaster and the decision to flatten her feet. Ruth considers asking to see a financial statement but reminds herself that Malibu Barbie and Hot Wheels have been huge sellers. The numbers are encouraging, and the timing is perfect with Toy Fair right around the corner.

Oh, Toy Fair. The mere thought of it fills Ruth with despair. If she could, she'd gladly skip the whole thing. Jack isn't going this year, which is a first. They've decided to send Barcus instead. She's not looking forward to the meet and greets, the shocked looks on everyone's faces when they see the change in her from the year before. There's more gray in her hair, more padding around her middle, as she's gone up another dress size since last year. Not that it matters. Her figure's shot. She hates shopping for clothes because everything she likes is too low-cut, too tight across the hips. She'll never be able to wear the kind of outfits she used to. Not even with the prosthetic that Peyton Massey made for her. And the thing is, she can see ways to improve it—just some tweaks would make it so much better—but she's too exhausted to even broach the subject with Peyton.

The only bright spot about going to Toy Fair is that they'll see Ken, Suzie and their grandchildren while they're in New York. But the night before they're expected to leave, Ethan Clark in investor relations; David Larsen, their new general counsel; and Simon Richards turn up on their doorstep.

What in the hell is so urgent that they're here at our home? It's late. Ruth's in her bathrobe without her prosthetic. She's already taken off all her makeup and feels naked. A dish of ice cream with two spoons sits on the coffee table melting. Elliot's in a pair of pajamas. Everyone politely pretends to ignore this intimate look into the Handlers' private lives.

"What the hell's going on?" asks Ruth, pinching her bathrobe closed.

"Something rather damaging has been brought to our attention." Ethan pauses, a clenched fist pressed to his lips. "I know you're both aware of the press release that went out about two weeks ago. It talked about a big turnaround in gross profits and painted a rosy outlook for the first quarter revenues. Since you approved that press release, Elliot, we're here to ask you where you got your information from."

"Where else—from Rosenberg," says Elliot. "Seymour handles all the forecasting now."

"And do you recall how he delivered that information to you?" asks David.

"What do you mean, *how*?" Ruth feels like Elliot's being cross-examined. "It was in Rosenberg's press release," she says.

"Well, the financial statement was less than accurate. You should know that the press release Mattel issued was full of misleading projections," says David.

They don't like the sound of this, but Ruth and Elliot aren't yet fully understanding what David's saying.

"Whose idea was it to implement this bill and hold strategy?" asks Simon.

"It was Seymour's," says Elliot, recalling the day Rosenberg called an emergency meeting because he was worried about the sales numbers. Rosenberg said they needed orders on their books.

"Even more than money in the bank," said Rosenberg, "what we need are the orders. We can't afford to disappoint our stockholders. So what we're gonna do is implement a bill and hold strategy. We'll have the sales force write up the orders—that's the *bill* part—and instead of shipping right away, we store the merchandise in our warehouses—that's the *hold* part. *Bill and hold.* It buys us time. It's a Band-Aid, but trust me," said Rosenberg. "I know what I'm doing here."

"Bill and hold's a perfectly kosher practice," says Elliot defensively. Rosenberg didn't invent that. Ruth has been using bill and hold for ages.

"Yes, it is kosher," says David, nodding, fully agreeing, fishing some documents out of his briefcase. "But offering cancelations and returns on bill and hold orders while still keeping them on your books is not only *not* kosher," he says, "it's illegal."

"Wait a minute," Ruth says. "What are you talking about?"

"*Someone* directed your entire sales force to offer customers the option to return or even cancel their bill and hold orders," says Simon. "But those orders are still on your books as sales."

She and Elliot both look clobbered. Their minds are scrambling to piece together this onslaught of accusations.

"Look here"—Ethan points to a line item on a financial statement—"on June 8, 1971, Sears placed a Hot Wheels order for $600,000. Any idea what the actual total was for their order?"

She and Elliot shrug. They have no idea.

"The final order for Sears came in at $65,000. Yet over here"— he turns to another document—"we're showing $600,000 as revenue."

"Maybe it's a mistake," suggests Elliot.

Ethan goes back to the first document. "Here we have FAO Schwarz. April 18, 1971. Order for hold is listed at $120,000. That final order amounted to $35,000, and yet"—he shifts to the second report—"we have $120,000 in revenue. Here's another order placed on March 21, canceled on August 5. Ordered on May 3, canceled on July 9."

"There's a pattern here," says Simon.

"And all together," adds Ethan, "we're claiming over $14 million in bill and hold orders—the majority of which were either canceled or returned. Mattel didn't fulfill even a fraction of those. So unlike the press release we issued and the story the *Wall Street Journal* and other financial papers ran, not only are we *not* going to see an increase in revenue for first quarter—we're actually going to be showing another substantial loss."

Ruth covers her mouth, thinking she might actually throw up.

"We need to get out in front of this," says David. "We need to issue a correction. Pronto."

Ruth knew something was off about that press release and curses herself for not having checked the financial statement. But what good would that have done? The release had already been sent out.

"Get Rosenberg on the phone," she says to Simon. "I want to talk to him."

But after several attempts to reach him, both at the office and at home, Rosenberg is nowhere to be found.

She calls her secretary instead, waking her up. "Get a locksmith," she says. "First thing in the morning I want the locks changed on Rosenberg's office door. And when that sonofabitch shows up tomorrow, have security escort him off the premises."

The Whistleblower

Ruth and Elliot have drafted half a dozen different press releases with Ethan and David before coming up with the correct wording that reports a decidedly more realistic and gloomier forecast than the claims they made two and half weeks before.

The release goes out and the first domino falls. The price of Mattel's stock takes a nosedive. Some shareholders feel they've been misled. Ruth loses track of how many people either are threatening or have already filed lawsuits against the company. The board of directors opens an internal investigation, trying to get to the bottom of what really happened and figure out who is responsible. Mattel's in-house counsel is overwhelmed. David sends for reinforcements by way of an outside law firm, but Simon is still working round the clock. He's hardly spent any real time with Stevie over the past few weeks.

One evening while Simon's working late, Patsy knocks on his door. "Do you have a minute?" she asks.

"Sure." He carefully closes his folder and does a quick scan of his desk to make sure nothing is visible that shouldn't be. He sits in a wingback chair at a stately desk surrounded by shelves upon shelves of leather-bound legal books. It's a sharp contrast to the jovial, playful decor of the other offices.

Patsy explains she needs to talk to him because David's already gone for the day. "And if I don't say something now, I might lose my nerve." She smokes a cigarette and proceeds to share a treasure trove of information with Simon. "As far as I can tell," she says, "the problems started a few years ago. Back in January of '71. I remember Rosenberg was worried about the merger with Ringling Brothers. I know for a fact that they inflated the financial records. And that if the circus found out, the whole deal would have blown up. They knew they'd get sued."

"Who's *they*?"

"Rosenberg for sure. Possibly Loomis. But Rosenberg for sure. He had us doctor invoices. We had tons of invoices that went into these *Do Not Mail* folders."

Simon, who's been taking notes, looks up, eyebrows spiking.

"Yep," she says. "Oh, and the books are an absolute joke. There's two sets of them, you know. One has all the real accounting, and the other is complete and utter fiction."

"Hmmm. That's, ah . . ." Simon shakes his head. His poker face is vanishing. He's writing as fast as she speaks, filling up pages of his legal pad.

"And I know of one case for sure where they forged a customer's signature on a bill and hold order."

Simon sits back and rubs his eyes. "Were Elliot and Ruth aware of all this?"

"I'm sure Elliot had no idea." Patsy looks down at her hands before gazing back up. "I don't know about Ruth. I'm not the best person to ask about her." Patsy is forever protective of Jack and will never forgive Ruth for the way she's treated him. She's even been encouraging him to go ahead and sue for lost royalties, arguing that Mattel's a mess right now anyway, so who cares if they fire him. "But c'mon," says Patsy, "Ruth has her hands in everything. How could she have *not* known?"

"But she never—*Ruth* never asked you to falsify any documents?"

Patsy shakes her head. "No. That came from Rosenberg." She pauses for a minute and then says, "Did I do something wrong? Am—am I in trouble?"

He sets down his pen. He doesn't want to scare her, because technically, yes, she's exposed. Technically there *could* be consequences, but he also knows that corporate crimes typically stop with the company officers. What he tells her is, "You did the right thing by speaking up."

When Patsy leaves his office, Simon consults his watch. It's late. Almost eleven o'clock. But this can't wait till morning. He calls David at home. "You're not gonna believe this."

The following week the board of directors is holding a special meeting, and beforehand, Ethan, David and Simon sit down with Ruth and Elliot.

"We don't want you going in there and getting blindsided."

"Blindsided by what?" asks Elliot.

"Some new and frankly disturbing information has come to our attention," says David.

Ruth wants to know what kind of disturbing information.

David and Simon turn to Ethan, who says, "Turns out Mattel has more to answer for than merely the cancelations and returns on the bill and hold orders. There's errors in the routing and delivery paperwork. Discrepancies in the invoicing, too."

"It's obvious," says David, "that someone's been fudging the numbers."

"Maybe it was Rosenberg," adds Simon with a shrug.

"Maybe it was Rosenberg and other people, but whatever the case," says David, "you should know that the board's been looking into this themselves, and I know this isn't what you want to hear, but we met with them and—"

"You met with the board?" Ruth asks. "Without us?"

David's hands fly up as if she's holding a shotgun on him. "We felt it was in everyone's best interest."

"I can't believe you went behind our backs."

"Ruth, this isn't about you personally," says Ethan. "These are some serious allegations. We're trying to protect the company. Which is why the board felt it was necessary to conduct their own internal audit."

"We never heard about this," says Elliot. "Arthur Andersen never said a word."

"The board had another firm conduct the audit," says Simon. "They went to Price Waterhouse."

"Why? Why not go to our accountants?"

"Well," says David, "frankly, they don't trust Arthur Andersen. Think about it"—he shrugs—"how could all these errors have possibly slipped by them? Price Waterhouse took a good hard look at Mattel's books and the accounting going back to 1971, when you first showed a loss."

"So now what?" Ruth asks. "What happens next?"

The men exchange looks that say: *Who's going to tell them?*

Finally, David speaks up. "We had to alert the Securities and Exchange Commission."

"The SEC?" asks Elliot in disbelief.

Ruth goes limp in her chair. A fog rolls in all around her. She barely hears David saying, "I'm afraid things are going to get worse before they get better."

The emergency board meeting that follows is a nightmare. Ruth and Elliot don't even recognize some of the men sitting in *their* conference room. Awkward introductions are made, and for the first time, she and Elliot learn about meetings that have been taking place with their bankers, with some of Mattel's top executives, even with the SEC.

"The SEC insisted we put new blood on our board of directors," says Irwin Brash, someone they've only just met ten minutes ago. He's tall, lanky and has an icy manner about him. "We've been hand selected, preapproved, if you will, by the SEC to serve as board members of Mattel. And now"—he shrugs—"now we need to make some changes. Ruth, we need you to step down."

"I beg your pardon?" She glares at him.

"We need to replace you as president. We've discussed it and we all think Art Spear is a better choice, given the circumstances."

"No way." Ruth shakes her head. "Absolutely not."

Art speaks up. "With all due respect, Ruth—"

"Art"—she cuts him off—"you're a vice president of operations. You're very good at what you do, but you don't know the first thing about running this company. You have no grasp on marketing. You've never worked with our ad agency, you've never even been on the floor at Toy Fair."

"It's the only way," says Irwin. "The banks have already said that without a change in leadership, they won't issue the company another line of credit. They'll call in all the loans. It'll be a disaster. So as you can see"—he has the nerve to smile—"we have no choice."

And though she continues to argue for the next half hour, fighting for her professional life, it's obvious that she doesn't have a choice, either.

By the time they leave the meeting, a vote has been taken. The new board members have spoken, crowning Art Spear as Mattel's new president and CEO. Ruth emerges from the meeting having been demoted to cochair, a title she'll share with Elliot.

She feels like a robot when she walks down the hallway of Mahogany Row. Elliot hasn't said a word. Neither has she. They sit in his office and stare at each other. Elliot has always been her rock, there for her when Sarah died, when she had her surgery, when things went badly at work. But strong as he is, there's nothing he can do or say to make this less of a disaster, less scary. She's clammy and dizzy. It feels like someone is striking matchsticks against her stomach lining.

Eventually she goes back to her office, opens her top drawer and fishes two quarters out of a compartment where she tosses loose change. She gets up from her desk, and without a word to anyone, without being able to focus on anything other than staying upright, she takes a long walk down to the cafeteria. She drops her quarters into the cigarette machine, selects a package of Winstons and pulls the knob.

The Glue Factory

Ruth still can't believe how her world is unraveling. Thanks to Rosenberg, that sonofabitch, she's under suspicion, smack in the center of an investigation by the SEC. She's sick to her stomach. She can't eat and has lost all the weight she gained since her surgery and then some. The prosthetic breast Massey made for her no longer fits properly. It slips and shifts; it rubs her skin raw. She needs to go back to him to get another mold made, but she's too busy trying to keep a hold on her own company.

One morning she goes to meet with Art Spear to discuss a marketing question. His secretary says he's in a meeting. She goes to Loomis next and is told that he, too, is in a meeting. Turns out everyone of note is in that meeting. Everyone but her. They all see her as useless now—the old mare heading for the glue factory. The message is loud and clear: *You're not wanted anymore.* It's her mother all over again, only this time there's no Sarah to be handed off to. But she built this company, ran it for years. Her identity has always been defined by Mattel, and now they're taking away a major part of who she is. Without her work, she is lost.

She returns to her office and tries to find something to busy herself with, but all her responsibilities have been stripped away. She watches the clock tick away, five minutes, ten, fifteen . . . When she can't take it anymore, she heads into David's office.

"This is bullshit," she says. "Art's avoiding me. So is Loomis. They're holding meetings without me. They're making all kinds of decisions that I'm not privy to. I can't take this. I'm quitting. I'm turning in my resignation."

"You can't do that," he tells her. "Not while this investigation is going on. I need you to appear as normal as possible. I want you to continue to come into the office every day, try and keep yourself busy. Or look like you're busy. Try and smile, hold your head up. You can't afford to let anyone know you're beat up. You can't afford to appear guilty."

"I'm *not* guilty," she barks.

David nods but doesn't say anything to indicate that he believes her. All he says is, "Trust me. For your own good and the good of the company, it's what you have to do."

So each morning Ruth gets up, drives to work in her Rolls-Royce and enters through the turnstile. Other than the guard, few people are even willing to make eye contact with her. The walk to her office might as well be a mile long. Her secretary gets her coffee because Ruth can't bring herself to go in the kitchen, where she'll have to face people. With her door closed, she sits wondering what to do with herself. She reviews sales forecasts and piles of Barbie hate mail. The only good news she's received lately is word that the SEC is investigating Rosenberg, too.

Usually by ten o'clock, she's out of things to do. Some days she leaves, claiming she has an off-site meeting when really, she's at the country club playing bridge or canasta with friends, which she finds just as boring as sitting in her office. Something else she does to pass her days is go to lunch. She always ate in the cafeteria or at her desk unless she had a business lunch. Now she goes to lunch with Barbara every Tuesday. Her daughter's cleaning girl comes that day and Barbara needs an excuse to get out of the house.

But today there's nothing on her calendar and so she sits, reading a magazine. As she flips through the pages of *Town & Country*, there he is again: *Jack Ryan, Hollywood's Favorite Host*. She groans, wondering what on earth he's said this time. Apparently, he's hobnobbing with Zsa Zsa Gabor these days. Ruth shudders and flips through the pages to a series of photographs of the two.

There's a knock on her door. "You got a minute?" asks David.

"That's all I've got," she says, tossing the magazine aside. "Nothing but time on my hands." He tries forcing a smile and it makes her stomach knot. "What is it? What now?"

"I just heard from Jack Ryan's lawyers."

"Oh, for Christ's sake." She rests her head on the heel of her hand.

"I'm sure you know what's coming. This probably isn't a big surprise, but he's suing Mattel."

"You've got to be fucking kidding me. What balls he's got—he works in the next office, and he's suing me?"

David nods, giving her a moment to let it sink in. "He's suing the company for $25 million in lost royalties."

Ruth doesn't even hear the rest of what he's saying because she's seething. The blood is thrumming in her eardrums, drowning out everything else. This lawsuit is just one more pile-on, and after David leaves, she can take no more. Fortified by the need to kick someone, all her anger and frustration over the past few months—even years—is now funneled into something ballistic, and she's aiming it straight at Jack.

"Well, well, well," says Jack, when she storms into his office and slams the door behind her. "What brings you here?" This is the first time in months that she's stepped foot inside his office.

"You know damn well why I'm here, you smug piece of shit."

"Ah, so you must have heard from my lawyers."

"You got some nerve. How dare you pull a stunt like this."

"What did you expect me to do, roll over and take it? You screwed me out of millions on my royalties."

"Don't give me that bullshit—we overpaid you for years. You were only supposed to get royalties for the products you patented. Not for *everything*."

"It was right there in my contract." He pounds his fist on his desk.

"Give me a break, Jack. You were getting paid for toys you had absolutely nothing to do with besides signing off on the final designs."

"I'm entitled to 1.5 percent of everything I was involved in," he protests.

"You took advantage of us for years. All I did was put things right."

The two of them are talking over each other. He's shouting at her; she's shouting right back.

"You'll never win this suit. You'll never see a dime," she warns him. "And I'll tell you something else: for the last time, you did not invent Barbie—I did."

"*You* invented Barbie." He laughs. "Tell me how you did that. Are you an engineer? Are you a designer?"

This strikes a nerve, going straight to the tenderest part of her insecurities, the fear that she'll be overlooked and that all her contributions to Barbie will be dismissed and forgotten.

Jack is still laughing at her, right in her face. "The only thing you know how to do is make people miserable—and you're quite good at that. You know what you are?" he hammers on. "You're a greedy huckster—oh yeah, and a felon, too. That contract is still binding. You still owe me for my royalties. The SEC isn't your only battle. You want a fight? I'll give you one."

Calling her a felon and bringing up the SEC is the final straw. She lunges for the phone on his desk.

"Oh, what, you're calling in Elliot?"

"No, I'm calling security. I want you out of here. For good." She switches the phone to her other ear. "I need you down here in Jack's office. Now."

"Oh, that's just swell," says Jack. "Who do you think I am, Rosenberg? I thought I was nuts, but you—you're out of your goddamn mind."

"And you're out of a job."

By now the guard is in Jack's office.

"Collect his badge," she instructs. "Get his keys, too, and get him the hell out of the building."

"Oh, give me a break." Jack looks at the guard, whom he's given boxes of cigars and bottles of scotch to for no reason at all. And he's also greased him well at Christmas for the past eighteen years.

The guard looks bewildered. Unsure of whom he's supposed to listen to.

"You heard me," Ruth says. "Collect his shit and get him off the property."

"Don't bother," says Jack. He yanks the badge off his shirt, reaches into his pocket and throws the keys on his desk. "I'll show myself out."

Twist My Arm

Word travels quickly. Jack Ryan is gone. Unbelievable. The end of an era. No one can imagine Mattel without him. They can't believe Ruth fired him. *No, no*, others insist, it was the other way around. Jack resigned. No one knows for sure. Even Ruth isn't quite sure how it happened. The whole thing got so heated and went sideways so fast. She can't remember who said what, but she does remember calling the guard. Her staff definitely doesn't know about the lawsuit, and Ruth has to admit she doesn't mind people thinking she did the firing. Let them assume she still has some authority.

And while life at Mattel carries on without him, Jack's been huddling with his lawyers, plotting his revenge. He's just returned to the Castle after a meeting with them. Audrey, his new girlfriend, is waiting for him, there to keep him company while he works on a new project. He's taking apart one of his many cars, wanting to reengineer his Mercedes, certain he can get it running over 120 miles per hour. It's one of those things he's been wanting to do but never had the time. But now, he has nothing but time. He has all day to do nothing but tinker. His lawn is strewn with pistons, spark plugs, belts, cylinder heads, the crankshaft, drive shaft. The sun is starting to set but he keeps working, even in the dark. At one point he wipes the grease from his hands on a clean towel and asks Audrey to fix him another drink while he lays out a few more lines of cocaine.

Dr. Klemes would definitely categorize this as a manic episode. At their last session, he talked about upping Jack's medication and possibly admitting him to a hospital. *Just for observation.* Jack has since canceled his next two appointments.

Stevie is worried about him. "The last time I saw him, he looked like hell," she says to Simon one Friday night while they're in her kitchen, making dinner together. Technically, he's making dinner—chicken Kiev—and she's relegated to making the salad.

It's one of those rare evenings, a Friday night when he's not working late. She's opened a bottle of wine and Tom Waits's *Closing Time* is on the hi-fi. With shirtsleeves rolled to his elbows, Simon is chopping garlic and fresh parsley. She is washing a head of iceberg lettuce and a tomato.

"Think I should go over there after dinner and check on him?" she asks, now rinsing a cucumber under the tap.

"No."

"No?"

"No." He pauses his knife.

"Really?"

He sighs, wipes his hands on a dish towel. "Obviously you want to, so just go."

"Hey, Simon—"

"How many times are we gonna have this conversation?"

She shuts off the water and leans against the sink. "But Jack listens to me."

"No, he doesn't. That's the point." He tosses the towel on the counter. "Jack doesn't listen to anyone. He doesn't even listen to his shrink. I honestly don't know what you think you're gonna be able to do for him."

She doesn't know, either, but she knows she wants to take away Jack's demons. She wants to put him back the way he was when everyone respected and practically worshiped him. "I just can't give up on him. You didn't know him when he—"

"When what? When you were sleeping with him?" Stevie's expression hardens, her eyes turn cold and Simon immediately wishes he could take it back. "I'm sorry. I shouldn't have said that. I'm just worried about you thinking you can fix him. He's sick, Stevie. The guy needs help. Professional help. He needs to go somewhere and dry out."

"I just can't give up on him," she says again, softer this time. "I'm sorry, but I just can't."

Morale at Mattel is at an all-time low. Everyone misses Jack. They miss Elliot's stupid marching music, too. There's no levity. No spontaneity. No one stages Barbie orgies on their desks anymore. There's no more beach volleyball games and bonfires, either.

Rumors about Ruth are buzzing like swarms of bees. No one knows how they're supposed to act around her. Is it okay to say hello? To run the marketing budget past her? Get her opinion on a package design? Some, like Patsy, have already decided she was the mastermind behind *everything*, though no one knows what *everything* is. Others, like Stevie and Charlotte, stand by Ruth, giving her the benefit of the doubt.

No one understands why they made Art Spear, of all people, president and CEO, and no one likes the new management.

They've implemented practices that amount to little more than busywork. Suddenly everyone is required to complete weekly timesheets, and all vacation requests must be put in writing and submitted a minimum of nine months in advance. *Who plans that far ahead?* they grumble.

And then there's Barbie. Poor girl. The women's movement is on the attack, saying Barbie is evil and vapid. They blame her for the rise in silicone breast implants and cancer cases—to which Ruth takes great offense. They blame Barbie for eating disorders and the fad diets that appear in every women's magazine. They say Barbie's the culprit, the one responsible for every slight, every inequality imposed upon women. It's as if she's on the chauvinists' side. And the latest is a bunch of avant-garde artists skewering Barbie's body, slashing her with razor blades, even setting her on fire. And through it all, Barbie keeps a smile on her face.

But not Ruth. Ruth wants to scream, *It's just a doll. She's just a plastic figurine.* No one is destroying their Easy-Bake Ovens, their Liddle Kiddles, Mrs. Beasley or Raggedy Ann dolls. Those are just toys to be played with and left in the middle of the floor for someone to step on. There's no attachment to those objects because they are just that, objects. They don't evoke love or hate. But Barbie is different. Barbie is both friend and foe.

With Jack gone, Lewis now oversees all doll design for Mattel. He and Barcus call a meeting one afternoon with Charlotte and her design team, eager to share a new doll they've been working on in secret. The room smells of clashing aftershaves, cigarettes, plus one pipe and one cigar.

They allow Elliot to join them as well, but when he suggests getting Ruth in there, Lewis says, "No offense, Elliot, but why?"

"You're kidding me, right?" Elliot laughs, lacing his hands together, resting them on the table. "Let's not forget, Ruth is the reason we're all here. Don't discount her instincts when it comes to Barbie. She was right about Barbie from the start, when everyone—myself included—doubted her."

Charlotte agrees. "If we're talking about a new doll for the Barbie line, you *have* to include Ruth."

And so Lewis and Barcus relent, and Ruth joins the meeting. Stevie can't get over how rail thin she looks, even smaller than usual. She seems tired, worn out. The lines in her face are more pronounced, and her eyes are hooded, with dark circles beneath them.

"We have a new Skipper doll," Lewis announces, standing at the head of the table, his hands clasped behind his back. He gives a long preamble about the doll's history before finally unveiling a prototype that looks like every other Skipper.

"Allow me." Barcus takes the doll from Lewis. "This Skipper is very special. She's two dolls in one. Just watch. See what happens when I raise and lower her arm."

Barcus demonstrates as little Skipper suddenly grows taller and sprouts breasts. They're modest breasts. Just young burgeoning mounds. Nothing like her big sister's, but impossible to miss. Barcus lowers her arm, and the breasts disappear.

"Well? Pretty groovy, huh?" says Lewis.

Elliot's hand goes to his forehead. Charlotte and the designers exchange horrified looks. *Is this some sort of joke?* No one says a word. Lewis, misreading the room, thinks they're speechless in a good way. "She'll need two separate wardrobes," he says. "One for the little girl Skipper. You know, her usual wholesome knee socks and school uniforms, that sort of thing. But the second wardrobe—when her boobs are out—"

Stevie half coughs, half chokes.

Lewis shoots her a look but keeps going. "As I was saying, when her boobs are out, we need to show 'em off and—"

"Are you fucking kidding me?" Ruth says. "We are not releasing that doll."

"What's the problem?" asks Barcus, no longer afraid to stand up to her. "It's a brilliant concept. Like I said, it's two dolls in one."

"Twice the fun," adds Lewis.

"If I have to explain what the problem is," says Ruth, "then you have no business working in the doll division."

"She's right," says Elliot. "That doll . . ." He shakes his head. He can't find the words.

"Well, I'm sorry, Elliot," says Lewis, "but we're not asking for your approval. Or Ruth's. This doll's already in the works. And we already have a name—Growing Up Skipper. We're releasing her next year. We think she's brilliant."

"Oh yeah?" says Ruth. "Well, I think she's insulting. How would you like it if I twisted your arm to make your dick grow?"

On Being Insubordinate

1975

Stevie lies beside Simon in her bed. It's late and she's afraid her tossing and turning will wake him. Eventually, she slips out from beneath the covers and wanders into the kitchen to make a cup of tea. Leaning against the stucco wall, she stares into the flames licking the bottom of the kettle. There are bags of chips and pretzels on the counter, bottles of Pepsi and 7 Up in the icebox, all preparations for the consciousness-raising meeting she's hosting at her place the following night. Because of her job, Stevie's starting to feel a little sheepish among this group of women.

Without Ruth at the helm, Barbie and her friends have lost their way. Now there's a bunch of men running the show, and they're out of step with the times. A lot of what Barbie stands for these days are things Stevie just can't get behind. As predicted, as soon as Growing Up Skipper was released, she came under fire, and Stevie is horrified to even be associated with the doll.

The day after Lewis and Barcus introduced the team to Growing Up Skipper, Stevie went into Lewis's office and shut the door. He was seated in his wingback chair, his feet up on the desk, ankles crossed. Expensive loafers. Three lines on his telephone were

flashing red. He was something right out of central casting—
Asshole Boss.

"I can't design clothes for Growing Up Skipper."

"Why not? Your workload too heavy?"

"Because"—she slapped her hands to her thighs—"it's degrad-
ing to women. It's humiliating. It's just wrong."

He smiled unkindly. "You wanna know what's *just* wrong? Being insubordinate." He leaned forward, waving his finger at her.
"You women, you take everything so damn personally. Every little
thing makes you burst into tears."

"I'm not crying," she informed him.

"Everybody's out to get you, aren't they?" He reached for his
stapler, clamped hold of it like it was a hand grip and started firing
off dead, spent staples. "The world is against you, well, boo-hoo.
Poor little you. I'm sick and tired of all of you women complaining
about how unfair the world is." He shot off another round of staples.

"A doll like that is going to ruin the Barbie line."

"I don't recall asking for your opinion, young lady. Don't think
you're irreplaceable around here. Remember, Jack's not here to protect you anymore. Now, get this straight"—he started with his
finger wagging again—"your job is to work on a doll that grows tits.
And if you don't wanna work on a doll that grows tits, then leave.
There's the door." He gestured.

Stevie wanted to quit right then and there but lost her nerve,
worried about how she'd pay her rent, her bills. She slinked back to
her office, kept her head down and went back to work, feeling more
like a robot than a designer.

Since then, Carol Spencer got lucky and was temporarily moved
to boys' toys to work on the new Big Jim project. But the other designers regularly huddle together outside of Mattel, going for coffee, sometimes drinks, far away from eavesdroppers, where they

can openly complain about the men now running the Barbie team. They commiserate. They feel like hypocrites.

Stevie hasn't been this conflicted about her job since the early days, when she first started and wondered what she was doing there. Now she's come full circle—*What have I gotten myself into?* She's starting to think she's perpetuating the problem. She works on Barbie, a name as recognizable as Liberace or Charo. You say *Barbie* and everyone knows who you're talking about. But what started as a great message for girls is now being turned inside out, and she blames the men at Mattel for that.

The teapot whistles and she pulls it off the flame before it wakes Simon. She's in a trance, dunking a tea bag in the hot water, which is growing darker, murkier.

The next morning, she slaps the alarm clock off and rolls over. She drifts back asleep, only stirring when Simon asks if she's okay. He's already dressed, reaching for a tie, slinging it about his neck.

"I just didn't sleep very well last night."

"Again?" He pulls the wide end of his tie through the loop and, after tightening the knot, goes over and places his hand on her forehead. "You're not warm."

"I'm okay," she says. "Just go ahead. I'll drive myself later."

After Simon leaves, she thinks about a meeting she has that afternoon with Lewis to discuss more Skipper outfits. How is she expected to go from that to hosting a consciousness-raising group? That's when she contemplates something she's never done before—calling in sick. Just the thought of not having to deal with Lewis and Barcus, with Puberty Barbie, as some have come to call her, would be such a relief.

But if she calls in sick once, she knows she can do it again and again, with diminishing guilt each time. She can already picture herself growing apathetic, and though it's counterintuitive, she knows that doing anything half-assed is more exhausting than giving something your all. Once again, for the umpteenth time, Stevie entertains the thought of resigning but, again, talks herself out of it, doubting she'll ever land a design job that's half as lucrative as this one. Plus, she can't imagine not working with Charlotte or Ruth and Elliot. A wave of nostalgia washes over her, remembering when she first held Barbie in Charlotte's office, when she designed her first outfits and saw them on that television commercial. She's studied Ruth through the years and her sense of determination has become ingrained in Stevie. It's like a muscle that's been worked and flexed and has grown more dominant through the years. She can't give up on Barbie just like she can't give up on Jack.

She pulls back the covers and prepares to bounce back. She's not only going into work today. She decides she's going to reverse course, turn this all around and call for the men in charge to discontinue the Growing Up Skipper just like they did the Allan doll. And Midge, too.

After getting showered and dressed, she arrives at Mattel and heads straight to Ruth's office. Her argument to the men will be much stronger if she has Ruth's support.

It used to be you had to go through Ruth's secretary and try to get on her schedule within a reasonable amount of time. But now Ruth is accessible, humiliatingly so. When Stevie gets to Mahogany Row, Ruth's secretary is away from her desk, but Ruth's office door is open, just a crack. Stevie's about to knock when Ruth looks up from her pink sofa and invites her in.

"Are you okay?" asks Stevie, closing the door behind her. Ruth seems brittle and frail. She looks older than fifty-nine. Her hair is as dull as her eyes. Her nail polish is chipped, her red lipstick bleeding into the lines around her mouth. There's so much coming down on Ruth, Stevie shouldn't be surprised to see her crack—but she tells herself it's just that, a crack. She's confident that Ruth will find a way to bounce back. She won't be broken. Not ever.

"I'll be fine," says Ruth. "Eventually. More importantly"—she rearranges herself on the couch, patting the cushion, indicating that Stevie should sit down—"how are you? And how's Jack?"

This second question takes Stevie by surprise. She sits down and shakes her head. She can't keep track of Jack's shifting moods. One day he's hyped up about starting his own design group, the next he's sobbing about being all washed up. One day he's throwing a party, and then he turns around and kicks all the UCLA boys out of the Castle. He's draining her patience, and she can only imagine how exhausted he must be. "Poor Jack," says Stevie. "He's a mess."

"Well, that makes two of us." Ruth lets out a sound, part whimper, part laugh. "He and I really screwed things up, didn't we. We had a good thing going and we messed it up."

There's a long silence, and Stevie looks about Ruth's office, at the shelves housing all the Barbies they've ever made, from the original Barbie #1 with her ponytail and chevron swimsuit to the Barbie with the bubble cut hairstyle . . . there's Ken and Midge, Allan and Skipper, the Francie dolls, and Christie . . . there are Barbies that bend, that twist, that talk. Every Barbie and all her friends are present, all the way up to the newest Malibu Barbies. Stevie turns back to look at the woman who started it all and thinks it's a strange legacy but a legacy nonetheless. Stevie wants the line to continue, which is why she explains her thoughts about discontinuing Growing Up Skipper and why she feels so strongly about it.

Ruth listens but is not really focused. She picks at her nail polish and then at a cuticle. When Stevie's done speaking, all Ruth does is shake her head. "This isn't the company that hired you. This isn't the Mattel I created. And for that, I'm sorry."

"It's not your fault."

Ruth looks as if maybe it is. "We've worked together for a long time," she says. Surprising them both, she reaches over and takes Stevie's hand. "You're smart and you're talented." She pumps her grip for emphasis. "Do what you need to do. Look out for yourself. Don't go down with the ship."

Later that day Patsy tells Stevie that Jack is missing. No one knows where he is. Stevie, fearing the worst, finally tracks him down in Las Vegas.

He's at Caesar's Palace with Zsa Zsa. That alone is concerning. Zsa Zsa loves spending Jack's money, and there's no better place to piss it all away than Vegas. Two days later he returns having lost about $8,000 at the tables, but at least he's gained a wife. After dropping another $12,000 on a diamond ring, Jack is now the sixth Mr. Zsa Zsa Gabor.

"Why did you do that?" asks Stevie the day he returns. They're in Jack's office at the Castle. The shag carpeting is covered with contracts and all the royalty statements he'd pulled for his lawyers before jetting off to Vegas.

"Because I love her," he says, kicking a pile of papers out of his way before joining her on the sofa.

"You do not love that woman."

"Are you jealous?"

"I'm not going to dignify that with a response. Seriously, why did you marry her? A wife is not an impulse purchase."

He laughs. His eyes look glassy but not tearful, just more unfocused than anything else. He's drunk, or maybe high. Knowing Jack, it's probably both. Not having the UCLA boys living there anymore hasn't slowed him down a bit. And she knows he's not taking his medicine.

"*Schteevie!*" Zsa Zsa is standing in the doorway, knuckles ground into her hips. She's wearing a sheer lime-green negligee-like getup that only Zsa Zsa could get away with. "What is *Schteevie* doing here?"

"Relax," says Jack. "She just came by for a visit."

"It's okay," says Stevie, getting up. "I was just leaving anyway."

"No, don't go," says Jack, taking her hand, pulling her back down onto the sofa.

"See, Jack?" says Zsa Zsa, pouring herself a drink. "*Schteevie* was just leaving."

"I really do have to go," she says, getting back up. "Besides, I don't want to disrupt the honeymoon."

As she heads for the stairs, Stevie overhears Zsa Zsa laying into Jack. "I don't want you to see that *Schteevie* ever again. You're married to me now. You can't have a mistress."

"Jesus, she's not my mistress. She has a boyfriend now. She's my friend."

"Well, I don't want your *friend* in my house."

"This is *my* house," he tells her.

"Fine. If that's the way you feel, I'll stay at *my* house tonight."

Stevie darts out the front door just as Zsa Zsa, in her negligee, gets into her Jaguar, nearly sideswiping Stevie's car as she floors it, chewing up the lawn between the Castle and her place next door.

Stevie grips her steering wheel as tears cloud her vision and her head fills with pressure that can find no way out. Her friend is destroying himself and it's tearing her apart. Such a waste. Jack is one of the most talented people she's ever met. What happened to the guy who inspired everyone around him? Who brought energy and fun with him wherever he went? The guy everyone wanted to be around? Now he's all alone. No UCLA boys to distract him. Even Zsa Zsa is gone. It's just Jack and his Castle, surrounded by booze, pills and cocaine. And there's not a damn thing she can do for him. She can't babysit him, can't keep watch on him twenty-four hours a day. Even if she cleared out his liquor cabinets, dumped all the booze and flushed the pills and all the cocaine, he knows how to get more. And he would.

There's a silent scream firing off inside her head as fresh tears trundle down her cheeks and her chest squeezes so tight it hurts to breathe. Just when she thinks she can't handle another second of this awful, heavy sinking, something else takes over. A new space starts to open up inside her chest. *That was the worst of it*—it can't hurt any more than it just did—and as she's working her way to the other side, she's greeted by a certain clarity. It comes to her like a rescue. Stevie gets it now, and the conclusion she's coming to is not the same as giving up. She just realizes that she can't save Jack any more than she can save Ruth or Mattel. But she can still save herself.

Falling into Place

When Bob Mackie hears that Stevie resigned from Mattel, he invites her to lunch at Scandia on Sunset Boulevard. They start off with the famous Viking Platter: delicate aquavit pancakes topped with dollops of sour cream and caviar. They reminisce about their days at Chouinard and he asks about Charlotte and some of their classmates. He tells her about working for Carol Burnett and how he started dressing Cher for the *Sonny & Cher Comedy Hour*.

Over Danish sole and their second glass of wine, he turns the conversation to her. "So, what are your plans now?" he asks.

That's a very good question. She's not sure. She only knew that she couldn't stay at Mattel. The decision to leave was both hard and easy. Easy because it was obvious that she had nothing more to give, the inspiration had run dry and she could squeeze no more joy out of the work. Hard because she has nothing else lined up, which now makes it scary, possibly even stupid. She's stirred up her life—she's a human snow globe that's been shook up; bits and pieces of her existence are spiraling, swirling in all directions. Her coworkers threw her a going-away party with toasts and tributes.

Even Jack was there, and somewhat sober, which she was pleased to see. He and Ruth circled around each other the entire night, like jungle animals deciding whether to strike or retreat. Thankfully neither one of them made a scene, but it would be the last time they'd all be together under one roof.

"Are you planning on taking some time off?" Bob asks, leaning in, resting an elbow on the table, earnestly interested.

She ponders this as she touches her napkin to her mouth. "Not if I can help it. I'm just taking a little time, trying to figure out my next move. But really, if I'm being honest, I'm not good with downtime. I'm going crazy being at home. What can I say"—she shrugs and offers a wee smile—"I like to work."

"So you're ready to jump back into the rat race?"

"Oh yeah, definitely," she says, nodding.

"Well, I'm glad to hear it, because you see, there's a reason I wanted us to have lunch today."

"Ooh, and what might that be?" she asks, anticipating a bit of juicy gossip as she reaches for her glass.

"I want you to come work for me."

"What?" Stevie sets down her wine before she spills it.

"I need a new designer. I've got more work than I can handle, and I love what you did with Barbie. And besides, we Chouinard dropouts have to stick together."

"But Bob, I thought we were just having lunch to catch up. I wasn't expecting this. I'm very flattered," she says, which is an understatement. Her former classmate has become one of the most celebrated fashion designers in the country, possibly in the world. He's dressed everyone who's anyone, from Mitzi Gaynor to Diana Ross and the Supremes, and a host of other celebrities.

"Well, don't just be flattered," he laughs. "Say you'll do it."

She takes another sip of wine and sits back, breathing, just breathing it all in. Life is certainly full of surprises, and by definition, a surprise is something you don't see coming. Seventeen years ago, when Charlotte, Jack and Ruth walked into that diner, she had no idea how much her life was about to change. She accepted the job with Mattel by default, never thinking that Barbie would give her the ammo and confidence to pursue her dream. It took time for that to become apparent, and it's never been more obvious than right now. Charlotte said, *You put in two years with Barbie and you can write your own ticket.* It's certainly been longer than two years, but Stevie has leapfrogged to the head of the class, more than making up for lost time.

Bob mentions something about matching her salary, health insurance and other perks, but she's already heard all that she needs to know. There's no weighing the pros and cons here, because all those little shimmering particles inside her snow globe are coming into view, floating in one direction, getting ready to land and falling into place exactly where they belong. Bob Mackie's offering her a once-in-a-lifetime opportunity. It's just like when she was offered the job at Mattel. It was $200 a week—what was there to think about? Bob Mackie wants her to work with him—what is there to think about? Her life has just advanced to the next slide.

Ruth has lost so much weight due to the stress she's been under that she needs to be fitted for a new prosthetic. As she sits on the examination table in Peyton Massey's office, the tissue paper rustles beneath her each time she moves. Sunlight is peeking in through the venetian blinds, bouncing glaring stripes off the metal cabinets. While Peyton prepares the plaster for the breast mold,

Ruth is reminded of all the casting molds they went through to get Barbie's breasts right. There's an art to making a perfect breast. And Peyton is close, but he's not there yet.

"Can we change the nipple this time?" she asks.

He cocks his head to the side, making sure the plaster is securely in place. "It all comes down to the mold and the impression we get."

"Well, then put a Band-Aid over my nipple. Or do something. I don't want a torpedo sticking out of my chest, and you always keep this place so damn cold."

He laughs. "Okay. I'll do what I can to adjust that after we get the impression."

"And the smell. Peyton, please, you gotta do something about that. Isn't there a different plastic you can use? Something that's not so heavy, so rough. It rubs against my skin."

"Is there anything else?" he says, sounding more amused than annoyed.

"As a matter of fact . . ." She proceeds to give him a laundry list of things he should change. He takes it all in good humor.

Two weeks later, when she goes back for her final fitting, they're both impressed by how much more natural this new breast looks.

"See," she says, "I knew I was right about that nipple. Now, if we can just find you a different plastic."

"Ruth, I'm more of a limb guy. I'm not in the prosthetic breast business."

"Well, maybe you should be. Do you know how many women need these? They aren't available. Anywhere. Trust me, you can't just walk into a department store and buy them. What they have on the market now is awful."

He laughs. "Ruth, even if I was interested in making breasts, I'm afraid they'd be very pricey."

"Not if we mass-produce them."

"We?" He laughs again. "You think *we* could mass-produce prosthetic breasts?"

"That would bring down the cost significantly. I've been thinking about it for a while now." And she has, ever since that first day she and Barbara went looking for prosthetics. "Oh, Peyton, this is a good idea. Let's do it. Let's go into business together."

"What? Ruth, be realistic. We can't."

"Why not?"

"A woman's breast is highly individualized. They're like fingerprints. No two are identical—not even on the same woman. And then you factor in how different each mastectomy is. It's way too complicated."

"Oh, I've heard that before. I figured out how to make Barbie's boobs, I can sure as hell figure out how to make yours. All I need from you is your talent, your artistry. You design 'em and I'll figure out the rest." As she says this, she realizes that Peyton Massey could become her new Jack Ryan. They could work together to create something that would benefit women everywhere. Yes, Peyton is skeptical, but so was Jack in the beginning. She can persuade Peyton, just as she persuaded Mattel to create Barbie.

It's all so clear to her now. A new path is unfolding before her, and for the first time in years, ever since this whole business with the SEC started up, she can see beyond the investigation—my God, she can even see something for herself beyond Mattel.

The Second Act

1976

R uth enters the conference room carrying the pink sample
case that accompanied her on the flight from Los Angeles.
Dressed in a royal blue Oscar de la Renta pantsuit with a
camisole underneath, she stands before the Neiman Marcus
decision-makers at their flagship store in Dallas. It's been years
since Ruth's felt this kind of rush, has taken on this kind of challenge.

As she sizes up the room, her adrenaline amps up even more
and she's ready to knock their socks off. There's the regional manager in his bolo tie, and next to him is the heavily sideburned district manager, and another man in bell-bottoms and platform shoes
whose title she never caught. At the other end of the table sits the
head buyer, a smartly dressed woman with a red scarf about her
neck. She is next to the merchandise manager, another woman
with long, frosted hair, who sits across from the lingerie specialist,
who is also a woman.

After the introductions are made and handshakes and pleasant-
ries are exchanged, it's showtime. This idea has been years in the

making, and now here she is with the answer that so many women need to help them feel whole again.

There were a million reasons not to mass-produce Peyton's prosthetic breasts, just as there had been a million reasons not to create Barbie. And yet, look at what Barbie has done for little girls the world over. It wasn't easy, but Ruth will never regret how hard she fought to get Barbie made. Something that she invented has helped shape a whole new way of thinking about what girls can do, what girls can become. Because of Barbie, Ruth's helped to reset the expectations and lift some of the limitations placed on young girls. And despite what the women's liberation movement and the feminists have to say, Ruth will not apologize for any of it. She may have fallen short as a mother to her own children, but that doesn't negate what she has accomplished. She's proud and humbled to have played even a small role in helping to raise a generation of women to be stronger and more independent than the one that came before them.

It's been twenty years since she started this journey, and those same little girls who once played with the original Barbie, the first doll she ever created, are now grown women, grown women who might have or might someday develop breast cancer. When Ruth and Barbie first came into their lives, they were young, and all possibilities lay before them. Back then they might have dreamed they'd fall in love someday, they'd marry and have children and that was just part of their story. They also might have dreamed—if Ruth got her way—they'd become doctors and lawyers, professors and chemists. They might have dreamed they'd grow up to be artists and dancers, musicians and singers. Maybe they'd wanted to pilot a jet airplane or circle the moon, or climb to the summit of Pikes Peak, watch the sunset in Machu Picchu. They had so many dreams back then, and none of them included developing cancer.

Two decades ago, Ruth knew what those girls wanted, and now, so many years later—and after her own experience—she also knows what these women need. As she unsnaps her sample case for Nearly Me, the prosthetic breasts she and Peyton created, Ruth turns a wide smile to the room. She has important work to do.

Take Your Toys and Go Home

Barbie is more popular today than ever, and Mattel boasts that three Barbies are sold every second.

Ruth Handler was found guilty of financial fraud and sentenced to 2,500 hours of community service and a $57,000 fine. In 1976, she formed the Ruthton Corporation, which produced Nearly Me, a line of prosthetic breasts for cancer survivors. This new venture became another multimillion-dollar company and is still going strong today. Ruth died in 2002 at the age of eighty-five due to complications from colon cancer.

Jack Ryan divorced Zsa Zsa after just one year and would remarry three more times. His lawsuit with Mattel was eventually settled out of court for $10 million. In 1991, two years after suffering a stroke, Jack took his own life. He was sixty-four.

Elliot Handler resigned from Mattel in 1975, just six months after Ruth left the company. He spent much of his retirement painting and visiting with his children and grandchildren. Elliot passed away in 2012 at the age of ninety-five.

Charlotte Johnson retired from Mattel in 1980 after being diagnosed with dementia. She passed away in 1997 at the age of eighty.

Seymour Rosenberg was convicted of conspiracy, mail fraud and falsifying financial documents to the SEC. Like Ruth, he was ordered to pay a $57,000 fine and sentenced to 2,500 hours of community service.

Ken Handler died in 1994 at the age of fifty. His family attributed the cause of death to a brain tumor, but others claim it was due to complications from AIDS.

Barbara Handler Segal went on to form her own linen business and is now retired. She's eighty-four years old, and no, she was not the older woman featured on the bench in the *Barbie* movie.

Bob Mackie is a longtime Barbie designer. What began in 1980 and continues till this day has resulted in the creation of nearly fifty collectible Barbies.

Stevie Klein, my fictional character, went on to fulfill her lifelong dream of being a fashion designer. She married the fictional Simon Richards and the two lived happily ever after.

AUTHOR'S NOTE

As you'll see mentioned later in the Readers Guide, this book was in the works long before the *Barbie* movie came out and Barbie-mania began sweeping the universe. I got the idea for a Barbie book in 2019 after someone from Mattel's doll division told me about Ruth Handler. Because I had two books already in the pipeline, I wasn't able to start writing *Let's Call Her Barbie* until the spring of 2022.

The story of Barbie and Mattel is as complex and controversial as it is fascinating, and it would have been impossible to cover everything in one book, let alone a novel. I do want to make it clear that this novel has not been written or developed in conjunction with Mattel. It is a work of fiction based on the facts as I found and interpreted them.

While conducting my research, I found myself reliving my childhood and even uncovered a bit of fascinating family lore. Over lunch one day, my cousin Gail Levinson told me that her relatives invented the Magic 8 Ball, which Mattel later bought and sold. Something else I discovered during my research was several inconsistencies in Barbie's history, making the truth a bit murky in places, depending on who was doing the telling. Because this is a novel rather than narrative nonfiction, and because it includes an ensemble cast of Barbie heroes and villains as well as a timeline spanning three decades, I have taken some creative license, which I will share with you here.

First and foremost, let me acknowledge Charlotte Johnson's immense contributions to Barbie's success. Charlotte was singlehandedly responsible for Barbie's magnificent wardrobe in those early years. Eventually other designers were added to the team, including Carol Spencer, who joined Mattel in 1963. But for the purpose of this novel and the narrative flow, I introduced the fictional Stevie Klein to assist Charlotte. While I have Stevie playing an active role in creating some of those early iconic outfits, make no mistake about it, that was all part of Charlotte Johnson's genius. I can't imagine what Barbie's wardrobe might have looked like without her.

Barbie is certainly a mononymous figure, but there are varying stories of how Mattel arrived at the name. What we do know is that Ruth's daughter and Jack's wife were both named Barbara, and some accounts say they both went by the nickname Barbie. I also saw that they had originally wanted to call her the Barbara doll and the Babs doll, but those names were already taken.

It's also true that Barbie was inspired by the Bild Lilli doll based on the adult risqué German comic strip character in the *Bild-Zeitung* tabloid. Due to her popularity, Lilli was later turned into a novelty gag doll for men. In 1961, two years after Barbie's debut, Greiner & Hausser, the creators of Bild Lilli, along with Louis Marx and Company, its licensee, sued Mattel for patent infringement. The case was settled out of court in 1963 and Mattel went on to secure the patents for Bild Lilli for $21,600. Twenty years later, Greiner & Hausser and Louis Marx and Company were out of business.

A word about Jack Ryan: Depending on who you talk to, you'll get a slightly different take on who he was. It was true that he did work on the Hawk and Sparrow missiles at Raytheon before joining Mattel in 1955. In addition to Barbie, Jack was instrumental in developing Chatty Cathy and Hot Wheels. Brilliant as he was, Jack was also severely dyslexic and bipolar and had an addictive personality, which he fed with a steady diet of women, alcohol and drugs. His parties at the Castle were legendary and on par with Hugh Hefner's at the Playboy Mansion. Jack is a tragic figure, but no one can dispute his contributions to Barbie and Mattel. There was immense animosity between Jack and Ruth toward the end of his tenure with Mattel. As a result, Jack did end up suing Mattel over disputed royalties. It's also true that Jack was Mattel's Casanova and never lacked for female companionship. Barbie represented his ultimate fantasy woman, and it is well-documented that he paid for cosmetic surgeries and fitness trainers for several women in an effort to transform them into the doll's likeness.

This brings us to Ginger, who is fictional but based loosely on Linda Henson, Jack's secretary turned Mrs. Ryan #3 after his split from Zsa Zsa Gabor. When Jack divorced Linda, she became severely anorexic, and like Ginger, Linda died of a heart attack while only in her thirties.

Throughout the years, Barbie has been no stranger to controversy, but certain dolls have drawn more negative attention than others. One prime example—depicted in this book—was Growing Up Skipper. She was issued in 1975, and with the twist of her arm, the doll grew taller and sprouted breasts. You might wonder, who came up with this preposterous idea? While some say Ruth had her hand in it, others insist the doll was created by Steven Lewis after Mattel had begun phasing Ruth out of the company. I gave Ruth the benefit of the doubt and set her firmly on the side of the feminists, making a statement similar to the one issued by NOW, which, according to Jerry Oppenheimer's *Toy Monster*, challenged Mattel to create "a male doll with a penis that grew when his arm was cranked."

Here are some miscellaneous items that I want to point out for Barbie aficionados. The first Barbie television commercial began airing in March 1959 rather than June 1959. I moved the timeline for the sake of pacing. According to the Hawthorne Historical Society, in 1959 Mattel moved from its previous location at 5432 W. 102nd Street in Los Angeles to 5159 Rosecrans Avenue in Hawthorne, California. For purposes of streamlining the narrative, this novel takes place at the Hawthorne location throughout.

Ruth was raised by her older sister Sarah Greenwald. Some accounts say Ruth's mother became ill after giving birth, which is why Ruth was raised by Sarah. Others say Ida Mosko was simply too tired to care for another baby. In Ruth's biography, she glosses over this slight, claiming she wasn't impacted by her mother's abandonment. Despite attending a different school and a different synagogue than her siblings, Ruth claimed she was close with her brothers and sisters. Perhaps that was true, but there's little indication to suggest she had much of a relationship with her mother, who spoke no English and was also hard of hearing. Regarding the ten-count indictment that plagued Mattel executives in the late 1970s, it should be noted that Ruth maintained her innocence throughout her lifetime.

As mentioned previously, while conducting my research, I found that different books gave a different slant to Mattel's history. Some authors were sympathetic to Jack; others sided with Ruth and barely mentioned him. If you're a fan of business capers, I highly recommend *Toy Monster* by Jerry Oppenheimer and *Barbie and Ruth* by Robin Gerber. Ruth Handler's own biography, *Dream*

Doll, paints yet another version. I leave it up to the reader to decide what really happened.

In July 2022, I attended the National Barbie Doll Collectors Convention, where I was introduced to the world of Barbie collecting. You would be hard-pressed to find a friendlier and more upbeat group of people. I've included a list of some key collectors and Barbie influencers and encourage you to follow their social media feeds. Their posts are guaranteed to lift your spirits.

In 1959, there were two Barbies: a blonde and a brunette. In 1961, they added a redheaded doll. Through the years, Mattel has moved toward diversity and inclusion for its Barbie line. In 1968, they introduced Christie, the first "Black Barbie." Fast-forward to today and Mattel now offers a wide variety of skin tones—thirty-five at last count—along with nearly one hundred different hairstyles and nine different body types. By recently creating Barbies with disabilities, Mattel continues its quest to craft a doll that everyone can relate to.

As of the writing of this book, there's talk about a *Barbie* sequel, but whether or not *Barbie 2* comes to the big screen, one thing is certain: Barbie is evergreen.

SUGGESTED READING

Eames, Sarah Sink. *Barbie Fashion: The Complete History of the Wardrobes of Barbie Doll, Her Friends and Her Family. Vol. 1, 1959–1967.* Paducah, KY: Collector Books, 1990.

Feder, Karan. *Barbie Takes the Catwalk: A Style Icon's History in Fashion.* San Rafael, CA: Weldon Owen, 2023.

Gerber, Robin. *Barbie and Ruth: The Story of the World's Most Famous Doll and the Woman Who Created Her.* New York: Harper Business, 2009.

Lord, M. G. *Forever Barbie: The Unauthorized Biography of a Real Doll*. New York: William Morrow, 1994.

Oppenheimer, Jerry. *Toy Monster: The Big, Bad World of Mattel*. Hoboken: Wiley, 2009.

Ryan, Ann P. *Dream House—The Real Story of Jack Ryan: The Father of Barbie*, 2022.

Shannon, Jacqueline and Ruth Handler. *Dream Doll: The Ruth Handler Story*. Stamford, CT: Longmeadow Press, 1994.

Spencer, Carol. *Dressing Barbie: A Celebration of the Clothes That Made America's Favorite Doll and the Incredible Woman behind Them*. New York: Harper, 2019.

BARBIE INFLUENCERS ON SOCIAL MEDIA

Matthew Keith posting as @DollsOnTheBrain on Instagram, TikTok and Facebook

Azusa Sakamoto posting as @AzusaBarbie on Instagram, YouTube and X

Tonya Ruiz posting as @GrandmaGetsReal on Instagram, TikTok and Facebook

Nicanor Aquino's Barbie Haus of Chic posting as @Plastic_Chic on Instagram and Facebook

Julia Renkert posting as @MittenStateBarbie on Instagram

Janice McLean posting as @Barbie_Vintage_RetroFun on Instagram

Jared Mijares posting as @LifeInPlasticBlog on Instagram, TikTok and YouTube

Laura Maar posting as @MidgeFan73 on Instagram

ACKNOWLEDGMENTS

I'd like to thank everyone who helped me take this story from an idea to a finished book. So here's to Chanel Cleeton, Stacey Ballis, Alison Hammer, Jamie Freveletti, Julie Anixter, Keir Graff, Stephanie Nelson, Tasha Alexander, Andrew Grant, Abbott Kahler, Melanie Benjamin, Lisa Barr, Barbara Sapstein, Andrea Peskind Katz, M. J. Rose, Lisa Kotin, the Tall Poppies, and my agency sisters, the Lyonesses. For early reads and invaluable feedback, I'm indebted to Mindy Mailman, Stephanie Thornton, Kerri Maher, Heather Webb, Lauren Margolin (Good Book Fairy), Olivia Meletes-Morris, Karen Call and especially Andrea Rosen, who read more drafts of this manuscript than I can possibly count.

To Captain Fun, Rich Rosen and cohorts Karen and Michael Rosen, who turned my mother's living room into a Barbie photo studio and taught me that "perfect is the enemy of the good." To Fred Stern, who went above and beyond, vetting the book to make sure I had the L.A. landscape correct, and for the extra fact-checking with the Hawthorne Historical Society.

My thanks also to Azusa Sakamoto (Azusa Barbie), who fully embraces the Barbie lifestyle and is a ray of sunshine. I also owe much gratitude to Matthew Keith (Dolls on the Brain), whose gorgeous photos are included in this book. And to Carol Spencer, one of the original Barbie designers, who shared many wonderful stories of her adventures with Barbie. Carol lent an air of authenticity to this book that I could not have otherwise captured.

To my publishing team, who work tirelessly behind the scenes and have given this book their all. My wonderful agent, Kevan Lyon, possesses more superpowers than anyone I know. My rock star editor, Amanda Bergeron, is *always* right, even if I can't see it at first. Sareer Khader keeps everything moving seamlessly and is always on hand to jump in and help whenever I need her. My thanks also to Ivan Held, Christine Ball, Claire Zion, Craig Burke, Jeanne-Marie Hudson, Tawanna Sullivan, Patricia Clark, Elisha Katz, Danielle Keir, Dache' Rogers, Theresa Tran and Jordan Jacob.

To my family, for cheering me on every step of the way: Debbie Rosen, Pam Rosen, Jerry Rosen, Andrea Rosen, Joey Perilman and Devon Rosen. And lastly, to my one and only, John Dul, who read every word, always told me the truth and continues to make every day special just because I get to share it with him.

LET'S CALL HER *Barbie*

RENÉE ROSEN

READERS GUIDE

A CONVERSATION
WITH RENÉE ROSEN

A lot of readers might assume that you decided to write this book in reaction to the Barbiemania that took hold alongside the Barbie movie, but in truth, you've been wanting to tell the Barbie story for quite some time. Can you explain where you got the inspiration?

The idea to write a novel about the creation of Barbie had been percolating in my mind since 2019. Right before *Park Avenue Summer* was published, I was introduced to someone in Mattel's doll division who told me the story of Ruth Handler, and I immediately got goose bumps.

With a little more research on my own, I learned that Ruth was only part of the Barbie story, and I knew without a doubt that this had the makings of a novel. At the time, however, I had two other books, *The Social Graces* and *Fifth Avenue Glamour Girl*, which would have to come first, but Barbie was always there in the back of my mind, and I was champing at the bit to get to it.

So did the movie's success influence your book at all? And what did the timing of the movie do to your own publishing plans?

The movie had zero influence on the writing other than having me change a line where *my* Ruth uttered the same words as Rhea Perlman: "I am Mattel." But otherwise, my novel was already pretty far along by the time the movie came out, and I knew where my story was heading. I wanted to take readers back to Barbie's inception and the early days of Mattel, which I found fascinating. Fact is certainly stranger than fiction. What the movie did do, however, was influence some of our marketing decisions. We knew, for example, that we needed a pink cover; we knew we needed to have *Barbie* in the title; and we knew we wanted to feature Barbie herself.

During the height of Barbie being in the zeitgeist, I admit that I was in a state of full-on FOMO, and while we discussed rushing the book to press, we also recognized that it was more important to get the novel right rather than try to chase the moment. I kept reminding myself that Barbie has been around for sixty-five years. She ain't going anywhere. And I hope that readers will enjoy this take on the creation of the world's most iconic doll.

Did you play with Barbies when you were growing up?

Oh my, yes! Growing up, I was a serious Barbie player. I never went to a friend's house without my Barbie case, complete with all her outfits and accessories. I had several Barbies, a couple of Kens, Skipper, Midge, the original Barbie Dream House—the whole bit. I even borrowed my brother's G.I. Joe so I'd have another boy doll for the girls.

In some ways, I attribute my becoming a writer to playing with Barbie. While friends were more concerned with wardrobe changes,

I was preoccupied with the various storylines. I remember thinking, *Barbie and Ken can't jet off to Paris. First of all, they're having financial problems, and secondly, they're in the middle of a fight. All that needs to be resolved before they can travel to Europe.* So yes, my fascination with Barbie goes way back, but I never even thought about the people who created her and what kind of obstacles they had to overcome to bring her to market.

Can you talk about the research for this novel?

The research for this book was pure joy, filled with nostalgia and wonderful memories from my childhood. After I got the green light from my publisher to write this book, I delved into reading everything I could get my hands on. As you saw in my Author's Note, not all accounts line up and there are definitely three sides to the Barbie story: Ruth's, Jack's, and the truth.

My friend and fellow author Stacey Ballis pointed out early on how crucial Barbie's wardrobe was to the doll's success, and it just so happens that Stacey's good friend Helga Scherer makes doll clothes in 1:6 scale. We went to Helga's studio, and she showed me some of the tricks of the trade and how she had converted a paper binder into a Barbie pocketbook, which I ended up using in the book.

In July 2022, I hit the research jackpot by attending the National Barbie Doll Collectors Convention. While there, I came to appreciate just how extensive and diverse the Barbie collector family is. There were women and men, young and old, all walking around with Barbie dolls. And I'd never seen so many Barbie accoutrements: Barbie sneakers, purses, jewelry, jackets and more. It was like I had crossed into a magical world. Everyone was happy and kind and beyond generous. It seemed like every time I sat down for a meal, my table host, Jared Mijares, showered me with Barbies and accessories. During the convention, I also met Barbie influencers and several Barbie designers, but nothing compared to meeting Carol Spencer, one of the original Barbie designers. Carol is Mattel royalty. They even had a pink throne for her up on the stage. Carol was gracious enough to have lunch with John and me and shared many stories of her journey with Barbie. I will forever be grateful for Carol's generosity and her contributions to countless hours of play during my childhood.

What was the writing process like for you with this book?

I think the hardest part about writing this novel was deciding whose story it was. Ruth and Jack were constantly vying for attention on the page, and I also felt it was critical to introduce a fictional designer to round out the various themes of the book. I was frequently going back and forth—*Is this Ruth's story? Jack's story? Or Stevie's story?* In the end, I realized it had to be all their stories as well as Elliot's, Charlotte's and that of all the little girls out there. I think it made for a richer story all the way around, but alas, also a long story.

When I turned the manuscript in, one of the first challenges my brilliant editor gave me was to cut one hundred pages from the book. I went in with a scalpel and struck every unnecessary word, scene and repetition until it was down to a lean, mean, manageable size. And that's when the *really hard* work began. Once we pulled out all the weeds and excess, we could start to shape the narrative arcs and streamline what is a very complex story into something that would be entertaining as well as informative. To say that this book was a labor of love would be an immense understatement.

QUESTIONS FOR DISCUSSION

1. Despite Ruth's intention to create a doll that would empower young girls, from the very beginning Barbie has been both celebrated and vilified. Do you think of Barbie as a feminist icon or a dangerous role model for women?

2. Throughout this novel, you get a behind-the-scenes look at the development and creation of Barbie. For example, you learned the real reasons why her waist is so tiny, her feet are so small, her neck is so long, etc. Barbie's creators never lost sight of the fact that she was just a plastic figurine with anatomically impossible body measurements. And yet some people thought they were supposed to look like her. What is it about Barbie that you think separates her from other dolls and toys and has this effect on people, both positive and negative?

3. Ruth was certainly a nontraditional woman for her time. She tried to have it all—a husband, children and a career. What are your thoughts about her as a mother and her relationship

with Barbara? How do you think her own childhood impacted her views on motherhood?

4. Jack Ryan was the unlikely Romeo of Mattel. What do you think it was about Jack that the women found so appealing and irresistible? What did you think about his relationship with Stevie? What did you think about Ruth and Seymour Rosenberg's attempts to shortchange him on his royalties and phase him out of Mattel?

5. Growing Up Skipper came under fire—rightfully so—from the National Organization for Women as soon as she was released. Can you cite other Barbie controversies through the years? What do you think about the Barbie line today, which is based on diversity and inclusion, with a multitude of skin tones, hairstyles, body images and other more representative features?

6. Barbie has had more than 200 careers, from fashion model to astronaut. What do you think were the most important milestones for Barbie, and how was she ahead of her time?

7. How did you feel when you learned that Barbie was inspired by Bild Lilli, a German prostitute gag doll? Did that surprise you?

8. Ruth and Jack were both instrumental in the creation of Barbie. Ironically, they each had a Barbara in their lives and took credit for the name and the doll itself. After Jack's tragic death, Ruth did a little revisionist history and downplayed if

not erased his contributions to the doll's success. Did you think Jack had a right to claim he created Barbie?

9. Ruth developed breast cancer in 1970, which led to the creation of her next enterprise, Nearly Me. She saw her prosthetic breasts as a way to help millions of breast cancer survivors. What did you think about her coming full circle in terms of her relationship with creating breasts for a doll for little girls and then creating breasts for grown women?

10. Ironically, many Barbie collectors say it's because they weren't allowed to have a Barbie when they were growing up that they became involved in collecting. Did you play with Barbies as a child, or did you shave off all her hair in a fit of protest? Were you allowed to have Barbies, or did your parents forbid you to play with "that" doll?

Barbie in her iconic black-and-white swimsuit (#850). Barbie was introduced to the world at New York's Toy Fair on March 9, 1959.

Barbie wearing her first wedding gown (Wedding Day Set #972, issued in 1959): a long-sleeved dress with a double-tiered skirt, designed in white satin and tulle that shimmered with silver glitter.
Original accessories included open-toed white pumps, short white
gloves, a blue garter, a "pearl" necklace, a tulle veil and a bouquet.

Barbie and Midge in the first Barbie Dream House, wearing Sweater Girl outfits (#976, issued in 1959): sleeveless shells beneath matching wool cardigans with gold buttons, and flannel pencil skirts to complete the look. The Midge doll (#860) was introduced in 1963. Sweater Girl was issued in two colors: blue, as pictured here on Barbie, and orange, as worn by Midge. Barbie's Dream House, issued in 1962, was originally priced at $4.44.

Also known as the bubble dress, this Gay Parisienne outfit (#964, issued in 1959) was designed in dark blue polka-dot taffeta and embellished front and back with bows. The matching headband and veil, along with the white rabbit fur stole lined in satin, made this the height of fashion. The Barbie Fashion Shop, issued in 1963, was constructed of sturdy cardboard and originally priced at $4.47.

This pink satin full-length gown with its glamourous train and white rabbit fur stole (Enchanted Evening #983, issued in 1960) remains a favorite among Barbie collectors. Original accessories included elbow-length gloves, a "pearl" choker, "pearl"-drop earrings and clear open-toed pumps flecked with gold glitter.

Solo in the Spotlight (#982, issued in 1960) was a formfitting full-length gown in a glittery black knit, featuring a red silk rose sewn onto the ruffled tulle hem. The pink chiffon scarf, long black gloves and microphone stand completed this nightclub ensemble.

Barbie's Movie Date blue and white striped sundress (#933, issued in 1962) had a sheer organdy overskirt and included decorative matching trim along the hem and bodice. Midge's Garden Party pink floral and pindot cotton dress (#931, issued 1962) had a full skirt with an eyelet inset panel. Skipper's School Days ensemble (#1907, issued in 1964) included a short-sleeved white blouse, a pink wool cardigan sweater with gold buttons and a pink flannel pleated skirt. Skipper, Barbie's little sister (#950), was introduced in 1964.

Ken's swim trunks were made of red poplin, featured a white stripe down the side and came with a matching red and white striped top. The Ken doll (#750) was issued in 1961. Allan's dark blue cotton swim-suit came with a gold, blue, green and red striped jacket. The Allan doll (#1000) was issued in 1964. Both Ken's and Allan's swim outfits came with color-coordinated cork sandals.

The white sleeveless blouse for the Crisp 'n Cool ensemble (#1604, issued in 1964) was enhanced with three decorative red buttons down the front and a red and white polka-dot ascot. The outfit also came with a red pencil skirt and a matching red and white bag with vinyl handles. This was Carol Spencer's first Barbie design, inspired by First Lady Jacqueline Kennedy.

Black Magic (#1609, issued in 1964) was a black silk sheath dress with a matching tulle cape that fastened at the neck with a satin ribbon. It was inspired by one of Ruth Handler's favorite real-life outfits.

Photo by Julie Kaplan Photography

RENÉE ROSEN is the *USA Today* bestselling author of *Fifth Avenue Glamour Girl, The Social Graces, Park Avenue Summer, Windy City Blues, White Collar Girl, What the Lady Wants,* and *Dollface.* Renée lives in Chicago.

VISIT RENÉE ROSEN ONLINE

ReneeRosen.com

f ReneeRosenAuthor

⊙ ReneeRosen_

Ready to find
your next great read?

Let us help.

Visit prh.com/nextread

Penguin
Random
House